When We Believed

in

Dragons

Of Gods and Dragons
Book 2

Liminal Books

When We Believed in Dragons

Of Gods and Dragons
Book 2

Colleen McMillan

Other books by Colleen McMillan

Men of the Year

The Falls

Of Gods and Dragons Series

Unbreakable

When We Believed in Dragons

To Roxy, no, I will not italicize the sexy chapters

Dramatis Personae

Khresh Bashima – Sun God, husband to Alaric
Alaric Shina – Dragon-touched, husband to Bashima

Bell "Tengu" Cypress – Forest God, partner to Oken
Oken Cindras – demigod, partner to Cypress

Raijin Cabari – Lightning God
Jace – demigod, son of Veles

Alora – Moon Goddess
Garyn – Messenger of the Gods

Vaultus – King of the Gods, husband to Hastia
Hastia Cypress – Goddess of Spring, wife to Vaultus
Savos – god-touched of Vaultus

Cindras – Fire God, Chief Elemental God, father of Oken
Marlana – god-touched and official concubine of Cindras, mother of Oken

Torstan – celestial, mentor of Vaultus
Falkar – celestial, mentor of Orn
Orn – Augury, student of Falkar

Daruk – Dragon-touched, partner to Loralei
Loralei – demigod, partner to Daruk

Veles – God of the Dead, husband to Niall
Niall – Voice of the Gods, husband to Veles
Nim – demigod, daughter of Niall

Shako – demigod, friend of Jace
Resk – god-touched, ward of Cypress

There is no God of Love, for love cannot be controlled

Prologue

Cypress

The storm helped, but the Forest God was relying on the Fire God's absence from his temple. Dressed in a long cloak of concealment he'd borrowed from another god, Cypress's presence was further dampened by the camouflage charm he'd invented. It kept his godly power from radiating off him like a beacon, which would have alerted the god-touched the instant he stepped near the Temple of Fire. He thanked the torrential rain for the extra cover. He'd have to tell Cabari that he was doing an excellent job. The cloak kept off the rain too, so he wouldn't drip water everywhere once he got inside.

The cloak didn't make him invisible; it made him blend in with his surroundings, a sort of camouflage. The hood covered his messy, dark green hair and ram's horns, but his wide green eyes peeked out, trying to decide the best course of action. He pictured the temple map in his mind and knew to avoid the main entrance and the servant's entrance in the back, leaving him with few options. There was an access point near the throne room, but Cypress wanted to avoid the Fire God's power base. There was no telling what sort of traps the god might have set up when he was absent.

Cypress snuck past a greenhouse covered in massive windows. It made Cypress pause; what Forest God could ignore a greenhouse? Inside flourished countless plants and flowers, mostly a beautiful lavender bloom that resembled an autumn bell flower. Cypress couldn't help but be impressed with the greenhouse's variety and upkeep.

Cypress noticed someone inside the greenhouse: a woman with long, light blue hair sit ting on a bench near a large growth of the lavender flowers. The Forest God panicked. It was her, the Fire God's concubine, which meant that Cindras either hadn't left the temple or he was closer than Cypress thought. He might have to give up for the moment and come back another time, but a buzzing filled his head, threatening to smother his senses. No, it had to be tonight.

The god-touched woman stirred, hands going to her cheeks, wiping something away. Cypress focused on her, stiff posture and impassive face covered with tears. She showed no other emotion but let herself cry, moving occasionally to rub her eyes. She seemed desperately unhappy, and Cypress's resolve cracked. She might be able to help him. To help her son.

He slipped inside the greenhouse, careful not to brush against the plants. Many of them called out to him, trying to communicate, but Cypress didn't have time. He needed to focus on his mission. He sent out calming energy, and the plants' voices quieted. Edging his way through the walkways, he kept alert, listening for nearby disturbances that would signal the Fire God's return.

When he neared the woman, he whispered, "Are you Marlana?"

So lost in her suffering, his sudden appearance didn't startle her. She turned toward his voice, eyes red and glistening with tears. "I can't quite see you," she said, voice quiet. "What do you want?"

The air around them turned colder, and Cypress recalled that she had an ice ability. Puffs of air formed as he breathed out. Hoping to calm her, he pulled the hood back.

"My name is Cypress, the Forest God," he said. "I'm here to help Oken."

The air returned to the warm and humid greenhouse atmosphere, and Marlana said, "Oken? How can you help him? I can't even help him."

"I…" Cypress stammered. He hadn't thought that part through, besides the rescue itself. "I can take him away from here."

"And go where?" she asked. "He'll find Oken wherever he tries to run."

Cypress's face fell. He'd thought to take the demigod to his own temple, but Cindras would definitely look there first. Cindras knew the Forest God had a soft spot for his son. Ask one too many probing questions about his family, and that got the Fire God's attention fast.

"Why attempt a rescue at all?" Marlana's sad gray eyes stared right through him, and Cypress's heart broke for her. No one had come to her rescue, after all.

"I can't ignore what the Fire God is doing to Oken," Cypress said, standing tall. "I'll take him to a friend's to hide, somewhere even Cindras won't dare attack."

He needed to think of that place, and quickly. He couldn't involve Vaultus more than he already was, so the King's Temple was out. His friends were his age and no match for the Fire God. Except maybe one.

"I won't say where we're going," Cypress said. "Then he can't make you tell him."

Marlana nodded. Though she had only seen Cypress once, he hoped that she would trust him. If she didn't, it was going to take even longer to get inside the temple.

She said, "Just promise me that you'll do your best to protect him."

"I won't let anyone hurt him," Cypress said quickly. He didn't intend for Oken to ever be afraid again.

She smiled that sad smile once more. "I love that you think he'll never be hurt again."

She reached out and brushed her hand over Cypress's cheek, her fingertips cold, but he didn't pull away. He wondered if she ever interacted with her son or her other children, or if she was stuck wandering the Temple of Fire by herself. Cindras may have tied her to him with the god-touched ceremony, but he could go far enough away from her to cause pain from the separation. He doubted that the Fire God paid attention to the pain on his end, preferring it to being in her presence.

"Come with me," she said and led Cypress from the greenhouse. "Keep your cloak up. There won't be many shades around this time of night, but one or two god-touched will be on guard."

She took Cypress around the back of the temple, past a massive water garden with flames dancing across it, alchemy keeping it afire. The light danced in his eyes, and he thought of the place he would take Oken once they got away. It would be the perfect hiding place. He hoped that he'd be welcome, but it was never a sure thing with gods.

They passed the servant entrance, Marlana continuing to a solid wall of black marble. She walked right through, and Cypress's eyes widened. He followed, unsure what he was getting himself into.

"He made this pathway for me," she said when he caught up, her steps assured in the darkness. "So I wouldn't have to face the other servants if I wanted to go outside. He'll probably seal it up when he finds out that I helped you."

Cypress shuddered. "You don't have to do this," he said, though he was grateful for her help.

"Don't I?" she asked. "I can't be around my own children because of what I did to Oken. I'll do what I can to make sure Oken has a chance to be happy."

They didn't speak for a long time, Marlana leading the Forest God on a winding path through the temple. Eventually, they reached a wall of lit torches, and Cypress's eyes needed time to adjust. It didn't seem to bother Marlana. Her dress was made of a thin gossamer material, and Cypress worried that it might go up in flames when she got close to the wall, but she avoided the torches by mere inches each time.

They reached another wall, which Marlana walked through. On the other side had to be her room, which was fairly large and filled with plush furniture and many filled bookshelves. The lavender flowers in vases filled the room.

Catching his stares, she said, "It's the only thing he knows that I like, this flower." She reached out and took a single bloom from the closest vase and held it out to Cypress. He took it, uncertain what to do with it.

"They are infused with my essence," she said. "It will help you mask Oken's presence in the temple. The servants avoid me if they can." He tucked it into the cloak and started to speak, but she stopped him. "Oken's room is near the throne room. I assume you at least knew that, since you were breaking in. Or are you the reckless type?"

Cypress grimaced. He knew the layout but not from his current location. "If you can show me to the throne room, I can find Oken from there."

"Stay close to me," she said. They didn't meet anyone on their way to the throne room, the halls illuminated by the occasional torch. Cypress preferred the gentler candles used in the Temple of the Forest. The candles changed with the seasons, smelling like evergreen in winter, flowers in spring, apples in autumn, and sweet berries in summer.

The Fire God's temple smelled like burning pitch and ash.

They reached the throne room, and Cypress felt hostile energy coming from within, the locus of the Fire God's power. It was hot and intense; he doubted anyone could enter when Cindras wasn't there.

Marlana stopped and touched his shoulder. "His room is down the hall to the left. Cindras likes to keep Oken close."

"He's, uh, not here is he?" Cypress wondered why Marlana was at the temple. Cindras might be only a few shifts away.

"No," she said, face pained. "But he will return tomorrow morning. So please make haste. And don't tell Oken that I helped you. He might not leave if he thinks I have."

Cypress wondered why the demigod would stay if he thought his mother had tried to help him, but he didn't have time to ask. He didn't think she would tell him either.

"Thank you for your help," he said and moved away down the hall, leaving Marlana touching the throne room door, her ice-covered hand sizzling on the blisteringly hot surface.

Cypress reached the only door in the hallway Marlana sent him down and almost knocked. He didn't want to burst in on Oken, but he couldn't risk anyone hearing him, so he tried the handle, which turned readily. Cindras probably wouldn't allow Oken to lock his door, but he'd expected the Fire God might lock him in.

Oken's room was about the same size as his mother's but sparsely furnished. What furniture he had was simple with clean lines, and he liked the color blue. The walls were coated in royal blue, and the bed was draped in blue bedding and pillows. A few art pieces hung on the walls, abstract and unusual. Had Oken chosen them?

"I told you I didn't want to see anyone, Dahlia," came a voice from farther in the room behind a traditional paneled screen painted with rolling waves. The voice held little intonation but was clear and pleasing, though Cypress could tell Oken was annoyed.

Oken came out from behind the screen, shirtless, trousers loose around his hips, and Cypress yelped. He was still the most beautiful person the Forest God had ever seen: striped hair, black with shining white; brilliant turquoise eyes, and a large birthmark-like scar that ran through his face but didn't detract from his angelic cheekbones. A chest and shoulders marred by scars but could sever Cypress's heart from his body. Cypress tried to keep his eyes on Oken's face and failed.

"Who are you?" Oken asked, looking directly at the Forest God. Who he definitely shouldn't have been able to see.

Cypress inhaled too fast and choked on his own breath, pushing back the hood of the concealment cloak. He coughed into his hand and waved, tears coming to his eyes. When he was able to breathe normally, he lifted his head and smiled, hoping he looked competent.

"Oh, it's you," Oken said, head tilted. "The Forest God."

"Yes," Cypress said. "I'm here to rescue you."

"Oh," Oken said again, frowning. "I don't need to be rescued but thank you."

Cypress had been expecting a variety of responses from Oken, except the one he got. Sputtering where he stood, Cypress said, "What?"

"I don't need rescuing. I can escape on my own. If I want to."

Maybe Oken was kidding. Maybe he didn't understand that Cypress was there to take him away from the temple, away from his father.

"But I've come all this way to help you," Cypress finally got out, incredulous.

"I didn't ask you to come," Oken said, tilting his head to the other side.

"Well, no…"

"So, you can go," Oken said and walked toward his bed, grabbing a tunic and pulling it over his head. Cypress yearned for Oken's chiseled physique and held back a groan. The demigod frowned as he focused back on the Forest God.

"I'm fine on my own." Oken pulled back the duvet on his bed and almost climbed in until he noticed that Cypress hadn't moved. "Good-bye."

"I can't just leave you here with him!"

Oken rejecting his rescue operation had not been part of the plan. How was he going to convince Oken to leave?

"Leave me with who?"

"Your father!" It was like talking to a brick wall, although a wall might be easier to communicate with.

"Oh, him. It's not ideal, but, like I said, numerous times, I can escape on my own. When I need to."

"Why not now?" Cypress asked, putting his hands on his hips. "I want you to come with me."

That made Oken pause. "You want me to? Why?"

Why indeed, Cypress thought.

He still wasn't quite sure what had made him hatch the rescue plot. Maybe it was the feeling he'd gotten when the Fire God paraded Oken around at the last gods' summit, making Oken show off his powers, not paying attention to him otherwise. Like Oken was a prize animal being sold at auction. It might have been the defeated look in Oken's eyes when he thought no one was watching him. Cypress didn't think anyone should ever look that miserable. Though when Oken realized Cypress was watching him, a defiant expression had crossed his face, and the demigod lifted his head high and went back to his father's side. So, not entirely defeated.

"What your father is doing to you is wrong," Cypress said, clenching his fists, trying not to shake.

"No one else seems to think so," Oken said, moving closer to the Forest God. Cypress wasn't sure what to do, but he stood fast, bottom lip quivering. Having Oken that close was frightening, but he also felt a surge go through his body, like he wanted nothing more than to hug the demigod and tell him everything would be okay. And also kiss him. Yes, that would be nice.

"I like your horns," Oken said when he was close. He reached out and touched one, making Cypress freeze. Oken was touching him. The most gorgeous person in the world put his finger on the Forest God's body.

Don't panic, he thought, while he internally screamed.

"Are you okay?" Oken asked, putting his hand down. Cypress felt like he might cry if the demigod never touched him again.

"I'd be better if you agreed to come with me," Cypress said, coming back to himself. They had to leave. Now. "There isn't much time. I know you can get away on your own, but wouldn't it be easier with two people?"

Oken looked him over, frowning, thinking. "I suppose it would be simpler. And if we get caught, I can blame you."

His deadpan delivery made Cypress sweat. If he was caught in the Temple of Fire, he wouldn't come out in one piece, eternal life or not.

"I was joking," Oken said, blinking. "No one can ever tell when I'm joking," he muttered to himself.

"I'm sorry!" Cypress said, putting up his hands. "It was funny!"

"Don't say it was funny if you didn't know I was joking," Oken said. "I don't like when people lie." He stepped back a bit, eyeing Cypress like he wasn't sure about his character.

"I have a tendency to try and make people feel better," Cypress said, rubbing his hair and biting his lip. "I've been working on it…for a few thousand years."

Oken laughed, a short clear tone that made Cypress jump. "You're funny, Forest God."

"Thank you?" Cypress said. Having a conversation with the demigod was surreal and also getting them nowhere. He had the feeling that once he got Oken talking, he might not stop. "We really should go, that is, if you want to. I won't make you."

He watched Oken's face for any emotion or decision but didn't see anything. Oken was inscrutable.

"Okay," Oken said. "But I should pack something." He moved around the room, gathering a few things, some clothes, one small painting from near his bed, a stuffed animal Cypress hadn't spotted before. Then Oken started stripping.

"Oh, my gods!" Cypress said and turned around, blushing.

"I shouldn't wear my pajamas, Forest God," Oken said, as though it was obvious that one never wore pajamas while making a desperate escape.

"Cypress," he said, trying not to have a heart attack, picturing Oken naked. "That's my name."

Or whatever passes for a god's name, he thought.

Oken actually had a proper name, given to him by his formerly human mother. He was even technically a prince on his mother's side. Or at least a duke. Maybe a marquis? Cypress wasn't sure how human titles worked.

"Isn't that your formal name?" Oken asked, somehow right behind Cypress.

The Forest God nearly jumped out of his skin and spun around, pressing up against Oken, who didn't move. He was bare-chested again, and Cypress's hands were on that chest. Oken was much taller than Cypress, so he looked up, cheeks flushed.

"What's your informal name?" Oken asked, unconcerned that Cypress's sweaty palms were on him.

"Um, it's, um..." Shit. What was his name? Think, damn you! "Bell!" he finally spit out, much louder than he intended. "You can call me Bell, if you want." No one called him that except his mother and Vaultus on occasion. It would be nice if someone else used it.

"Bell," Oken said. "That's a nice name. Bell, can I kiss you?"

"WHAT?" Cypress dropped his hands and backed away to the door at great speed.

"I felt like I should, for some reason," Oken said. "You ran away though, so I guess it wasn't the right thing to ask." His shoulders slumped and Cypress came right back like he was on a tether.

"It's okay! You just surprised me. We can, um, kiss later. Right now, we should leave."

"All right, Bell," Oken said. He went to the bed and grabbed a new tunic, put it on, then grabbed his pack. "Where are we going?"

"That's a great question," Cypress said. "Let's get out of the temple first, then we can plan the next move."

"This isn't a very efficient rescue," Oken said. Maybe Cypress wouldn't let the demigod kiss him after all.

They approached the mountain from the forest, crossing the wide valley, moonlight guiding them. Oken walked behind Cypress like a shadow, his footfalls soft. Leaving the temple had been easier than

Cypress expected. No one had seen them. Perhaps the lavender flower tucked in Cypress's cloak helped. Either way, he was glad to shift them away once they were a safe distance from the building.

It took them six shifts to reach the mountain, leaving Cypress drained. The concealment charm plus shifting took everything he'd had, and now that they were so close, he couldn't get them up to the temple. When they cleared the safety of the trees, Cypress collapsed, panting.

"The temple is up there," he said, pointing at the black mountain in the distance. "But we'll have to walk from here. I can't do another shift."

"I can," Oken said. "My father recently taught me how. I'm not very good at it yet, but if it will help."

Before Cypress could stop him, Oken grabbed his arm and shifted them onto a footpath about halfway up the mountain. Not too bad, except it didn't matter that Oken shifted them; the added pressure from the concealment charm sapped the rest of his strength, and Cypress passed out.

He wasn't sure how long he'd been out, but it must not have been long, because Oken had only gotten them to the temple doors. Cypress felt sluggish and his mind reeled. Had Oken dragged him there?

"Bell," Oken said gently, crouching down where Cypress lay. "There's no handle. How do we get inside?"

"Ugh, my head," Cypress said. "Get me up so I can knock. It might let us in."

Oken nodded and helped Cypress stand. He put his palm on the door and whispered a greeting to the temple, asking it permission to enter. Oken looked stunned, as though he had no idea you should ask a building permission before going inside.

It didn't take long for the great doors to open, and Cypress breathed out. Oken put Cypress's arm over his shoulder and walked them inside. The doors shut slowly behind them, and they were enveloped in soft candlelight. It smelled of sage and citrus. Finally feeling a little at ease, Cypress relaxed into Oken's side.

The easy part was over. Now he just had to talk to…

"What the fuck are you doing here, Tengu?"

Bashima.

Chapter One

Cypress

"And that's how Bell and I met. Besides him spying on me at the summit," Oken said, sipping his water. He was the only one at the table who didn't drink alcohol, and Cypress was glad for it. Maybe the others wouldn't remember every part of the story Oken had told, particularly the part about kissing someone you'd just met. These many years later, Oken still didn't know that his mother helped in the escape. Cypress had planned on telling him, but it never came up in their years together.

"Wow," said Cabari, the Lightning God, staring at Oken. "How had I never heard that story before?" Cabari glared at Cypress who shrugged and gulped his wine.

"I'm surprised you didn't know," said Oken, tilting his head. "It's well known that Bell broke into the temple to kidnap me."

Cypress spit wine across the table as Cabari cackled. Bashima rolled his eyes, bored with the entire dinner party. Alaric Shina, a true saint, asked Cypress if he was okay and glowered at his husband, who shrugged and pushed grapes around his plate.

"You know what, Cypress? Oken?" said the Lightning God, rubbing mirthful tears from his eyes. "Jace and I are just like you. Two star-crossed lovers trying to make it in this judgmental world."

Jace didn't skip a beat before saying, "Just because my dad doesn't like you doesn't make us star-crossed lovers."

"Star-crossed lovers," Cabari said again, sighing, staring at the ceiling.

"Babe," said Shina, still glaring at Bashima, "Did you really almost make them leave? They came to ask you for help!"

The Sun God crossed his arms, scowling. "I don't remember inviting Tengu to stop by with a fugitive whenever he wanted. I let them stay. Eventually."

"Bashima hadn't seen Bell in quite some time," Oken said, "So his behavior was understandable. Although he was rather rude about the whole thing."

Cypress could see where the conversation was going, and it wasn't going to end well. Bringing up Bashima's past and how he treated people was never a good dinner topic. Or a good anytime topic. The Forest God could almost see smoke coming from Shina's nostrils.

"It's really okay," Cypress started, but Shina cut him off.

"And you hadn't seen Cypress in five hundred years? Why the hells not? He's here all the time now!" Cypress didn't have the emotional strength for what was coming, but he was stuck. He wished he could liquefy himself and sink beneath the table.

"Yeah, and the last time he was here, I strictly recall you yelling at him to leave," countered Bashima, temper flaring.

"Well, we were busy," Shina said, flushing redder than the wine Cypress had spit out.

The Forest God recalled vividly why they'd been busy, the memory coming back to him, making him space out from the current conversation:

Cypress, running from the throne room, eyes covered: "Can you two NOT have sex for one damned minute? Just because you just got married doesn't mean you have to be on each other's dicks all the time!"

Oken, having followed Cypress out: "We have sex all the time, Bell."

Cypress: "You're not helping!"

Bashima, fuming, slamming the throne room door: "Now you've embarrassed him, and I'm gonna hear about it for weeks."

Cypress: "Seriously? It's during work hours!"

Bashima: "Not my fault, when he bites his lip like that, I can't help it."

Cypress: "He does that on purpose!"

Bashima: "…And?"

But Cypress's reverie wasn't meant to last. Jace tapped him on the shoulder, and said, "Don't you think you should say something?"

"Huh?"

Shina, who had been sitting at the foot of the table, was now standing, hands on the table, eyes wide, said, "YOU BEAT HIM UP AND TOLD HIM NEVER TO COME BACK?"

Bashima, at the head of the table, also standing, light racing across his skin like comets, said back, "He wouldn't stop asking if I was okay! How the hells was I supposed to be okay?"

"He was trying to be a good friend! Say you're sorry!"

"He knows I didn't mean it!"

"APOLOGIZE RIGHT NOW!"

"LIKE HELLS I WILL!"

Cypress glanced around the table. Oken watched the argument like it was an almost-entertaining tennis match. Cabari was at the edge of his seat, eyes gleaming yellow, while Jace sat back in his chair, trying to look as small as possible.

"Gods, it's like watching my dad and Niall fight," Jace said, picking at his fingernails. "You know what comes after a big row like this, right?"

Unsure what Jace meant, Cypress cleared his throat and said, "Shina, it's okay —"

Shina whipped his head in the Forest God's direction, and Cypress froze, because the redhead's eyes had changed color, blown full crimson. Everyone grew quiet, including Bashima. Cypress felt a crackling intensity coming off Shina that he'd only witnessed once, and he saw Cabari move fractionally across the table from him, Cabari's eyes on the redhead. The movement drew Shina's attention, and his grip on the table surged, diamond-hard claws emerging from his fingers. He snarled low in his throat, and Cabari's face tensed.

Shit, Shina was losing control. He hadn't had an incident since the Temple of Time. At least Bashima hadn't mentioned anything. A faint golden glow emanated from Shina's back, in the vague shape of Bashima's Sun God symbol. Cypress had never seen a god-touched brand glow like that, but it wasn't a normal brand.

"What the hells is going on?" whispered Jace.

A lot of things happened at once. Shina roared, causing Cabari to fly across the table and tackle Jace off his chair, directing a bolt of yellow lightning at the transforming redhead. Bashima let off a string of curses and leapt from his seat, small flames popping in his palms.

"Oken!" Cypress yelled.

They'd planned for this scenario multiple times, trying to gauge what would work best against Shina in his dragon-touched form, and had settled on trying to keep him in one place until he could calm down. Fire would have little or no effect on him, and Bashima was hesitant to use his powers on his husband. So, Oken formed ice handcuffs that trapped Shina's hands on the table, the ice running up his arms to his shoulders.

It didn't hold him for long, but it gave Cypress time to grab Oken away from the table. Shina bellowed again and tore his arms free, the ice clattering across the floor, and his body erupted in ruby scales, shredding his clothes. He seemed to grow larger, muscles rippling, a gold chain tightening across his chest. In glimmering golden scales, Bashima's brand burned like a beacon on Shina's back. Even Shina's hair and eyes transformed into large, unbreakable shards.

Bashima jumped onto the dining table, drawing Shina's attention by waving his arms and yelling challenges. Shina hissed, crouched down, and leaped up, barreling right into the Sun God, scattering food and dishware. Bashima wrestled with his husband, directing small light blasts in Shina's face, which only enraged him more.

"Bashi!" Cypress yelled when Shina's claws raked up the Sun God's arm, golden blood splattering on the table. Bashima flinched from the blow and backed away from the dragon, clasping the wound.

"You asshole!" he yelled. "It's me!"

"I think he knows that!" Cabari shouted from the wall, pinning Jace behind him. Probably smart not to turn their backs and run for the door, but the Lightning God should have shifted away. Cypress had the feeling that Cabari wanted to help, but he was leaving Jace in danger.

"Everybody, get down!" Bashima yelled. Cabari grabbed Jace and hit the floor, covering him, and Cypress fell on top of Oken, who was covering his ears.

"Close your eyes!" Cypress shouted.

A massive light bomb engulfed the room, explosive power mostly contained, but the blast ruffled Cypress's hair, and he gripped Oken tighter.

A soft scream came from the table when the light went off, then there was silence.

As Cypress's eyes adjusted, he could make out simple shapes. He blinked, trying to clear his vision. Even closed, his eyes hadn't fared well against Bashima's light blast.

When the black spots disappeared from his sight, Cypress saw more than he wanted: Shina's scales were slowly fading, but he was naked, his (very nice, but still) ass on full display. Bashima was beneath Shina, his thighs holding the redhead away from his body, hands holding up his shoulders, a surprised sneer on his lips. Shina's body shook, and tears fell silently from his eyes. He and Bashima were covered in food, and plates and candlesticks littered the floor. The Sun God's blood trickled down his arm in thin rivulets.

Cypress was very glad that no shades were in the room. Shina's attendant, Matthias, might have lost his mind.

No one moved. Cypress heard Shina's muffled sobs and nothing else. Bashima wasn't trying to comfort him; he looked afraid that his husband might transform at any moment, chest heaving.

"Hey everybody!" A yell came from the doorway. "Sorry we're late, Garyn wanted to stop for dessert and HOLY SHIT!"

Alora and Garyn entered the dining room. The Moon Goddess clutched two wine bottles against her chest, her large black eyes wide. Her blue skin paled at the state of the dining room. Garyn, who held nothing — where was the dessert? — stood beside Alora, wings on his elbows and ankles fluttering rapidly. He grabbed Alora's elbow. The rest of Shina's scales dissipated, and he was back to his normal size.

"Stay where you are!" Bashima shouted. "Don't move! You might startle him."

"What the fuck, Bashima?" Garyn asked, his calm voice a pitch higher than normal. "Are you into some weird food orgy thing we didn't know about?"

"I would have been fine with an orgy," said Cabari, covering Jace. "This isn't that."

"Why is Shina naked?" Alora asked, worried. "Cabari, why are you almost naked?"

Cypress looked, and Cabari was shirtless. When the hells had that happened?

"Should we really be focusing on me right now?" the Lightning God asked, and Jace stirred beneath him, his eyes fearful and mint-green hair askew. "Don't move, Jace," Cabari said.

"Hey, Alaric," Bashima said, his hands on Shina's face, eyes intent. He released the redhead, letting him fall slowly down, hugging him. Shina continued whimpering, not saying anything. Bashima pushed his hands through his husband's hair, whispering soothing things. "Everything's okay," Bashima said. "Everyone's okay."

"Speak for yourself," said Garyn. "I just got here and I'm traumatized."

"Shut up," Alora said, elbowing him. She thrust the wine bottles into Garyn's hands and shook her head. "This is going to take some explaining." She inched toward Cabari and Jace, keeping an eye on the dining table, but Shina seemed spent. He didn't move, letting Bashima pet him. The Sun God's blond hair was plastered to his head, the usual spiky explosion covered in sweat and food.

After Bashima took Shina to their room, Garyn descended on Cypress, questions toppling from his lips. It was disconcerting seeing the Messenger of the Gods so agitated; Garyn was normally mellow, laid back, didn't let much affect him.

"What the hells was that? Shina looked like a monster! Then he was normal again...Is that what destroyed Chronas? Wasn't that god-touched shit under control? Did you know about this?" He directed the last question at Alora, who bit her lip and averted her eyes. Garyn blew out a frustrated breath. "Great. You knew."

"I told you everything," Alora said, bottom lip stuck out. "At least, everything I could..." She looked at Cypress, eyes accusing and hesitant.

Shades came to clean the dining room once Bashima left with Shina, so the dining table was clear. Cypress thought it odd that Kuroi hadn't checked on them, but he would be worrying about Bashima and Shina, probably trying to keep the shades calm.

They sat around the table, couples gathered together. Cabari kept glancing at Jace, who was quiet and contemplative. The Lightning God twitched as though he was desperate to leave the room, but he also wanted to hear what everyone said.

Alora and Garyn were on the opposite side of the table, unscathed but anxious. Alora knew about Shina's transformative ability, having seen it firsthand at the Temple of Time, but she didn't know the specifics. Her eyes boring into Cypress said she was done with the story they'd fed her. This wasn't a god-touched thing. Humans who went through the ritual and exhibited powers got used to them quickly, within days, sometimes a couple weeks at most. It had been months since Chronas branded Shina, since Bashima had drawn his own symbol on the redhead's back, since their wedding. A god-touched would not have flown out of control that way. Not after all that time.

"You know what's going on, don't you?" Alora asked, speaking for the others.

Oken shifted uncomfortably next to Cypress, taking his hand under the table. Cypress wasn't sure what to say. It wasn't his story to tell.

"We should wait for Bashima," Cypress said, and Garyn rolled his eyes. Alora nodded, accepting his reply but still unhappy. Cabari tried to put his hand on Jace's shoulder, but the demigod shook him off, crossing his arms and sitting back in his chair.

It didn't take long for Bashima to return. He stalked into the room, clothes fresh, hair clean. The claw marks on his arms stood out in the candlelight, bright red on his pale skin. The wounds had closed but looked raw and angry. He'd been slashed across his chest as well; the marks visible near his shirt collar. Cypress noticed that the older bite mark on his shoulder looked vibrant, much like when Shina first claimed him. Bashima's eyes were murderous.

"If any of you tell a single soul what you saw, I will kill you," Bashima said, fists clenched, colored light traversing his skin in waves. His eyes glistened with barely contained rage.

"We won't say anything," Cypress said, but Garyn stood up, his chair falling back.

"Speak for yourself," he said, leaning over the table. "You invite people to your temple with a gods-damned monster living here?"

Bashima was so quick, Garyn didn't stand a chance. The Sun God grabbed Garyn's throat and got in his face. "Call him a monster one more time, and I'll tear those wings off."

Garyn shoved Bashima away, buffeting him with his wings. He said, "I got the gist from Cabari and Alora. Sure, a god-touched might throw a tantrum when they're first created," he glanced at Oken, which provoked Cypress. Green light crackled across his body, and Garyn held up a hand, apologetic. "But what happened tonight wasn't normal. What if we'd gotten here a few minutes earlier? Cabari said he nearly took your head off."

Bashima glared at the Lightning God, who shrugged. Cabari said, "He's not wrong. I thought that was a one-time thing at the Temple of Time. But you, Cypress, and Oken were a little too prepared." He looked at Jace beside him, and his usually carefree face hardened. Jace wasn't immortal, and it seemed like Cabari finally realized that. "You could have warned us that he wasn't safe."

"Bashi," Cypress said, "maybe we should explain —"

"Shut up, Tengu," Bashima warned. "This is all your fault."

"What?" Cypress asked, perplexed. Oken had been in danger from Shina's episode, just like Jace. Cypress had the right to be pissed off too. "If this is anyone's fault it's yours! Shina's right. You never apologize to anyone, for anything, and you've done a lot of shitty things. But do any of us ask for apologies? Of course not. And they aren't even asking for an apology, just an explanation. But no, can't ask the Sun God for anything!"

"Bell…" Oken said and reached for his arm. Cypress yanked it away, anger growing. He was done with Bashima's bullshit. Done covering for him.

"It's one thing for us gods to be around Shina when he loses it, but he could have killed Oken or Jace." Cypress was breathing hard and talking fast, but he needed to get it out. Everyone at the table stared at him, open-mouthed, even Bashima. He kept going, "And it's irresponsible to keep it from them. Should you tell everyone? Of course not, but if you can't trust the people in this room, then you might as well hide in your temple for another two thousand years."

"I don't like talking about it when Alaric's not here," Bashima mumbled, arms crossed and eyes down.

"We've kept quiet," Cabari said, nodding at Alora. "It wasn't fair to keep it from Garyn and Jace, but we did, besides the story you fed us, the one we told everyone. Because you asked us to. We thought it was weird that Shina wasn't affected by Veles's alchemy, and I barely fazed him with my lightning." The Lightning God narrowed his eyes at Cypress. "But you obviously told Oken everything, when Bashima asked us to keep it to ourselves."

Cypress flushed, averting his eyes. He hadn't thought about it that way. He didn't consider Alora and Garyn to be an actual couple, and Cabari and Jace hadn't made their thing official yet. Cypress had been with Oken for fifteen hundred years, and it was difficult to hide things from him, but now that Cabari brought it up, he should have tried to keep the particulars secret. Even if Shina was okay with it, Cypress hadn't asked him if it was.

"He's right," Oken said, voice clear. He looked at the others around the table, settling on Bashima. "Since my life was in danger, even though I wasn't worried, they are. I think it's only fair to tell them that Shina is a dragon."

Silence greeted the room. Bashima and Cypress stared at Oken, shocked at his honesty. The others looked at Oken as though he'd lost his mind. Jace moved in his chair, uncomfortable. Cabari and Alora glanced at each other, unsure what to make of it. Garyn looked pissed.

"What the hells does that mean?" Garyn asked.

"Zebra Head doesn't know how to keep his damn mouth shut," said Bashima, face flooded with red and gold light.

Cypress stood up, blocking Oken, his face firmly set against the Sun God. He said, "Isn't it better to have more people to protect Shina's secret? More people who could help when he gets like that?"

Bashima looked ready to fight, but he was also afraid. He didn't know how to help Shina any better than Cypress, who at least had done research on the dragon-touched. There wasn't enough information on the topic for them to plan strategies. If their friends knew, at least they could jump in if Shina transformed again.

"He's not exactly a dragon," Cypress said, gauging Bashima's reaction. Bashima slumped in his chair and made a "go ahead" gesture, flicking his hand. Cypress continued, "But he is dragon-touched. We don't know a lot about it, but having dragon's blood gives Shina incredible abilities."

"Like what?" Garyn asked, unimpressed. Alora nudged him, and he rolled his eyes. "What? They've all lost it. Dragons? Who's seen in a dragon in a million years?"

"Fifty thousand," Cypress muttered, "but that's beside the point. As you all saw —"

"Oh, we saw all right," Cabari said, and Jace smacked the back of his head, focused on the Forest God, eyes alert. Bashima leveled his intense gaze at Cabari and flexed his hands, ready to smash Cabari's face into the table.

"AS YOU SAW," Cypress continued, "his strength and speed increase, and he grows scales. We're fairly certain they're impenetrable and immune to most godly powers. Cabari wasn't lying about his lightning. I hit Shina with my power in the Temple of Time too, and it only knocked him off balance for a moment. And Veles's alchemy had absolutely no effect on him."

"Seven hells," Garyn said and rubbed his eyes. "If Veles doesn't have a chance against him…And you knew nothing about this?" Garyn asked Alora.

"About Shina being a fucking dragon?" she said, scoffing, "I think I would have remembered that."

Garyn turned to Bashima, whose face was a storm cloud. "And your brand does nothing?" he asked. "You can't control him?"

"He doesn't need to be controlled," Bashima growled, palms igniting.

"Fighting isn't going to solve anything," Cypress said, holding up his hands. He was still furious at Bashima — and none too happy with himself — but going back and forth wouldn't solve a thing. "Shina turned back to his usual self, and he's safe now, right?"

Bashima nodded, not looking away from Garyn. Cypress sighed and said, "We're tired and overwhelmed, and we were all staying here tonight anyway. I think we should turn in and hash this out tomorrow."

Garyn looked mutinous, but Alora stood up, the wine bottles in her arms. She whispered in Garyn's ear, and he bit the inside of his cheek, maybe wanting to say more. Instead, he stood too and they shifted away, hopefully to their room. Cypress wanted to explain things better, but Bashima was right: Shina needed to be part of the conversation.

"I guess that's our cue too," Cabari said, attempting his usual smile. "I suppose it would be better from the dragon's mouth anyway." Jace sighed at the Lightning God's poor attempt at a joke and grabbed his arm, shifting them away as well.

"I know this isn't how you wanted them to find out," Cypress said to Bashima.

"I never wanted them to find out," Bashima sneered, leaving his seat. He stomped to the door, not acknowledging Cypress or Oken as he left.

"Should I not have said anything?" Oken asked, eyes calm but shiny. Oken hardly showed outward emotion, so this was a rare occasion.

"It was going to come out eventually," Cypress said, though he wished Oken hadn't blown Shina's cover so indifferently. "And it would never have been the right time."

"Can we go to my room now?" Oken asked. He reached for Cypress's hand, and the Forest God sighed. It wouldn't help to be angry with Oken. He'd meant well and had only wanted to help ease the situation. And maybe tearing off the bandage was the only way to do that.

Chapter Two

Alaric

Alaric woke in the middle of the night, burning with fever, covered in sweat, and breathing hard. He was aware of nothing but Bashima beside him, the Sun God giving off intense heat, like his skin was scorching. He smelled like citrus and honey and grass after a long rain. Intoxicating. Alaric felt the urge to grab his husband, flip him onto his stomach, and tear into him with all his strength, hold Bashima down with his body, bite onto his shoulder, use Bashima until the desperate feeling inside of him was gone. It was like his entire body exploded with the need to rail Bashima until they both fainted.

He was strong enough to do it…all he had to do was reach out.

A soft glow came from his back, his brand luminous, and Alaric realized what he'd almost done. The ravenous feeling remained, but he had a hold on it, barely. He was afraid to move, because if Bashima reacted in his sleep, Alaric wasn't sure what he'd do. Part of him still screamed in his head to satisfy his urge, but that wasn't the real him.

Alaric loved Bashima and wouldn't hurt him, couldn't hurt him. Not like that.

What the hells was this ravenous feeling inside him?

Then he remembered what happened at dinner; Bashima's slashed arm and chest, the golden blood driving him mad, having the same impulse to fuck the Sun God raw. He might have succeeded if Bashima hadn't detonated the flare bomb in his face, which pulled Alaric out of his rage spiral. It hadn't mattered that other people were in the room; all the better that they knew Bashima was his. In that moment, he hadn't cared what they saw, and that scared him. But not as much as the horrific thing he'd almost done in their bed.

Alaric needed to move, to leave, to do something, but he was frozen. As though sensing his distress, Bashima scooted closer to him, and Alaric groaned. The exact opposite of what he needed. He started shaking, not sure if he could hold back much longer. He was already hard, and the need was overwhelming. His teeth ached in his gums, saliva pooling in his mouth.

"Hey," said Bashima, voice soft and slightly slurred from sleep. "What's-a-matter?"

Alaric didn't answer. He focused on restraining himself, clenching his fists behind his back. The brand's light intensified and Bashima said, "Don't worry about tonight, we can fix everything with those morons tomorrow. Get some rest."

He reached back and awkwardly patted Alaric's arm, and Alaric grabbed his wrist in a vice-like grip and jammed his chest into Bashima's back, wrapping his legs around his husband's and thrusting forward with his hips. If they'd been naked, he might have succeeded in whatever quest his dick was set on.

Bashima tensed, fully awake, and light flew over his skin, illuminating the room. "Alaric…"

"Don't talk," Alaric said, trembling. It took everything he had to say those two words, then his mouth filled with more saliva, dripping from his lips, and he felt his teeth growing.

No, no, no, not now!

Through their bond, he sensed Bashima's heartbeat speed up, as well as his interest, though the desire was layered with apprehension. Drool dribbled down Alaric's chin, and he bit back a snarl. Bashima wanted to be fucked, Alaric could feel that, but Bashima didn't understand what Alaric was dealing with. He might not be able to stop fucking the Sun God.

When Alaric thought he was about to lose control completely, Bashima relaxed in his arms and bombarded him with soothing soul energy. One of the techniques that they'd figured out together: they could perceive each other's emotions and even push their own wills outward, which Bashima usually deployed to calm Alaric down. He hadn't needed to do it in a while — Alaric had hoped he'd never need to do it again — but it worked. Feeling everything his partner was feeling encased Alaric in Bashima's deepest inner workings, and while some of Bashima's thoughts were fearful and angry, they weren't his dominant emotions. Knowing Bashima was there for Alaric no matter what helped. Bashima was trying to fill Alaric with concern and love.

Alaric let out a huge breath, loosened his hold on Bashima, and rolled over so he was facing away, which made Bashima flip and envelop Alaric with his own body, still sending the calming feeling and stroking Alaric's hair.

He intertwined their legs and whispered, "It's all right, Red. You're okay."

Alaric's teeth receded into his gums, back to normal, and he panted heavily, Bashima's chin on his shoulder, hands clasped over Alaric's heart. "Just you and me here."

"I'm sorry," Alaric said, tears falling. He felt like all he'd done that evening was argue with Bashima and cry, as though every fiber of his being wanted to instigate a reaction. Anything to get his husband to pay attention to him. The hot tears fell onto Bashima's arms, sizzling on his skin, which alarmed Alaric. Bashima wasn't the one who was on fire. Alaric's tears were boiling.

"You don't have to apologize, I'm here," Bashima said, running a hand down Alaric's back, stroking the brand, which also calmed him, their connection most focused when the Sun God touched him there.

"Yes, I do," Alaric said. "I almost…I'm awful."

"What do you need?" Bashima asked, hand drifting to Alaric's pants, dipping below the waistband. Alaric's hips rolled toward Bashima's waiting hand, his hardness meeting warm flesh, and the Sun God took hold of him and stroked, hand firm but gentle.

"Harder," Alaric said, jutting his hips forward again.

Bashima increased the pressure, holding his husband's body close with his other arm, restraining Alaric while he helped. Bashima let Alaric use his fist, hips jutting up, sharp teeth biting down on the arm that encircled Alaric's neck. Bashima grunted, and Alaric felt his husband's hardness against his back. He lurched harder, trying not to focus on his husband's ready and willing dick. But it was too much.

"You need to fuck me now," Alaric said, "Or I think I'll lose it."

Bashima didn't need telling twice. He pushed down Alaric's trousers and lined himself up. Though Alaric hadn't prepped, he felt no pain when the Sun God pushed into him; it was like he'd been ready for years, and Bashima felt perfect inside him. His husband's hand pulsed on Alaric's cock as he fucked him from behind, every motion in sync, and Alaric shoved his hips back in unison, aching for Bashima to go deeper and harder. He urged Bashima on, releasing the Sun God's arm, lest he bite too hard.

Alaric felt Bashima's skin heat behind him, and his brand blazed with light. It wasn't enough. Everything Bashima did felt amazing, he was the perfect lover, but it wasn't what the base part of Alaric's mind craved. That part wanted to be dominant, to show the Sun God who was really in charge. Alaric battled with that part of himself constantly, usually enjoying when it took over, but now wasn't the right time. It felt insatiable, like he might destroy the Sun God. This voice hadn't been so insistent before.

When he could hold back no longer, Alaric let himself go.

Alaric growled and rolled them both off the bed. Bashima let out a startled "oof" when they hit the floor, and Alaric skittered away from him on his hands and feet, back arched, eyes igniting crimson. It was different from the other times his dragon-side tried to take over. He was more aware, more hyper-focused on Bashima's scent and the sounds in the room. He was done relying on sight. His body wanted to take control, to transform and show who was more powerful.

We're equals, his saner mind warned, he's just as strong as you.

That thought only spurred his desire.

"You better not transform," Bashima warned, palms igniting in bright light. He stood near the bed, eyes glimmering gold and orange, tongue licking his bottom lip. "You want me, come and get me."

The invitation was all Alaric needed. He sprang at Bashima, much faster than the Sun God expected, Alaric's reflexes honed after months with the dragon-touched body. Alaric slammed the Sun God into the bed, and a forceful light flash went off, but he hardened his face in time, and it had no effect. He let the scales fade back into his cheeks and kissed Bashima, hard but closed-mouthed, and the Sun God melted beneath him.

"I need you," Alaric begged, panting in Bashima's mouth. "I don't know why, but I need…"

"If you're going to fuck me, you better do it before I kick your ass," Bashima growled, pushing him back. Alaric's body howled in outrage and he swept his husband to the floor, turned him over, and pulled off his soft trousers. Bashima pressed back, ready, snapping at him, clawing up Alaric's arm. Light flashed over his skin, the arousal colors, dark reds like blood.

Knowing that his mate was accepting him but still defiant filled Alaric with a euphoria he wasn't prepared for. Bashima was perfect. He never made Alaric feel lesser because of who he was. The Sun God protected him every day, protected them every day. So, he couldn't fuck him like some random stranger.

Alaric ran his hand down Bashima's back, making the Sun God shiver in anticipation. He grabbed one hip and leaned forward, running his tongue over the claiming bite on Bashima's shoulder, linking them, pulling them together. The Sun God's passion released, vibrating through their bond, a nonverbal invitation, and Alaric thrust forward, Bashima sighing loudly, asking for more.

Alaric wasted no time. He leaned into each thrust, pulling Bashima closer, his strength increasing, almost pulling Bashima off his hands and knees. Bashima was just as strong, and he planted himself, taking everything Alaric had, grunting approval, the red light a dazzling display along his back and neck.

"Gods," Bashima said, "my dragon, so strong."

Alaric nibbled at his husband's neck as he pulled out then rammed home again, Bashima taking it, not flagging. Something inside Alaric burst, the ache, the want, needing to be inside his mate forever, and he came hard. He usually had time to warn Bashima, but it hit him like thunder. They pitched forward from the force, Bashima landing on his stomach with Alaric pulsing into him until he was spent. They lay still,

Bashima underneath him, Alaric still inside the Sun God, ruby-colored, shining cum seeping beneath them. That was new.

Neither of them spoke as their light shows dimmed. Bashima's' skin lost the shining colors, and Alaric's brand stopped glowing, leaving them in a dim bedroom.

After a few minutes laying together on the floor, Alaric stirred. "Um…" Alaric said, "I think I need to go again."

"You're still inside me," Bashima said, his voice flat but satiated. "Just keep going."

It turned into an insane late night and early morning for the Sun God and his husband. Alaric's lust couldn't be tempered. They roved around their chambers, Bashima tired and irritable, Alaric lascivious and slightly embarrassed, each giving what they could, mostly Alaric taking what Bashima offered.

When the sun started rising, they were entangled on the floor in the sitting room, furniture overturned, Bashima on his back and Alaric lying on top of him, breathing hard.

"I think," Bashima said, unable to move, "that I lost count."

"Of what?" Alaric asked, tongue hanging out of his mouth. His dick finally quieted, and he wasn't sure how they'd ended up on the floor in the sitting room.

"Of how many times you tore into my ass, idiot," Bashima said, trying to push Alaric off. It didn't work, and his arms fell to his sides. "Can you get off me so I can get ready for work?" He flicked Alaric's forehead.

Tired and sore himself, Alaric huffed and said, "Take the day off. Who even cares." The moment he said it, he regretted it, and Alaric covered his mouth with his hands, eyes wide, staring down at his annoyed husband. "I didn't mean it!" Alaric said, talking through his fingers. "I don't know what's wrong with me. I'm exhausted but my skin feels like it wants to jump off my body."

His cock twitched between them, and Bashima's eyes flashed gold.

He gathered his strength and shoved Alaric away, saying, "If we keep this up, I really will mess up." Bashima gathered himself, stood, and backed away from his husband. "Don't look at me like that, I have to go. The Sun God doesn't get days off."

Alaric hadn't realized he'd been making a face, so he shook his head, trying to hide his desire and self-consciousness. Bashima saw him naked all the time, but Alaric hadn't felt so vulnerable in a long time. Even as his dragon strength rallied, his blood running hot, Alaric felt ashamed.

"Fuck," Bashima said. He knelt beside Alaric and cupped his chin, raising Alaric's face so their eyes met. "I always want to be with you," Bashima said, "But I can't be with you every second."

Alaric knew Bashima was trying his best, but he didn't know what was happening. This feeling wasn't normal. Alaric had a healthy sex drive, but he already felt himself overheating again. Something was off, and Bashima didn't realize it. Alaric was amazed; wouldn't Bashima have thought having sex all night was odd? They hadn't stopped for hours. Even with Bashima's innate healing ability he would be staggering around the temple.

Alaric exhaled roughly, and smoke tendrils came from his nostrils, causing them both to pause. Bashima looked at him askance, and Alaric touched his nose, but it felt fine. It wasn't hotter than usual.

"We're going to discuss that later. Do you feel up to hanging out with the moron squad while I work?" Bashima asked. "Or do you want to stay here?"

"I should at least try and explain myself," Alaric said, sighing. "Although I won't be able to explain it any better than Cypress."

"You're living as a dragon-touched. Fucking Tengu can theorize all he wants, but that doesn't make him an expert." Bashima patted him on the shoulder and sniffed, nose wrinkling. "We definitely need to wash up or the entire temple will reek."

Alaric giggled. They smelled terrible, although it was enticing to his overtaxed brain. Bashima leaned in and kissed him then limped from the room, saying, "We better go separately. I don't think I can handle more right now." He said it in a joking manner, but it riled Alaric a bit. There was an odd sense of pride coming from deep within his mind, that he'd put his mate in this condition. He bristled, but the Sun God shifted away to the baths, out of his reach.

For all the powers the dragons blessed him with, Alaric couldn't shift on his own. His body could deal with the strain, but it was beyond his reach to perform the trick. He usually didn't mind, but this morning he wanted nothing more than to follow the Sun God and make him limp more.

After throwing water on his face from their bedroom washing basin and wiping himself down as best he could, Alaric huffed around the room, trying to set furniture right, cleaning up. He couldn't leave their mess for the shades.

Everything they'd touched smelled like Bashima, and Alaric had to sit down multiple times to collect himself.

You need to calm down, he thought, frustrated with his delinquent cock. Getting hot and bothered while Bashima worked wouldn't do either of them any good.

After he'd cleaned up, Matthias came in with Alaric's breakfast, a concerned expression marring his usually pleasant features.

"Alaric," the shade said, looking around the room, "Kuroi said there was an incident last night. Is everything okay?" The shade set

Alaric's tray down on the table he'd just set back up. "He asked if I would bring up your breakfast. Gods! You're covered in bruises!"

"You should see the other guy," Alaric joked, leaning his head back so it hit the back of the sofa. There were some odd red stains on the ceiling.

"That's not funny," Matthias said and stomped over, hands on his hips. "What the hells did you do to each other? Wait. No. I don't want to know. You two are incorrigible."

"Sorry," Alaric said. "Do you know if everyone is still here? They may have…seen me transform last night."

Matthias rubbed his face with a hand and shook his head. "That's more than an 'incident.'" He glanced at Alaric, who felt guilty for worrying his friend. He'd made things difficult for Kuroi as well. Matthias said, "The others are still here, though none of them have called for breakfast yet."

"Maybe we could eat together?" Alaric wondered.

It would be better to talk to everyone while they were in a group. They might feel safer than if Alaric spoke to them one-on-one, and he doubted Cabari would let him get anywhere near Jace alone. He remembered a few things from the night before, mainly scents, and underneath his usual woodsy scent, Jace had smelled like ozone and rain and sour lemons, just like the Lightning God. Cabari marking his territory, Alaric guessed.

"I'll see what I can do," Matthias said, a small smile touching his lips. "It will be all right. Everyone here knows Master Bashima, and they adore you. Tell the truth, and they'll accept it."

Or maybe they wouldn't.

Kuroi and Matthias set up breakfast in the conservatory, which Alaric thought was an excellent idea. The atmosphere was quiet and serene, and more importantly, it wasn't where Alaric lost control in front of them.

Bashima was in the throne room, meditating, but Alaric could handle this by himself. His husband needed to focus on the sun, not on Alaric's issues. The possessive urge remained as well, so all the better that Bashima stayed away.

Alaric entered the conservatory and heard them chatting near the main fountain, voices subdued but not fearful. The shades had set a long table with an assortment of food and drink, but the others hadn't eaten much.

"Shina!" Cabari yelled when Alaric came into view. "Glad you decided clothes weren't optional, not that I'm complaining. Ow!" Jace smacked the Lightning God on the back of the head, and Cabari grinned, shrugging. "I mean, if you were going to give us dinner and a show, you could have advertised." He dodged another blow from Jace, who looked exhausted, though it wasn't much different from his usual disposition.

"Shut up, you ass," Alora said. She got up and beckoned Alaric over, enveloping him in a hug. "You okay, hon?" She shoved him into a chair. Grateful to her, Alaric smiled.

"I'll be okay," Alaric said, "but I need to apologize to you all."

He looked around the table. Cypress was nervous and fidgety, but he knew everything, so Alaric figured it wasn't about his transformation. Something else was weighing on the Forest God. He'd have to ask later.

Oken ate a piece of toast, not paying attention, which made sense too; he also knew almost every detail of Alaric's abilities. Oken looked into the fountain, watching the koi fish swim beneath the water's surface.

Cabari and Alora smiled, encouraging. Alaric noted that Jace and Garyn were sitting with their respective partners, but their body language was less agreeable. They leaned away from Cabari and Alora, their arms crossed, expressions serious. Since they'd been the most in the dark about Alaric's condition, it made sense. They were confused and upset, but at least they weren't afraid of him.

Alaric thought maybe they should be. He had control at the moment and the obsessive pull toward Bashima had lessened. It still beat a steady rhythm in his chest, clenching his heart, but was manageable.

"I'm sorry you saw me like that," Alaric said, voice gaining strength. "I lost control, and that's unacceptable. I don't understand exactly what happened to me at the Temple of Time." His voice broke a bit when he mentioned the temple, and he felt a slight twinge on his back. He winced and shifted around in his seat, making Cypress focus his attention on him. Alaric hated that they had to be tense around him, but it was a reasonable reaction. He was glad they'd agreed to talk with him at all.

"I wasn't afraid of you," Oken said, staring at the koi. Cypress glanced at his partner, as if he were trying to tell if Oken was being truthful.

"Thank you," Alaric said, "I understand if anyone else was, though."

Jace met his eyes, unfathomable, and Garyn remained on edge.

Alaric continued, "I don't know what Cypress told you, but he's probably the only one who gets what's happening to me. A few months ago, I was a normal human, and now…"

"You're part dragon?" Cabari asked, excited. "That's incredible!"

"But what does it mean?" Garyn asked. "We don't know you very well, and you seem like a good guy, but expecting us to just roll with this..."

Alaric put up his hands in surrender. "You shouldn't have to! It's weird and scary and I would understand if you didn't want to be my friend."

"Of course, we're still your friends," Alora said and nudged Garyn. "We just want to know what's going on and if we need to watch out for anything."

"We're supposed to keep it secret?" Garyn asked, glaring at Alora. "Even from the king? Cypress, can you keep it from your mother?"

They looked at the Forest God, whose expression was firm. His eyes shined and his green freckles stood out on his flushed cheeks. He said, "It's of the utmost importance that no one else knows about Shina. Even Vaultus and my mother can't know." When Garyn looked like he might counter, Cypress said, "Shina is a unique being. There aren't many dragon-touched in the entire world, if any at all. We don't know the extent of his powers, but I'm sure there are people who would love to find out. And they wouldn't do it gently. I don't want him to be some experiment or stuck in a cage for eternity. Because we don't know how his life expectancy has been affected by this." He paused, as though wondering if he should say the next thing. "The gods killed all the dragons who chose not to ascend. We hunted them down, and now there are no more dragons. Shina has more right to be angry with us, even though none of us had anything to do with that."

Alora's eyes widened in horror and Garyn looked down, realizing what Cypress said was true. Cabari picked at his fingernails, and Jace said, "I have absolutely no idea why we're having a discussion. Shina is our friend. He's probably the most valuable person in the world, right? We should protect him if we can."

Alaric hadn't expected that from Jace, and Cabari looked at the demigod like he'd never seen him before. He scooted closer to Jace and laid his head on the demigod's shoulder. Jace rolled his eyes but allowed it.

"Thanks, Jace," Alaric said. "I would tell everyone if I could. I don't like keeping secrets, especially if they put others at risk. But I also don't want to be poked and prodded either. I need to find a way to control my emotions better."

"That'll be easy, married to Bashima," Cabari said and snorted. When they glared at him, he said, "What? It's true. We've all wanted to beat the shit out of him at least once."

"Not me," said Oken, and Cabari waved his response away.

"Okay, everyone besides you." He raised an eyebrow at Alaric. "How are you supposed to keep your temper when you live with the biggest asshole in the pantheon?"

Alaric laughed, clutching the table. "Yeah, he's a pain in the ass, but I did marry him. I suppose I should give him a chance." He wiped away a mirthful tear and said, "He's pissed me off without me flying out of control, so I don't think the argument was the trigger last night."

"Then what?" Cypress asked, curious.

Alaric didn't know what to say. It probably had something to do with his ravenous…appetite, but he didn't want to mention that. He was embarrassed enough.

Alaric sighed and said, "We'll figure it out. Thank you, all of you. It's a lot to ask."

"If it's between you being hunted down like an animal and us keeping quiet, I think we can handle a secret," Garyn said. His elbow wings fluttered, his face pensive but resolved.

Alaric nodded, grateful. Though more people knew about his dragon side, at least no one but Cypress knew about the soul bond he shared with the Sun God. If the wrong god found out and believed it, it could be infinitely worse for Alaric and Bashima.

Chapter Three

Bashima

After a week of Alaric attacking him the instant the sun set, Bashima was feeling the strain. He'd sent an urgent letter to Maida, the Fertility Goddess, asking what the hells she thought might be the reason for his husband's insatiable, aggressive behavior. His stressful incantation to Garyn — as the Messenger of the Gods, Garyn controlled the magical flow of letters between the gods — worked, because Maida replied with haste.

"Greetings Sun God,

Another letter in such a short span of time, and sent express no less! What exactly are you getting up to these days? Besides a glorious amount of sex, that is. I suppose, with your duties as Sun God, your husband's appetite will start to wear thin over time. I enjoy these delicious questions and am intrigued yet again by your god-touched man. Although, it seems less like he's god-touched and perhaps something else.

Is Shina an animal hybrid? The enhanced libido and protective or obsessive nature suggests that he may be in a rut or heat. It's common among many animals, though I'd have to look into human-animal hybrids. I do know that it's an occurrence with no discernible schedule and can last for days or weeks, depending on the animal. Unicorns have a similar instinct, if we're adding magical creatures to the list, and full adult dragons were known to rut for months. It's a breeding thing, and they became quite savage when their time came. Grown male dragons would tear anything apart that came near their mate while in rut.

The cum being a different color points to the magical option as well. That is quite unusual. Have you tasted it yet? Since you're a god, it shouldn't hurt you, though there may be some interesting side effects. If you do happen to ingest his cum, please document its effects.

As always, if you need assistance on the sexual front, just send another note.

Maida, Goddess of Fertility"

Bashima thought of Maida's letter as he hoisted Alaric's legs onto his shoulders. At least the redhead allowed Bashima to shift them back to their chambers before attempting to tear Bashima's clothes off, but they hadn't made it to the bedroom. Alaric tackled him to the ground the instant their feet hit the floor and tried to pin him, but Bashima flipped him onto his back, his own need cascading through his mind.

Knowing his husband wanted him so ardently made Bashima hard almost immediately, but he wasn't sure how long Alaric would let him be in control. The answer was: not long. Alaric tried to shove Bashima off, but the Sun God used all his strength to drive his husband back onto the floor, hands pressed on the redhead's shoulders. Alaric's eyes rolled back, accepting Bashima's dominance for now, fingers growing sharp claws that gauged the floor.

Fuck, Bashima thought, at least he didn't claw me this time.

Bashima's body was covered in claw marks, healing at varying times. His torso looked like a crudely drawn map.

Bashima leaned down and connected their lips, tongue searching for purchase, evading Alaric's sharp teeth, which nipped at him. He touched their foreheads together, releasing the redhead's mouth and moaned with pleasure. Alaric's eyes snapped open, full crimson, and he pulled Bashima closer, widening his legs, Bashima's hips slamming into him. He reached between them and stroked his length and Bashima thrust deeper, clenching his teeth. Alaric's soul walls fell, encasing Bashima in red swirling desire and aching need. It was like falling into an abyss.

Hit with the entire blast of his husband's emotions, Bashima came hard, and Alaric followed. Some of the ruby-colored fluid got in Bashima's mouth, coating his tongue with the taste of pomegranate and smoke, and he felt an instant euphoria. It was like when Alaric took him cloud-dancing, soaring into an open sky, nothing to hold them down. Just them, together.

Taking advantage of Bashima's stunned state, Alaric pried his husband off and tossed him over the back of the couch, draping him ass-up. Bashima groaned, his head swimming with the taste of Alaric lingering in his mouth. His husband knelt behind him and licked him everywhere, a rumble forming deep in his chest and vibrating out. Bashima melted into the couch, his husband's tongue soothing him, another new phenomenon from the last week that he needed to ask gods-damned Maida about. Soothing spit? A weird concept.

While it seemed like Alaric was always prepped now, ready for sex at a moment's notice, Bashima didn't have that ability. Luckily, his husband usually remembered that fact, but today was not that day. As soon as his tongue left, Alaric thrust forward, bending over Bashima's back and licking the claiming mark, which sent Bashima tumbling into another passion. His husband's brand glowed, enveloping them in golden light, and Bashima's skin ignited as well, glimmering in yellow and orange.

With a grunt, Alaric lifted Bashima bodily from the sofa, arms bound around Bashima's chest. He heaved the Sun God into the air and fucked up into him. Bashima's toes curled from the sensation and realization that Alaric was strong enough to pull off the move. He held up the Sun God as though he weighed no more than air. Bashima wrapped his feet behind Alaric's thighs, holding on. He leaned his head back and closed his eyes as Alaric drove into him again and again.

Alaric's breath came hot and rapid on Bashima's neck, and he nuzzled his husband, whimpering in his ear, "Best mate. Best husband. Love you." Alaric came again, with less force than before. He gathered Bashima in his arms and laid him on the sofa before collapsing onto the floor beside him. Spent, or at least for the moment.

"Fucking hells," Bashima said after a few minutes of them panting, chests heaving. "Where the fuck you learn that?"

"I have no idea," Alaric said, dazed. "I wanted to do it."

They were both covered in sweat, Bashima's blond hair plastered to his forehead. Alaric reached up and caressed Bashima's arm, interlocking their fingers. His eyes were back to normal, which was a good sign that he was done for a while, and Bashima sighed in relief. Even with his husband's healing tongue baths, Bashima's body was wrecked. Covered with scratches and bruises, everything felt sore and beaten. Alaric's body was also littered with wounds, but his — rut, it's a damn rut — current condition helped him heal faster. If Bashima were another dragon, he might not be having these issues. Oh, to be a dragon.

"We have to figure this out, Red," Bashima said, voice hoarse. "I nearly fell asleep in the throne room today, and gods knows what would happen if I did."

His husband didn't answer, running his fingertips over Bashima's knuckles. Alaric also knew it had to stop, but Bashima didn't think he could help it, not with his baser urges in charge. Bashima continued, "I got Maida's answer today."

"You did?" Alaric yelled, sitting up, dislodging their hands. "Why didn't you say something?"

"You were a little busy jamming your tongue down my throat and your dick up into my damn stomach," Bashima growled. He didn't bother sitting up. His head spun, and pomegranate whirled through his senses. It was so alluring that he almost gave in and reached for Alaric to kiss him, but they needed a break.

"I told you," Alaric said, pouting, "I can't seem to control myself. It's like there's a bow inside me and someone keeps drawing the string back. But I'm so tired." He leaned his chin down onto Bashima's chest, staring at him with those massive eyes. Bashima couldn't resist the pained gleam and long lashes, and he stroked Alaric's cheek, smiling.

"We have at least a few answers, but I want to double check with Tengu. I figure we can take a short trip there tomorrow after the sun sets."

"What did she say?" Alaric asked, hand inching across Bashima's waist. The Sun God slapped his husband's hand, and Alaric hissed, "Ow! You didn't have to do that." He sat back on his haunches, bottom lip sticking out.

"If we go again, I might not have any brain cells left to tell you what that rabbit-eared goddess said." He sighed and finally sat up, body protesting. They'd have to clean the sofa again. It was the fourth time that week.

"I'm shifting us to the baths, okay?" Bashima said, and Alaric's eyes gleamed. "Not for that! We need to clean up and go to bed. And not have sex," he added. "Can't take anymore right now."

Alaric's face fell, but he nodded. "I think I'll be okay for a while," he said, sounding cranky. It would be different if Bashima could satisfy Alaric with his hands or mouth, but the damn dragon wanted to come inside him every time. It didn't matter that Bashima couldn't possibly carry children; the breeding drive must be too strong to ignore.

Bashima beckoned his husband over, and Alaric grabbed his hand. They went straight to the baths, Alaric collapsing into the hottest pool and swimming around like a damn shark, Bashima going for the medium heat. He might fall asleep in the hottest bath. After they washed, Alaric dove into Bashima's pool and swam circles around him. Bashima held up a finger, seeing the eagerness returning to his husband's eyes.

"No," he said, and the firmness stopped Alaric, who whimpered but stopped swimming. Alaric settled for them sitting on the ledge so he could mess with Bashima's hair, massaging his scalp. So long as he was at least touching the Sun God, he seemed okay.

"All right," Bashima said, "Maida probably knows you're not god-touched now, but there's not much we can do about that." Alaric stiffened behind him, his grooming paused. Bashima glanced at him and said, "She doesn't know the specifics but asked if you're an animal hybrid. She's curious, obviously, but she won't say anything. The other gods think she's nuts, remember?"

"Uh huh," Alaric said and continued running his fingers through Bashima's hair, fluffing it up, settling himself behind his husband. He didn't get too close, which made Bashima sigh in relief. At least Alaric was listening to him when he said no.

"She mentioned that animals go into this thing called a rut or heat."

"Oh, yeah," Alaric said. "The sheep and goats do that, makes them really…hard to handle." As though realizing something, he stopped touching Bashima and backed away. "Is that what's happening?"

"Maybe, but I doubt sheep or goats get as insane as we've been. Maida said magical animals have this rut thing, unicorns and shit." He turned around to look at his husband, who seemed surprised that unicorns were real. "She said dragons did it too and were savage fuckers when it happened."

"Oh," Alaric said, hugging himself, blushing scarlet.

"Hey, it's not like I don't appreciate a rough fuck every now and again," Bashima said, "but she said adult dragon ruts could last for months."

"What?" Alaric yelled. He launched himself out of the pool and ran to his changing room, closing the curtain and screaming into the bunched-up fabric.

"I can hear you, you know," Bashima said and rolled his eyes. "At least you're the one who gets to do most of the fucking. I feel like I can't walk half the time after we're done."

Alaric's feet shuffled under the curtain, and Bashima got out of the pool slowly, his muscles creaking. He walked over to the curtain and tapped where he thought his husband's forehead might be. His finger connected, and Alaric whined, kicking out from under the curtain. He didn't hit Bashima, which made the Sun God laugh.

"You're not a full dragon, so maybe it won't last that long. Either way, I can't take many more nights of constant fucking. We need to check if Tengu has any solutions before we ask Maida again."

"Okay," Alaric said quietly. He opened the curtain a bit, peeking out. "Maybe I should sleep in my old room tonight." He sounded so sad that it made Bashima furious, both at his husband and at himself. He held back a sharp retort, remembering to take a deep breath. Alaric couldn't help what was happening, and they were both weary.

"Hells no," Bashima said. "You're sleeping in our bed. We can make a pillow wall or something."

"That might work," Alaric said. "I suppose I can hump a pillow. Better than doing it to you in your sleep."

Bashima rubbed a hand down his face, expecting a difficult night's sleep. But he wouldn't banish Alaric from their bedroom. At least, not yet.

Interlude

Oken

The Forest God fainted, falling from Oken's grip, and fell to the temple floor. Oken stared down at his would-be savior and had to admit that he was kind of attractive, if ram's horns were your thing. Apparently, they were Oken's thing, because he couldn't stop looking at the god's closed eyes, gaping mouth, and wild green hair. The irritated Sun God didn't bother him; Oken had a much scarier god in his own home, so posturing meant little to him. The Sun God had no intent to harm them, even though he was enraged.

"Oh, perfect," the Sun God said, and Oken noticed that his kilt was crooked, as if he'd put it on in great haste and had been naked moments before. How odd. The god glared at Cypress on the ground then at Oken and said, "Who the fuck are you, Zebra Head?"

"My name is Oken. Oken Cindras, not Zebra Head. If you're referring to my hair, that's not a very creative insult."

"What the fuck else would I be referring to?" The Sun God crossed his arms, eyes narrowed. "Did you say Cindras? Fuck me, you're one of the Fire God's spawn, aren't you?"

"That's also fairly offensive, but accurate," Oken said. He knelt down beside the Forest God and brushed his hair back, feeling his forehead. "He's slightly feverish. I think we shifted too quickly. He also muttered about having a spell running. That might have sapped his strength."

He looked up at the Sun God, who didn't seem impressed. Oken cleared his throat and said, "May we come in?"

The Sun God didn't speak, but pretty colors raced across his skin: yellows, oranges, and reds. Oken wanted to touch the god's skin but thought it might be rude. Most people didn't like to be touched unasked.

After a while, the god grew fidgety and huffed, "You're already inside. Might as well make yourselves at home. Fucking waking people up in the middle of the night, fucking ridiculous. Kuroi!"

What an odd thing to yell, Oken thought, then a man appeared out of nowhere next to the Sun God.

He was fairly tall, though still a head shorter than Oken, with bushy black eyebrows and fathomless pitch-black eyes. Oken tilted his head. The Temple of the Sun got stranger with each moment.

The man — Kuroi — raised an eyebrow at Oken, unsure who he was and probably annoyed by the late hour of their arrival. But his eyes widened when he saw the Forest God splayed on the floor, cloak of concealment askew.

"Master Cypress?" he said, shocked. He looked at the Sun God, uncertain what to do. "What would you like me to do, Master Bashima?"

"Fuck if I know," the Sun God said. "You're the one who's supposed to be good at this hospitality shit. This asshole with him is a gods-damned Cindras. Why the fuck would Tengu bring him here?"

"We'll have to wait until he's conscious to ask him, Master," Kuroi said. "Master Cindras? Can you enlighten us?"

Oken looked from the black-eyed man to the Sun God. What did they want to hear? People always wanted explanations, reasons for the things he did. He wasn't even sure why he'd followed the Forest God, just that it seemed a better alternative to being stuck in the Temple of Fire all day and night.

"I know you're not fucking deaf," the Sun God said.

"Bell broke into my father's temple to rescue me," Oken said, and Kuroi's mouth dropped open. The Sun God snorted and rolled his eyes. Oken didn't know what else to say. "It's the truth. I didn't really need rescuing, but he made a good point. It was easier to get away with two people."

"I already have a fucking headache," the Sun God said, stomping away. "Put them in the guest wing, I really don't care."

Once the god was gone, Oken turned to Kuroi and said, "I'd rather stay with the Forest God, if that's okay. And please, don't use my father's name. I'm Oken."

"There are many rooms in the Temple of the Sun," Kuroi said, voice filled with pride. He stood tall and inclined his head. "I shall find one that suits you."

Oken was glad. He didn't like sleeping alone.

Chapter Four

Cypress

"Bell? Do you think they'll be okay?"

Cypress and Oken arrived back at the Temple of the Forest, having shifted from the ill-fated dinner party's aftermath. Cypress used fewer shifts than usual, so he was tired, but he'd wanted to get home and relax and try not to think about dragons or other gods' problems.

"I think they'll be fine," Cypress said, rubbing his eyes. He was ready to fall into bed and sleep for an entire day.

They walked into the temple, Oken quiet again. He'd hardly spoken on the way back, but Cypress was grateful not to need to think much. He could grasp Oken's hand and shift them.

The Temple of the Forest was made from trees shaped into livable structures. Oaks, maples, and birches mingled together. Cypress worked on coaxing the trees into the necessary shapes for centuries, honing his skills as he made his home. It wasn't easy, because trees were fairly stubborn, but he was very polite, and they were strong and withstood the elements. Perfect for Cypress's planned home.

While not as large as most gods' temples, Cypress could call it his own creation. Most gods had no talent to create with their powers; they could control and manipulate but not create. Another example was Pressa, the Goddess of Music, whose job was literally to create and inspire creation. That was one thing the celestials made sure most gods couldn't do, and Cypress wasn't certain why they'd given his mother the ability. He was even more adept at it than his mother, who relied on a seasonal schedule with three other gods. Cypress did most everything on his own.

It gave him job mobility, being able to use his power in any forest in the world. He could reach out to the forests all over the world and help them regulate when needed. He often coordinated with other minor earth gods, but he did the bulk of the work. No one else had his gift with the trees and other plants, and forest animals adored him. They'd been waylaid on their way back to the temple by a flock of geese who were eager to share a massive amount of gossip.

After entertaining the birds, Cypress felt even more weary.

The temple doors opened for him and Oken, and his head shade, Dasari, was at the door. Her long black hair hung like a waterfall down her back, and her large brown eyes were alert.

"Master Cypress, Master Oken," she said, inclining her head. "I assume that you need to retire at once to your chambers?"

Cypress laughed. Dasari knew exactly how he felt after returning from Bashima's company. "Yes. We'll go right to our room. Can you please have some dinner sent up? Oken, do you want anything special?"

The demigod shook his head, still silent, and Cypress furrowed his brow. Oken usually liked talking to Dasari when they got back. Maybe he was more exhausted than Cypress had thought.

They walked through the halls. Covering the ceiling was a canopy of everlasting leaves that changed with the seasons, a gift from the temple. Oken liked the spring colors the best, and he enjoyed decorating the dark browns of winter with his ice. He made no comment on the new colors as they went to their room, shuffling along behind Cypress. Something weighed on him, but Cypress didn't have the emotional strength to ask. Maybe in the morning.

Their bedroom was made of cherry wood and decorated with earthy tones; the bed covered with soft sheets and blankets that beckoned Cypress. He was always glad when he didn't have to wear formal or ceremonial clothes, and a dinner party and sleepover hadn't counted as a special occasion. He stripped off his travel tunic and tossed it to the floor, face-planting on the bed. It felt amazing. Staying at the Temple of the Sun was fine, but nothing beat his bed. He rubbed at the bases of his horns, groaning.

Oken sat on his side of the bed and drummed his fingers on the duvet.

"Bell?" he asked, voice hesitant.

"Hmm?" Cypress said, thinking whether he should just sleep on top of the blankets and not bother unmaking the bed. Oken probably wouldn't mind.

"Why aren't we married?"

And Cypress was fully awake. He stood up, lightning quick, not sure what to do with his hands, and stared at Oken.

"What?" It wasn't the best reply, but he was tired and unprepared.

"I thought the question was clear, but apparently not," Oken looked at him, brow furrowed. "I would like to know why we're not married."

Cypress thought he might lose consciousness. What was Oken talking about? They'd been together for fifteen hundred years. Why suddenly ask about marriage? He thought back to a few months ago to Oken's fascination with Bashima's and Shina's wedding. He'd asked so many questions that day, wanting to know everything about the ceremony and why people got married. Cypress hadn't thought much about it at the time, but now he realized it had been something noteworthy. Shit.

"Why we're not…"

"Married," Oken said, concerned. "Are you having trouble hearing? Do I need to get the ear cleaning kit?"

"No, I heard you," Cypress said. He felt the blood draining from his face and imagined that his freckles were standing out in stark contrast. "I just…do we have to talk about this now?"

Oken tilted his head, brows contracting. "I think so, yes."

"I'm really tired, you're tired."

"I'm not tired," Oken said, "I've been thinking about asking you for a while. I thought you might say that we needed to wait for a better time to discuss it, but when would a better time be?"

"Literally any time besides now?" Cypress said, ruffling the back of his hair. Leaves fell to the floor and he looked down at them. Dammit. He swept the leaves under the bed, wanting to pay attention to anything besides Oken.

"I don't want to wait," Oken said. "You'll find an excuse not to talk about it."

Oken had him there. Cypress was trying to brainstorm reasons to postpone the discussion. Could he say that a forest was in danger somewhere and flee?

"You're thinking of leaving." Oken stood up and faced Cypress, frowning. "Why are you panicking? Isn't this something couples talk about?"

"I had no idea you wanted to talk about it," Cypress admitted. Oken was putting out an annoyed energy, something Cypress rarely felt from him. Oken was usually calm and even-tempered, reliable.

"You've never asked," Oken said, obstinate.

"Why does it have to be on me?" Cypress asked, pointing to his chest. "Is this because Bashima and Shina got married?"

"Not entirely," Oken said, voice lowering. "You're saying everything about our relationship is up to me? You're thousands of years older than me."

"What's that supposed to mean?" Cypress asked, huffing.

"It means that you've never made an effort. I don't even live here, Bell."

"What? Yes, you do!" Cypress didn't like the octave his voice had reached. Were they fighting? They were fighting. Fifteen hundred years together and it was the first time.

"I stayed over one night and didn't leave," Oken pointed out. "You never asked me to live with you."

"Are we seriously fighting?" Cypress asked, needing to clear it up. He was used to brawling with Bashima and had argued with Vaultus and his mother on numerous occasions, but he didn't know how to handle a disagreement between him and Oken. He hadn't thought it was possible.

Oken looked at him like he'd lost his mind. "Of course we're fighting. You don't want to marry me. You can admit it, you know."

Cypress's mouth fell open. He had no idea how to respond. How was he supposed to answer when he'd never thought about it? He tried to speak, but no words came.

"I'm fine to have sex with and keep at your temple but not to marry," Oken went on, and lowered his eyes. "Is it because I'm part human?"

"What are you talking about?" Cypress yelled, much louder than he'd intended. "That's not it at all!"

"You're a god," Oken said. "You could be with anyone. So why are you with me?"

"Because I love you!" Cypress was lost. Where was this coming from? Oken had been thinking about it a while? Had he been waiting for Cypress to ask? "I didn't know you wanted to get married!"

"You never —"

"Stop saying I never asked!" Leaves rained off his body, forming a pile at his feet. "Argh! These leaves!"

"It's true," Oken said. "I know you think you love me, but you shut me out a lot. And I don't understand why. If you loved me as much as you think you do, why won't you listen to me right now instead of trying to shut me up?"

"That's not what I'm doing!" Cypress said, and green energy crackled over his skin, his ire rising. He scorched the leaves at his feet and smoke rose into the air. Oken's eyes widened, and Cypress choked on a breath and calmed himself. The green light faded. "I'm sorry," he said. "I do love you. And you do live here. With me. I thought that's what you wanted. Isn't that enough?"

Oken looked at him, expression unreadable. He eventually took off his tunic and walked over to his changing screen, grabbing his pajama bottoms on the way. "Let's go to bed," he said from behind the screen. When he came out, he wouldn't meet Cypress's eyes. He climbed into bed and tucked the blanket under his chin, facing away from Cypress's side of the bed.

Cypress changed into his sleepwear too and eased under the covers, careful not to disturb Oken.

Only when he was almost asleep did Cypress realize why Oken wanted to talk about marriage so much. His mother lived with the Fire God, had his children, but she was more of a nuisance than anything to the Fire God. After everything she'd done for him…he hadn't married her.

Oken didn't bring it up the next morning or the next day. Or the next. He went about his normal routine: reading, chatting with the shades, shadowing Dasari when she let him, waiting for Cypress to finish working so they could have dinner. The Forest God didn't have as strict a schedule as the Sun God, but he preferred to work during the day. If there was a crisis while he was asleep, he would wake instantly.

The only thing Oken wasn't doing was showing Cypress affection. Oken liked to hold hands. A lot. He enjoyed grabbing Cypress's hand as they walked from the throne room to dinner and when they retired to their room. He snuggled up to Cypress the instant they were in bed, giving off a calming warmth. He'd find excuses to touch Cypress whenever he could, but he must still have been miffed from their fight. Cypress didn't say anything, didn't want to call attention to it. He didn't want to make Oken feel bad by calling him out on his behavior. Or lack of behavior. They hadn't gone without sex for more than a few days the entire time they'd been together.

Did you ever even ask him out on a date?

Cypress's brain was a traitor, trying to find all the things he'd missed or done wrong in their relationship. Surely, he must have at least done that. But he couldn't remember any particular dates. It was like they'd always been a couple, ever since that first stay at the Temple of the Sun. Oken was so easy to fall for, so willing to be loved. He said awkward things on occasion, but Cypress found it endearing, even if he was sometimes embarrassed by it. It wasn't Oken's fault; his father hadn't taught him much besides how to use his power and fight with it. Not that Oken liked to use his power. The ice was one thing, but Cypress knew something would have to be terribly wrong for Oken to use his fire.

If Oken needed some space, Cypress would give it to him. He wouldn't bother Oken with his inadequate words. He'd only make things worse. Because he wasn't sure he ever wanted to get married. He wanted to be with Oken forever. His soul called out to Oken's, another thing they'd never talked about. Oken seemed in tune with Cypress's feelings for the most part, but he never asked if that was odd, he simply accepted it as fact. Maybe it was time to bring it up. If Oken knew they were soul-bonded, that might be enough. Cypress would pledge to be with him forever, to protect him and love him. Yes, that's what he would do. When he got up his courage.

About a week passed and Oken finally took his hand when Cypress met him outside the throne room. He relaxed and gripped back, a smile rising. He finally felt like things were back to normal. Had he been that agitated all week from Oken not touching him? He could feel desire coming off Oken, which nearly caused him to trip. Yup, he was starving for Oken.

All through dinner, they made conversation, but Oken kept up the simmering passionate energy assault, driving Cypress crazy. Oken didn't seem to notice the effect he was having, because he kept bringing up mundane things, asking if they could go visit Jace soon. Oken hadn't been to the Underworld in a while, and he liked the other demigod's company. Cypress wasn't sure why. Veles's son was interesting but very unusual. When Oken mentioned Jace, his energy did something strange. It sent a spike of emotion at Cypress, a sense of belonging, of kinship. Jace knew what it was like to be a demigod, and one from an unorthodox union. That connection was something Cypress couldn't give Oken.

"Of course we can go. Are you sure you want me to go with you?"

Oken gave him a confused look and said, "Only if you want to."

"It'll be good to check in with Veles on some things," Cypress said, thinking. There were a few questions he'd been meaning to ask the God of the Dead. It would be the perfect time to do that while Oken spent time with Jace.

"I see," Oken said. "Are you finished? There's something I've wanted to do all week."

Another burst of sexual energy came off Oken, making Cypress drop his silverware. He said, "I'm definitely done."

Oken was on him the instant they entered their room, hands in Cypress's hair, pulling him in for a kiss. With his soul wall down, even just a little, Cypress felt helpless and melted into Oken's lips and tongue. His breath was icy tonight, sending shivers through Cypress's body, and he moaned into Oken's mouth, his need naked. Careful not to release all his soul energy, Cypress felt every part of his body reacting to Oken's touch.

Oken broke away and took off his tunic, and Cypress eagerly followed suit, reaching for Oken, but he shook his head. "I want to try something different."

Excited but a little nervous — sometimes Oken got weird ideas about sex, not that it didn't always turn out in their favor — Cypress nodded. "What were you thinking?"

"Remember that overly-personal gift Cabari gave us a few years ago?"

Cypress's eyes glazed over. He'd been dying to try that. How had Oken known? He hadn't thought the demigod would ever be into it, but he'd been wrong about the damn marriage thing, so maybe he was seeing Oken's hidden depths.

"I, um, remember," Cypress said, his dick hardening by the second. He needed to get himself under control. It would take some concentration to set up the contraption, though a construction incantation would probably do.

Oken smiled, his eyes soft. "Do you know where we put it? I thought you might have thrown it out."

"Nope, I know right where it is." Cypress snapped his fingers, and the collection of leather and cloth straps materialized between them and hit the floor.

Oken giggled, a sound Cypress wanted to hear forever. He looked at Cypress, blushing. "Have you ever used something like this?" Oken asked.

"What? No!" Cypress said. "I barely had normal sex before I met you." He stumbled over the words. Oken knew his history, short as it was. Cypress shouldn't be shy about it.

"Okay, then how do we…"

"Oh! I can try the construction incantation. Usually does the trick." Cypress gathered his power and closed his eyes, muttering the spell under his breath. Green lightning flew across his skin as he concentrated. He needed to focus on setting it up right, not fast. He didn't want them falling. Even if they weren't that high off the ground, it would ruin the mood considerably.

A whoosh and a gust of air told Cypress that it was done. Hanging from the ceiling, a safety line connecting to the wall, was a swing. The tree-wall and ceiling would hold anything for a long time, so that was at least sturdy enough to hold them up.

"Wow," Oken said, eyes wide. He stared at the swing like it was a mountain to conquer, then he glanced at Cypress, perhaps estimating their combined weight.

"I seriously have no idea what I'm doing," Cypress said, but Oken grabbed him and kissed roughly, his hands tugging at the Forest God's trousers. Cypress's hands ran up and down Oken's bare back, touching every familiar muscle, letting the demigod have his way. Oken pulled away from their kiss and knelt, taking the trousers with him. Cypress nearly fell from the force of Oken's eager tongue, his hands gripping Cypress's ass hard. Cypress held in gasps, his eyes bulging, and he grabbed Oken's hair, scraping his nails against Oken's scalp.

"You're gonna make me come too fast," he warned. Oken released Cypress and picked him up by the thighs, tossing him into the swing.

Well, I'm in for a rough night, Cypress thought, head swimming.

"We can't have that," Oken said, but there was something off about his voice. Cypress opened his eyes, and the demigod who stood before him was vastly different from the one who'd suggested the kinky sex detour. Gone was the never-ending desire. In its place was fury, like nothing Cypress had ever felt from Oken.

Before Cypress could react, Oken blasted him with a wave of icy wind, which pitched him up toward the ceiling, cutting off his breath for a moment. Coughing from the cold, Cypress opened his eyes and stared straight down at the floor. Oken had pinned him to the ceiling with a layer of thick ice. Every inch of Cypress's skin screamed, and he shook from the chill.

"Oken! What the hells are you doing? Let me down! This isn't funny!"

"I didn't intend it to be humorous, but seeing you up there is the first thing that's made me laugh all week," Oken said, glaring up at him, icy air rising. His right hand and arm were covered in sparkling crystals up to his shoulder.

"I'm freezing!" Cypress couldn't move an inch. He tried to summon his power, but it was too cold, and he knew the ice would be too strong. It was the same color as Oken's turquoise eyes, the coldest and strongest ice Oken could produce.

"You'll be fine," Oken said, crossing the room and taking a small pack from beneath the bed. "It'll melt. Eventually. Or the shades will get you down. Maybe if you ask nicely, the temple will release you."

Cypress watched in horror as Oken opened the pack. It was already full. He'd been planning this! The only thing he added to the pack was the threadbare stuffed cat he'd taken from the Temple of Fire the night Cypress rescued him. It normally sat on the table next to Oken's side of the bed.

"Wait, what are you doing?" Cypress asked. "You're not going to leave me here!"

"Why should I stay? You've given me no reason to."

"I told you that I wanted you to stay here!" Cypress yelled, trying to wiggle his body, but nothing moved. The only thing Oken left exposed was his head. It would be harder to use his power without his hands free.

Oken shot him a seething look, indifferent to Cypress's plight. "You couldn't bring yourself to talk to me when you knew I wanted to. When I asked. You ignored it, pretended I never said anything at all."

"I didn't want to make things worse!" Cypress said. "Please, Oken!"

"No," Oken said. He fastened the straps on his pack and hoisted it onto his back. "I'm going to my actual home for a while. You know, the one where I was actually invited to live."

Cypress was dumbstruck. Oken would rather go to the Temple of the Sun than stay with him? Oken was making no sense. He was pissed and frustrated and overreacting. It would pass the instant he had to deal with Bashima's and Shina's bullshit. Maybe it would be good for him to see that marriage wasn't the end-all-be-all in the world.

"Fine!" He yelled, voice shaking. "Do what you want!"

"Don't follow me," Oken said. "I don't need rescuing this time." He slammed the bedroom door, leaving the Forest God stuck to the ceiling, naked, in a sex swing.

Oken

He wasn't going to turn around. No. Not this time. He'd let Bell get away with everything for too long. The Forest God had ignored him for the last time.

But he almost turned around.

Storming out of the bedroom felt liberating. Marching down the halls made him feel powerful. Asking the doors to open and let him out into the world was freeing. And yet, when the doors closed behind him, Oken felt like shrieking into the forest. Something tore inside him, his heart beating rapidly, making him stumble. He stayed upright, barely, and set down the pack for a moment. He and Bell rarely left each other's side. This was the first time he'd thought about going somewhere without the Forest God, and it felt awful.

Why?

It wasn't supposed to feel like that. He was supposed to be striking out on his own, claiming his independence. He didn't need someone to hold him up. Not his father. Not Bell. He glared at the temple and stomped away. He wouldn't give in. Not just yet. Let Bell stay up on the ceiling for a while and think about what Oken had said. Not that he would. He'd stew over it, blame Oken, and call him unreasonable.

Well, Oken was done being reasonable.

He shifted away, taking their usual route toward the Temple of the Sun. He'd stay there for a while and try to stay out of Bashima's way. Shina would talk to him and tell him stories and make him feel better. They always welcomed him when he came back. Oken was fairly sure the temple liked him.

He reappeared in a dark forest den and sighed, stretching before taking the next shift.

He thought about Bashima and Shina, the Sun God and the special half-dragon. Their relationship seemed miraculous to Oken, considering how different they were. Bashima was irascible and preferred to keep to himself, while Shina was sociable and optimistic. But there was no doubt that they loved each other. Everyone could see it, could feel it. The way they looked at each other, how Bashima came to his husband's defense so quickly, or Shina's steadfastness even though Bashima was difficult.

Once, when Bell and Oken had been walking to the temple to visit the new couple, they'd come across them in the valley. Their horses were nearby, grazing, and they were just being together. Even from a distance, Oken could see that Bashima had his head laying in Shina's lap, the redhead weaving a crown of flowers to put in his husband's hair. Despite his acidic nature, Bashima would do anything for Shina, even allow him to shove the make-shift crown onto his blond hair.

Shina noticed them first, his head snapping up, alert, red light pulsing in his eyes. For a moment, Oken had been afraid, seeing Shina's dragon side assert itself so quickly. Gone was the kind, gentle man. A dragon sat in his place, protective and dangerous.

Bell had seen as well and moved in front of Oken, shielding him. Once Shina recognized them, he went back to normal. It took less than a few seconds, but Oken had seen more devotion in those moments than he'd ever seen in his life.

And he knew that their marriage wasn't perfect. No marriage was. But they made showing how much they loved each other seem effortless. Even when they argued at the dinner party, the instant Bashima thought Shina was being threatened or insulted, he nearly exploded.

Oken didn't want the exact same thing for him and Bell. For one thing, Bell was nothing like Bashima, like day and night, although they were both annoyingly stubborn and obtuse about certain things. Maybe it was because they were gods. He'd have to ask Shina how he dealt with their differences. Maybe he'd have some advice for Oken on what to do about his own relationship.

Oken had such a difficult time understanding how people were supposed to interact with each other. And Bell was the one who usually taught him.

He needed time to think. Could he stay with the Forest God as things were? Probably, considering the aching pain in his chest from Bell's absence, but he didn't want to feel like he'd given in. Bell had to compromise on something. Oken wouldn't stand one step behind him anymore, even if a god was worth more than a demigod.

Thoughts of his mother floated through Oken's head, making him pause and run his fingers along his scar's outline. Why was he thinking of her? Her long hair and sad eyes, a large smile just for him. He hadn't contacted her since the summit, after his father had tried to take him back to the Temple of Fire. Perhaps it was time to reach out, but he wasn't sure how to meet her without having to go through his father. He'd find a way. His sister Dahlia could help. Maybe.

Two more shifts had him at the Temple of the Sun. He stood at the main doors and gazed back over the valley to the forest. He wouldn't miss the Forest God. Not yet. They'd barely been separated. He thought of Bell's ready, lopsided grins and nervous hand-twisting and tried not to smile. The piles of leaves he'd find around the temple most days when the Forest God was preoccupied and muttering about one thing or another…

He didn't even ask the temple to be let in. The doors swung open slowly, and Kuroi stood behind them, confusion infused in his posture.

"Master Oken?" Kuroi said." His eyes darted about, probably searching for Bell. He didn't ask why Oken was there, didn't pry.

"May I come in, Kuroi?" Oken asked, finding it difficult to speak for some reason.

The god-touched man raised an eyebrow and saw the pack at Oken's side, perhaps understanding what had happened, at least at a basic level. Oken hoped that Kuroi didn't think he was running away. That wasn't it. He was showing that he could be on his own. That he was just as capable as anyone.

"Of course, you don't need to ask," Kuroi said. "This will always be a home for you."

Oken collapsed into Kuroi's surprised arms and sobbed, hugging the god-touched man fiercely.

Chapter Five

Cabari

Jace didn't say much before they shifted away from the Temple of the Sun. All four of them traveled to the same spot where they'd separate to go to their temples, and Jace would go back to the Underworld. They appeared on an open plain, the strong wind tousling their clothes and hair. Jace's wild mint green hair danced around his head, his eyes far away and pensive.

Cabari tried not to look at him for too long, but it was impossible. Jace drew the Lightning God's attention like no one had done for centuries. He'd had plenty of lovers, none that lasted long, all beautiful, none very bright. Jace was the first person he'd spent more than a few days with, and some of those times they hadn't even had sex. Which baffled Cabari. Wasn't that the point once you showed someone you were interested? But Jace was a tough nut to crack. He'd held out for an obnoxious amount of time, making the Lightning God work for it. And he laughed at Cabari, a lot. Not in a mean way, but he had a quick wit and didn't hold back.

Cabari should have expected it from Veles's son. The Lord of the Underworld was sarcastic and severe, and his son hadn't strayed far from that personality. Some days it was downright eerie how much Jace looked like Veles, and Cabari feared the God of the Dead would somehow find him and remove his soul from his body for messing with his son. But Jace had a lightness that Veles lacked, a willingness to interact with people, a need for acknowledgment. Luckily, Cabari was great at optimistic support. He wasn't used to being someone's long-term support however, and he wasn't quite sure if Jace appreciated it, but he smiled fairly often in the Lightning God's company. That had to count for something.

Jace's grip on his arm didn't lessen; maybe he wanted Cabari to stay, let Alora and Garyn leave so they could talk, but they lingered, wanting to speak with Cabari. Garyn had hinted that he wanted to continue their conversation from the morning once they left the temple, and he'd made sure to not include Jace in the invitation.

"Well, that sure was interesting," Cabari said, rubbing the back of his neck, pulling his arm gently from Jace's grasp. Jace glanced sidelong at him, eyebrow raised.

"I better get home," Jace said, taking the hint. As a demigod, he was used to being excluded. Cabari didn't like to leave things that way, but his friends might have something important to tell him. Jace leaned in and gave Cabari a quick kiss, nodded at Alora and Garyn then shifted away. Cabari felt the ghostly presence of Jace's lips, wishing he'd ditched the other gods and asked Jace to sneak him into the Underworld instead.

"This better be good," Cabari said. "I just missed getting laid."

Garyn snorted, "Sure, keep telling yourself that. He's pissed at you."

"What? Why?"

"Did he let you put one finger on him last night?" Garyn asked, arms crossed. Alora shuffled her feet, uncomfortable.

"Well…no," Cabari admitted, but they'd seen Shina turn into a dangerous monster, and Jace had no idea what was happening. He'd been so stunned that he'd allowed Cabari to shield him during Shina's rampage. Cabari was chastising himself for not shifting Jace away when Shina went berserk, but he'd completely forgotten that the demigod would be in danger, and he'd wanted to try and help. Not that he'd done any good.

"Exactly," Garyn said, huffing. "You can get your piece of demigod ass later." Before Cabari could protest, Garyn held up a finger and said, "I'm pissed at you too. Both of you."

He glared at Alora, who looked contrite, but Cabari knew she wouldn't have changed her decision to keep certain things from Garyn. He felt bad for keeping Jace in the dark too, but Bashima never asked for anything, and it would be stupid to go against his wishes. Keeping Shina safe seemed like the top priority, especially after seeing what the God of Time had done to him. Cabari shuddered; thinking about Shina's broken body lying in the middle of Chronas's throne room would always haunt him.

"We did what Bashima asked," Cabari said, voice firm. "Don't you think you would've done the same?"

Alora made a face at him. Maybe it was the wrong thing to say, but he wouldn't be blamed for helping out a friend. At least he thought he and Bashima were friends.

"Maybe, but I wasn't given the option," Garyn said, muttering something Cabari couldn't hear.

"It's not our fault you weren't around when the summons came," Alora said.

"Let's not get into that argument again," Garyn said, rolling his eyes.

"You two weren't even there when Shina transformed this time," Cabari said, biting his lip. "It was terrifying. Like watching all the person drain out of someone. And there was nothing I could do to help. I stood there like a moron, didn't even shift Jace out of the room."

"You really like him, don't you?" Alora asked, happy to pivot to a new topic, especially when it was one she'd orchestrated. She'd had the notion to set Cabari up with Jace in the first place.

"What? I don't know what you mean," Cabari said, avoiding her eyes. "He's cool, I guess."

"Then why do I actually know his name, unlike the rest of your conquests?" she teased, sidling closer. "I couldn't even keep up with your last parade of pretty idiots."

Garyn groaned, but Alora had the scent of a wounded animal. She said, "You're spending an unusual amount of time with him." She got right in his face, grinning. "And you're willing to face Veles's wrath to date him. That's not the Raijin Cabari I know. It's too much work." She poked him on the nose, and he shoved her back, cheeks burning.

"He's just a great fuck, all right," Cabari said fuming.

Before Alora could press the issue, Garyn cleared his throat and said, "I get why Bashima wants to keep this under wraps. Shina would have a huge target on his back." He winced, maybe thinking of the massive golden brand on Shina's back. "Poor choice of words. But it's gonna get out, and then we'll be in deep shit. Vaultus knows who was at that rescue, and he sure as hell knows who we're all fucking."

"Meaning?" Cabari asked, looking at his fingernails.

"Meaning," Garyn said, snapping his fingers under the Lightning God's nose. "That we would be in trouble if he found out we knew and didn't say anything. He knows Alora helped rescue Shina, so who would she tell about that? Me. And you'd tell Jace, I suppose."

"Whatever," Cabari said, "Vaultus thinks the sun literally shines out of Bashima's ass. He won't care. He'll probably tell him it was a good idea to keep it secret."

Garyn shook his head, as though Cabari was the dumbest person he'd ever met. "We're. Not. Bashima. You think Vaultus will let it slide that we knew and didn't report it? Especially if he thinks Shina's dangerous to gods? Chronas deserved it but look what happened to him. He's never gonna wake up. I don't care what Shina is now; it will look like a human did that to a god. It could start a panic about whether there are other dragon people out there, and there'll be a fucking slaughter. There must be records of the places dragons used to protect. Think about it."

Cabari didn't want to think about what that could mean. Wholesale destruction of human villages, just to eliminate a threat that might not exist. Vaultus might not act rashly, but other gods might take it upon themselves to rid their world of a threat.

Alora touched Garyn's shoulder and said, "He's an asshole, but I trust Bashima's judgment. And Cypress's. If Vaultus finds out, then those two will take the blame and back us up."

Cabari wasn't so sure about the Sun God, but Cypress would definitely stand up for the decision. He'd been so sure of himself last night, and there was no way Vaultus would ignore the Forest God if his mind was made up.

"And it's not Shina's fault," Cabari said. "You weren't at the temple, Garyn. What Chronas did to him…I'll never forget that. I'm amazed he survived, let alone almost tore him to shreds. And according to Bashima, Chronas was about to put him out of commission too. Why would Bashima lie about that? If Shina had to become a monster to beat the Time God, more power to him."

Alora nodded, probably recalling Shina's body covered in blood and bruises and that horrible brand.

"Yeah," Garyn muttered, "except now we're relying on two demigods to keep the Locker shut and time not cracking apart."

"Come on," Alora said. "Time mostly takes care of itself, and Niall's daughter is really stinking cute." She put her arm through Garyn's and pulled him closer. "Let's go. I'll let you do that thing you like when we get to my place."

Garyn smirked and said, "You said that last time. Later, Cabari."

Alora winked at the Lightning God before disappearing with Garyn.

For a few moments, Cabari studied the spot where they'd stood. Slightly jealous of them, he kicked a rock and it skittered across the ground, disturbing some birds who flew away into the wind.

At least someone was getting laid.

Garyn did have a point, but there was nothing they could do. He'd rather eat a pile of shit than piss off Bashima for no reason. As Cabari was about to shift, Jace's indigo eyes flashed in his mind, and his stomach did a flip.

Stop it, he told himself. Jace was great, but it would take a lot more than a sardonic attitude and a nice ass to keep the Lightning God's attention.

Chapter Six

Cypress

Cypress wasn't sure how long he'd been on the ceiling, but it felt like ages. His body had gone numb, and he'd tired after thrashing around. Dasari had come in when he'd called her, face unreadable. When he begged her to help him down, she'd said, "None of us shades are powerful enough to melt the ice. Maybe you should think about that the next time you upset Master Oken." Then she'd shifted away, ignoring Cypress's bellows of betrayal.

No other shades ventured into his chambers, and he realized that they were on Oken's side. How the hells did they even know they had to take a side? And why weren't they on his? He was the Forest God! The Lord of the Trees! Not that titles would defrost his balls. Couldn't Oken at least have finished blowing him before sticking him to the ceiling?

As he contemplated how long he'd be frozen, he heard the outer chamber door open. He breathed in deep and shouted, "Dasari! Please help me! It wasn't my fault! I need to go find him!"

Rapid footsteps sounded, much too heavy for a shade. Oh shit. Who was in his chambers?

The bedroom door burst open, and Shina rushed in, hitting a fighting stance once inside. Bashima walked in casually behind him, looking bored, his cloak over one shoulder. He looked around the room and edged past his husband, patting his arm. "Down, boy," he said, and Shina tried to shove him, but the Sun God danced nimbly away.

"Shina! Bashi!" Cypress said and struggled within the ice. They could get him down, but he was also very naked under the ice. And currently trapped in a sex swing. His face flushed and he shook his head, saying, "Wait! Forget you saw me. Leave me here to my fate."

Shina and Bashima looked up at the same time, Shina's eyes wide, Bashima's flashing with mirth.

"What the fuck, Tengu?" Bashima asked, snickering. "Is that ice?"

"Where's Oken?" Shina asked, searching the room. As though Cypress would be on the ceiling, encased in ice, if Oken was there.

"Not here," Cypress said through clenched teeth. Bashima and Shina shared a look, already so familiar with each other, so close. Cypress had to admit that he resented them a bit. Okay, more than a bit. They had a shorthand that eluded Cypress and Oken, maybe because of their soul bond. Either way, it was really annoying when they were so in sync.

"Well, where is he?" Bashima asked, hands on his hips. Shina left Cypress's vision, probably searching the inner rooms.

"He went to your temple," Cypress said. "Didn't you see him?"

"Must have just missed him," Bashima said.

"Sorry we didn't come right here," said Shina, still out of sight. "We stopped at my village first to see my parents."

"Isn't that nice," Cypress said. "I've been hanging here while you got a hot meal and a nice bed to sleep in."

Bashima said, "As if I'd stay away from the temple overnight." Which meant that Cypress hadn't been on the ceiling that long.

Shina wandered back into view. He looked worried. "Why would Oken stick you to the ceiling?" he asked, scratching his chin.

"We kind of had a fight," Cypress said.

"Ha! And here I was, thinking you were the perfect couple," Bashima said. "Maybe we should leave him up there. If he did something bad enough to piss off Zebra Head, he probably deserves it."

"Bashi!"

"Come on, babe, don't be a dick," Shina said, shoving his husband lightly. "Just a second, Cypress." Shina closed his eyes, and Cypress had no idea why. Bashima rolled his eyes and took a step back, crossing his arms and tapping a foot.

Shina stood very still, concentrating. What the hells could he do? Sure, he was strong, but he couldn't get up to the vaulted ceiling. Their best option was to have Bashima propel himself into the air and somehow destroy the ice. Shina left the ground and floated straight up, the golden brand shining through his tunic.

"Holy shit!" Cypress yelled, panicking. "You're flying!"

"Technically, he's cloud-dancing," Bashima said in a know-it-all voice.

"He can do that now?" Cypress asked, shocked.

"Yes, he can do that now," said Shina, eyes narrowed. He was right below Cypress, surveying the ice. "And he's about to get you down, so stay still. I don't want to nick your skin."

"What?"

Long claws emerged from Shina's fingers, hard red scales encasing his hands. The scales' spread stopped, which meant that Shina's control had improved immensely since the wedding. Cypress couldn't wait to ask him about his progress.

"What are you going to do?" Cypress asked.

"I thought it was obvious," Shina said. "I'm going to cut you out." He slashed forward, and Cypress closed his eyes, hearing the ice tinkling and cracking from Shina's blows. He slashed into the ice again and again, making slow progress. He stuck to Cypress's torso section, avoiding where Cypress's limbs might be. As he broke more chunks away, he slowed. Bashima moved farther away, getting out of the falling ice's strike zone. His grin faded, instead he stared at his husband with reckless attraction, red and gold light cascading over his skin, eyes an intense orange. Cypress looked away, feeling like he was interrupting a private moment.

Ice pieces skittered across the floor, glittering cold dust floating in front of Cypress's eyes. He felt movement near his chest as a large chunk fell away. It was like Shina hit a fault line. Once that big piece was gone, the rest started cracking. Cypress eyes grew huge, realizing what would happen. Shina moved out of the way, and Bashima stepped under the Forest God, intending to catch him.

"Oh no," Cypress mumbled, and the ice gave way, freeing him but also the swing. He fell about halfway down before the safety line caught, letting out a low twang, and the swing pitched him out. Landing out of Bashima's range, Cypress hit the floor with an "oof," planting on his stomach and chest.

"Why are you naked? And what the hells is this thing?" Shina asked, sounding mystified and a bit repulsed. Bashima devolved into a laughing mess, toppling to the floor, clutching his stomach, tears raining from his eyes.

"I was wondering how Zebra Head got the drop on you. Mystery solved," Bashima said, pushing out words between cackles.

"Very. Funny," Cypress said, face on the floor. Shina landed next to him, feet light. He draped a blanket over the humiliated Forest God and didn't say anything. Cypress was grateful. Hearing Bashima split his lungs laughing was quite enough. He got up the courage to turn his head and look at the Sun God and dragon-touched man. Such an odd couple, and yet Cypress envied their easy rapport in that moment. Bashima leaned against his husband, clutching his tunic, sniggering into his shoulder while Shina looked down at the Forest God with kind pity.

"And here I thought we'd be discussing our sex life," Bashima said, still laughing.

"Don't get any ideas," Shina said, eyeing the swing with suspicion.

"What do we need that for when you can fucking fly?"

"Don't mention that right now," Shina said, an edge in his voice, and Bashima quieted in an instant. He backed away from his husband, and Shina took deep breaths.

"While I lay here in my embarrassment," Cypress said, "is there a reason you're here?" Anything to divert his attention from Oken and his own plight.

"Um, would you like some clothes first?" Shina asked. "Or a fire?"

"If you breathe fire, Shina, I might lose my mind," Cypress said, and Shina chuckled. Cypress stood, holding the blanket closed around him, and teetered to the nearby armchair, crumbling into it. "I'll be all right. What do you need?"

"Well," Shina started, then turned bright red and clammed up. He wrung his hands, moving from foot to foot.

"I don't know why you get like this," Bashima said, tutting at his husband. "He's the sex expert. Just tell him."

Shina's eyes flashed crimson but he got under control fast. "Do you know anything about dragons going into heat or anything about ruts?" He said everything so fast that Cypress only caught every other word, but the words he did hear made him grimace. He knew why Shina and

Bashima kept coming to him about these things, but it didn't make the situation any less horrifying. And since when was he a sex expert?

"I'm sorry," Cypress said, rubbing his eyes. "I was just frozen to my own bedroom ceiling. I didn't quite catch all that."

"He's been fucking me raw every damn night since the dinner party," Bashima said. "And he can go for hours. My ass is prime real estate for his dick. Then he fucking licks me, and it kind of heals, but then he's ready to go again. He'll let me fuck him, but not for long, and he's a real jerk about it, snarling at me the whole time. Oh, and his cum is red now. That's fucking new."

Shina looked as though he'd passed out standing up, his face and eyes blank, hands curled in front of his body.

"That's...a lot of information that I previously did not have," Cypress said, voice even. He tapped his fingers together, unsure how to tackle the problem. A rut? "Did you ask Maida about this?" he asked, trying not to fall off the chair.

"You shouldn't be so squeamish," Bashima said. "We just caught you trapped in your own sex swing."

Shina dissolved into a coughing fit and had to excuse himself from the room.

"And yeah, we asked Maida. She suggested the rut thing, but I wanted to double check with you." Bashima quieted and glanced at the doorway Shina had gone through. He marched over to the armchair and got in Cypress's face. "Tengu, I'm fucking exhausted, and he's not much better. He attacks me the minute the sun goes down and doesn't stop until it comes back up. And Maida said dragons did this for months. I'm at the end of my fucking rope."

"Months?" Cypress squeaked. Bashima did look tired. His normally alert eyes were half-lidded, and now that Cypress watched closer, he was limping slightly. "I can't tell you much more than what I assume Maida said. She's the actual sex expert, you know. Wait, why did she bring up dragons?"

"She's too sharp," Bashima said and sank to the floor, drawing his knees up to his chest. "I only told her the basics, and she said it was more like Alaric's an animal hybrid than a god-touched human." He rubbed his eyes with the back of his hand. "She doesn't know exactly what he is, but she mentioned magical creatures who go into these ruts, particularly dragons."

Cypress nodded. Even if Maida was onto Shina's secret, she wouldn't say anything, and the other gods would laugh at her if she did, thinking she had gone crazy. Dragons were almost myths now, let alone dragon shapeshifters.

"Don't get mad…" Cypress said, eyes darting toward the Sun God. Bashima grunted, not moving. Cypress went on, "But I think it might be time for Shina to look for the other dragon-touched. If Togarashi isn't talking to him, it would be the best option. At least the other one would know what was happening, or at least have an idea. We're scrambling around in the dark here."

Bashima bowed his head, resting his chin on his knees. "I know," he said, voice low. "I just didn't want to be the one to say it." He sighed. "I'm pretty sure Alaric's been thinking it too. I keep feeling like he's pulling away from me. Not in a bad way, but like part of him is looking for something I can't give him."

As though realizing he was getting too intimate, Bashima glanced at Cypress and sneered, "What the hells did you do to Zebra Head anyway?"

Cypress's face reddened, and he spat back, "Nothing! Well, not nothing, but he got carried away. And it's all your fault, you and your damn husband."

"How the fuck you figure that?" Bashima said, leaning away, appalled.

"You and Shina were together for what, a millisecond? And now you're married?" Cypress asked, fuming.

"So? What's that got to do with you and Zebra Head?"

Cypress opened his mouth to speak, but he stopped. Bashima would make fun of him, or tell him to shut up, that he didn't want to hear about the Forest God's problems.

"You proposed or something and he turned you down?" Bashima asked, barking a laugh. When Cypress didn't answer, the Sun God quieted. "Is that it?"

"No. Pretty much the opposite." Cypress said. "You're such an asshole."

"I didn't need to get married for you to know that," Bashima muttered. "Sorry."

Cypress leaned his head back, flexing his hands and feet. They were sore and chilled, but he was slowly warming up. "Well, that's a first. I guess Shina has rubbed off on you." He sighed, trying not to think about Oken. "Why did you have to get married?"

Bashima checked to see that his husband wasn't coming in yet and said, "Oken might be fine waiting around for your dumb ass, but I didn't think Alaric would. Soul bond or not, I still have no idea why he said yes." Cypress nodded. Bashima went on, "I sure as hells don't deserve him. Maybe you don't deserve Oken, but he's with you, right?"

Cypress chuckled and said, "Maybe not anymore."

"It's not like most of the other gods our age are married or whatever," Bashima said, maybe trying to make Cypress feel better. "Alora and Garyn obviously don't give a shit about marriage. Cabari…let's just pray for Jace, that stupid fucker. But I guess you found a guy who cares about that stuff."

They were both silent for a while, and Bashima muttered, "Don't you want to be with him?"

"Obviously! We've been together for fifteen hundred years."

"Then you have to figure out if you want to be with him enough."

"Sorry," came Shina's voice from the doorway, "I needed a minute. Got a little too, uh, excited." He coughed into his hand and rocked back and forth on his heels. "Cypress? There's a really nervous-looking guy outside. He's pacing back and forth in front of your door."

"Resk," Cypress said, slapping a palm to his face. "Now I do need clothes." He staggered from the chair and went behind Oken's changing screen, grabbing a too-long shirt — one of Oken's — and a pair of his pants that were behind it.

"Who's Resk?" asked Bashima, now standing next to his husband, suspicious.

"It's kind of a long story," Cypress said, glancing at Shina, not sure how to explain. Shina cocked his head to one side, curious.

"He seemed concerned about you," Shina said. "All he would say was that you needed help."

"He's kind of codependent at the moment," Cypress said. He called out, "Resk! You can come in, I'm okay!"

A young man stuck his head inside the doorway, blue-black hair hanging around his face, wire spectacles secured around his eyes by a leather strap Cypress had fashioned. When the Forest God waved him in, he entered but stood right next to the door, looking down at the floor.

"Resk, don't be scared. You can come in farther," Cypress said, exasperated but trying to sound calm and reassuring. "This is Bashima, the Sun God, and his husband, Alaric Shina. We've talked about them before, remember?"

"The Sun God?" the man asked, adoration shining in his eyes.

"What's on his face?" Shina whispered to Bashima, who snorted.

"They're called eyeglasses," Cypress said, as Resk covered his eyes, hiding the glasses. "They help him see. There was an issue with his eyes. I thought these would help. Seriously, you humans need to catch up."

Shina huffed and said, "Maybe the gods should be a little more helpful and give some of these treasures to the humans."

Bashima snorted again and held in more laughter.

Resk's head shot up and he said, "I used to be human!" His voice was loud and clear, a nice baritone that fit his stature but not his usually meek nature. Cypress wasn't used to hearing him be loud. As though realizing he'd spoken, Resk's eyes bulged, and he started making jerking hand motions as he said, "I apologize for speaking out of turn, Master Cypress! It won't happen again!"

"Sheesh, where'd you dig up this shade?" Bashima asked.

"I am not a shade!" Resk said, getting more comfortable with talking now that there were people listening to him. "I am a god-touched!"

"What?" asked Bashima, who went up to Cypress and smacked him in the back of the head. "You promised you'd never make any god-touched. The fuck is wrong with you?"

"Ouch! As if you can talk!" Cypress said and rubbed his head. "He's not my god-touched! He's just staying here while he rehabilitates."

"From what?" Shina asked. "Are you okay, Resk?"

As though shocked by the question, Resk took a deep breath, thinking. He looked at Cypress then refocused on Shina, and his eyes brightened. He'd figured something out.

Oh shit, Cypress thought. I really did not expect this to happen so soon.

Resk marched up to Shina, took his hand, which made Bashima hiss, and said, "I know you, sir! I must apologize for the horrendous treatment you received at my former master's temple."

Cypress held his breath and stood still, hoping that nothing would happen, that Shina would brush off the comment and leave with Bashima as quickly as possible. Cypress was too exhausted to deal with the questions and yelling that were sure to come.

Shina looked confused and lifted an eyebrow, while realization dawned on Bashima's face. His eyes pierced Cypress like blades, and the Forest God flinched backward, almost falling over his own feet.

"I also must give you my most sincere regrets that I assisted in taking you from the forest. I don't remember much, but I know I did that, and I am sorry." Resk's voice was strong and his words clipped, and he still clasped Shina's hand.

Dark orange colors stained Bashima's skin, and he wrenched Shina's hand from Resk, enveloping his husband in a massive hug. Cypress wasn't sure why until Bashima screamed, "RUN!" He must have felt a dam burst in his husband's soul, because Shina the person was gone, and a vengeful creature was in his place.

Bashima

Bashima wanted to murder Tengu, but there wasn't time. The instant the idiotic god-touched mentioned his former master, Bashima had known. And then he dug himself in further and admitted the horrible truth, and Bashima felt a wild pulse release from Alaric's body. Bashima thought it might disintegrate everything it touched, that was the strength of his husband's wrath. But fucking Tengu and the god-touched didn't move. So Bashima flung himself at his husband and told them to fucking run. Not that it would do much good if Alaric broke free.

His husband's body shook in his arms, and Bashima rested his forehead on Alaric's shoulder, whispering calming words and trying to push out his soul, but Alaric blocked him, like a door slamming shut with incredible force. Bashima had nothing left. He couldn't pull saved sun energy from his body, since he'd used most of it to shift them to Tengu's fucking temple.

Bashima felt Shina's body changing but didn't let go. Alaric's tunic tensed across his body and sharp scales shredded it, revealing a golden chain stretched across his chest. Heat came off his body, intense as a solar flare. Gods, Bashima needed to stop his husband before he did something he would regret.

"Alaric," Bashima said, "This isn't you right now. You don't want to hurt that bastard."

His husband growled but didn't move, claws growing from his fingers. Bashima felt hot breath on his neck.

"Remember what Veles said about the Temple of Time shades. They were tortured and turned into shells." He took a breath and Alaric's teeth grew, slicing through his gums. Bashima went on, "I should have told you this. Veles said that all the god-touched eventually died. They were too far gone without Chronas to keep them alive." Alaric stopped growling. Maybe Bashima was making a difference. "I'm guessing this is the only one that survived. He didn't mean to hurt you. God-touched are compelled to obey. You know that. In here."

He tapped his husband's chest over his heart, catching the golden chain with a finger. He pulled on it lightly, and Alaric's attention flashed to the Sun God.

Fuck, he thought. Tengu better not still be in this room.

Cypress

What the hells was happening? One moment they were in Cypress's chambers, and the next they were outside the main entrance. Cypress was unceremoniously slung over Resk's shoulder, and the god-touched man's body heaved, like he'd shifted them from the room that contained the beast. But they hadn't shifted. Cypress would have felt that. Hells. Had Resk run outside?

"Resk! Put me down!"

"Apologies, Master Cypress!" Resk said and set the Forest God on his feet, brushing off his tunic.

"Did…did you just pick me up and run away?" Cypress's mouth hung open. Did everyone have some secret power?

"I believe I did, sir," Resk said, wringing his hands. "I was an able runner as a human, but the god-touched ceremony made me much faster."

"I'll say," Cypress said, rubbing his arms. His scarred arm was sore, which made him think of Oken.

"I believe my ability was the only reason Master Chronas, I'm sorry, not Master anymore. He valued my ability, so he didn't use me as much as the others."

Resk hung his head, shoulders slumped. Dammit, Cypress worked so hard on getting Resk to forget the things Chronas used to say, the things the Time God had done. He clasped Resk's shoulder and said, "It's an incredible skill for an incredible person."

"I said the wrong thing to Master Shina," Resk said, despair in his voice. "He meant to kill me. When his magnificence the Sun God said to run, I didn't hesitate."

"I'm glad you didn't," Cypress said, gazing into his temple through the front doors. "We might be red and gold blotches on my nice floors."

Dasari appeared at the doors, and Cypress took a step back, running right into Resk.

"Master," Dasari said, cheeks flushed. "There are very loud noises coming from your chambers. I'm thankful you're not inside."

Resk's mouth became an embarrassed thin line and Dasari clicked her tongue, disapproving.

"Loud noises?" Cypress asked, then smacked his face. "Bashi better replace everything they break."

Interlude

Cypress

Cypress's eyes fluttered open. Unfamiliar ceiling above. Unfamiliar smells wafting through the air. An open window letting in birdsong and a cool breeze. A hard bed with black and orange bedding. Shit.

His body protested when he moved, but it could have been worse. He hoped that his horns hadn't pierced the pillows in the night. When he tried to reach for them, one hand didn't move. He found out why in a hurry.

Lying next to him on the bed on top of the covers was Oken, asleep, his fingers intertwined with Cypress's. His tall frame was curled up, feet angled toward Cypress. The Forest God's eyes went wide, and he attempted to keep it together, but Oken was absolute perfection, even in sleep. His breath came evenly, his hair almost covering the scar on his face. How was Cypress supposed to stay calm when Oken was beside him? Why was Oken beside him? That would be his first question, but Cypress didn't want to wake him. Questions could wait.

It didn't feel quite right to stare so openly at Oken while he slept, so Cypress sighed and glared up at the ceiling. They were somehow still in the Temple of the Sun, and he had no idea why Bashima let them stay. The last time they'd seen each other hadn't gone well. A fresh wave of guilt washed over him, and Cypress tightened his grip on Oken's hand, a reflex. The demigod squeezed back but didn't wake. He mumbled something under his breath, not moving.

Their hands fit so well together.

Then the bedroom door blasted open, and the spell was broken. Oken was on his feet in a blaze of cold air, launching over Cypress's side of the bed. He moved like a blade thrown from a sure hand, lithe and graceful as a dancer, and he met the Sun God as he plowed into the room, Bashima's palms popping with small light bursts.

"Get out of my way, Zebra Head," Bashima snarled, eyeing the demigod's upturned hands.

"I won't," Oken said, shifting to a defensive stance, eyes calm.

Cypress gaped from the bed, entranced. No one stood up to Bashima.

"You," Bashima said, pointing at Cypress. "The fuck is wrong with you? Cindras hears about this, and he'll make sure you never walk again, let alone use that pathetic excuse for a dick again."

"His dick is very nice, I'll have you know," Oken said, and Bashima's attention shifted back, his lip curling. Cypress blushed and looked under the covers. Yup. Naked. Hells, had he and Oken…

Oken continued as though he'd read the Forest God's mind, "We didn't do anything, but your clothes were doused with sweat. Warming you up was easier without them."

At least Cypress hadn't forgotten their first time together. No. He couldn't think like that. There wouldn't be a first time for them. Bashima was right about that.

"Bashi," Cypress said, "It's not like that."

"The fuck it's not," Bashima said, and bright colors played over his skin then faded. He lowered his hands and looked contemptuously at both the Forest God and the demigod. "You better figure it out quick. And not in my house. Get the fuck out. Take him back where he belongs." Bashima stalked out, muttering about idiots.

Tika, Bashima's personal shade attendant, appeared next, her hair in a severe bun, eyebrow raised at Oken. She said, "We won't kick you out just yet." Slight smile on her lips, she put her hands behind her back. "Would you care for some breakfast?"

Bashima may have been the most mercurial person Cypress knew, but his shades were second to none and covered for most of his social deficiencies. Tika stood, waiting.

"Thank you, Tika," Cypress said. "I'm not in the best shape at the moment."

"So I can see," she said. "I'll have something sent up." She looked Oken up and down, appraising him, then spun on her heel and shifted away.

"This is a strange place," Oken said. "Who are we supposed to listen to?"

"Not Bashi," Cypress said and winced as he sat up straighter.

"You're in pain," Oken said, suddenly at the Forest God's side. He placed one hand on Cypress's forehead, the other clasped his hand. Cypress screamed internally, but he pulled away from Oken.

"I'll be fine," he said. "We shouldn't...can you go into the other room while I put some clothes on?"

Oken listened right away, leaving the bedroom. He hummed as he went, a pleasing voice on top of being handsome and attentive.

Great, Cypress thought. Just perfect.

Bashima could fume and yell all he wanted.

There was no way Cypress was taking Oken back to the Temple of Fire.

Chapter Seven

Cabari

"Hey, where are you going, Jace?"

"If I didn't know you, I'd be insulted."

Not Jace's voice.

Cabari jerked awake and sat up in his bed. Sitting on the edge was Pressa, and he remembered sending her a message the day before, asking what she was up to that night. She'd cut her dark violet hair shorter, skimming her sharp cheekbones, and it suited her. She was slender, the tanned skin of her back smooth, which she covered with a long-sleeved robe. She turned around, flashing Cabari a sly smile full of pity. The twin beauty marks under her eyes mocked him.

"Shit," he said, rubbing his eyes. "Sorry."

"I'm fine, hon," she said, tossing a hand, zero concern in her voice. "But I have a feeling you're not. Isn't Jace from the Underworld? Veles's son? I didn't know things were getting serious between you two."

"They're not," Cabari said, defensive. There was a pang in his chest, uncomfortable and annoying.

Cabari knew what Pressa was thinking when she arched an eyebrow: then why did you say his name when you woke up?

"Probably for the best," Pressa said and shrugged. "He's like, what, four hundred years old?"

"Three," mumbled Cabari, and Pressa grinned. Cabari rolled his eyes and slumped down in bed. Pressa smacked him on the stomach, getting perilously close to his cock. "Don't get me excited again," he said, cranky.

"If I were you —" she said.

"You're not."

"I would break things off with the demigod as fast as I could." She pulled on ornate gold sandals, her toenails painted black. Cabari was a sucker for nice feet, and Pressa's were fantastic. She snapped her fingers in under his nose and said, "Before things go too far. He's too young to know how you operate. He won't understand."

"I'm sure his father's gone hoarse warning him about me," Cabari said, pouting. "It's not like who I am is a secret."

Jace had admitted that Veles didn't like Cabari, not that he needed the reminder. The Lord of the Underworld had never been a fan of storms in general, and one chasing after his only son was probably his worst nightmare.

"And how well did you listen to your parents?" Pressa asked, smirking.

"I don't know what you're talking about," Cabari said, checking his fingernails. "I was a delightful child."

"I'm sure," Pressa said. She went over to Cabari's washing table and poured warm water from the jug into a waiting bowl. After splashing her face, she dried it, fingers tapping the towel in a beat Cabari couldn't hear. She'd already moved past last night. Onto the next rhythm, the next song. It was the thing Cabari liked most about the Goddess of

Music: she didn't want to be tied down, had no interest in it at all. She controlled her own life, she'd once told him. No one would dictate it for her.

"Like you can talk," he teased. "What about Morgain? How's she doing?"

Pressa tutted, but her cheeks flamed. "She's away at the moment, but she knows I need an open relationship. She knows who I am. Your demigod child might think he's ready for you, but it always hurts to find out they're not the only one."

"He's not a child, hells. You make me sound terrible."

"Raijin. You are terrible," she said, checking her hair in the large mirror Cabari had suspended over his bed. "Let me know how your confession goes. Talk to you later."

With those words, Pressa shifted away, leaving Cabari with a sinking feeling in his gut. Confession? Did she think he was going to tell Jace?

Not that it mattered. Jace knew the score, hells, he was the one who said he didn't want anything serious from the Lightning God. Numerous times. Not that it stopped Cabari from pursuing him. That was the fun part, the chase, the prey resisting. Though no one resisted the Lightning God for long. Jace was the first person to turn him down more than once. Was that why Cabari liked him so much? Shit, he didn't like him that much. He'd called Pressa, hadn't he? Didn't that mean it was time to move on? That was his usual pattern: find someone attractive, seduce them, fuck them a few times, get bored, ask Pressa if she was busy, never see the other person again.

But then why did he keep thinking about sneaking into the Underworld to see Jace?

He looked up, seeing himself in the mirror. His hair was all over the place, the lightning bolt highlights swooping everywhere. Did he look guilty? Did he feel bad? Hells, he kind of did. And he'd never felt bad about having sex, not once. He'd never thought about what the consequences could be, and why would he? He was a damn god! He had no reason to feel guilty about chasing his pleasure.

Ugh, he thought. I'm too pretty for this bullshit.

He shoved his hair into his eyes, hiding his guilty reflection.

Why did it have to be such a hassle to get laid?

The Underworld wasn't as dreary as people assumed. Sure, it was permanently night, the general mood somber and quiet, but Veles married someone bright and full of life. Niall's influence was all over the Underworld, from the welcoming fanfare shades received when they arrived to the brilliantly shining structures where the shades worked and lived.

The Temple of the Dead was more to Veles's taste, simple and elegant and made from dark blue stone that looked almost black. It had high ceilings, and the walls were covered in glittering everlasting candles, throwing light and shadow around the halls and rooms. It smelled of ancient incense, a recipe lost to time.

Not that Cabari had seen much of the temple, but he'd glimpsed a few rooms whenever Jace snuck him inside. It was kind of exciting, making clandestine trips into a realm he knew almost nothing about. Veles wasn't known for entertaining, much like Bashima, and the godly summits never took place in the Underworld. There were too many shades around, too much hustle and bustle. Jace had warned Cabari which areas to avoid, the ones where lots of shades worked, because they doubled as Underworld guardians, telling Veles everything they saw. Jace said they mainly ignored him; Underworld shades only spoke to Veles, or Niall on occasion. And he was only a demigod, after all.

One good thing about having so many shades and god-touched around: it made it easier to hide a full god in the Underworld. The denizens gave off so many different energies, so Veles wouldn't notice if one god entered his kingdom unless they made themselves known.

Niall was away from the temple much of the time. As the Voice of the Gods, he traveled over the world with his god-touched, settling minor godly disputes, interpreting various godly laws, and overseeing the smaller shrines. Humans loved him as well, showering him in gifts of ripe fruit and gems. It kept him very busy, for which Jace was thankful.

Jace didn't talk about his home life much, but Cabari could tell if Niall was at the temple, depending on Jace's mood. Alora asked if Jace had facial expressions besides bemused boredom and apathetic handsomeness. When Niall was in the temple, Jace's eyes drifted more, and he often disappeared into his own thoughts. On those days, Cabari tried his hardest to make Jace smile. He'd even dragged out a laugh once or twice.

Jace had shown Cabari a secret way into the temple, a path he often took when he wanted to escape his stepfather's attention, and Cabari crept up the path now. Ignoring their usual routine, he hadn't sent a message ahead of time. Cabari didn't want Garyn knowing that he was going to see Jace right after he'd been with Pressa, and the nosy bastard definitely read the Lightning God's urgent messages. Being the Messenger of the Gods would be so boring without gossip.

He hoped Jace was in his room, otherwise Cabari could be waiting a while, and lingering in the Underworld was a bad idea. Veles hadn't stopped his treasured son from seeing Cabari. What they did outside the Underworld was one thing, but traipsing into his realm uninvited was another matter. Especially if it was to seduce that son.

He still wasn't sure why he was there, but something kept nagging at his mind, a persistent nudging. He'd tried to go about his day, but Cabari couldn't lose the feeling that he needed to see Jace, even if it was only for a moment. He wore a dark cloak, feeling very dashing, like a thief, which stirred his desire, and thinking about seeing Jace helped that along too.

Calm down, he told himself, you're just here to see how he's doing, then you're going to leave.

He reached the temple wall undiscovered and let out a deep breath. Taking one last look around, Cabari tapped the side of the wall five times in a rhythm Jace had taught him, and the stone shimmered, revealing a secret entrance. When he'd asked Jace about the entrance and how Veles didn't know about it, Jace shrugged and muttered about a god-touched "helping" him make it. Which probably meant Jace used coercion on someone.

Jace's power also intrigued Cabari. If he activated his ability, Jace could coerce anyone who spoke to him, making them do whatever he asked, within reason. He couldn't talk someone into killing or hurting themselves, for instance, but he could get them to answer questions or do certain tasks. As far as Cabari knew, it didn't work well on gods. Not that Jace would try. The punishment for using a demigod power on full gods was severe. He'd never seen Jace use his power on anyone, but he wanted to see it. He'd bugged Jace about it a few times, but Jace always changed the subject. He didn't like talking about it, so Cabari dropped it eventually. Lest the angsty demigod try to coerce him.

Cabari loosened up once he was inside. The hard part was over. He followed the tunnel to Jace's room. Yellow lightning crackled over his skin, providing some light. He didn't want to call too much attention to himself, but Jace said it was okay to use his power at a lower level. He traveled along the path, delving deeper into the temple, and heard various rumbles from the stone. The temple didn't like that he was there, Cabari could feel an annoying scraping against his skin, but it accepted his presence, having remembered when Jace led him through the passage numerous times. Still, Cabari could feel Veles's influence in the stone like thousands of eyes watching him. He shuddered, trying not to think about the God of the Dead.

He made it to Jace's room unscathed and stuck his head through the camouflaged wall, looking around. Jace's bedroom was large but modestly furnished. He didn't have many possessions or furniture, but he had a cache of musical instruments, including a violin and flute. His music station was situated in the corner near a large window that let in soft candlelight, his stands and sheet music organized and neat. The scent Cabari associated most with Jace filled the room, deep and woodsy with a slight sweetness.

But the demigod wasn't there.

Shit. Now what? He could wait and see if Jace came back, but it would have to be short. He should have risked Garyn snooping and sent a message. He was about to withdraw his head and wait in the passage when the bedroom door opened.

Jace stalked in and threw something on his bed, slamming the door behind him. He ran his fingers through his messy hair, breathing hard. After a few moments, he composed himself and dropped onto the bed face-down and lay there, not moving. Cabari had never seen Jace show so much emotion, and it made him pause. Gone was the sardonic demigod who could care less what people thought. In his place was someone who expressed frustration.

Cabari stared, unsure what to do. It would be awkward either way, leaving without saying anything or barging in and announcing his presence. He usually avoided this kind of thing. He didn't need the negativity, the "realness." But he couldn't make his feet move back down the passage.

Cabari cleared his throat and stepped through the portal, and Jace didn't budge, though the Lightning God was sure he'd heard.

"Um, hey," he said, making his way over to the bed. Might as well go for it. Cabari was terrible at half measures.

"How long have you been lurking in there?" Jace's muffled voice asked, his face remaining on the bed.

"I just got here, actually," Cabari said and jumped onto the bed, leaning back on some pillows, arms crossed behind his head, crossing one ankle over the other. Jace's bed was comfortable, covered with simple bedding and soft pillows.

"What do you want?"

Cabari didn't know how to answer, so he reached to grab what Jace had thrown on the bed, a disheveled scroll. Jace's hand shot out, grabbed the scroll, and tossed it across the room. Cabari watched it hit the wall and drop to the floor, and he grimaced.

"I'm really not in the mood," Jace said.

"For what?" Cabari asked. He started humming, hoping to redirect Jace to a happier state of mind.

"For any of this," Jace said, gesturing to Cabari's entire body.

"Well, that's rude," the Lightning God said. "I'm a delight."

Jace sighed and turned his head to look at Cabari. His indigo eyes were heavily lidded, the usual bags under them more pronounced than usual. His face etched with sadness. Jace inched up the bed until he was next to Cabari and leaned in. Closing his eyes, Jace kissed the Lightning God, and Cabari marveled at his dark purple eyelashes and the hunger in Jace's lips. He kissed back, tongue pressing forward, and Jace opened his mouth, sighing. He moved slowly, straddling Cabari's hips, hands in Cabari's hair, eyes clamped shut. Cabari sat up and wrapped his arms around Jace, pulling him closer.

Jace had been the most difficult person to get to, seemingly indifferent to Cabari's considerable charms, but persistence was the Lightning God's dominant trait.

After the summit at the Temple of the Sun, he had waged war against Jace's emotional defenses, wrote him letters and poetry, sent him invitations to parties, and asked about the things Jace enjoyed. The last one was hilarious, because Jace answered that he enjoyed "being left alone." Which only made Cabari try harder.

He wasn't sure what broke through Jace's indestructible walls, but the day the demigod sent him a message reading, "Fine. One dinner," had sent a jolt of glee through Cabari.

Closing the damn deal had been harder than he expected. Jace seemed immune to his charisma and sexual innuendos. So, Cabari tried to impress him. Nothing worked. Bashima's and Shina's wedding had been the real breakthrough. However, he still had no idea what he'd done to change Jace's mind. He'd apparently given a very drunken speech, fell off the stage where Jace caught him, and invited Jace to stay at the Temple of the Sun after the wedding. Not that they'd had sex that night. Cabari had woken up with a severe hangover, trousers still on unfortunately, and the demigod had been in the bed with him, sleeping peacefully, a small smile on his lips. Fully clothed.

Trusting the Lightning God.

Fuck, Cabari thought, as Jace's hands pulled at his tunic. Jace trusted him. He really shouldn't.

He pulled away from Jace, breaking their kiss, and Jace's eyes popped open, annoyed. He leaned back, sitting between Cabari's legs and said, "What's wrong?"

"That's what I should be asking," Cabari said, glancing at the scroll Jace had thrown. Color rose in Jace's cheeks, and he looked away, scowling. Cabari rubbed Jace's thighs and said, "It must be bad. You usually make me work for this."

Jace's eyes darted back to Cabari, purple light flashing in their depths. He grunted and pushed Cabari's hands away, getting off the bed and walking toward the scroll. He leaned down and grabbed the crinkled parchment, rolling it back up, then he tossed it into the rubbish bin in his music area.

"It's nothing," he said, arms crossed.

"It must be something," Why was he pushing? Why was he asking? "I've never seen you this pissed off."

"If you're not going to fuck me, what the hells are you doing here?" Jace said, avoiding eye contact.

Fine, Cabari thought, affronted, if he doesn't want to tell me, that's just fine.

"I'm all for a rage-fuck," Cabari said and patted the bed. Jace raised an eyebrow at him, lips an angry line. "Or not," Cabari said. He blew a breath out through his nose.

"Seriously," Jace said. "You didn't say you were coming over. You might have been caught, so what's going on?"

Cabari felt the urge to jump off the bed and kiss Jace until he forgot he'd asked the question. His body screamed at him to do that instead of what he'd come to do. Never take responsibility for how other people might feel. That was their problem, not his. But a small voice in his mind told him that Jace deserved to know exactly what he had gotten into with the Lightning God. Especially if Cabari wanted to keep sleeping with him, which, apparently, he did.

The mental effort was exhausting.

"I wanted to see you," he started, but he didn't know what to say next.

"But you didn't send a message," Jace said.

"I didn't want Garyn to read it," Cabari mumbled, which made Jace snort.

"He's probably read every message you've sent me, and some of them were pretty explicit. I believe there was one where you said you wanted to wear my ass as a hat? Then there was the one where you said your favorite food was my dick. Not exactly subtle, so why couldn't you send word ahead today?"

Jace was too sharp. There was a reason Cabari pursued the beautiful, stupid ones. They rarely asked questions or wondered why he did the things he did. Jace was plenty beautiful, but he definitely wasn't stupid.

"Because he would have given me a hard time," Cabari said, running a hand through his hair. "And he would've told Alora."

"Since when do you care what either of them think?" Jace asked. "It's not like they don't know we're a thing."

"That's just it," said Cabari. "They don't know how much of a 'thing' we are."

Jace took a deep breath and sunk into a chair near the one window. "I already told you," Jace said, rubbing his eyes, "I don't need you to be my boyfriend or whatever —"

"I slept with someone last night," Cabari blurted out.

Jace's mouth hung open from what he'd meant to say before Cabari interrupted. The color drained from his face, and his lips settled into a disappointed smirk. "You can sleep with whoever you want," he said, voice low. He looked out the window, jaw trembling.

"It didn't mean anything," Cabari said, not sure why he'd said it. Did Jace need to know? Did he need an explanation? "She's just a friend." Why did he keep talking?

"I don't care who you fuck," Jace said, still not looking at him. His shoulders stiffened, the muscles tense.

Cabari wasn't prepared for the hurt in Jace's voice. He almost didn't catch it, layered beneath cultivated indifference. Jace's wall was going back up, stone by stone. Cabari's guilt vanished, and he clicked his tongue, indignant.

"You hang out with Shako all the time," he said. "How is this any different?"

Jace's cold eyes met Cabari's and he took a step back. He said, "I'm not fucking him, for one, although I guess I should have been. I could have. He's liked me since we were young."

"Why are you getting so mad?" Cabari asked. "You're the one who said you didn't want anything serious. You were pretty specific about it."

Jace's eyes widened, fury surging off him. "You're blaming me for the fact that you slept with someone else? Aren't you supposed to be the mature one?"

Cabari huffed and said, "I should have known better than to fuck around with a damn demigod." When Jace's eyes shined with barely contained tears, Cabari added, "Pressa was right, you are just a kid."

A knock came on Jace's door, and they both startled, Jace flying from the chair by the window. He went to shove Cabari through the disguised portal but wasn't fast enough.

"Can I come in?" The door eased open. The Lord of the Underworld stepped inside and he said, "I know you saw Niall's letter." He stopped speaking when he saw the scene in front of him.

Jace stood next to Cabari, hands on his back, mid-shove, tears in his eyes, face pale. Cabari's cheeks were red from frustration and shame. He couldn't believe what he'd said to Jace. It had slipped out, his tongue unguarded. Now Veles stood in the doorway, shocked, one hand on the door handle.

Veles's hair stood on end, swept back in rage, and his eyes crackled with red light. He swept into the room and slammed the door. "What the fuck are you doing here?"

"It's not what it looks like!" Cabari said, putting up his hands and backing away. Veles was much older than him and could definitely kick his ass. He wouldn't even need to use alchemy against the Lightning God's power.

"It looks like you've made my son cry," Veles said, advancing. "You had to know that if you courted my son and hurt him that I'd end you."

Jace stepped in front of Veles, his hands raised. "Dad, stop. I'm not mad at Cabari, I was crying because of Niall. He just happened to be here."

Cabari closed his mouth in surprise. Why was Jace covering for him? He could let his father beat the shit out of him.

Veles didn't stop glaring holes through Cabari's body, but his hair fell and the red gleam left his eyes. He touched Jace's arm, jaw clenched and said, "He needs to leave. Now. I'll speak with you when he's gone." Before he opened the door and left, he pierced Cabari with one last look and said, "You are not welcome in my home. Don't ever come back here."

When he was gone, Cabari took a deep breath and let it out. He said, "Whoa, thanks for that."

"You should go," Jace said, his voice bereft of any inflection.

"Jace..." Cabari said, wanting to make some peace between them before he left.

"Don't call me that." Jace's voice was icy and dangerous. Using a demigod's first name was common. Gods didn't use honorifics with them or bother with last names. They rarely had a god's surname, either.

Jace hardly used Cabari's chosen name. Raijin, Cabari's chosen name, wasn't even real, but Jace's was, given by his mother. It held power and intimacy, something the Lightning God didn't really understand, yet he used it all the time, never thinking to treat Jace with godly respect. He had no idea what Jace's family name was, if it was his mother's or if Veles allowed Jace to use his.

"Come on," Cabari said, flustered. "Don't be like this. I didn't mean…"

"Don't say another word. I'll use my power on you, I fucking swear. Just go away. Don't come back."

Cabari didn't want things to end between them like this. His heart beat quickly, and he started sweating. This couldn't be the last time they kissed. He said, "Can't we get past this? This is who I am, which you knew." He bit his lip. "It's not like I cheated on you."

Jace didn't spare him a glance. He walked toward his bedroom door and said, "Fine, I'll go. You're not worth getting into trouble over. You know the way out."

He closed the door quietly as he left, and Cabari stood in the middle of the room. Was this what it felt like to break up with someone? He wouldn't know, since he'd never done it.

I guess it's over, he thought and went to the hidden passageway. Before he went through, he paused. Cabari took the rolled scroll from the bin and unfurled it.

It was a letter from Niall to his friend Fiona, the Goddess of Dreams and Sleep. Cabari's hands tightened on the scroll as he read:

"We missed you at the summit, but I guess I forgive you. The southern one is so much closer to you. I'll visit next month, but Veles can't come this time. He's too busy, and dragging all his god-touched along is a huge chore. I know you wanted to see him, but there's too much to do around here. You'll have to plan a visit here soon, but I'll be glad to get away. With Nim staying at the Temple of Time, I can't bear to be in the Underworld for very long. Before you get all scandalized, Veles and I are fine. But his son has been giving him a heart attack daily, messing around with Cabari, of all the gods. It's all he's been talking about since the summit, and it's driving me crazy. What do I care if his kid wants a lightning rod shoved up his ass? Not that it'll last very long. You know how Cabari is. He'll toss Jace out like garbage the second he gets bored. I'll be so glad when Veles finally makes him move out."

Cabari stopped reading and sent electricity coursing through the letter, disintegrating the paper to dust.

Interlude

Torstan

Torstan was too old for this shit. It wasn't his job to watch the gods. He'd earned his retirement far to the north, away from prying eyes and constant questions. But something had gone wrong, he could feel it. When he meditated, shadows filled his thoughts, a lingering presence with a vicious laugh. He knew that laugh, knew it meant a coming conflict they might not be able to handle. Not with Vaultus's strength diminished and his student ill-prepared. Torstan had trained the boy as well as he could, the rest had been up to Vaultus, but it seemed like their preparation had been in vain.

Perhaps he shouldn't have left before the task was complete.

He arrived at the temple in the early morning, fog rolling off the lake that surrounded it, shrouding the building. Torstan drew back; the temple looked haunted, covered in mist. A place that was usually bright with life and laughter now made him pause. He took a deep breath and ran across the lake, hardly skimming the water's surface with his bare feet. The fog parted from his speed, though the curtain closed once he was through. There was no alchemy to it, so the fog wasn't for protection. More ominous thoughts filled Torstan's mind.

The King of the Gods lived in a magnificent sandstone temple covered in meticulous gold leaf. A towering ziggurat stood in the temple's center, buttressed by shorter towers and adorned with statues so detailed they appeared alive. Multiple staircases led up to the temple, which sat on three giant sandstone platforms layered atop each other. A monument to the king's strength. Vaultus had always been ostentatious.

Torstan surveyed the quiet gardens, taking in the Goddess of Spring's creations: exotic topiaries, fruit trees full to the brim, hedges and flower bushes everywhere. A sandy area hosted cacti and other succulents. Soft buzzing came from a collection of beehives near the temple. Even the garden was soundless, though not serene. The queen's presence was diminished as well.

The silent courtyard agitated Torstan. Long ago, he would have found his student running drills in the main training square, other warriors watching in disbelief and awe. Vaultus had been the celestials' finest creation: strong, agile, powerful, athletic. He'd also had a brilliance, a charisma that drew others to him and made them swear fealty. Where were those warriors now? Those confidants and comrades?

"Off in their own temples," Torstan muttered, stalking through the courtyard. "Or gone."

He passed many shades on his way through the halls, and they didn't bother him. Many gave him curious looks, the younger ones who had never seen him. A few nodded, and Torstan recognized them from centuries ago. He came across no god-touched, which was for the best. If they accosted him with questions, he would have been forced to react. His haste was too great.

Torches burned in the hallways leading to the throne room, and Torstan thought about the last conversation he'd had with Vaultus after the confrontation with the former Sun God.

He had said, "With injuries like this, I don't know how much time you'll have. And it could hit you at any moment."

"You talk like I'm dying," Vaultus had scoffed, golden blood covering his muscular body. When he coughed, his hand came away shining with it. He wiped the blood on his tattered cape, unconcerned. He'd bled before, what was one more injury?

"You can't die," Torstan said. "But that doesn't mean you can't lose control over your body. You will succumb to these wounds someday, probably when you least expect it."

The King of the Gods hadn't answered. Instead, he surveyed the host of incapacitated gods and demigods who lay in the gardens waiting for care. The Sun God's war was a costly one.

Mighty hands on the windowsill, Vaultus had said, "I don't intend to lose anything."

Now, Torstan pushed the throne room doors open. Vaultus was at least awake, though the hour was early, but he wasn't alone. Standing beside the throne was a tall, lanky man with an aquiline nose and severe expression, glowering down at the king, a hand on the king's cheek.

"Savos," Torstan said, loud enough to carry across the room.

The god-touched man and Vaultus jumped as if they'd been shocked and turned toward the doors. Savos let his hand drop slowly, and he took a step back from the king.

"Torstan?" the king asked and stood. He nearly stumbled, and Savos made a slight gesture to help, but Vaultus waved him away. "It's been..."

"Too long," Torstan said. He marched across the room until he was in front of the throne. "I need to speak with you. Now." He threw a glance at Savos, who inclined his head and shifted away. Torstan shook his head, disappointed. "Is that what you should be focusing on right now?"

"I don't know what you mean," Vaultus said, though he wouldn't meet Torstan's eyes. He wasn't dressed to greet guests, clad in a loose-fitting toga, the fabric fairly plain. His feet were bare. Very unlike him not to be ready at all times.

"I didn't come here to discuss your complicated marriage," Torstan said. "Why didn't you send for me immediately? I heard it second-hand from Falkar. Falkar."

His former student's face contorted, his large black eyes guilty. Vaultus asked, "What do you know?"

"A celestial got out of the Locker." Vaultus winced and nodded, and Torstan sighed and said, "Somehow the God of Time lost control?"

"An incident with a god-touched ceremony," the king said. He walked back to his throne and tumbled onto it. "Other gods corrected the issue, but they weren't fast enough. He escaped."

"And when were you going to tell me?" Torstan waited for an answer that didn't come. "Is the boy ready, or have you neglected his training while pursuing other things?"

"Young Cypress is well-suited to the task," the king growled, glaring at his mentor.

"The celestials didn't give you their power just to see him rise again and destroy everything they built."

"You speak like you're not one of them," Vaultus said, waving a hand. "We're preparing as well as we can. I've sent word to the old gods, the ones who were there when he was defeated."

"But you haven't spoken to the boy?"

"I won't burden him if it can be settled quickly and quietly."

Torstan snorted and said, "You believe that this will be easy? The instant he escaped, you should have alerted the remaining celestials. We could have helped."

"Right," the king said, sarcasm leaching into his voice. "You were such a big help the last time." He winced and grabbed his side, grumbling under his breath. "Present company excluded of course."

"You've been entrusted with this world, Vaultus," Torstan said, ignoring the king's comments. "How you choose to protect it is up to you, but I won't sit back and watch it be destroyed because of your stubbornness."

The king remained silent, drumming his fingers on the throne's arms.

Torstan said, "Send for the Forest God. I need to see how he's progressed. You may need to give him more of the celestials' gifts."

The king bent his head, dark hair covering his face. "I know," he said.

Chapter Eight

Jace

Jace sat in his father's study, eyes downcast. A fire burned low in the fireplace, warming the usually chilly room. Veles didn't mind the cold, but his husband and god-touched weren't as accepting of low temperatures. Veles kept fires going in most of the temple's rooms, though his study was usually an exception.

"I'm not an idiot, Jace," his father said, voice calm but authoritative. "You think I didn't know you've been sneaking Cabari into the Underworld? I don't know how you've been doing it, but it stops now."

"It will," Jace muttered, drooping lower in the chair across from Veles's desk.

"Excuse me?"

"I ended things with him, so he won't be coming here anymore."

Veles stared at his son, eyes glittering red. "Did he do something to you?"

"No. Doesn't matter," Jace said. He wanted to shift out of the study and hide in his room, but he wanted to make sure Cabari was gone first, and he needed to smooth things over with his father. "He didn't do anything."

The study door opened and Niall barged in, eyes blazing. He spotted Jace and pointed at him, saying, "Where is it?" His long, pink hair was loose around his shoulders and danced across his back in erratic waves. His rose-colored skin was somehow pinker.

"This isn't the time," Veles said, leaning back in his chair, voice tired.

"It most certainly is," Niall said. "I know he took that letter. What the hells was he doing in my office?"

"I sent him to look for you," Veles said, his hair floating slightly. "It was almost time for dinner."

Niall fumed, looking from his husband to Jace, who bit his lip, wishing he could make himself invisible. It was much better when Niall ignored him. He shouldn't have taken the letter. The words were burned into his mind, and he wished he could leave the Underworld, but where would he go? The temple had been his home for most of his life, and he doubted he'd be welcome anywhere else.

"He knows better than to go snooping around my office," Niall said, pretending Jace was no longer in the room. He put his hands on his hips and glared at Veles, expecting him to agree.

"He won't intrude on your space again," his father said, rubbing his eyes. Veles turned his attention back to Jace and said, "Are we clear on the other matter?"

"Yes," Jace said and stood up to leave. The Lightning God must have gone by now.

"What is it?" Niall asked, crossing his arms. Jace thought about the letter, how his father had been worried about him dating Cabari. He didn't want Veles to have to keep anything from Niall.

"Cabari won't be an issue anymore." The words felt like ice on his lips, burning and painfully cold.

Niall rolled his eyes and tutted. "Well, your father did warn you."

Jace felt a hotness in his gut. Niall had called him garbage, something the Lightning God would throw away when he eventually lost interest. Jace hated that his stepfather was right. For a short moment, he'd thought Cabari wanted to be with him, thought he'd braved sneaking into the Underworld because he couldn't stay away. For just a heartbeat, Jace thought the Lightning God wanted him more than he wanted his freewheeling lifestyle. Thought maybe Niall had been wrong.

He should have known better, but his stepfather didn't get to tell him that.

"Shut up," Jace said, standing tall, his voice clear.

His father and Niall gaped at him, stunned.

"Don't pretend that you know anything about me," Jace went on, balling his hands into fists, his shoulders shaking. "I'd leave right now if I had any place to go. I hate you." The words slipped out easily, and it felt like a massive weight lifted off him. He looked at his father and said, "Sometimes I hate you too."

He stormed out of the study before they could stop him and shifted to his room. Jace grabbed his bag from under the bed and started packing. He would leave, even if it was for a few days. He couldn't traipse off forever like Oken had done. He'd have to come back eventually. Oken. He would go to his friend at the Temple of the Forest. Cypress wouldn't turn him away. Jace could take some time to think about everything.

The scent of burnt paper filled his nose when he went to his music area and grabbed the flute.

Weird, he thought, looking at the small fireplace on the opposite side of the room. A small fire burned, almost out.

As he went to walk through his secret tunnel so he could shift out of the Underworld, he realized that he hadn't checked if Cabari was lingering before he went in. He needed to stop worrying about the Lightning God and where he might be. It didn't matter anymore.

Veles

"This has to stop," Veles said as he stood and closed the door to his study.

"I agree," his husband said in a huff. "Did you hear what your son said to me?"

"I'm not talking about Jace," Veles said. "What was in that letter?"

Niall flushed but looked defensive. Veles stared at him, wishing his husband would be honest with him. Had nothing really changed in the three hundred years since Jace was born?

"He shouldn't have been in my office in the first place."

"Stop," Veles said. He held up a hand and walked around his desk and sat. "That's not the issue. Whatever was in that letter upset him, and he didn't deserve that."

"Veles —" Niall started, but Veles cut him off.

"I don't want to get into the same fight we've been having for three hundred years." Veles knew that his husband could argue for hours, days, weeks, however long it took to think he'd won. "I've spent centuries apologizing to you, and I'll keep apologizing, because I made the mistake. Me. Jace didn't ask for this life, so stop taking everything out on him. He's a child."

"And now's when you throw Nim in my face," Niall said, deflecting what Veles had said.

"I wouldn't do that," Veles said. "I adore Nim. She's as much my daughter as yours."

"And you want me to treat Jace the same way?" Niall asked, lip curled. "That's not going to happen. You let him live here in our home. Every time I see him, I think about what you did." He turned away, eyes filling with tears.

Veles knew his husband felt guilt as well, which he didn't deal with well. He stood and walked to Niall, turning him back around.

"I won't ask you to love Jace," Veles said. "But he's my son, and I won't make him leave for your piece of mind. That would be cruel."

"I've never asked you to make him leave," Niall said, pulling away.

"But you've made damn sure he knows you don't want him here, and I won't stand for it any longer." Veles squeezed his husband's arm and walked past him, leaving his study before Niall could make a dramatic exit.

Jace

Jace arrived at the Temple of the Forest and thought he'd made a mistake. He hadn't messaged them, so they wouldn't be prepared for guests. Cypress didn't strike him as the sort that would be angry, but it would've been polite to warn them that he ran away from the Underworld. And also told his father that he hated him.

What a mess. What could he possibly say to make that better?

He sighed and walked up the wooden stairs to the main doors and knocked. A shade with a massive smile opened the door and peeked out, assessing Jace. She had a light, musical voice. "Welcome to the Temple of the Forest. How can we be of service?"

"Uh," Jace said, shuffling his feet. "I'm here to see Oken?"

The shade's eyes widened for an instant, then she was back to grinning. "Master Oken isn't here at the moment. Would you like to come back another time?"

Jace's shoulders slumped. He didn't have another idea of where to go.

"That will be enough, Twyla," said a new shade who appeared at the door. This one was diminutive with shining black hair and an impressive air of authority. The smiling shade nodded and scampered away.

"Master Jace? I am Dasari, Master Cypress's head of house. Would you like to come in?"

"Yes, thank you," Jace murmured and stepped through the doors. Some vines touched his shoulders as he went through, the leaves whispering.

Dasari motioned for him to follow her, and Jace easily kept pace with her small steps. The ceilings they passed under were covered with multicolored leaves and more vines, and Jace swore he could hear them gossiping about him. The shade led him to Cypress's throne room and let him inside.

"Master Cypress is preparing for a journey," she said, "but he will speak with you before he goes."

"Okay," Jace said, confused. If Cypress was at the temple but Oken wasn't...

Cypress's throne room was like walking into a forest glen. The entire room was covered in plants, trees growing from the polished floor, birds singing in their depths. Jace heard water running and assumed there was a stream or fountain somewhere, maybe a waterfall.

No, don't think about waterfalls.

The room teemed with life and the Forest God's care and attention.

The path to Cypress's throne was clear with shrubs and wildflowers lining it, and Jace walked toward the Forest God, whose green hair nearly blended in with the room. He was stooped over near his throne, speaking to a rose bush that bloomed white and black. Jace hadn't seen Cypress in his formal godly attire since the summit, and he looked commanding and a little frightening. Though shorter than Jace, the Forest God's chest was broad, his arms well-muscled. He exuded immense power, the throne room singing around him. It was like nature itself had melded to the god.

When Jace neared the throne, Cypress turned his gaze, with one last touch of the rose bush. The flowers settled back, resigned to losing the god's attention.

"Jace?" Cypress asked, large green eyes surprised but welcoming. "What brings you here?"

"Sorry to intrude, but Dasari let me in," Jace said, clutching his bag. Cypress noticed the bag and frowned out of concern.

"That's fine," the Forest God said. He walked down the stairs from his throne, which was shaped from a massive oak tree, and stood next to Jace, smelling like fresh-grown grass and just-turned soil. "I'll actually be leaving soon, but did you need to talk with me? Did your father send you?" The last question held a nervous edge.

"No, my father doesn't know I'm here," Jace said, awkward, and Cypress tilted his head. Jace went on, "I was hoping to see Oken."

The Forest God's green face blanched, his eyes crackling with emerald light. "Oken's not here."

"That's what your shade said." Jace took a step back, wary, but Cypress grasped his arm, eyes clearing.

"I'm sorry," Cypress said. "I haven't been myself for the last couple days. If you want to talk to Oken, he's probably at the Temple of the Sun. I'm sure he'd like to see a friendly face." Cypress's posture fell, and he seemed to shrink. The forest quieted around them, and Jace looked around, alarmed.

"Is everything okay?" he asked. Cypress's grip tightened on his arm for a moment, then he let go.

"If you see him…" The Forest God began then fell silent. He flexed his hands and stared into the trees, which hummed around the throne room, resonating with Cypress's mood. "Nevermind. He wouldn't want to hear it."

Jace watched the Forest God walk slowly back to his throne. He looked sadder than Jace felt.

"Do you need anything before you go?" Cypress asked.

"I should be all right," Jace said, uncomfortable. What had happened between Oken and the Forest God? Cypress nodded and waved, dismissing Jace.

Cabari

"Raijin," Alora said, annoyed. "It's the middle of the damn night. I'm working."

Cabari, a bit drunk, had shifted directly into Alora's throne room, unable to stay in his own temple with his thoughts.

"Please don't kick me out," he said and hiccoughed, sinking to the floor. He lay his face on the cool stone; it felt glorious.

Alora tutted at him and poked him in the side with her foot. "You could have warned me you were coming. It's a full moon, you idiot."

Alora's control over the moon was most difficult when it was full. That's when the moon became irritable and unwilling to listen. Alora's attention pulled away for a moment, her face full of concentration. "Dammit, she's such a bitch tonight," Alora muttered.

"Sorry," Cabari said and turned over so he was looking up at her. Her throne room was dark, a few candles illuminating the walls. Alora worked better in darkness, saying it helped her focus. She put her hands on her hips, gazing down at him with annoyance and pity.

"What did you do?" She asked. "The last time you showed up here drunk and depressed was...you've actually never been drunk and depressed."

"You need to help me," Cabari said. "I think I'm sick."

"Gods don't get sick," Alora scoffed. She sat on the floor beside him and flicked his nose. "So, what the hells happened? You're never this mopey. It makes you look ugly."

"You really know how to cheer me up," Cabari said and shoved her away. She teetered, pretending to fall over, then came right back and flicked him again, harder. "Ow!"

"Spill so I can get back to work."

"I have a headache and a stomachache and everything feels terrible and I think I'm dying."

Alora laughed and fell backward, her blue hair splayed out around her head. She scratched one of her horns and patted the Lightning God's shoulder. "There, there," she said, completely unhelpful.

Cabari crinkled his nose and breathed out heavily. "I saw Pressa the other night."

"And?" Alora asked, pushing at her cuticles. "How's she doing?"

"Fine. Still with Morgain, I guess."

"Good for her," Alora said. "But why would that make you feel sick? You've been whatever with her forever, and it's never fazed you before."

"That's not it." Cabari wasn't sure he wanted to tell Alora everything. She'd laugh at him for sure. "I told Jace, okay?"

Alora didn't say anything for a few moments. "And he took it super well, I'm guessing?"

Cabari bit the inside of his cheek and thought about the letter falling apart in his hands, Niall's unkind words tattooed on his mind.

"Tell me I'm a good person," he said, voice quiet.

"You're a good person," Alora answered immediately.

"Like you actually mean it, hells," he said and sat up.

"I don't know what you want me to say," Alora said. She put her arms under her head and gazed up at the ceiling. The moon shone down like a faraway beacon through the massive skylight. "You live the life you want to live. There's nothing wrong with that."

"But I've never felt bad about it before," Cabari said. "Why do I feel like this?"

"You really want to know?" she asked.

"Obviously," he said, snorting. It had been a mistake to come here. Alora was one of his best friends, but she'd never been good at advice. Not that he'd asked her for much advice during their long lives.

"You like Jace. And you hurt him." It was so simple. So easy. The words came to Alora quickly, and she unleashed them. She said, "He's the only person who's ever made you work for anything."

"Jace is a jerk," Cabari said, crossing his arms, face reddening.

"Welcome to having feelings. Sucks, doesn't it?"

"I DO NOT have feelings." Cabari stood up and started stalking away.

"Hey!" Alora chased after him, grabbing his arm. "It's not a bad thing."

"I don't want to have feelings," Cabari said, jerking his arm out of her hand. "We broke up or whatever anyway."

"Because of the Pressa thing?"

"I guess," he said, sulking. "Should have kept my mouth shut."

"Why did you call her?" Alora asked. "Isn't that what you do when you're done with someone? I thought you were really into Jace."

Cabari didn't answer. He'd called Pressa because Alora had teased him after the dinner party fiasco, but Alora wasn't the only reason. All she'd done was point out the obvious: the Lightning God liked someone enough to not ditch them after a few fucks. Jace's betrayed face flashed through his mind, those damn indigo eyes filling with tears.

"Veles caught me at the temple," he admitted.

"How are you still in one piece?" Alora asked, awed.

"Jace said he was upset about Niall, not me," Cabari said and ran his hands through his hair.

Jace hadn't needed to step in, to stand up to his father. The fact that he had done it meant something…right?

"Was he upset about Niall? I didn't know Jace could even get upset."

"He's always on edge about Niall, but I didn't know how bad it was."

Cabari was pissed that Niall nailed his character so well — the asshole who fucks around a while then disappears — but what really got under his skin was the way he'd talked about Jace. Cabari expected Niall to be pissed that Veles cheated on him, and with a human, but to despise Jace who'd done nothing but be born was some grade-A nastiness.

"That family is weird," Alora said. "I wouldn't wish it on anyone."

"And I made everything worse." Cabari looked up at the moon, wishing he could launch himself off the planet where all his troubles waited for him.

"Maybe you can make it up to him," Alora said. "Give him space, though. Don't go barreling after him like some love-starved moron."

"Who said anything about love?" Cabari asked, panicked. Alora rolled her eyes.

"Calm the fuck down," she said. "Since you're here, have you heard from any of the other gods recently? Our old crew?"

Cabari dragged his brain away from the word "love" and shook his head. "Nothing recently. A few gods were trying to get some reunion thing going a while back, but it kind of fell apart."

Alora nodded, deep in thought.

"Have you heard something?"

"Garyn's been really busy," she admitted. "A lot of urgent correspondence going back and forth between the older gods. Way more than usual. He doesn't dare read any of it," she added, answering Cabari's question before he could ask. "So he doesn't get tempted, he's been having his chief shades make sure everything gets delivered."

"You think something's going on?" Cabari was glad to have something to distract him from thinking about Jace.

"Now that the summit's over? Yeah, something's definitely up." Alora held her chin in her hand, pondering. The gods got into petty disagreements constantly, and they were so connected that a minor dispute was liable to spill over into many social circles.

"Could Garyn risk a peek? We won't have any clue unless one of the old assholes brings us into the loop."

"Yeah, I know," she said, distracted by the moon. She muttered a soothing incantation, her fingers fluttering at her sides. Alora looked like a different person when she worked, serene and contemplative. Cabari felt like he was intruding on her true self.

"I'll leave you alone," Cabari said. "Thanks for listening to me whine about stupid shit."

"It's not stupid," she said, eyes hooked to the moon. "No relationship is perfect."

"Relationship?"

"Yeah, honey," she said, smiling, not looking at him. "That thing you're in with Jace."

Chapter Nine

Bashima

Bashima couldn't feel most of his body. He hadn't bothered trying to shift away from damn Tengu's tree temple, accepting Alaric carrying him and flying home through the clouds. The redhead was distraught, ashamed that he was the reason for his husband's condition. They'd almost destroyed Tengu's bedroom, Bashima trying to subdue his husband's rage, Alaric trying to both get away from him so he could tear the god-touched — Resk — apart but also wanting to hump Bashima. They'd wrestled around the bedroom, crashing into furniture, Alaric shrieking to be released, Bashima cursing, not letting go.

Alaric's split attention meant that they at least hadn't fucked in Tengu's fucking bedroom, but Bashima was drained, his power ebbing. The brand on Alaric's back glowed bright as he flew, hugging his husband, keening low in his chest. Bashima tightened his grip around Alaric's neck and sighed.

"It's okay, Alaric, it's okay."

127

He'd been fighting a losing battle with consciousness since Tengu found them in the bedroom sprawled on the floor, Alaric's energy spent. Finally showing some intelligence, Tengu kept the obnoxious god-touched away, though Tengu wouldn't stop apologizing:

"Veles asked if I would take him in. I'm sorry I didn't say anything, but he was so frail, and he needed help. I couldn't turn him away. It was wrong not to tell you both. I'm so sorry. Dammit, what did you do to my bed?"

Bashima chuckled then groaned. Even laughing hurt.

"We'll be home soon," Alaric said, worried.

"Great, then we have to deal with Zebra Head," Bashima said and coughed.

"Don't worry about that," Alaric said, swooping lower in the sky.

Flying with Alaric always felt a bit odd, considering he didn't have wings — how the hells did he stay in the air? — but Bashima was too tired to tell Alaric to slow down. He wanted to get home just as much as Bashima.

"I'm not worried," Bashima said.

"Oken can stay as long as he wants," Alaric chided. "It would be good if someone else was at the temple while I'm…gone."

Bashima didn't want to think about that. After Alaric's strength had returned, he'd talked with Cypress about finding Daruk, the other dragon-touched. Alaric was mortified that he'd gone out of control about Resk, but the Forest God comforted him, saying it was understandable that he lost himself, since Alaric had no idea what was happening to him or how to subdue his anger.

Before Bashima passed out, he heard Alaric say, "I keep hurting him. I don't know what I'd do if I accidentally made him like Chronas."

Awake now in Alaric's arms, Bashima said, "Great, you get a vacation, and I get Zebra Head."

"At least your sense of humor is still intact," Alaric said, smiling for a second before turning serious again. "I might not be able to find this Daruk person."

Bashima was more worried that his husband would find the other dragon-touched. Since Alaric's abilities were new, and the other guy was probably much older and used to the power, anything could happen. He imagined Alaric brawling with a massive dragon-man, struggling to escape. It was more likely that the other dragon would try to fight Alaric or chase him off than accept him and teach him. Everything he'd read about dragons mentioned that they were cooperative with each other but also extremely territorial. And Alaric was going right to the other's home.

"You'll find him," Bashima said. "Just promise you'll be careful."

"Careful is my middle name," Alaric said and laughed at his own joke. "I promise I won't do anything rash. I know you're worried, and don't say you aren't."

Bashima snuggled closer to his husband's chest and kept silent. The cool night air breezed past them, and Bashima eased into a troubled sleep, his husband's grip tightening on his body.

The sun pierced the window and shone in Bashima's face. He groaned and covered his eyes, pulling the covers over his head. Grumbling, every muscle on fire, Bashima reached beside him, but Alaric wasn't there. Gods dammit. Bashima threw the blanket off and sat up, wishing he could sleep forever. Alaric had stripped him down and thrown his clothes on the chair near their bed, and there was a phial of healing potion on the bedside table. Bashima downed it, grimacing at the taste, and felt slightly revitalized.

Alaric poked his head through the bedroom door and said, "Good morning," his voice cautious. Bashima glared at his husband, light playing over his skin, eyes narrowed. Grin nervous and too wide, Alaric disappeared and didn't return.

As the potion worked through Bashima's body, only lessening the pain and not removing it entirely, he got up and threw on a pair of soft pajama bottoms, and he stretched, bending over to touch the floor. He was sure he heard something pop, but he was in no mood to try and figure out what. His torso was covered in scratches, luckily no bites. Alaric was pretty good about not biting, but he was less careful with his claws, especially if he was excited.

Out in the sitting room, Alaric stood over their dining table, muttering to himself, going through a pile of clothes and other supplies. He was packing. To leave the temple. A spike went through Bashima's heart and he nearly stumbled. Alaric was instantly at his side, holding him up.

"Whoa! What was that?"

"Nothing," Bashima muttered. "Just sore as hells."

Alaric frowned, his shoulders drooping. He let Bashima go, and the Sun God hobbled to the couch and sank down. "I need to get to work soon," he said, not wanting to move.

"I know," Alaric said and went back to the table to sort through the piles. "Will you be okay? Should Tika stay with you today?"

"Probably," Bashima said and scowled. He hated needing help.

"I'll let her know," Alaric said, wincing at his husband's tone. "I know you don't want me to go, but I think it's the best thing I can do."

"I'd rather you go and find out what the fuck's been happening than get railed every night."

Alaric stiffened at the table, his hands clutching the edge.

"You know what I mean," Bashima said, sighing.

The redhead nodded, back facing Bashima, and started stuffing clothes into his old pack. "The sooner I go, the sooner I come back," he said, sniffling.

"Just be sure you do come back," Bashima growled. "Some dragon nobody, tries kidnapping you, he'll answer to me."

Alaric snorted and closed his pack. He walked over to Bashima and leaned down for a kiss. "I don't think he'd be afraid of you at the moment, babe."

A knock came at the door, and Alaric went to let them in. Bashima watched him walk away, the golden brand visible through his thin tunic. If the other dragon did try to keep Alaric, Bashima wished him luck; his husband would rip the guy to pieces.

Alaric came back into the room, purposefully not meeting Bashima's eyes. He went back to packing, ignoring his husband. Fucking Zebra Head followed him into the sitting room, looking well-rested and most definitely not contrite.

"Hello, Bashima," Oken said, nodding at him. "I see you're home."

"Well-fucking-spotted," Bashima said, vexed. "How soon are you leaving?"

"Khresh," Alaric warned from the table.

"What? It's a valid question." He focused on the demigod, who observed him like he might a potted plant. "Although I gotta give you credit. Getting the drop on Tengu isn't easy."

"It is for me," Oken replied and sat next to Bashima on the couch. What the fuck? The slight praise hadn't been an invitation to make himself comfortable. Oken watched Alaric fussing with his pack, head cocked to the side. "Are you going somewhere, Shina?"

"He found out you were staying," Bashima said, barking laughter. He winced, grabbing his ribs. The potion wasn't working for shit.

"Don't listen to him, Oken. He's just cranky." Alaric put the pack on the floor and said, "You're welcome to stay as long as you need. But yeah, I'm going on a trip." He glanced at Bashima. "Are you okay?"

"I'm quite adequate," Oken said, face betraying no emotion. "Kuroi asked Emilia to be my companion, and she is most diligent."

Alaric laughed and clapped Oken on the shoulder. "That she is. If you need anything, just ask her, or ask Bashima." When his husband sent him a murderous thought, Alaric's eyes widened and he added, "But only when he's done working."

Gods dammit, that wasn't what Bashima had meant at all.

Alaric

Kuroi met Alaric outside the throne room after he'd deposited his irritated husband onto his throne. Tika stood beside Bashima, trying not to smirk as the Sun God had tried to stop Alaric leaving the throne room with the sheer force of his will. Shaking his head, Alaric had bent and kissed his husband, sending him as much calm energy as he could muster. It worked. A little. Bashima nipped his bottom lip as Alaric pulled away, possessive and displeased.

"I can take care of myself, you know," Alaric said. "I'll send word when I find him."

"Whatever," Bashima said, moping and crossing his arms.

Tika shrugged at Alaric as though saying, "You married him. No take-backs."

Alaric knelt in front of the throne and hugged Bashima, who grudgingly hugged back, resting his chin on Alaric's shoulder. "Better come back," he mumbled.

"Focus on healing, okay?" Alaric said. "And please try not to kill Oken while I'm gone."

"I make zero promises," Bashima said, eyes flaring gold.

When Alaric closed the throne room doors, he made sure to block the sadness that rumbled through his soul. Bashima didn't need to be hit with Alaric's emotions at that moment. Luckily, Kuroi was there, ready with a distraction: a parcel wrapped in lovely iridescent paper.

"What's this?" Alaric asked, taking the parcel.

Kuroi smiled and said, "It was supposed to be for your birthday, but Draiden and Shefu agreed now was a better time. Open it."

Alaric loved gifts. He loved giving them, he loved getting them. Wasting no time, he tore into the paper and unwrapped a long, rectangular scarf. He twisted it in his hands, marveling at its softness. It was dark blue and patterned with black asymmetrical stripes and flowed through his fingers.

"It's beautiful!" Alaric said and wrapped it around his neck in loops. Kuroi shook his head, mirthful, and fixed the scarf, straightening it and throwing one end over Alaric's shoulder.

"It's not just a scarf," Kuroi said. "Though it is a rather dashing design. We have imbued it with spells of our own creation."

"You can do that?" Alaric asked, stunned. He touched the scarf, wondering what powers it had.

"We can," Kuroi said, amused. "Shefu added her signature spell, which allows the scarf to store an endless supply of simple food. I believe it's chock full of jerky at the moment." Saliva flowed into Alaric's mouth at the mention of food, and Kuroi raised an eyebrow. "Simply tell the scarf that you're hungry, and it will provide. Draiden stored maps and some books he thought you'd enjoy. Give the scarf a simple instruction, like 'map' or 'book' and the item will appear. The maps will appear right on the scarf, while the books will emerge from the scarf whole."

"What about you?" Alaric asked.

"I designed the print," said Kuroi, who looked very pleased with himself. "It will offer you complete camouflage from anything. Finding spells, magical seeing devices, and of course the naked eye. No one will be able to see you. Simply say, 'conceal' and the scarf will do the rest."

Alaric enveloped Kuroi in a hug, and the god-touched man patted his back. "Now, now. No need to get emotional."

"It's like you don't know me at all," Alaric joked, wiping his eyes.

"Since we can't be with you, we will do everything in our power to protect you," Kuroi said. "Now, we also had a new pair of boots commissioned for you. I assume you'll fly to Kamaishi, but you'll have to walk at some point. Matthias wanted to give them to you, so let's get moving before he loses patience with us."

Bashima

Bashima had a long day. Alaric's absence weighed on him; he'd felt his husband getting further and further away from him as he flew south, and it was agonizing. It felt like his heart was tethered to Alaric's and it was being stretched to its limits. Their soul bond was useful for the most part, but he felt like half of himself was gone. He almost felt bad for Tengu and Zebra Head, who were probably feeling the same way. Almost.

Stupid Tengu still hadn't told the demigod about their bond, but Oken didn't seem fazed by the connection and its odd abilities. Hells, he didn't seem fazed by anything. Bashima was shocked that he'd had the balls to pull one over on Tengu, but it was hilarious. Until he remembered that Oken would now be in his temple indefinitely.

Speaking of Zebra Head, his inconvenient ass sauntered into the throne room once the sun set, didn't even knock. He looked up at the skylight, seeing the twilit sky, and said, "What's for dinner?"

"The fuck should I know?" Bashima growled. Tika, who stood beside his throne, cleared her throat. Bashima rolled his eyes and said, "You want to join me or something?"

"All right," Oken said. "You look tired. I can shift us to the dining room."

"Fine," Bashima said, pissed that he looked tired but grateful he didn't have to walk to the dining room. Oken walked up to the throne, and Bashima noticed the shade Emilia wandering back and forth on the other side of the doors. "You too?" he called. Emilia was next to them in a second, grinning. Tika grabbed Emilia's hand, shaking her head, and shifted them away.

"She's very inquisitive," Oken said, grasping Bashima's arm. Before the Sun God could answer, he'd shifted them to the dining room.

Where someone already sat at the table.

"Fucking hells," Bashima said, throwing up his arms. "What is this, a home for wayward demigods?"

"Hello, Jace," Oken said and waved.

The green-haired demigod looked extremely uncomfortable, seated on one side of the table. His glance darted to Alaric's empty chair, which made Bashima's heart ache. Jace was in terrible shape: heavy bags under his eyes, hair drooping, clothes covered in dust.

Kuroi walked into the room as Bashima sat in his usual place at the head of the table, though he'd gotten used to eating dinner in his chambers with Alaric. He'd almost forgotten they had a dining room.

Kuroi nodded at Oken, eyeing Jace. "Master Bashima, as you can see, we have a guest."

"I'm plagued by guests," Bashima said, voice sharp.

Oken paid him no attention, seating himself and putting his napkin in his lap. Emilia stood by the wall behind Oken, beaming. She held her hands behind her back and kept moving back and forth on the balls of her feet, immune to Bashima's glare. Jace at least looked repentant.

"Mmm," Kuroi said. Tika went over to Kuroi and whispered something. "I see. Master Jace, will you be staying the night?"

"Um…"

Bashima didn't know the demigod that well. The only times he'd bothered to pay attention were at the dinner parties Alaric liked to throw. Jace always seemed aloof, like he was bored with life and everyone in it. But he also inherited Veles's arrogant posture. Now, his shoulders were slumped, his eyes downcast.

Kuroi raised an eyebrow at Bashima, signaling that he needed to extend an offer. Bashima took a deep breath.

Don't explode. Don't explode. Don't explode.

"Just put him in the guest wing," he growled. Kuroi nodded and shifted away, but Bashima saw him smiling.

What had happened to the mighty, frightening Sun God? Alaric was making Bashima way too soft. His old self would have kicked the demigod out as soon as look at him. He picked up his fork and pointed it at Jace, saying, "Your dad going to come looking for you here?"

Jace's face tightened. "I don't think so," he managed to say after a moment. "Unless he knows Oken's here, I guess."

Bashima stared at Oken, who was sitting quietly in his chair, waiting for the food to arrive. "I hope there's cheese," he said to no one in particular.

Bashima smacked himself in the face and leaned back in his chair. It was going to be interesting with Alaric gone.

Interlude

Falkar

"Orn, I think that's it. Yeesh, it's not very subtle, is it?" Falkar flapped his silver wings, a few feathers flying downward, circling the temple. The thick black walls were surrounded by a fence of fire, except where a huge water garden hugged one side. The water was aflame; long rows of fire burning across the surface down the center.

"Like the very fires of the seven hells," Orn answered, cryptic as always.

Falkar ignored his student and swooped down, knowing Orn would follow. He brushed the treetops as he went down, soaring on an air current. Orn was kept aloft by his version of alchemy, which affected air currents, much like air-elemental gods, and Falkar watched him from the corner of his eye. It was almost night, and Orn became unpredictable once the sun set. It couldn't be helped. They needed to talk to the Fire God immediately.

He landed first, light on his feet, and swept his white-gold hair out of his eyes. He straightened his coat, adjusting the collar, waiting for his student. It was a nice day for a flight, and he wished the reason had been solely for his pleasure.

Orn landed lightly, his gaze focused straight ahead. One of Orn's innate abilities was threat detection, but he was calm. Focused but calm. Falkar breathed out, relieved. He folded his wings to his back. Orn's eyes swept the clearing and said, "All appears well."

"Things are rarely 'well' at the Temple of Fire," Falkar said, gazing at the main doors. He hadn't bothered masking their presence, so Cindras's god-touched knew they were there. "Let's get this over with."

Orn nodded, falling into step behind Falkar. They ascended the stairs, and the main doors swung open before they hit the landing. A woman stood before them, long hair unbound around her shoulders, a cold look in her eyes.

"Greetings!" Falkar said, making a slight bow.

"Celestial," the woman said, her voice full of ice. She glanced at Orn but didn't address him. An Augury, Falkar's protege usually garnered interesting reactions. Orn had the head of a bird of prey, sleek brown feathers and a long curving beak that could bite through almost anything. He could make his body appear human, though he preferred his clawed feet and hands to remain visible. He wore a long black cape that resembled wings. But the woman wouldn't be distracted by such a rare person. Not when a celestial was in front of her.

"You must be Marlana," Falkar said, and a cold breeze hit him. He fought shivering and kept his smile in place. Cindras's not-wife was known to have an ice ability, but Falkar wasn't sure how powerful she was. He kept his distance, letting her dictate how their interaction went. Though if she refused to admit them to the temple, Falkar would have to push her aside.

"We're here to see the Fire God. Urgent business."

"That's what they all say," Marlana said, not moving. Orn stirred beside Falkar, who put up his hands.

"Would a celestial drop in unexpected if it weren't urgent?" he asked, smiling.

"You'd be surprised," Marlana said, but her posture relaxed, and the cold wind died down. "I'll show you in, but don't expect a warm welcome."

"Was that a joke?" Orn whispered to Falkar as they walked through the doors. Falkar shrugged and sent a few feathers flying away. They soared through the hall and down separate passages.

"I can never tell with god-touched," Falkar said.

They trudged after Marlana, who was one of the most graceful and delicate women Falkar had ever seen. She was quite lovely as well, though he could sense a deep well of sadness that she kept buried within herself. He had great intuition for such things.

Marlana led them to a set of large black doors, heat coming off them, hot to the touch. She put her bare hand on one of the doors, and Falkar held Orn back when he made a move to grab her away. The hand she placed on the door became covered with ice, and it sizzled, but she showed no pain. The intense heat died and she stepped back.

"He will see you now," she said and turned to leave.

"Thank you, ma'am," Orn said, and she smiled, inclining her head. She walked so softly it was difficult to tell if she'd truly left their presence.

"You've never met the Fire God, have you?" Falkar asked his student, curious.

Orn had met very few gods, being from an island far to the north. His family preferred to keep to themselves, which made sense. Auguries were feared for being harbingers of death, and the misconception led to their exile on the island. People gave Orn strange looks when he and

Falkar went to a village or town that needed assistance. He'd gotten used to it, letting it slide off his feathers, but Falkar wondered if his student wished he looked more human. Falkar seemed human, but for the wings, so he didn't face the same problems as Orn. He was also astoundingly handsome.

"I have not," Orn said. "Is he as intimidating as they say?"

"He sure thinks he is," Falkar said, chuckling. "Don't worry. I could easily overpower him if he tries to attack us."

The doors opened, and they stepped into a furnace. Cindras had turned off the constant flames that encircled his throne room, but the residual heat hit Falkar like volcanic walls.

"I told you never to come here," came a booming voice from across the room. The Fire God stood next to his throne, arms crossed, glaring at his guests. He was a dormant volcano.

Falkar grinned and shrugged as he walked. "What can I say," Falkar called, "I love surprising people. Keeps things interesting."

Orn walked behind him, watching for possible attacks. Falkar was proud of his student. He knew exactly what Falkar needed from him and didn't have to be told. They worked as a unit, and it added an extra wrinkle to Falkar's plan of attack: Cindras wouldn't be able to split his attention well, not knowing how to defend against a celestial and an Augury.

"That's far enough," the Fire God said when they were halfway across the room. "Why are you here?"

"I heard a little rumor," Falkar said, smiling. "You're having a bit of an issue with the Locker."

The Fire God was good. Falkar hardly noticed his reaction, but it was there. Cindras blinked several times, his mouth hardening. He said, "Where did you hear this?"

"Here and there," Falkar said, looking around the throne room. "Really nice place you've got here. Your wife was kind enough to lead us right to you."

"She's not my wife," Cindras snarled. Flames flared along his body.

"Silly me, how could I forget?"

Keeping Cindras off his game was also necessary. He probably wouldn't chance an assault on a celestial, but better safe than burnt to a crisp.

"Anyway, it doesn't matter where I heard about your little problem. What keeps me up at night is why none of the gods bothered contacting the celestials."

He let his words sink in, and the Fire God's expression darkened.

"We don't report to you," Cindras said, voice low.

"Maybe not," Falkar said, and Orn tensed again. He touched his student's arm. Now wasn't the time to antagonize Cindras. "But you could have given us a heads-up."

"So you could ascend and leave us gods to deal with your mess?"

Cindras wasn't wrong. Most of the celestials left the mortal plane after the last major incident, ashamed that one of their own caused so much damage to the human world. But there wasn't time to linger over past mistakes.

"The few of us who're left are here to help," Falkar said, holding out his hands, palms up.

Mostly, he thought.

"Torstan went to see Vaultus," Falkar said. Cindras harrumphed, but Falkar continued, "I don't know about the others, but we're committed to keeping this world safe, just like you. Though I'd prefer the quiet life, myself."

Cindras eyed him, silent. Torstan might have been right. Falkar shouldn't have bothered with the Fire God. He was too old and set in his ways, but he was one of the most powerful and experienced gods in the world, and they were going to need him if things turned from bad to worse.

"I assume Vaultus has been in correspondence with the other old gods?" Falkar asked when the silence stretched on.

Cindras nodded. "He has."

"That's at least a step in the right direction," Falkar said. "What's his plan?"

Cindras raised an eyebrow and said, "You'd have to ask him."

That wouldn't do. The two most powerful gods needed to work together not stew in old grudges. "How about we ask him together?" Falkar asked.

Orn said, "Eternal darkness awaits those who hesitate."

Falkar wanted to smack his student, but he held back and waited for the Fire God's answer.

Chapter Ten

Alaric

Alaric landed near a large lake and stretched his back. Cloud-dancing was tough on his body if he flew for extended periods, but he was making progress. The map Draiden installed in his scarf was helpful, showing Alaric's location in relation to Kamaishi, and he was getting close. Maybe only a few hours away. He wished for the millionth time that he could shift there, because cloud-dancing was killing his back.

Walking along the shoreline, looking for a place to fill his water-skin, Alaric felt a pang in his chest. Bashima was missing him, reaching out a tendril of emotion, which Alaric answered with a wave of positivity, hoping his husband could feel it. He was amazed their connection cared nothing about distance. It was permanent and vaulted over forests, mountains, and rivers to gnaw at him. He closed the connection, otherwise he would fly straight back to the Temple of the Sun. Being far apart calmed his libido as well, though he still yearned to be close to his husband, to protect him. From what, Alaric had no idea.

His mind kept telling him that it was a foolish choice to leave Bashima's side.

After drinking his fill from the lake and filling the skin, Alaric took off, startling a group of deer on the opposite side of the water. They raced into the forest, and Alaric's stomach grumbled.

"Almost there," he mumbled to himself.

The hours drew on, and Alaric figured he should stop at the next village and rest. He had plenty of money to stay at an inn and get a hot meal. Bashima would kill him if he knew his husband ambled into an unfamiliar town with no idea what he'd find, but Alaric figured it was good for him, would build character. Meeting new people was fun, and he was curious about the region. He'd never been so far from his village, and most humans never got the chance to travel.

He dropped down into a clearing a few miles away from the closest village, which he was happy to see was Kamaishi when he checked the map. Perfect! He would get a nice night's sleep then ask around for someone named Daruk. It was an odd name; someone had to know where he lived.

He wrapped the scarf back around his neck and started towards the woods when he heard rustling behind him. Alaric spun around, growling low in his throat, and saw a woman across the clearing. She had long gingery hair tied back in a ponytail and wide green eyes, her mouth frozen in an "o" of surprise. Her blouse hung loosely off her shoulders, one of which sported an old scar that looked like a bite.

Before Alaric could take off his scarf to conceal himself, a loud snarl came from behind the woman, and she said, "Oh shit."

A huge man burst through the trees and barreled toward Alaric, silvery eyes enraged. Alaric threw down his pack and concentrated, trying to push off the ground, but the man hit him and they went down hard, tumbling through the grass. Alaric didn't have time to grow his scales, and the man sank his sharp teeth into Alaric's neck and shook him.

Alaric shrieked in pain, and claws burst from his hands, ruby scales growing over his body. He slashed at the man, but his claws screeched as silver scales erupted from the other man's skin, hard as steel. His long white hair hardened; his glittering eyes becoming diamonds. And he wouldn't let go.

Alaric would be seriously injured if he didn't act fast, so Alaric pulled his legs under him and pushed off, concentrating on keeping himself in the air.

Surprised by the sudden flight, the other man's eyes bulged, and he opened his mouth, releasing Alaric's neck. He fell to the ground, landing nimbly on his hands and feet. He glared up at Alaric, pacing and growling.

The woman ran over, dropping a basket of flowers and waving her arms. She yelled, "Daruk, you jackass! Stop it! It's another dragon-touched!" She sounded both ecstatic and pissed, and Alaric grimaced when she grabbed the man by the scruff of the neck and picked him up, twirling him around. Damned hells, she was strong.

"I know," the man — Daruk — snarled. "Smelled his rutting ass right away."

In the woman's grip, he kept his eyes on Alaric, who hovered in the air above the clearing, unsure what to do. He'd found him! He'd found Daruk! But the other dragon-touched looked like he'd rather do anything than welcome a fellow dragon to his home.

"Get your ass down here, you coward!"

Alaric snorted, and smoke tendrils trailed from his nose. His entire body felt warm, and he fought the temptation to swoop down and attack Daruk. The woman didn't deserve to get caught in a dragon brawl, though she might be fine going against them. She pinned the other dragon-touched to the ground, shoving his head into the grass, cursing at him.

"Loralei! Get off! He's dangerous!" Daruk shouted.

"Not more dangerous than me, you ass," she said and smacked his head. "Why don't you worry about yourself for once? He could have torn your head off!"

Alaric's eyes widened. He'd never do that!

"First dragon-touched we've seen in a thousand years and you attack him, that's just great!"

"Excuse me?" asked Alaric, lowering himself slightly, still out of reach, he hoped. They glared up at him, the woman on top of the man, both breathing heavily, and Alaric put up his hands. "I'm sorry! I didn't know you lived near here. I was heading into town."

"You stay away from my town!" Daruk bellowed and tried to shove the woman off again.

"Settle down or I'll knock you out," she warned, then she looked up at Alaric. "What do you want? As you can see, he's a little overprotective."

"I'm the exact right amount of protective," Daruk growled, but lay still, glowering at the woman.

"Well, uh," Alaric mumbled and rubbed the back of his neck, feeling shy.

"We don't have all day," the woman said.

"My name's Alaric Shina, from Togarashi, and I was looking for other dragon-touched," Alaric blurted. This was his one chance to talk with someone like him. If Daruk refused to speak with him, he had no other options.

The man and woman glanced at each other, and she released him, standing. "Togarashi? Wow, I'm sorry."

"Beg your pardon?" Alaric asked, affronted. What was wrong with his village? It was the most perfect place in the world!

Daruk laughed heartily and sat up rubbing his eyes. "You poor devil. Come down. I can't kill someone I pity."

"And you can't reach him," the woman said, hands on her hips, smirking.

"Don't remind me," Daruk grumbled and stood. He tried to move in front of her as Alaric landed, but she shoved him away.

Once Alaric was on the ground, the two dragons sized each other up. Daruk was taller than Alaric, seven feet at least, and built like a boulder. His shirt was shredded from his transformation, and fine, silvery hair covered his chest. His leggings were stretchy, encasing thick, powerful thighs. Silver-white hair hung to his shoulders in waves, and his eyelashes were thick, his eyebrows plush. He was like an arctic bear.

The woman coughed when the minutes dragged on, "This is very alpha-y and all, but we'll all be dead and dust before either of you move. I'm Loralei." She gestured at the bite mark scar on her shoulder and said, "And if you couldn't tell, I'm his mate, which is why he freaked out when he saw you."

"I didn't freak out!" Daruk said, throwing his arms up.

"And this is Daruk Darukson Helgason." At Alaric's confused face, she giggled and said, "It's a mouthful, so call him Daruk."

"Why do you always introduce me like that?" Daruk grumbled. He pointed at Alaric, accusing. "And you've got a lot of nerve coming to another dragon's territory uninvited. What the hells is wrong with you?"

Alaric winced and offered a contrite smile. "Sorry about that. I didn't know of any other dragon-touched."

"That's because there aren't any," Daruk said. "Coming here while you're rutting too. You're lucky I didn't kill you."

"That's why I'm here," Alaric said, because Loralei looked like she was going to chastise her mate again. "I only became a dragon-touched a few months ago."

Daruk and Loralei shared a nervous look, and she said, "So, this is your first rut?"

Alaric hung his head, embarrassed. "Yeah, and I don't really understand what it is."

Daruk shook his head at her, but Loralei smacked his shoulder and said, "Considering this is your first time and you're not a drooling mess, I'd say you're doing better than most. You're coming home with us."

Their home was a two-story stone cottage tucked into a picturesque glen surrounded by large oaks and maples. Off to one side was a barn. Chickens clustered outside, scratching the ground. Daruk paused to pick one up and cooed at it, but when he noticed Alaric watching, he clutched the bird to his chest and hissed.

"Stop it," Loralei said, and Daruk put the chicken down, watching Alaric with suspicion. She marched to the front door and pushed it open, beckoning to Alaric. "Come on in, you might as well be family."

Alaric perked up. He toed off his dirty boots outside by the door and loped inside, excited by all the new scents. The cottage smelled like fresh-baked bread, wood-fires, and something metallic. He didn't know where to look, his eyes darting around, taking in the home. It was old and well-loved. Two chairs sat next to a fireplace, and Alaric bounded over to them, sniffing. For some reason, he felt like jumping onto the larger chair and rubbing himself all over it.

"Don't even think about scenting in here," Daruk growled from the door.

"What does that mean?" Alaric asked, tilting his head.

"Lay off, hon," Loralei said. "He's just a pup. Shina, right? How old are you?"

"You can call me Alaric. I'm almost twenty-one," he said proudly, but Daruk snorted in derision.

"Seven hells, who the fuck activated you at that age?" The other dragon shook his head vigorously and wandered over to his chair, shoving past Alaric and settling into it. Alaric smelled the metallic odor again, more potent this time. He got in Daruk's face, eyes wide, but the other pushed him away. "You can't even control yourself!"

Alaric backed away, blushing. "I'm sorry! I don't know why I did that." He twiddled his thumbs.

"Fucking Togarashi," Daruk muttered. "Did he bother telling you anything?"

"Togarashi the dragon?" Alaric asked. "He mentioned some things."

"And when was the last time you saw him?" Loralei asked, looking concerned.

"Well…" Alaric said. Togarashi wasn't the best guide, but Alaric felt protective of him. "Not for a while."

"I knew it," Daruk snorted. "That flighty jerk activated a child then fucked off to wherever."

Alaric's cheeks flamed. "I'm not a child, and Togarashi didn't activate me."

They stared at him and Loralei said, "Then it was spontaneous? That hasn't happened since dragons were still around."

"I don't know about spontaneous," Alaric said, thinking about his husband, which warmed his belly. He purred, a deep rumbling in his chest.

"Cut that out," Daruk said. "You're putting out your scent like a lovesick pup."

"He has no idea what you're talking about," said Loralei. "Alaric, sit down please."

She dragged a chair from the other room into the sitting area and Alaric fell into it, cutting off the thoughts of Bashima. Loralei patted his knee, and Daruk growled low in his throat.

"Speaking of not controlling yourself," she said, cutting a scathing look at her mate. "It's obvious that Togarashi didn't prepare you for this, he's terrible at explanations. So, how did you unlock your abilities?"

Alaric's eyes widened and he crossed his feet at the ankles, clearing his throat. "I guess it all started when I met my mate."

"Thank the heavens, you've got a mate already," Daruk said. "Probably why you're not interested in Loralei, even in a rut."

"I don't think I'd be interested in Loralei whether I was or not," Alaric said, biting his lip, and Loralei snorted. "Not that you're not pretty!" he said when Daruk's face changed to bright magenta. "But I only want my husband. A lot. That's one reason I'm here."

He looked at them both, pleading.

"That shouldn't be a problem," Daruk scoffed. "Rutting is completely natural, and your husband should be fine with it. We do just fine, don't we?" he asked Loralei.

She chopped her hand across the back of his neck, and he yelped. She said, "Why don't you ask my vagina if we do just fine?" Refocusing on Alaric she said, "Please tell me your husband is a demigod or at least another hybrid."

"He's a god, actually," Alaric said, proud, trying to get as far away from the vagina conversation as he could. "The Sun God."

"You've got to be fucking kidding me," Daruk said, rubbing his eyes. Loralei drew back from Alaric.

"I'm going to grab you a new shirt, Daruk," Loralei said. She stood and disappeared up a nearby staircase, expression troubled.

"What's the matter?" Alaric asked.

"You purposefully married a god?" Daruk asked. "He didn't trick you into it?"

"Of course not," Alaric said, indignant. His brand let off a soft glow, illuminating the room, and Daruk's eyes bulged.

"What. Is. That?" He was up in an instant, pushing Alaric forward and lifting what remained of his tunic from their brawl. Alaric squawked his displeasure, but Daruk cuffed the back of his neck. The light intensified, and Daruk drew back, chest rumbling in anger.

"A god dared brand a dragon?" Daruk yelled, and claws formed from his hands. The metallic scent exploded around the room, and Alaric leaped from his chair, toppling it, growing his own claws.

Before they could move, water cascaded onto both of them, and Daruk grunted. Alaric calmed down right away, claws withdrawing. A few red scales had popped up on his arms, and he relaxed, sending them back into his skin.

"I leave the room for one minute, and you're already fighting again?"

"That GOD branded him!" Daruk said, grabbing Alaric and spinning him around.

"Hey!" Alaric said, and shoved Daruk away. He pulled his tunic down. "I asked him to, all right?"

Loralei coughed into her hand and threw shirts at both of them.

"I grabbed one for you too, Alaric. It'll be big on you but better than wearing that."

Alaric had been working on not tearing his clothes to bits when he changed, but it was difficult unless the tunic was oversized. Seeing that Daruk had the same problem made him feel a bit better.

"You let him do that to you?" Daruk asked, appalled.

"It's a long story," Alaric said, sighing. He slumped down in the chair, tugged off his ruined tunic, and pulled on Daruk's shirt. It smelled really nice, and he rubbed the fabric over his torso.

"You can keep that," Daruk said. "Won't be able to get your damn smell off it anyway."

He stalked into the kitchen and grabbed a mop. He squeezed water from his hair onto the ground and mopped it up, taking a turn around the room, getting rid of the water. Loralei thrust the bucket she'd used into his waiting hand. Alaric retied his wet hair into a bun and rubbed his hands on his leggings, which hadn't gotten too wet.

"Tell us what happened," Loralei said. She walked behind him and said, "Let me see." Alaric obeyed, pulling his borrowed shirt up in back. A sharp intake of breath came from behind him.

"It doesn't hurt," he assured her. "It was like he claimed me back, I suppose."

Daruk barked angry laughter from the kitchen. "You nibble on him once and he disfigures you? Seems fair."

"Shut up!" Alaric said and stood. Loralei grabbed his shoulders and forced him back into the chair.

"Don't make me drown you both in the well," Loralei said.

"He better not insult my husband or I'll —"

"What?" asked Loralei. "He might not look it but he's much older than you. So, stop being a big baby."

"Yes, ma'am," Alaric whimpered.

When Daruk laughed from the kitchen again, Loralei said, "And you, behave yourself. You're acting like a hatchling. What would Kamaishi say?"

Alaric heard muttering from the kitchen, but Daruk didn't come back to the sitting room.

"Should I wait for him or…"

"He can hear you just fine," Loralei said, taking a seat in her chair by the fireplace.

Alaric told them about Bashima, with a lot of editing. He didn't think Loralei and Daruk would be interested in his sex life, but he explained how he'd been initially activated, which made Loralei whistle.

"But you didn't change right away?" She asked, fingers tapping her teeth. "I guess that makes sense. It would take more than one time."

"I changed when I almost died," Alaric said quietly. Daruk poked his head back into the room, frowning. Alaric went on, "The God of Time, Chronas, he kidnapped me because of Bashima. Made me go through the god-touched ceremony and…branded me."

Daruk growled and Loralei shook her head. Alaric didn't want to remember what had happened to him. While the pain from Chronas's brand had faded to a distant memory, thinking about that day made him feel sick. But he needed to make Daruk and Loralei understand.

He said, "The Time God almost killed me. I think I passed out, and that's when Togarashi told me I could choose to become dragon-touched, though he didn't explain it very well."

"Shocking," Daruk said, sarcastic.

"So," Alaric said, cutting off the other dragon, "I transformed. I don't remember much. I saved Bashima and put Chronas in a coma, but I was still affected by the brand." He closed his eyes and shivered. "I wanted to die, the pain was so excruciating. Bashima wanted to help me, so I told him to change the brand to his symbol. It was all I could think to do, and it worked. I feel no pain from the Time God anymore."

"And because you're dragon-touched, the brand the Sun God made doesn't really affect you?" Loralei asked. "This is so strange. I've never heard anything like it. Daruk?"

The other dragon finally came back into the room, arms crossed, expression grim. "The other dragon-touched I've known were the same as me: village was in danger, had the dragon dreams, activated, did their duty." He paused and looked at Loralei fondly. "All the others are gone now, but I had Loralei, so I stayed."

Loralei rolled her eyes but smiled.

Alaric glanced at her claiming mark and bit his lip. "Did it hurt?"

"This?" She rubbed her fingers over the scar. "When he first bit me it did, but then it was like a wave of contentment washed over me. Dragon saliva has minor healing abilities," she explained, "so it didn't hurt for very long."

Alaric nodded. Bashima said something similar when Alaric asked about it. The Sun God hadn't been trying to make him feel better. It was the truth.

Loralei noticed his relief. "You thought you hurt your mate."

Alaric nodded, holding in tears. "I still am," he said. "I can't stay away from him, you know…even thinking about him now makes me want to…"

"Fuck him until you both pass out?" Loralei asked, and Daruk choked, running from the room. "Such a baby! Alaric, what you're feeling is normal. Your first rut will be the worst, and since you were so young when you activated, your human body was in overdrive too. Daruk was in his early thirties when he transformed for the first time, so he was calmer." She shifted around on her chair, eyebrows dancing. "Not that it matters when you're the one getting all the attention," she said, seeing his horrified face. "What is with you dragon-boys and sex?"

Alaric giggled nervously. "Thanks for saying that. It makes me feel a little better. When I heard dragon ruts could last for months…"

"Hells, if that were the case I would have moved out ages ago," Loralei said. "It's usually a few weeks, and it doesn't happen every year.

At least not with Daruk. Since you're younger, it might happen annually. There's a skilled textile alchemist in town. He can make a rut aid for you."

"What's that?"

"It's a toy of sorts, made with very soft leather. Put some oil on yourself, and you can hump that thing to your heart's desire so your mate can get some sleep."

Her bluntness made Alaric flush, and what he'd dubbed his "dragon brain" told him that was a ridiculous idea when he had a perfectly good mate, but it sounded great to Alaric. His formerly human side knew that Bashima could only take so much, thinking about how exhausted he was when Alaric left.

"I'll make some dinner for us. You can discuss your training with Daruk, when he gets his craven ass back in here."

"Training?" Alaric asked, tilting his head. They were going to let him stay?

"Can't have a feral dragon-boy running around," Loralei said, patting his shoulder.

Interlude

Cypress

Cypress was so nervous he might vibrate into a different dimension. Oken had asked to see his temple, and the Forest God readily agreed. Bashima gave him the dirtiest look before they left, judgmental and protective. For wanting to kick Oken out of the Temple of the Sun the first time he'd met Oken, Bashima transformed into a temperamental bear guarding his cub. He ordered shades to watch Oken when Cypress visited, because Cypress came during sunlight hours. Bashima tried to get Kuroi to spy on them, but the god-touched man had better things to do.

"Promise not to undermine my honor as a loyal servant and I will leave you alone," Kuroi had said through gritted teeth. Cypress agreed, terrified of Kuroi. "But if I hear even a whisper of you taking advantage of that boy, you will answer not to Master Bashima, but to me."

Oken wasn't put off by threats. He didn't care that Bashima and Kuroi watched Cypress like falcons ready to tear his heart out. Oken always sat as close to Cypress as he could, attempted to hold his hand,

and mentioned how attractive he thought the Forest God was. It was like battling a casually aggressive angel. Oken didn't mind when Cypress tried to move away or pulled his fingers from Oken's hand or sputtered at the complements. His face remained impassive and calm.

Apparently, he was done waiting after a few months of Cypress's chaste visits.

"It's very difficult to be alone here," Oken said.

"Alone?" Cypress had asked, green tea spilling from his cup down his chin. They were in the library, two shades shelving books nearby trying to be inconspicuous.

"Yes," Oken said, sipping his own tea. "Bashima is always busy brooding about the sun, and the servants don't talk much. Could we go to your temple? I'd like to see it."

"I'd like that very much," Cypress said before thinking. He covered his mouth with a hand, alarmed.

"I'll tell Bashima I'm leaving," Oken said, putting down his cup and shifting away.

"Wait!" Cypress shouted, too late. The two shades walked past him, shaking their heads in pity. They shifted out of the library, probably to report to Kuroi.

Cypress put down his teacup and raced toward the throne room. Maybe he could stop Oken before…

"FUCKING TENGU!" The roar flew through the temple like a blast of heated air, knocking Cypress into a wall. Candles flickered in their sconces on the walls, the wax melting fast.

So much for that idea. Cypress pushed his hands through his hair, dislodging numerous leaves, and walked down the halls to the throne room. Might as well get the fight over with.

He found Oken and Bashima in the throne room, the demigod silent, head tilted to one side as he watched the Sun God pace around the room like a caged tiger.

"I will still live here," Oken said, voice even. "Why are you so upset?"

"I'm not upset!" Bashima yelled, then he saw Cypress cowering near the door. "Tengu! What did I fucking tell you?" He was so fast. Light blasted across his skin, his palms glowing with rage. But Cypress had his own power. He sidestepped the Sun God's rush, skin crackling with green energy, and skidded away, landing in a crouch.

"Bashi, just listen —"

"Like hells," the Sun God spit at him, venomous. He charged Cypress again, but a large ice wall formed between them, and Bashima slammed into it. He fell backward and hit the floor, dazed.

"I cannot permit you to hurt Bell," Oken said, walking over to them.

"Fucking hells, Zebra Head," Bashima muttered from the floor.

"I will return, time uncertain," Oken said, grasping the Forest God's arm. "I think it's best if we leave now, Bell."

Cypress saw Bashima's jaw tighten and golden light flashed in his eyes. Judgment was thick in the air.

"Tengu, I fucking swear," was all Bashima got out before Oken shifted them away.

"Your temple is quite beautiful," Oken said, smiling at the building. He stood alarmingly close to Cypress, clutching his forearm, and Cypress shuddered, trying to find words. Any words. Oken was in front of his temple. Touching him.

Oken glanced sidelong at him and asked, "Can we go in?"

"Oh! Obviously, yes, it's my temple I suppose, ha ha," Cypress stammered, marching up the steps. He heard the curious plants that lined the stairs snicker at his utter lack of finesse. The old trees that surrounded the temple rumbled their approval.

Great, he thought, even the trees think I need to get laid.

Oken followed him through the main doors, looking around and making appreciative noises at the décor. Leaves fell from the ceiling around them and swirled in the air, billowing around the demigod.

"It's all so natural," Oken said.

"I am the Forest God," Cypress said, laughing.

Oken took it in stride and said, "It's nothing like my father's temple. Although my mother would enjoy the greenery."

Cypress looked at Oken out of the corner of his eye as he took in the temple's numerous flowers and trees. Not many people visited his temple, and the shades were accustomed to the work Cypress put into cultivating the plants, so watching Oken see it for the first time was invigorating.

"What would you like to see?" Cypress asked.

"Everything," Oken said, grabbing the Forest God's hand. Cypress felt a buzz sizzle through his body, and the hair on his arms stood up. He reached up and scratched a horn, laughing nervously under his breath.

Cypress gave Oken the tour and introduced him to the shades, most of whom grinned at the demigod and shook his hand. They were livelier than usual, and they didn't greet Cypress in the same way as Oken. They nodded at him, courteous as always, but they must have enjoyed seeing a new face. Dasari appeared in front of them as Cypress turned toward the throne room.

"Master Cypress," she said, raising an eyebrow at Oken. "I see we have a visitor."

"Um, yes, Dasari, this is Oken," Cypress said, blanching at her pursed lips. Dasari liked to have at least twenty-four hours advance notice for guests. "Oken, Dasari is my head of house."

The small shade looked Oken up and down, appraising him.

"She's a lot like Kuroi," Oken said. "Scary."

Dasari let out a huge belly laugh, which Cypress had never heard. He was so surprised that he took a step back. Dasari wiped a tear from her eye and said, "Kuroi wishes he was as good as me. Should I make up one of the guest suites, Master Cypress?"

"I'd rather stay with Bell," Oken said before Cypress could answer.

Dasari looked from Oken to the Forest God, and Cypress stared off into space, blind to her questioning eyes. She shrugged and said, "As you wish. Dinner will be ready in an hour or so." She shifted away to make preparations for two instead of the usual one.

"An hour should be fine," Oken said, contemplative.

"Um," Cypress said, unsure what to show Oken next. Maybe the lake by the back entrance? Or the library? He seemed to enjoy the library at the Temple of the Sun. "What?" he asked, vaguely aware that Oken had asked him something.

"Have you ever had sex before?"

Cypress tripped and nearly fell, but Oken grasped his arm and held him steady. He stepped away from the demigod, twisting his fingers, trying to make himself invisible. The mortification might destroy him. He was very old, thousands of years old, and yet he wasn't what the other gods would call "seasoned."

"Um, yes, but I'm no expert," he said, trying to smile, but he was sure it looked terrifying.

"I've never had sex," Oken said, unconcerned. "So, I don't think it matters that you're not proficient."

Now hold on a minute. He might not be an expert, but Cypress was at least pretty good at sex. Or so he'd been told. Not by many people, but still, more people than Oken.

Oken gave him an odd look. "You're angry."

"No, I'm not! I promise," Cypress said, flustered. He wasn't mad, just a little annoyed. Oken's bluntness threw him off, unprepared for that level of honesty. Oken didn't like lying, and he cut right to the heart of things.

"Would you like to kiss me now?" Oken asked, moving closer, his turquoise eyes shining. Cypress backed against the wall but otherwise didn't try to escape. Oken was taller than Cypress, but he tried to make his presence smaller when the Forest God backed away. Cypress had noticed him do it a few times at the Temple of the Sun; maybe Oken did it to make others feel better when they met him. Safer. A demigod with unknown powers would be enough to make an old god hesitate. Whatever the reason, Cypress didn't want Oken to feel like he needed to diminish himself for anyone.

Oken said quietly, "Since you weren't ready when you rescued me."

Bashima was going to kill him, but in that moment, Cypress didn't care. He didn't wait for Oken to close the distance. Cypress stepped forward and pulled Oken's lips down to his.

Chapter Eleven

Jace

Matthias shoved Emilia into the library, saying, "Damn your incessant questions!" Then he slammed the door, Emilia looking delighted.

She turned slowly, and Oken tilted his head and asked, "So, you've been with Matthias this morning? I was wondering where you were."

Emilia blushed and looked at the floor. She reminded Jace a lot of his sister, Nim. Brash and bold at times then shy if someone asked her a difficult question. Nim had taken to hiding under the dinner table when they tried to eat together in the Underworld "as a family." Jace was the only one who could make her come out, which annoyed Niall to no end.

"Maybe we can help with your question?" Jace asked, beckoning her over. Emilia's eyes widened, and an evil grin erupted on her face. Maybe giving her permission was a mistake.

"I was just asking why the master's still been limping around the temple even though Alaric's gone," she said, feigning innocence. She rocked back and forth on her heels, and Jace caught the gleam in her eyes.

Jace set his teacup down, trying to keep his face impassive. Oken crossed a leg over the other and went back to his book, but he said, "And Matthias didn't know?"

"He's just prissy," Emilia said. "He told me to stay with you, but do you mind if I go to my room for a bit?"

Oken shrugged and said, "I don't mind. But it's almost time for lunch, and Shefu doesn't like us to be late." Emilia nodded vigorously and shifted away, giggling.

"I don't even want to know what she's up to," Jace said, rubbing his forehead.

"She snuck some books out of the library the other day," Oken said. "So, she's probably reading where we can't comment on it."

"I suppose," Jace said.

Oken nodded then dipped his head toward the book in his lap. He was a good person to hang out with if you needed calm and quiet, not intrusive or loud. Jace missed the activity that usually irked him in the Underworld: shades and god-touched everywhere, always needing his father's advice; Nim asking him to play or tell her stories. He even wondered what his stepfather was doing. Niall often had interesting tales from his travels that he told Veles during meals.

Jace thought about Cabari's dopey smile. And stupid jokes. And his dumb lips and smooth hands and…other smooth things.

Jace slammed his book shut and sighed, drawing Oken's eye.

"You seem troubled," Oken said.

Thinking about something Cabari said the day they'd broken up, Jace asked, "Do you ever wish you were a full god?"

"That's an odd question," Oken said. "But I suppose I've thought about it before. I think my mother wishes that I was. Or that I was fully human. But I can't be either of those things, so why dwell on it?"

"My mom was so proud that I'm part god," Jace said, rolling his eyes. "She'd introduce me as 'Jace, my son, who's half god.' It was really embarrassing."

Oken nodded. "It must have been nice to meet people with your mom."

"Shit, I'm sorry," Jace said. He sometimes forgot that Oken's life was even crappier than his. Or at least his childhood had been. Niall was an asshole, but at least Jace had his father and had been able to spend time with his mom.

"It's all right," Oken said, matter of fact, "You can talk about your parents if you want. It's not your fault that mine are less than exemplary."

That was putting it mildly. Jace was fascinated by Oken's ability to let things go, to move past old wrongs and slights. He didn't think Oken harbored resentment toward his mother for scarring him, although he knew Oken hated his father. Which was an easy thing to do. The Fire God was a massive prick.

"I'll have to go back home eventually," Jace said. "My dad is probably pissed that I ran off. But he hasn't come after me, so maybe he's relieved that I left, even if it's just for a bit."

Veles never let Jace feel less than loved, so Jace felt hurt thinking his father would be more relaxed if Jace left the Underworld, but he wouldn't blame his father either. Veles wouldn't have to worry about Niall getting mad because Jace existed.

"I'd rather my father not come after me," Oken said, "but yours seems nice."

Jace nodded, biting the inside of his cheek. "At least you're safe here. I'd feel bad for anyone who tried to break into Bashima's temple."

Oken smiled and looked off out the window. "He's very protective."

"If that's what you want to call it," Jace muttered.

He hadn't asked Oken why he was at the Temple of the Sun. They'd spent a few days relaxing in each other's company, having dinner with the moody Sun God, who never spoke to them and pushed food around his plate. Then they'd go to their rooms. Jace's dreams were plagued by thunderstorms, and he often woke, sweating, wishing his stupid brain would stop.

"He's been like that for a long time," Oken said. "You should have seen the fit he threw the first time I left the Temple of the Sun with Bell."

Jace glanced over. He was curious about that dynamic. Oken told the story about Cypress rescuing him from the Temple of Fire at the last ill-fated dinner party, and they'd apparently been a couple since then. The god and the demigod.

"Did you two have a fight or something?" Jace asked. Oken knew Jace stopped at the Temple of the Forest before coming to Bashima's temple, but he hadn't asked Jace about it.

"Of a sort," said Oken, sipping his tea. "He ignored me for a week so I froze him to the bedroom ceiling in a sex swing."

Jace spit his tea all over himself and stood up, cursing.

"Are you all right?" Oken asked. "Hopefully the tea wasn't too hot."

Jace stared at Oken, shocked. He'd attacked a god? Was he insane? There were rules against it. Even if it was in self-defense, Oken could get in huge trouble.

"First of all," Jace said, wiping the tea off his tunic. "What the hells is a sex swing?"

Oken frowned. "Cabari gave it to us as a gift, so I assumed you'd know what it was."

Jace's face went scarlet and he sat down hard, the book poking into his back. He tossed it to the floor.

"I guess we hadn't gotten to that part of the relationship," Jace mumbled.

"Are you distressed?" Oken asked. He also hadn't pried into why Jace was at the temple and not in the Underworld.

"Cabari and I aren't a thing anymore," Jace admitted, running a hand through his hair. It hurt to finally say it. When he'd told his father that he'd dumped the Lightning God, it hadn't felt real. Admitting it to Oken made it real. It was for the best. Cabari could continue with his true calling: fucking everything in the world with a hole.

"That's too bad," Oken said, awkwardly patting Jace's shoulder. "If it makes you feel better, I don't know if Bell and I will be together much longer either."

"That doesn't make me feel better," Jace said, frowning. "You two are the best couple I know. If you can't make things work, how the hells can anyone else?"

"Best couple?"

"You two seem so in sync," Jace explained. "Like you know everything about each other."

"I thought I knew everything about Bell," Oken said, "but I don't think it's possible to know a person completely. I had no idea that he didn't appreciate me."

"What?" Jace was confused. It was painfully obvious that the Forest God adored Oken. The way he looked at Oken, not caring who noticed how enamored he was. How protective he was.

Cabari protected you from Shina too, his brain reminded him. Shut up.

"He doesn't want to marry me," Oken said, as if that explained everything.

"But you've been together forever," Jace said. "Does it really matter if you're married?"

Jace supposed that if Oken wanted to get married, that if it was something his heart needed, then maybe it did matter. Not that being married fixed anything. Jace's father and stepfather had a good relationship for the most part, but he didn't think it was because they were married. Oken had also seen the spectacle of Bashima's and Shina's wedding, and those two had permanent let's-go-fuck eyes, so maybe Oken thought it was the next logical step in a relationship. And Oken was very logical.

"Do you want to get married?" Oken asked, voice low.

How had this become about Jace? "I'm a little young to be thinking about that."

He recalled Cabari calling him a kid, so scornful and disappointed in how Jace reacted to him telling the truth about sleeping with someone else.

"But someday you might," Oken said. "And shouldn't you be able to talk about it with your partner without them avoiding the subject and not listening to you?"

He had a point, and from what Jace knew about the Forest God, that behavior seemed very in character. He said, "And you don't think you'll be able to talk it out?"

"Maybe," Oken said. "I told him not to follow me here, but I thought he would. I don't know if I want him to show up or not, but I do miss him."

Jace knew how Oken felt. He'd spent the last few days fighting the temptation to write to the Lightning God, just to let him know where he was and that he was okay. But Cabari didn't get to know those things anymore.

"He, uh, was planning a trip when I saw him at the Temple of the Forest," Jace said.

Oken glanced at him, surprised, "A trip? Where?"

"I'm not sure. I didn't ask."

Oken nodded and looked at the floor. "I haven't been able to feel him, probably because we're far away from each other."

Jace didn't know what that was about, feeling the Forest God, but Oken looked devastated, and Jace could rarely tell what the other demigod was thinking. He tried to cultivate the same kind of nonchalance, but Oken was the true master at hiding his feelings.

"Do you want to ask if Bashima knows?" Jace asked.

Oken shook his head. "No. Bell can do as he likes. He doesn't need my permission." He was silent for a few moments, and Jace didn't know what to say. Oken finally said, "Can I ask you something?"

"Sure."

"Did you like Cabari?"

"I suppose," Jace said, wondering where that question came from. Oken rarely showed interest in anything besides the Forest God, let alone other peoples' relationships.

"Why?" Oken asked. Jace stared at him, so Oken continued, "It's very mysterious to me, how people decide they like someone. For me, the first time I saw Bell, I knew. I didn't know exactly what I was feeling, but I saw him at a summit when my father was showing me off, and he was the only one who looked at me like I was a person. Like I mattered. That was a nice feeling."

Jace wasn't prepared for Oken's honesty. He'd never talked about Cabari with anyone; he didn't have many friends, besides Shako and now Oken. Shako made his feelings clear when he heard Jace was seeing the Lightning God, his jealousy ill-disguised. It was the last time they'd spoken in a while. Jace had gone to visit Shako at the Temple of Time, trying to cheer him up from the constant work of keeping the Locker closed.

Shako had started the conversation, talking about how fast Bashima and Shina married, searching out Jace's feelings: "It all happened so fast. And…So, I heard you spent the night at the Temple of the Sun after the wedding."

"I did," Jace said, uncomfortable. He knew Shako liked him. He was only a hundred years or so older than Jace, and they'd grown up together, but Jace only felt friendship for Shako, which he thought the other accepted.

"And?" Shako asked, eyeing his friend.

"I went home the next day," Jace ventured, hoping Shako would drop it.

"Niall was here the other day," Shako said. "To see Nim." Jace didn't like where the conversation was heading. Shako knew he hated talking about his stepfather. "He let slip that you're seeing a lot of the Lightning God, Cabari."

There it was. The one thing Jace wanted to avoid. He didn't say anything, and Shako snorted, shaking his head.

"Seriously? That guy?"

Jace's face had gone red. He knew his father wasn't happy with his choice, had already heard the warnings and seen the disappointed expressions. Jace hoped to avoid the topic with Shako, but that apparently wasn't going to happen.

"I've only been on a few dates with him," Jace mumbled.

"So, you're willing to give the Lightning God a shot? The guy who brags about how many people he's fucked? But you've never even thought about me?"

"Shako…"

"I just hope you know what you're in for," Shako had said. "He's going to use you up and spit you out. The gods are like that with us 'lesser beings.' Don't come crying to me when he drops your stupid ass."

Jace refocused on Oken, pushing the memory away. Why had everyone been right about Cabari? Why hadn't he listened to them? Was there something wrong with him? To fall for someone so wrong for him?

Oken's gaze was almost meditative, as though he could wait forever for Jace's answer.

"He reminded me of my mom," Jace said, pulling himself from the memory of Shako, and Oken's eyes widened. "He made me laugh. And he didn't make me feel bad about who I am."

Until he did.

Jace and Oken went down to the kitchens to see what Shefu planned for lunch. She usually made them bento boxes and tossed them out of the kitchens as quickly as she could. Emilia stood outside the door, peeking in, dancing on the balls of her feet.

"Emilia," Oken said, making her jump. "What are you doing?"

"Watching," she said, eyes gleaming.

"Watching what?" Jace asked, and something crashed in the kitchen. "What the hells?"

They pushed Emilia behind them and went in, and it was chaos. Bashima stood next to one of the large prep tables, hands on his hips. Shefu had slammed a massive copper frying pan on the table and glowered at him, a massive spill on the ground behind the Sun God that some shades frantically cleaned up. The other kitchen shades dashed around, trying to stay out of the way.

"All I asked was how your day is going," Bashima said, red-faced.

"And I asked if you're feeling okay," Shefu answered, face equally as red. "Gods can't get sick, so what is wrong with you?"

"There's nothing wrong with me!"

"Don't you raise your voice at me in my own kitchen, Master Bashima!"

"What is going on down here?" Kuroi shifted into the kitchen and stood next to Jace and Oken. His face was stormy, and Jace backed away.

Oken didn't move. He pointed at the scene and said, "Bashima is in the kitchen."

Kuroi glared at Oken, who didn't notice. His attention was back on the chef and Sun God. The shades scurried away, watching Kuroi from the storeroom like frightened mice.

"Master Bashima," Kuroi said, marching into the fray. "Can I help you with something? Did no one bring you your lunch?"

Jace snorted. As if the shades would forget to bring the Sun God a meal.

Bashima jumped at Kuroi's voice and looked like a scolded child for a moment before morphing back into a god. Yellow light flew over his skin, and he narrowed his eyes. "I wanted to see how everyone was doing down here," he said, and Kuroi tensed.

"Are you feeling all right, Master Bashima?"

"Why does everyone keep asking me that?" Bashima yelled, smacking his fists on the table.

"Master Shina can't come back soon enough," tutted Shefu, and she turned her attention to the kitchen shades. "What are you all gawking at? Get back to work." She pierced the Sun God and Kuroi with a frightening look and walked away.

Upon hearing Shina's name, Bashima deflated. Kuroi gripped his shoulder and whispered something Jace didn't catch. Oken hummed next to him, waiting, and Bashima noticed them. He shrugged Kuroi off and glared at them. "Why are you still here?" he grumbled.

Jace glanced at Oken, who didn't answer. He lived in the temple, so Bashima must have been talking to Jace.

"Would you two care to have lunch with Master Bashima?" Kuroi asked, and the Sun God's mouth fell open. He started to protest, but Kuroi pulled him forward so they were all standing together. "I'm sure he wouldn't mind."

"Whatever," Bashima said and shifted away, most likely to the throne room.

Kuroi sighed and rubbed his eyes. He muttered, "Who's turn was it to watch him? I'll have to redo the whole schedule."

Tika appeared in the kitchen, looking frazzled. "I'm sorry Kuroi," she said, looking at the temple head. "He got away from me."

"Was it your turn? Didn't I have you scheduled off during the mornings and early afternoons?"

"Yes, but Daphne was called away for a moment, and he shifted out of the throne room before I could relieve her."

"Blast it all," Kuroi said. He finally realized that the two demigods were still standing there. "Well?" he asked. "Get up to the throne room and someone will bring up the food."

Jace didn't need to be told twice. He grabbed Oken's arm, stepped back through the door, caught Emilia's arm, who squawked at him for disturbing her fun, and shifted them all away.

When We Believed in Magic

Interlude

Jace

The wedding was fine, though Jace had seen way more of Shina than he'd planned, and Bashima wouldn't stop pulling his new husband into far too intimate make-out sessions. Right in front of Jace's dinner. After seeing them grope each other for the fourth time, Jace left the pavilion to get some air.

It was the first wedding Jace had attended, and he wondered if it was more or less normal. Everyone seemed happy, or at least in a good mood. Free food and alcohol would do that, but the gods behaved themselves, clapped when they were supposed to, danced and chatted merrily. Some even started conversations with Jace, which hadn't happened at the summit. He'd been so bored at the summit until Shina and Oken wanted to hang out.

And when that loud idiot tried to hit on him.

Jace stood outside the pavilion and took a deep breath. He had no idea why he'd agreed to a date with the Lightning God. Maybe to change up his routine. The god was nothing if not persistent, and his poetry wasn't half bad. And he was pretty cute. Dammit, he was very cute. But Jace knew better. One date. That was it. He needed to tell the Lightning God that nothing was ever going to happen past that. Jace might be young, but he wasn't stupid. The Lightning God's reputation was well-known.

He remembered what his father said the first time he noticed Cabari talking to Jace at the summit: "Absolutely not. No loudmouthed gods. One is enough." He'd also mentioned that Cabari was notorious for chasing after things he thought he couldn't have. "He'll pursue you just to spite me," Veles had said, expression grim.

One thing was true: Cabari wasn't afraid enough of the God of the Dead. If Veles intercepted any of the letters the Lightning God sent Jace, Cabari would be in a full body cast for years. Jace had to admit that it was pretty hot that Cabari wasn't concerned about Veles's obvious disdain and disapproval.

And he looked really good in his formal armor, glistening yellow gold and black leather.

Tempting the fates, Cabari came right up to Jace when he arrived at the wedding with his father and stepfather. Cabari knew he looked good, huge grin and suggestive eyes, those blasted lightning bolt highlights in his hair flashing in the candlelight. Walking up to Jace, he'd draped his arm across Jace's shoulders, ignoring Veles's deadly gaze and Niall's raised eyebrow.

"Hey, Jace, how's it going? Dance card filled already?"

The attention felt nice. Even if he'd have to let the god down later, at least Jace would have a few hours of adulation. Except, the Lightning God stayed away. Jace watched for him in the crowd, the unique hair hard to miss, and Cabari smiled at him or winked but never came over. It had to be part of a strategy. Make Jace wonder why he had suddenly withdrawn his attention. Make him more interested. And dammit, it was working.

The Lightning God circulated the crowd with ease, talking to everyone, making them laugh. Even Bashima didn't blast him away when Cabari interrupted him kissing his new husband, though the Sun God had murder in his eyes. Shina was way too kind to let Bashima do anything to Cabari, and he'd gladly chatted as Bashima pouted beside him.

A light breeze played with Jace's hair, and he took a deep breath. Bashima had chosen an amazing spot for his temple. The mountain jutted up behind them, the temple glittering gold high above, and the valley was covered with tall grasses and wildflowers. Brilliant fire lilies dotted the base of the mountain, stunning red like Shina's hair, almost like the mountain had been waiting for him to arrive. As though he already belonged somewhere that he hadn't known about.

"You're quite the wallflower," came a smug voice behind him, and Jace barely turned. Cabari stood with his hands in his pockets, nonchalant and mischievous.

"I'm not much for crowds," Jace said.

"Ha, I couldn't tell," the Lightning God said, sarcasm dripping from his lips. "A bunch of us are gonna crash at the temple tonight. Do you want to stay and hang out?"

Jace arched an eyebrow, and Cabari grinned. Jace said, "I probably shouldn't."

He turned back to his view of the valley and forest. Tall evergreens swayed in the distance, but Jace couldn't focus on them. He felt something surging through him that he'd never felt before. The Lightning God was so close to him, could reach out and touch Jace's back if he chose, and Jace wasn't sure if that was what he wanted.

Cabari's voice remained bright and cheerful, saying, "Think about it." Then he was gone.

A few hours later, everyone was drunk. Except poor Shina, who couldn't seem to get drunk. He downed nectar and strong wine and beer but remained himself, if a bit louder. Bashima wasn't much of a drinker, and he watched the guests fall over each other with thinly veiled contempt. Jace guessed the only reason he remained at his own party was because Shina wanted it. Alora and Garyn were in the middle of the dance floor, swinging each other around, almost hitting other gods, but no one cared. They were just as intoxicated.

Jace sat at his assigned dinner table and watched his father and Niall slow-dance, eyes soft, whispering to each other. Niall laughed, and Veles's smile was ready and content. Jace loved to see his father like this, unconcerned with the matters of the Underworld, being present. He had one of the most difficult jobs, and it wore on him. Niall was a shining beacon for him, and while Jace knew his stepfather hated him, he couldn't bear much of a grudge when Niall made Veles so happy.

Cypress and Oken had already snuck away to the temple, which made Jace think about Cabari's suggestion that he stay over. To be asked to be part of one of the younger god groups was quite an accomplishment for a demigod. As far as Jace knew, no other demigods were welcome company for gods. Cypress was the only god in a relationship with a demigod. They mainly kept to themselves: the gods in their temples, demigods remaining with their human parents in the villages where they were born. Unless they had a skill the gods found useful.

"Hello everyone!" A loud, raucous voice shouted from the raised platform where Bashima and Shina had been married. The shade band quieted. "I know you said no speeches, Bashi, but how could I resist? Stop sucking Alaric's face for one second."

Oh no, Jace thought. Only one other person called Bashima that nickname.

The Lightning God held a champagne flute in one hand, waving it around so bubbly liquid spilled on the stage. The band watched him, backing away, eyes wide.

"Well, it was nice knowing him," said Vesper, the Air Goddess, who stood next to Jace. She floated away, moving closer to the stage. Everyone looked at Cabari, including a red-faced Bashima and a delighted Shina. Alora and Garyn seated themselves on the dance floor, rapt. They crossed their legs together and held hands.

"You all know me," Cabari said, winking down at the crowd, and there were some whistles and a lot of clapping. The gods lived for this shit, to see each other make fools of themselves. Jace watched a group of earth gods whispering excitedly together, their grins vicious.

Cabari caught Jace's eye, beaming, and Jace rubbed his face, alarmed. This was going to be a disaster. The Lightning God set his glass on the platform and narrowly missed kicking it off. Jace fought the urge to run and tackle him off the stage. It was Cabari's choice if he wanted to piss off Bashima.

"But what you might not know is that I'm a sucker for a good love story." Everyone let out a breath at once, and Jace was shocked. What the hells was Cabari talking about? He had to be wasted. Cabari said, "It's true! Watching two idiots make it work is one of the best things in the world. Sure, they'll only be able to have sex with each other for all eternity, but who am I to tell them how to live." He waggled his eyebrows and asked, "Unless you're into threesomes, Alaric. If you are, you know who to call."

Shina flushed across his entire body, but he giggled and held a death grip on Bashima's arm, who had alarming colors traveling across his skin in bursts. His palms glowed.

"I remember when Bashi and I were kids," Cabari said. "He used to brag about how he was the best god, that he could do everything better than us. Alaric? Can you confirm?"

Alora and Garyn toppled over, laughing hard and clutching each other. Bashima tried to stand but Shina pulled his arm and whispered something in his ear, and he sat down, shaking with rage. Cabari hiccoughed and waved toward the back of the pavilion where Jace stood.

"He's got jokes," said someone near Jace. Another god answered, "Yeah, and he's gonna be in a coma soon, look at Bashima."

Jace moved toward the stage. He wasn't sure why. He pushed past numerous people, including his father and Niall. Veles made to grab his jacket but missed. Jace felt like he was in a dream, moving in slow motion, as though he wouldn't make it to the platform in time. Why did he need to get there? Why did he care?

"Seriously though, their love story is ridiculous," Cabari said, "Who in their right mind marries someone after a few months? Are they insane?" He paused, and the audience leaned forward, waiting for him to flounder even more. "I mean, Alaric is one of the most attractive people I've ever seen, but come on. Months, people! His dick must be enormous!"

Jace was almost through the dance floor, and he heard Alora call his name, but he ignored her. He could almost feel the heat coming from the Sun God, an inferno waiting for Shina to finally have enough so Bashima could blast the Lightning God into next month.

"But," Cabari put up a finger, and the crowd murmured. Jace shoved through the last line of gods, and a few glowered at him, but he wouldn't be stopped. He was at the platform's edge, looking up at the Lightning God, who had yellow electricity encircling his arms, like he was preparing for an attack. He went on, "Have you seen how those two lovesick morons look at each other? Hells, Bashima can hardly keep his tongue in his mouth! It's sickeningly adorable to see him so happy."

The gods turned to look at the couple, and Shina leaned his chin on Bashima's shoulder. The Sun God's eyes were narrowed, but he wasn't as tense as a few moments before.

"And that's because of Alaric Shina," Cabari said. He stooped down, grabbed his champagne flute and raised it up. "I hope you two continue to make me sick with your love!"

He downed the rest of his champagne in one swallow then teetered a bit. Shit. He was going to fall right off the stage. Cabari spotted Jace and smiled, then he tripped over his own foot and crumpled off the platform and into Jace's waiting arms.

"You're so lucky Bashima didn't tear your face off," Jace muttered.

They walked through the Temple of the Sun toward the guest wing, Cabari leaning heavily on Jace's shoulder. The Lightning God was shorter than Jace by quite a bit, and his drunken state was making it difficult to get to the room Kuroi had assigned Cabari. Once he dumped Cabari into bed to pass out, Jace could go to his own room. His father hadn't been pleased that Jace wanted to stay, but Jace made the excuse that he wanted to spend more time with Oken. It was tough to find demigods to spend time with, and he could shift home the next day. Veles reluctantly accepted the reasoning but made Jace pledge to be home before lunch.

"Bashi loves me," Cabari said, shrugging.

"Ugh, why are you so heavy?" Jace asked, lugging Cabari around another corner. Were they almost to the blasted room?

"Why are you so pretty?"

Jace snorted. "Shut up, you're drunk."

"And so mean!" Cabari said, sputtering in feigned despair.

"Well, you're probably not going to remember any of this," Jace said, grunting as he propped Cabari up higher. "So, I can be as mean as I want."

"Oh, I'll remember," said Cabari. "Since it's you." He grinned wickedly and Jace shook his head at the god's audacity.

"Even when you're wasted you can't help yourself."

"Hells, you're really hard to flirt with," Cabari huffed.

"I try," scoffed Jace.

"Nah, I'm the one who's trying." Cabari leaned his head against Jace's shoulder and sighed. "It's a good thing you're so hot."

"That's the only thing you think about, huh?"

"What else is there?" Cabari asked.

"Maybe all the other parts of a person?" Jace snapped. Was Cabari kidding? What else was there?

"I like all your parts," Cabari said and giggled. Then he sounded a little far away, "That other stuff gets you attached."

"And that's bad."

"Really bad!" Cabari refocused on Jace, eyes shining. "That's a sure-fire way to…"

After a moment when the Lightning God didn't finish his statement, Jace said, "To what?" But Cabari didn't answer.

They finally made it to the room, and Jace grumbled in relief. He could finally go to bed.

"Here we are. Don't come out until morning or Bashima might get away from Shina long enough to murder you."

"Your voice is nice too," Cabari said, giggling again. "You can coerce me any time."

"Good gods," Jace said, rolling his eyes.

"That's what I'm talking about!" Cabari pulled away from Jace and stumbled. When Jace gasped at the sudden movement and tugged

Cabari up from falling, the Lightning God grabbed his face and shoved their lips together. Jace, outraged, planned to push Cabari away. But then he didn't. A shiver went through his body, making the hair on his arms stand up. He closed his eyes and kissed back, opening his mouth slightly. Jace wasn't sure how good he was at kissing, but Cabari seemed to think he was doing fine, humming into his mouth, tongue darting in and out, teasing. He pressed forward until Jace's back was to the door, fumbling with the door handle.

Spell broken, Jace parted their lips and pushed Cabari back. "That wasn't an invitation," Jace fumed. He wiped the back of his hand across his mouth, which tasted like tart lemons and champagne.

"I'm not sure if you noticed," Cabari said, "but you were kissing me back."

Jace blushed, making Cabari chuckle. Indignant, Jace said, "Don't laugh at me."

Cabari put up his hands, swaying on the spot. Jace had wondered if Cabari was faking being drunk to maneuver Jace up to the room, but he seemed pretty out of it.

"I'm not laughing at you, Jace," Cabari said. "I like you."

Jace narrowed his eyes, suspicious.

"You're really clever and smart."

"Those are the same things," Jace said, crossing his arms. He needed the Lightning God to stop talking and pass out already.

"And you don't put up with any of my bullshit!" Cabari said, raising his arms in the air and falling forward. Jace caught him, sighing.

"So it would seem," Jace growled. "I'm going to open this door and shove you through it, I swear."

"I'm sorry I kissed you," Cabari said, gazing up at him, some sort of drunk innocence plastered on his face. "But I really wanted to. And you're a good kisser."

Cabari rested his cheek on Jace's chest and let out a soft snore. Jace sighed, and shook the Lightning God lightly.

"Did you seriously fall asleep on me?" Cabari was silent. "Great," Jace said.

The room was nice, smaller than the one Veles had for the summit, but the bed was big, and there was cozy furniture and a large shelf filled with books. A few candles burned on the bedside table, making the room smell like citrus and sage.

Jace sat Cabari on the bed, holding him up while he stooped to take off the armored gold breast plate. As he pulled it off, grunting with the effort, the undershirts came with it, revealing Cabari's bare, well-muscled torso. He was lean and graceful, even in drunkenness, and Jace held his breath. He'd never been in such an intimate situation. With anyone. His fingertips brushed Cabari's bare skin, sending a tingling feeling up his arms.

Cabari's eyes fluttered open for a second, and he smiled, cupping Jace's cheek and rubbing his thumb across it.

He said, "You're way too good for me."

Stunned, Jace stared into the god's golden eyes. They were flecked with light green, so subtle you'd miss it unless you looked close enough. Cabari closed his eyes, kissed Jace again, softly, then fell backward onto the bed.

Unsure what had just happened, Jace stared down at the Lightning God, mouth opening and closing. Cabari snored happily on the bed, his legs dangling off the edge, hair covering his eyes.

Shit. Now what? Jace looked around the room, indecision flooding his senses. His brain told him to leave Cabari where he'd collapsed. He'd gotten away mostly unscathed. He would go to his room, crawl into bed, and leave in the morning.

You don't ever have to talk to him again, Jace thought. Keep it together. You have more sense than this.

Those thoughts came in Veles's voice, chiding, believing that the Lightning God was only paying attention to his son to embarrass him and tarnish his reputation. Jace was pretty sure Cabari was interested in him because of the chase, the idea of a conquest. He doubted the God of the Dead had entered much into the equation.

Cabari had admitted that Jace was too good for him. Was he? He was only a demigod. Cabari was ancient, with enough power in one finger to destroy anything he touched. Yet he never flaunted his power, had never brought it up in his countless letters or flirtations. He coasted on charisma and luck.

Jace watched Cabari's chest rise and fall with his breath, mouth finally at rest. He looked peaceful and content, things Jace rarely felt. What was it like to fall asleep so easily?

He sighed and climbed onto the bed, pulling Cabari into a better sleeping position against the pillows. Cabari wore tight leather trousers, but there was no way Jace would attempt to take those off. He thought about what it would be like, if Cabari were awake and hungry for him. Those gold eyes heavily lidded with desire.

Clearing his throat, Jace started to edge off the bed, but Cabari turned over and snuggled closer to him, small snores tearing at Jace's resolve.

What did it matter if Jace happened to fall asleep there? Who would know besides a shade or two? He could sneak out before dawn and go to his room, no one the wiser.

Jace leaned back on the pillows, arms behind his head at first. Tiredness fell over him, a heaviness he couldn't ignore. Lugging Cabari through the temple hadn't been fun, but he hadn't wanted to shift with a drunk god. Who knew what might happen if he tried? Now his muscles were reaping the consequences. As he drifted into sleep, Jace's arm fell from behind his head and draped over Cabari's shoulder.

Chapter Twelve

Alaric

"Take that out of your mouth! What did I just tell you?"

Alaric growled and Daruk pounced on him, trying to drag the blanket from his teeth. There was a struggle, sharp teeth snapping, claws drawn, and the fabric ripped, sending a horrible sound tearing through the cottage.

"What the hells is going on down there?" Loralei's voice came from the upstairs bedroom.

Alaric and Daruk looked at each other, toward the stairs, then at the blanket, which had become two blankets. Loralei emerged wrapped in a robe, hair wet from her bath. She glared at them, Alaric's teeth clamped around one half of the blanket, the other half in Daruk's hands.

"He did it," Daruk said, pointing at Alaric.

"What the hells?" Alaric said, spitting out the fabric. "I was just looking at it!"

"Then why were you rubbing it all over your naked torso?" Daruk yelled. "You look with your eyes!"

"Outside, now," Loralei said, rubbing her temples. "I was trying to have a relaxing bath, and you've ruined it."

"But —" Daruk started, pouting.

"Don't be such an asshole." Loralei got in his face, well, his chest, but Daruk's posture crumbled under her withering gaze. "Alaric is basically a baby. Explain things to him instead of yelling at him. He's the first dragon-touched you've met in gods knows how long, so be nice. Don't ruin this alone time for me!"

She stomped back up the stairs, muttering.

Daruk called up, "But that quilt was over two hundred years old!"

"I don't give a rat's ass about the quilt!" Loralei shouted. "Outside!"

Daruk turned a burning glare on Alaric, who grinned, awkward. "Uh, sorry about the quilt. I got a little excited."

Daruk grumbled, walked by Alaric and grabbed his arm, dragging him outside. He marched them away from the cottage toward a circle of stones, and Daruk tossed Alaric into the center and said, "Your job is to stay in the circle. No matter what I do or say. Keep your ass inside."

"Why?" Alaric asked, confused. He scratched his nose, feeling apologetic for getting them kicked out. Daruk didn't need to be so mean, though.

"You'll see."

Daruk stalked around outside the stones, and Alaric cocked his head, wondering what this was about. Was it a lesson? Or was the other dragon fucking with him?

Daruk kept circling and started to growl, the sound low in his throat, increasing in volume as he walked. It didn't bother Alaric. At first. After about five minutes of the constant threatening noise, Alaric felt a stirring in his mind like a snake coiling, preparing to strike. His instincts were preparing for an attack, and he felt scales growing on his arms and legs, though he hadn't been concentrating on doing that.

Surprised, he looked down and studied his arms, turning them over. Daruk watched him, back bent low, snarling.

"Stop," Alaric said, covering his ears. He forced himself to sit down and crossed his legs, humming, trying to keep the sound from his mind. He closed his eyes and willed himself away. He didn't want to attack Daruk, but his inner self screamed. Another dragon was nearby and wanted to hurt him. But it wasn't true. Daruk was pissed at him, but he didn't want to hurt Alaric.

Taking deep breaths, Alaric concentrated on making his scales withdraw. After a few minutes, they receded, leaving Alaric panting on the grass on his hands and knees.

"Not bad," Daruk said, the growling gone. "You regained control. Not fast enough, though. Eventually, you should be able to drown out that distraction." He crouched down outside the circle, and plucked the grass. "What did you do to retract your scales?"

Alaric, still breathing heavily, said, "I knew you didn't want to hurt me, so I focused on that."

"Well-reasoned," Daruk said. "But you could have come to that conclusion quicker if you'd read my scent. I wasn't putting out any hostility, was I?"

"I…I don't know," Alaric admitted. He didn't understand the entire scent concept yet.

"You've never had to pay attention to it before," Daruk said. "Remember what I said before. Dragons were able to communicate with each other through scent. That way, they could send messages over longer distances. Or tell other dragons to stay away. Like how I knew you were in my territory that day Loralei was picking flowers. Your scent was everywhere." He grumbled something else then said, "You can probably pick up on emotions and intentions from other people, just from their scent, but only if they're projecting hard."

"I can sense Bashima's feelings just fine," Alaric said, sticking his bottom lip out.

"Obviously," Daruk said. "The god is your mate, so that's easy. I know that Loralei is still pissed at me, for instance, even though she's trying to block it. It's hard to do when you're mated. And she's not dragon-touched, so it doesn't work as well."

"Is Loralei a demigod?" Alaric asked. She had to have some power to handle Daruk, and she'd displayed incredible physical strength.

Raising a bushy eyebrow, Daruk said, "Yes. Why?"

"Just curious," Alaric said and struggled to stand up.

"Loralei's strong," Daruk said. "She can tear stones apart, trees, steel." Seeing Alaric's wide eyes, he added, "So, don't mess with her."

"I wouldn't," Alaric said.

Daruk snorted and shook his head. He stood up, stared at Alaric, and said, "How do you know your god is staying faithful while you're gone?"

Alaric's face paled. "Why would you say that?"

"Gods are fickle," Daruk said, voice cruel. "How do you know he hasn't had his eye on someone else. He promised he'd be faithful, right? You said the vows, did the wedding dance, let him fuck you, fill you up with his pureness. I'll bet he's giving it to some poor fucker who caught his fancy the instant you left."

Alaric's vision went scarlet, and his body moved, darting at Daruk like a spear. How dare he insult Bashima?

Daruk caught him by the neck and slammed him to the ground, and breath fled Alaric's lungs as Daruk squeezed his throat. Alaric clawed Daruk's scaled hand, which did nothing. He tried to shriek, but no sound escaped. Daruk's grip tightened, and Alaric stopped struggling.

"Well," Daruk said. "You failed that test."

Alaric relaxed fully, furious.

Daruk scratched his chin, other hand still around Alaric's throat, and said, "Didn't think it would be that easy, but at least your scent isn't fearful or jealous. You're just mad I slighted your god's good name."

Alaric grabbed Daruk's hand and ripped it away. He stomped back into the circle, back facing the other dragon. He needed to calm down, but Daruk's words rang through his head. He needed to defend his mate's honor, no matter what.

He was slammed into the ground again, Daruk on his back. "Never turn your back on an enemy," Daruk said. "If you'd been paying attention, you would have heard me coming. Get up."

"What's the purpose of this?" Alaric asked. He rubbed his arms and knees, getting back on his feet. "You're not teaching me anything."

"When you first came here," Daruk said, crossing his arms, "I attacked you. I lost my head. Should have known you weren't a real threat by reading your scent better. Haven't had to deal with anyone coming out here in a long time. I'm rusty."

"And?" Alaric snorted, and smoke curled from his nose. "And what the hells is with the smoke?"

Daruk laughed and shook his head. "That happens from time to time. Don't worry, we can't breathe fire, but the smoke can come out if we get too agitated." He paused and looked Alaric up and down. "As for teaching, I'm doing exactly what my master did: subjecting you to various scenarios, trying to get you to react."

"And it worked," Alaric said, head down.

"Dragons were quick to anger," Daruk explained. "Especially if their mate was threatened. Even simple taunting could set them off. Some were worse than others." He eyed Alaric and continued, "And you have the blood of the Ruby Dragon, one of the prickliest fuckers who ever lived."

"Is that bad?" Alaric asked. Togarashi hadn't explained his past to Alaric, and had skipped many of the important details of being dragon-touched.

Daruk clicked his tongue, "It's not great for your temper issue, but you can work on that. Your normal state is very pleasant, easy-going."

Alaric blushed, saying, "I wanted to rip your head off. How's that 'easy-going?'"

"You'll work on that. You'll be no use to anyone, including your god, if you can be goaded into attacking without thinking. Just because they say mean things about him, which he probably deserves." Daruk said the last part under his breath, but Alaric caught it.

"Don't say another thing about Bashima," he warned.

"It's better that I tell you this, instead of you finding out later," Daruk said. "Gods killed the dragons. Wiped out every single one that didn't ascend. Hunted them down for sport. Laid waste to nests, slitting hatchling throats as they slept."

"Bashima didn't do any of that," Alaric said, though he knew gods had killed many dragons. Daruk's words made him wince, and he wondered if any god he'd met had murdered baby dragons.

"Maybe not," Daruk said. "But you can't trust them. They're old and savage and don't care about anything but themselves."

"Don't talk about my husband," Alaric said, leaving the circle. "You don't know him. And I don't care if I failed another test. I need a break." He walked away, leaving Daruk behind but listening for approaching steps if the other dragon chose to pounce.

Loralei was in the kitchen making lunch when Alaric came in and slammed the door behind him.

"Going well?" she asked when Alaric came in, sniffing the stew she was making. She shoved him away as he bent over the pot, interested.

"Hells, you're just as bad as Daruk. It's not ready." Alaric stared at her, and she laughed. "Don't use those huge eyes on me. I'm sure it works on your husband, might even work on Daruk, but it won't work on me."

Alaric slumped into a chair at the kitchen table and sulked, which only made Loralei laugh louder.

"You're back a little earlier than I expected," Loralei said, stirring the stew.

"Yeah, well, your mate is a jerk."

"Did he rile you up already?" Loralei asked. "It's not even noon."

"I failed the circle test or whatever," Alaric said, putting his arms on the table and leaning his chin on them. What Daruk said about the dragons prodded his heart. Cypress had told him that gods killed dragons, but so had humans, and probably demigods too. He supposed it was easier to blame the all-powerful gods than think about other beings who might have aided the destruction.

"Oh?" Loralei asked, not looking at him.

"He said I can't trust my own husband," Alaric said, scoffing. "He doesn't get it. Bashima would never hurt me. At least not intentionally."

"Perhaps," Loralei said. "Daruk only wants to protect you."

"I don't need protection from Bashima," Alaric said, though he pushed away thoughts of the Sun God's pitiless sneers from when they first met, his initial disdain and predatory behavior. His rough hands, grabbing Alaric, shoving him against a bookcase and the mountain shaking...

"Are you okay?" Loralei asked and sat down beside him, touching his trembling arm. Alaric pulled it away slowly. It wasn't Loralei's fault that he was thinking back on that horrible day. The brand glowed subtly, peeking through Alaric's tunic.

"Bashima...he's not easy," Alaric said. "He's said and done awful things. To me." He paused and noticed that Loralei was holding her breath, her hands clamped on the table. Not wanting her to break the table, Alaric went on, "But I forgave him, and we moved past it. I'd be dead if it wasn't for him, or enslaved to the sort of god you're worried about. I love him, and he loves me. If he could die for me, he would. I know nothing is ever perfect. I'm not stupid. We're going to have fights, probably hurt each other, because an eternity is a long time. But I'd rather spend it with him than anyone else."

Loralei sighed and released the table. "I can't pretend that I approve and I can't tell you what to do. Just remember that gods can turn on you in an instant. Maybe not your husband. You've claimed him, so he's bound to you, but be mindful of the others."

"None of the gods are safe," Alaric said, echoing Matthias's old advice. He knew it was true, especially now that more of them knew his secret. He wanted to believe none of them would betray him, that their loyalty to Bashima would keep them from doing so, but he kept a kernel of worry inside his heart, waiting for the day one of them would accidentally spill his true identity. He hoped it would never happen.

"Exactly," Loralei said, patting his arm. "Why don't you head back outside. Daruk's waiting for you."

She was right. Daruk stood outside the stone circle, arms crossed, gazing off into the surrounding evergreen grove. Waiting, as though he knew Alaric would return. He didn't turn at Alaric's approach and didn't speak when Alaric was right beside him. The wind blew past them, and Alaric bit his lip as the minutes ticked away. He wondered what Daruk was looking at, so he also watched the trees. They looked like normal trees, needled branches full and dark green, almost black.

"Close your eyes," Daruk growled, so Alaric did, trusting the other dragon wouldn't attack him if he'd given a direct order. "Let down your warding."

"My what?" Alaric asked, peeking out one eye at Daruk.

"Close your damn eyes," Daruk barked. "You put up wards to block your senses, to keep your mate out, I assume? But that also blocks your ability to perceive everything around you."

Alaric didn't want to do that. He didn't want to pummel Bashima with his feelings when he couldn't be beside him. Bashima might be far away, but their soul bond connected them as though he were only a few rooms away. Not that he could explain that to Daruk.

"I don't want to keep him out," Alaric said. "I'm trying to protect him."

"Over this distance it shouldn't be more than a pang of emotion," Daruk said. "And he needs to get used to it. What if you have to leave him for an extended period of time again? Doesn't he have duties?"

That's what Alaric was afraid of. He imagined Bashima trying to meditate with the sun and getting a blast of Alaric's faraway emotional flashes. Would he be okay? Another part of him scoffed. Of course, the Sun God would be fine. He was strong, not easily brought down. He was the best mate. The perfect husband.

"Okay," Alaric said, and Daruk nodded. Alaric withdrew all his blocking — the warding — and sent an apology to his husband. He tried to do it with care, but the slow trickle turned to a downpour. A massive surge of energy hit him, like the sun had turned all its attention on him, and Alaric stumbled to his knees, eyes opening.

Babe, he sent out, I'm sorry but I have to do this. Block me. Now. There was a flicker deep within him, a pained yearning, like a hand reaching for him. I love you, don't worry.

Then Bashima was gone, like a whisper on the wind.

"Well," said Daruk above him. "That was interesting. That god has you trapped good."

"I'm not trapped," Alaric snapped, leaping to his feet, body nearly pressed against the other dragon. "Don't bring him up while we're training. Or I'll rip your arms off."

Daruk's eyebrows were almost to his hairline. "Fine, I won't. But you need to learn to control your scent when you're connected to him. Even gods might be able to detect it."

"What do I care if gods know I love my husband? I think marrying him gave that away."

Daruk barked a laugh, saying, "Fair enough. New mating bonds are always strong, but the shit you're sending out is making my nose hair burn off."

"How do I stop it?" Alaric asked.

"With a lot of practice. Now that your wards are down, stand beside me, eyes closed. Reach out with your senses to the world around you. Start small. Pick one thing to focus on or you'll overwhelm yourself."

There were a lot of things in the yard surrounding the cottage. The chickens pecking the ground near their coop, the nearby trees, or maybe he could try and sense Loralei.

Alaric chose Daruk. He closed his eyes and tried to focus on his teacher. Taking deep breaths, he allowed the energy that surrounded the other dragon to seep into him, but he couldn't stop the flow, much like when he'd tried to let down his wards. A riot of images and scents assaulted him: Daruk as a young boy with teary eyes, a small village market, two women with kind eyes and matching grins, a house ablaze, scents of ash and vanilla, then Loralei's smile as Daruk bent to kiss her, and then a booming explosion and massive eyes made of boiling silver.

"Stop!" Daruk's voice rumbled through Alaric, his iron grip on Alaric's arms, shaking him. Alaric opened his eyes, the smell of burning wood fresh in his nose. Daruk glowered at him and said, "Hells, don't focus on me! Reading a complex being is dangerous when you don't know what you're doing." He dropped his hands, seeing Alaric's contrite expression. "It took me a minute to push you back," he muttered. "I really am out of practice."

"Sorry," Alaric said, rubbing the back of his neck. A pain gnawed at the center of his forehead. Was it from being inside Daruk's mind? "What should I focus on?"

"Anything but me," Daruk growled. "An ant, a tree, a rock. They all give off energy that you can read."

Alaric looked at Daruk out of the corner of his eye. The other dragon was flustered, jaw clenched, eyes flashing with silver light.

"Was that Kamaishi? In the vision? Your dragon?" Alaric asked.

"Hmm? Oh, yes." Daruk glanced at him, annoyed. "Steel Belly Dragon. He activated me when I was in my thirties, because our village was being attacked constantly by bandits. They'd come, steal from the surrounding farms, but didn't hurt anyone. More of a nuisance than anything. Until one day, they came to the town and burned houses. Didn't bother to take anything, just set peoples' homes on fire."

Daruk looked away, fury rising in him. Alaric picked up the metallic odor and wrinkled his nose.

"After I caught them, which was quite a feat for a newly transformed dragon-touched, they told me that a god coerced them. That it was a punishment for our village. They were lucky that Kamaishi had a good grip on me, or I would have killed them and torn the bodies to pieces."

Alaric recalled the burning buildings from his visions of Daruk and shuddered. What if that had happened to his village? How would he feel if a god caused destruction to his home?

"I'm sorry," Alaric whispered.

Daruk grunted and shook himself as though ridding his body of water. He said, "It's in the past. I've protected my village since then, and nothing bad has come again."

"I can smell you," Alaric said.

"I'm sure you can," Daruk said and turned an eye to him. "Notice how you're not trying to roll all over me like you did to my chair this morning?"

Alaric blushed and took a couple steps away.

"That's not entirely your fault, although you didn't have to tear up the pillows," Daruk muttered. "You have no idea what you are or what powers you have."

"It's not like I don't know anything," Alaric said. "I can cloud-dance."

Daruk snorted. "Congratulations, the one thing I can't do. Gotta keep bringing it up huh?"

"Since it's all I've got, yeah."

Daruk shook his head and pointed to the circle. "Get in there. We're going to try something. It's a little advanced, but you're pretty strong for a newly-turned."

Excited, Alaric leaped into the circle and sat down, gazing up at Daruk.

"Hells, your eyes are enormous," Daruk said. "You look like a pup begging for dinner."

Alaric grinned and shrugged. Daruk joined him in the circle and sat in front of him, scooting closer so their knees touched.

"I'm going to lead you into a dragon trance. Once you can do them on your own, you'll be able to communicate with Togarashi, though I'm not sure how much good that will do."

"Why are you so mean about my dragon?" Alaric asked. He flicked a stone out of the circle and glared at Daruk.

"Once you meet my dragon, you'll understand." Daruk clasped Alaric's hands and set them on their knees. "Close your eyes and focus on my scent. Don't try to dig in like you did before, that's not what we're trying to do."

"Okay." Alaric shut his eyes and took a deep breath, searching for the metallic odor, finding it easily. He was getting used to it, and it felt familiar and comforting. He pictured curling up in Daruk's chair and hummed deep in his chest as Daruk laughed.

"Yeah, yeah, keep it to yourself, kid," Daruk said. "Match my breathing and let yourself relax. Follow my scent."

Once their breathing synchronized, Alaric heard a whooshing sound and felt the earth fall away from them. Them? He was alarmed to find Daruk in his mind but didn't push him back. He wondered how much Daruk could perceive. Could he feel Alaric's determination, his fear of losing control, the beating center of his being where Bashima lived? Daruk was only a vague shadow to him, not like when Alaric infiltrated his defenses before, but he was a solid presence.

"Alaric, open your eyes," Daruk said, voice serene.

They were still seated on the grass within the circle, but everything around them sang with vibrancy. It was like Alaric had never truly seen the world until now. The colors! The sounds! The grass beneath him burst with life, and he could feel each blade against his body.

"This is incredible!" Alaric said and almost released Daruk's hands.

"Nope! Don't do that or the trance will break," Daruk warned, grip tightening. "This isn't the real world. We're projecting into a space where the dragons can reach us."

"It's beautiful," Alaric said, listening to the songs of hundreds of birds, hearing water cascading from a distant waterfall. He could almost feel the mist rising from the waterfall's pool, taste the clear water.

"Kamaishi will be here in a moment," Daruk said, staring at Alaric. "You did very well."

"It wasn't too hard," Alaric said, looking around. "I reached for you, or the you that's in my head, I guess."

Daruk shook his head as though to clear his ears.

"That's a good way to put it," Daruk said. "But it's usually difficult. For a pup, you have a talent for this. Now I can see why Togarashi took an interest in you."

Alaric perked up at the mention of his dragon. "Is Togarashi really that bad?"

"He's not bad," said Daruk, blowing hair out of his eyes. "He's just erratic and impulsive."

"How do you know that?"

"I've met him. He and the other dragons from this area often meet with a new dragon-touched, even if it's just for a moment. Togarashi was supposed to teach me how to cloud-dance when Kamaishi's lessons didn't work. But he grew tired of me after a few days and I haven't seen him since."

Alaric winced and said, "I'm sorry. I guess he didn't have to teach me. I did it in my dragon dreams and sort of figured it out on my own."

"It's okay," Daruk said and laughed. "Good thing you're an independent learner, otherwise you would be even more of a mess than you are now."

"Hey!" Alaric bristled. He thought he was doing all right. "At least I can cloud-dance!" He stuck out his tongue at Daruk, who sighed in irritation.

"Daruk Darukson Helgason. Have you forgotten our talks about managing your frustration?" A new voice, low in timbre and soft. Alaric looked around for the source and spotted a silvery flash across the clearing. Daruk bowed his head, teeth bared.

"Yes, teacher, I remember," Daruk said through clenched teeth.

"Apparently not," the voice said, then a massive form was beside the stone circle. Silver scales gleamed in the sunlight, brighter than the dawn, though the dragon's tufted mane and beard were thick and golden. Kamaishi was much larger than Togarashi and thicker across the chest. His legs were corded with powerful muscle, thicker than ancient tree trunks, and curved silver talons pierced the ground. A long tail coiled around the stone circle, tapping the ground in a rhythm, and the dragon flicked Daruk's head with his tail, whapping him smartly.

Alaric giggled and the dragon turned to him, which made Alaric zip his lips. While Togarashi had seemed both mighty and funny, Kamaishi was different. This dragon exuded ultimate calm but also a commanding strength that brooked no fools. His tail wrapped around Alaric, touching his shoulders and hair, searching for something.

"Ah, you are Togarashi's," he rumbled, raising a huge golden eyebrow. "How fitting that you should also lack discipline and find amusement where you should be bending every part of your being to your studies."

"He's very young, teacher," Daruk said. Alaric sent Daruk a silent thank you, which made the other dragon-touched smile a bit. It was good to know that Daruk would defend him, even from his master.

"I am very aware," Kamaishi said and released Alaric from his tail's grip. "Activated by a god no less? Intriguing and also irritating. Are you under the sway of this god, hatchling?" His tail tugged at the back of Alaric's tunic, revealing the brand, which started glowing. "Oh..." Kamaishi's voice trailed away, and he withdrew his tail as if burned. "That is another unfortunate wrinkle. No matter. You can rid yourself of that easily enough."

"Teacher?" Daruk asked, confused.

"Never you mind, Daruk." Kamaishi snorted and shook his head, smoke tumbling from his nostrils. "Somehow I think you don't want to be rid of your god?"

Alaric paled, realizing Kamaishi must have figured out the soul bond, but he hadn't told Daruk. It really must be dangerous if the dragon couldn't tell his own blood.

Alaric cleared his throat, glared up at the dragon, and said, "I don't."

"You speak so firmly for one who doesn't truly understand," Kamaishi said. "Perhaps with time you will realize what a mistake it was to take a god as your mate."

"I doubt it," Alaric said, defiant.

"At least you have conviction," Kamaishi said. "Daruk, why have you summoned me? Is it because of the hatchling?"

"My name is Alaric Shina," Alaric snarled. Daruk squeezed his hands, but Alaric paid him no attention. The dragon could tear him to bits, but Alaric wouldn't let Kamaishi dismiss him so quickly.

"I know," the dragon said, his great head lifted, silver eyes glittering down at Alaric. "Togarashi could hardly shut up about you for months. It's too bad that he's neglected your education. Didn't bother to teach you how to regulate your tongue."

"Teacher," Daruk said, shooting Alaric a dirty look. "He came to find me, seeking guidance. I wished him to meet one great as yourself, to better understand what has been gifted to him."

"An excellent idea, but will he learn from me? I can feel the fury writhing under his skin. And his scent...he's in his first rut. Hardly a good time for listening and contemplation."

"But isn't it remarkable that he has this much control during his first rut?" Daruk pointed out. Alaric looked from Daruk to the dragon and back. He wanted to chime in but felt resistance from Daruk. Shut up, and let me handle this. Daruk went on, "And he taught himself to cloud-dance."

Kamaishi tutted, saying, "Stop praising him. He's already an obstinate child. He doesn't need you to tell him what a good boy he is." The dragon gazed at Alaric, who tried his hardest to keep his emotions at bay. "You can't control your scent, child. That should have been the first thing Togarashi taught you." He lifted a clawed hand to his chin and looked away. "But perhaps you aren't unteachable."

He started to amble away, no concern in his careful steps.

"You're leaving?" Alaric asked and Daruk hissed at him.

"I have decided to assist Daruk with your teachings," Kamaishi said. "But there are other matters we dragons attend to that mere humans cannot comprehend. Remain vigilant until my return. Don't make me regret my choice."

That night they ate a quiet dinner. Loralei attempted conversation a few times, but Alaric and Daruk gave short answers or grunted, so she gave up. She reached for Daruk's hand and held it on the table as they ate, rubbing his knuckles. Alaric watched them, taking in the little touches, the smiles, the way Daruk looked at Loralei. They reminded him of his parents: the ease of their companionship, reading each other's moods, knowing when to push and when to hold back. He hoped that he and Bashima could reach that place, that level of knowledge. Even if it took a million years, Alaric was willing to try.

After Alaric cleared his plate and excused himself, he left them alone in the kitchen. In his room, he noticed that he'd left his scarf across his chair and went back. The book he wanted to read was still stored in the scarf. He heard muffled voices and paused. Probably discussing what happened with Kamaishi. He'd grab his scarf later and let them talk.

"I'm worried," Daruk said, loud enough for Alaric to catch. "Kamaishi wouldn't tell me what's going on, but that has to be it. That connection is too strong. You should have seen him when he lowered his wards. From that distance, it shouldn't have that much effect."

"Maybe it has something to do with the brand? Maybe there's a way we can get him to stay with us," Loralei said. Alaric held his breath.

"I have no idea about the brand. It's a little too perfect though," Daruk said, troubled. "What if it was all planned? That Sun God basically made him. If a god can command a dragon…"

Furious, Alaric entered the kitchen and growled, making Loralei jump and sending Daruk bolting from his chair. Alaric held his fists at his side, trying to regain some control.

"Bashima doesn't command me any more than Loralei can command you."

They stared at Alaric, Loralei's mouth quivering. Daruk's head was lowered, his back hunched, ready to attack if needed.

Alaric let frustrated tears fall and he said, "If that's what you're worried about, Bashima's compulsion thing stopped working on me when I was human, so I doubt it works now. And even if he tried to command me, I wouldn't obey blindly. Is that what you think of me?"

"Alaric," Loralei said, reaching out her hand.

"Compulsion didn't work on you?" Daruk asked. "That's impossible."

"I guess not," Alaric said, the tears running down his face. "I know how you feel about gods, and I'd be pissed too if one of them tried to destroy my village, but don't try to drive a wedge between me and my husband. I will return to him."

"We wouldn't try to take you from him," Loralei said and stood. "You're mated. It would be cruel and basically impossible to keep you away from him. We're just concerned —"

"Don't be," Alaric said. "I need you to train me, not dissect my marriage when I'm not in the room."

"Alaric," Daruk said. "You masked your scent from me."

Surprised, Alaric took a step back and looked down at himself. He didn't feel different, besides being mad at the couple.

"I didn't know you were in the next room," Daruk said. "But damned hells, you reek now." He waved a hand in front of his face. "Look, we only want to help you. What did Kamaishi mean when he said you could be rid of it?"

"That's none of your business," Alaric said, wiping the tears away. "It doesn't matter, since I won't leave Bashima. No matter how many people tell me I should. It's not happening. He's mine and I'm his. End of story."

Loralei looked at Daruk and sighed. She sat down and beckoned for Alaric to sit beside her. "I know that the mating instinct is very strong, Alaric. I'm half of a set myself." She smiled, and it was full of sadness. "Please, come sit with us."

Suspicious but not wanting to disappoint Loralei, Alaric gave Daruk a scathing look as he rejoined the table. Loralei took a deep breath, and Daruk sat beside her, nuzzling her head. She leaned into him, and Alaric wanted to look away to give them some privacy.

"Daruk and I met a long time ago," Loralei said, scratching her mate's head, threading her fingers through his hair. "He's not the only one who worries about gods. When he found me…"

"Loralei," Daruk started, but she patted his hand.

"It's okay. Alaric should know. He's so new to this world." She wet her lips, thinking of how to begin. "I'm a demigod. My mother is a goddess. My father, a knight of some sort. I never knew who he was, just a passing fancy to my mother. She hadn't planned on becoming pregnant, especially not with a half-human child, but she decided to have me. A new way to alleviate her boredom, maybe."

Daruk stood and went to the stove to prepare tea. He stood with his back to the table, and Alaric noticed the tense set of his shoulders. The metallic odor intensified before disappearing.

"He'll be okay," Loralei said. "I can't pick up on the scents like you, but I can feel him. He's heard this story plenty of times."

"Doesn't make it easier," Daruk said.

"I wish I could say I entertained my mother enough, but that wasn't the case," Loralei said. "When I was about one hundred years old, she brought me to a human village and left me there."

Alaric inhaled sharply and looked at Daruk, who was shaking.

"I was taken in by a man. He fed me, gave me a place to stay, but once he saw my strength he made me fight people. How I earned my keep, I suppose. He didn't speak much to me, but I won every time, so he was pleased. Until one day, I went up against a demigod. I didn't know. I thought it was another human who I could take out easily, but this guy was different."

"And if I ever find him, he's a dead man," Daruk said.

"He'd seen me fight in another town," Loralei explained. "So, he started following us. Town after town, fight after fight. I looked like this innocent girl, so there were always people who agreed to fight me. The guy looked young too. No way to tell exactly how old he was, but he was a fire-type. The instant I got close, he grabbed my arms and created a circle of fire around us, blocking us from view."

The kettle shrieked, and Alaric jumped. Daruk brought the kettle over and three cups, pouring them tea. The steam rose above their heads, and Alaric felt a blazing hate from Daruk before the other dragon blocked himself again.

"He wanted me to join him," Loralei explained and sipped her tea. "Said that demigods needed to stick together. Gods hated us. Humans were animals. The usual bullshit. Like I needed him to tell me that some humans were awful or that gods couldn't care less about us. He said he knew other demigods who felt the same way, and that I would be welcome with them."

"I'm sorry, Loralei," Alaric said, head down. He had a feeling what was coming next.

"I refused to join him, of course. He had this look in his eyes, pure madness. You get used to that kind of look, considering the work I was doing. I had a feeling that going with him would be worse than staying with my human captor. He gave me a pitying look and told me that I was doomed to be a slave. He broke my arms like it was the easiest thing in the world, burned my skin, then he released the flames and disappeared. I screamed. I screamed until my lungs gave out. But it's what saved me." She touched Daruk's cheek. "This big lug heard me. We were near Kamaishi at a makeshift fighting ring. He came out of nowhere, this silver boulder, scattered the humans who probably thought he was a monster. He picked me up, trying not to hurt me more, and brought me to his cottage."

Loralei noticed Alaric's shocked expression and joked, "It looked like shit when I got here." Alaric snorted and Daruk rolled his eyes. Loralei patted his cheek roughly and said, "He got to me in time to save my arms." She showed Alaric her forearms, which were burn-free. Daruk purred next to her, and Loralei laughed. "Yes, you did a good job."

"That's awful," Alaric said. "All of it. How could your mother abandon you like that?"

Loralei shrugged. "That's what gods do. At least the ones I've heard about. When you're immortal, things stop having meaning. You're left with endless existence stretching into eternity. Some of them choose to be savage pieces of shit. Some are like my mother, indifferent and cold."

Alaric had to admit that Bashima was brutal when they'd first met, that he'd seen a ruthless side to his husband more than once. Or they were like Chronas, reveling in their power over lesser beings, using their power against anyone weaker than them. But some of them were loyal, brave, and thoughtful.

"They're not all like that," Alaric said. "My friend Jace is a demigod, and he lives with his father. Lord Veles would do anything for his son."

"Does this Jace have a useful ability?" Daruk asked, as Loralei rubbed his arm. Daruk looked at her but shook his head. "No, he needs to hear this too. Demigods aren't allowed to use their abilities without a god's permission. They could be tossed in the Locker or worse if they do. Even in self-defense, it gets tricky."

Alaric thought about Oken fighting his father at the summit, which had definitely been self-defense. When he examined the memory closer, he hadn't actually seen Oken use his power against his father. He'd been ready to, but he didn't threaten his father until the Fire God hurt Cypress. Oken probably got away with it because Cypress was the king's stepson.

Jace could coerce people and read minds. The gods were using Shako to keep the Locker closed. Nim would train to be the new Goddess of Time, even though she was so young.

Loralei leaned back in her chair. "I'm sure there are gods who aren't bad, but I've yet to meet one. Veles — the God of the Dead, right? — he might care about his son. But if his son's also useful, that probably makes it easier. Gods don't usually keep their demigod children."

Alaric shook his head. Jace never complained about his father, had only mentioned that Veles didn't like Cabari, which seemed like a dutiful fatherly thing to do. The Lightning God was mercurial and unlikely to stay with Jace for very long, so of course Veles didn't like him.

"They can't all be bad," Alaric said. "Just like all humans aren't bad or good. And all demigods aren't the same. You're completely different from the bastard who burned you. Shouldn't people get a chance to change, if they really want to?" Bashima's eyes flashed through Alaric's mind, orange as two blazing suns, his smile radiant. "If they find a reason to be better, some people can change."

Loralei nodded, but her expression was full of doubt and pity.

Daruk grunted and said, "Would have to be a damned big reason."

Chapter Thirteen

Cypress

Cypress hit the stone wall and slammed onto the ground, breath rushing from his lungs. The whip-like vines pulled back into his skin, slithering like aggravated snakes. Cypress could almost feel the disappointment wafting from Vaultus and Torstan, who stood at the opposite end of the training area.

Vaultus hid his face in his hand, covering his eyes. Torstan eyed Cypress, celestial foot tapping the grass.

"That was certainly something," Torstan said. "I barely moved."

"You're a celestial and much faster than me," Cypress said, staggering to his feet. He was on his ass again in a second, Torstan's blow coming out of nowhere.

"That's no excuse." Torstan was back at Vaultus's side. "You're undisciplined. Unfocused."

"I'm sorry," Cypress said, rubbing his chin where Torstan punched him. That would leave an angry bruise.

"Not sorry enough to train, it seems," Torstan said, but he was glaring at Vaultus, whose hair drooped around his face. Cypress hadn't seen his mentor so disheveled in a while, but they were at his temple, secreted away from prying eyes. The only ones who knew about Vaultus's true condition were in the training area. Except Savos, who Torstan chased away with his mere presence, and Hastia, who refused to watch her son be pummeled.

"How is he supposed to adapt to the additional strength if he hasn't mastered what you've already given?" Torstan walked over to Cypress and gazed down at him, the breeze ruffling his long, gray hair. Torstan might look like an old man, but he was hardly weak. As a celestial, he had more power than almost anyone, including Vaultus.

"I'll get better," Cypress said and stood, bracing himself on the wall. Torstan shook his head, blowing out a huge breath.

"You don't have time to 'get better.' You should be well past this part of your training. What have you been doing for the last two thousand years?"

"I think he needs a break," Vaultus said, appearing at Torstan's side. "Hastia will want us to join her for lunch."

Torstan nodded, but Cypress could tell he wouldn't let this go. If Cypress was being honest, he'd been more interested in Oken than using the celestial power Vaultus had given him. The vines manifested after the gifting, and he had yet to master them. Sometimes the vines emerged of their own volition, usually when Cypress was angry. He wielded his own power as a god, but it didn't do much good when the foreign celestial power had a mind of its own.

And then there were the parts of his mind that Oken inhabited.

The instant Cypress kissed Oken the first time, it was all over for him. Their lips meeting opened a floodgate, sending the Forest God into an intoxicated spiral from which he would never recover. Why hadn't it felt that way when he kissed anyone else? Cypress hardly knew Oken, yet he was drawn to the demigod like the tide to the shore.

He recalled Oken's first trip to his temple, when Cypress had shifted them to his chambers as they kissed, which hadn't fazed Oken one bit. He didn't even lose his kissing concentration. They were less than graceful making their way to the bedroom; knocking into every piece of furniture as they kissed, sending a priceless vase crashing to the floor, upending Cypress's washing table, which spilled water everywhere. They tugged at each other's clothes, trying not to break their lips apart. Cypress ripped Oken's shirt clean off in frustration at the buttons. Then his tunic got stuck on one of his horns, making Oken beam with laughter. Cypress hadn't seen Oken smile like that, and he grabbed the demigod by the hips and pulled him in.

"We have an hour," Oken said, confusing Cypress.

"What? We have however long we want."

"Dasari said food would be ready in an hour, and it would be rude not to eat what was prepared."

Oken looked dead serious, and Cypress laughed. Oken tilted his head. "Was that funny?"

"No, you just amaze me," Cypress said, rubbing his hands up and down Oken's back. He was lean, whip-thin but strong. Cypress wanted to keep touching Oken forever.

"And that's funny?" Oken asked. Cypress snorted and shook his head.

"I'm mainly laughing at myself," Cypress said. "You're amazing."

Oken smiled again, genuine and elated, and dipped his head to kiss Cypress. "You have a lot of scars," Oken said, taking in Cypress's body. Cypress flushed and stepped away.

"Yeah," he said, self-conscious. Magical scars from his training that would never heal. Though he shouldn't have felt weird about them with

Oken, whose own scars were impossible to hide. Cypress didn't know if Oken's mother had done all the damage, but Oken's shoulders and torso were littered with the birthmark-colored scars like the one on his face.

"I like them," Oken said, tracing one on Cypress's chest. Cypress's breath caught in his throat and he nearly choked. "Do you enjoy that?" Oken asked, and Cypress nodded.

Oken went over his upper body, finding every scar, every mark, running a finger down each one, and Cypress felt himself getting harder by the moment. Finally, Oken noticed his arousal and slid his fingers down the back waistband of Cypress's trousers.

"Do you have any scars down here?"

Cypress's pupils blew, dark green flashing across them. He picked Oken up, wrapped Oken's legs around his torso, and threw them both on the bed. Oken's eyes went wide at Cypress's strength, looking up at him in passionate surprise. He gripped Cypress's biceps and squeezed, and snowflakes started to fall from above them. Cypress hardly noticed the snow.

He tore off his trousers and slid one hand down Oken's body. Fuck, he was too excited. He withdrew his hand, willing himself to slow down, but Oken wasn't interested in slowing down. He flipped Cypress over on the bed and shed his trousers, wild hunger in his eyes, and he bent and kissed the Forest God, biting his lower lip, which made Cypress thrust his hips up.

Oken made a primal sound deep in his chest, and Cypress reacted, taking back control. He grabbed Oken by the ass, sat him forward and pinned him, so he was back on top. He needed to feel Oken. Sliding his fingers across Oken's body was exhilarating, and Oken's jaw clenched at the sensation, pulling Cypress back down for another savage kiss.

Oken's tongue searched inside Cypress's mouth, battling for dominance.

For not knowing what he was doing, Oken seemed to have a pretty good idea. He reached between them and stroked Cypress. The touch was too much for Cypress, who pressed Oken back onto the bed. He buried himself inside Oken without needing a hand to guide him, and Oken's back arched, his hands held down by Cypress.

Damned hells, it felt like Cypress had been missing a vital piece of himself when he thrust inside Oken and felt muscles tighten. The sensation might send him over the edge too fast.

He leaned down to whisper in Oken's ear, "Let me know if I'm hurting you."

"I don't think you can hurt me, Bell," Oken said, kissing his brow, and Cypress melted. He gathered Oken in his arms and thrust slowly, reading Oken's hip movements, listening to the catches in his breath, burying his face in Oken's shoulder. Oken held onto Cypress's back, his hands roving to the back of his neck to play with green hair, then down to his ass, cupping and squeezing, getting to know his new lover's body. He tried not to wrap his legs around Cypress but failed once the Forest God found his pleasure center. Oken closed his eyes and pressed his head back onto the bed, grasping the sheets.

Cypress paused, pulling his face away from Oken's shoulder, looking down at the demigod. Was he okay?

"Don't. Stop," Oken said. So, Cypress didn't.

After an hour, they lay next to each other, breathing heavily. Oken leaned over and kissed Cypress's sweat-covered brow. He ran his hand down Cypress's chest and said, "After we eat, I'd like to try that again."

An aggravated shout brought Cypress back to Vaultus's temple. His hand slipped off his chin, and his face nearly hit the table. His wine glass teetered, but he caught it. Cypress didn't recall getting to the table. Had his mind wandered that far?

"Glad you could join us," Torstan said, and Vaultus stared at Cypress with wide eyes. He made a face, admonishing Cypress for daydreaming while the celestial was there. Cypress noticed, to his horror, that he was halfway to being hard, and he was grateful for the napkin in his lap.

"I'm sorry, sir!" Cypress said, blushing.

"Every day, you're getting farther away," Torstan said. "You know what's at stake and yet you're distracted. And what is an Oken?"

Cypress's cheeks blazed and his mother coughed. Vaultus's eyes pleaded with him to keep it together.

Torstan observed every detail; his perception was second to none, and he caught their reactions. He said, "Or is it a person? Have you been wasting time on romance instead of focusing on your inherited powers?"

"That's not —" Vaultus started.

"Fair?" Torstan asked, keeping his aged gaze on Cypress. "Is there anything fair about this situation? We celestials meant for Vaultus to keep the power that was bestowed upon him, not pass it on to someone less worthy."

Hastia's posture straightened, but she didn't speak, and Torstan eyed her, waiting for a reaction. He said, "Bell is a fine boy, but he wasn't made for this power. He has to work a thousand times harder than Vaultus, and he's not putting in the effort."

"You won't tell me everything," Cypress interrupted, grimacing at his bravery. He knew Vaultus and Torstan kept things from him to try and protect him, but he was a god and was entrusted with celestial powers. Didn't he deserve to know what was going on?

"We tell you what you need to know," Torstan said, sipping wine.

Hastia huffed next to Vaultus and said, "If you two are going to subject my son to this torture you call training, then I agree with him. What exactly is he preparing for?"

"Hastia," Vaultus said and reached for her hand, which she snatched away.

"Don't 'Hastia' me," she said, and Cypress paled and sat back in his chair. Torstan pretended that he was very interested in his salad rather than get involved in the brewing argument. Hastia said, "I've gone along with it because you promised to protect him, but how are you supposed to do that in your condition?"

"Bell won't be alone," Vaultus said, though he looked defeated. "The gods will stand behind him, no matter what. And the celestials too."

"That's just it," Hastia said, and threw down her napkin. "He'll be out in front with a huge target on him. It doesn't matter who fights alongside him, he's the one taking all the risks." She rose from her seat, prompting them all to rise. Cypress grabbed his napkin just in time and held it in front of his crotch, hoping no one would look at him.

"Please, sit," Hastia said. "I must attend to my duties in the gardens."

She inclined her head at Torstan and touched her son's arm as she left but spared no second glance for her husband. Savos passed her as she left, and Hastia whispered something to him, and the god-touched man nodded.

Vaultus slumped back in his chair as Savos made his way to his side.

"I grow weary," Vaultus said, his hand on his brow. Savos stood beside him, face impassive, though Cypress saw light flash in his yellow eyes. Savos gave him one withering glance before settling with his hands behind his back.

"Perhaps we should take a break," Torstan said.

Seeing that his erection problem had abated, Cypress excused himself from the table and fled, glad to be away from them. Cypress knew Savos didn't approve of Vaultus passing his abilities to him. The god-touched man had a better candidate in mind, though Cypress didn't know who, and he didn't blame Savos. Cypress was just the Forest God, not an Elemental, not an old god. Almost anyone would have been a better choice than him.

Walking down the hallway toward his room, Cypress almost ran into someone. He stepped back, startled, saying, "Oh! Excuse me!" Then his voice caught in his throat and he jumped, landing in a crouch ten feet away. "What are you doing here?"

The Fire God glared at him with disdain, flames dancing around his head and arms, his shoulders bent like he wanted to charge. Next to him was a handsome man with large silver wings and a bird-headed person wrapped in a black cloak.

"Forest God," rumbled Cindras and raised a fist. The winged man grinned and clapped his hands once.

"Cypress, is it? Splendid!" His voice was relaxed and musical, and he approached Cypress with a bounce in his step. The bird-headed person followed in his wake, taking in the surroundings, while the Fire God remained where he was, eyes narrowed.

"Who are you?" Cypress asked. The winged man didn't seem like a threat, but Cypress couldn't be sure. He seemed too at ease in the king's temple.

"The stories of my exploits don't reach the forest, huh?" he asked, winking. He stood in front of Cypress, about the same height, though he wasn't as broad in the shoulders. His silver wings ruffled behind him, and a few dislodged themselves and went flying. Most of them circled the man's head, but a few flew away as though a wind had passed through the hall.

"You're Falkar," Cypress said. Great. Another celestial. "Vaultus won't appreciate you spying on him." He nodded after the flying feathers and Falkar shrugged.

"Gotta stay informed somehow. This is my student, Orn."

Up close, Orn resembled an eagle, but his feathers were spikier. He was very short, a little over five feet, but he exuded a quiet confidence.

"A pleasant experience, to find myself in the halls of greatness," Orn muttered, and Cypress glanced at Falkar, who shrugged again, smiling.

"If you're here to see Vaultus," Cypress said, "he's busy." He positioned himself in their way.

Falkar laughed and clasped Cypress's shoulder. "Don't worry, we're not here to cause trouble. That's already afoot, if the rumors I've heard are correct."

He watched for Cypress's reaction, reminding Cypress of Torstan. These celestials were always a huge problem. Why couldn't they ever speak plainly?

"He was speaking with Torstan," Cypress said.

"Excellent!" Falkar said. "What perfect timing. Cindras? Shall we?" Falkar passed Cypress, his student close behind. Orn nodded at Cypress but said nothing else.

The Fire God hadn't moved, so Cypress walked toward him. Vaultus and Torstan could handle themselves. He wanted nothing to do with them meeting with the Fire God. Had they known he was coming? Cypress hoped Vaultus would have mentioned it if he knew. Either way, the Fire God wouldn't attack him in the king's own temple.

"Is Oken here?" the Fire God asked when Cypress tried to pass him, his voice like a cave-in.

"No," Cypress said and made to push past.

"You wouldn't tell me if he was," Cindras said.

Cypress stopped, fists clenched at his sides. "He's not here."

"If he's not with you, then where is he?"

"Not that you deserve to know, but he's safe with Bashima. Remember? The one who kicked your ass at the summit?"

Cindras growled, the flames billowing off him. Cypress's eyes flashed green, and bright green lightning traveled across his body. He was in no mood to deal with the Fire God.

"So long as he's not with you, I'll take that as a consolation," Cindras said, striding away.

Cypress felt rage boiling inside him. Remembering the Fire God's hand around his neck at the summit, Oken on the floor, covered in golden blood. A father standing over his son who couldn't defend himself without facing severe consequences. Cindras had picked the perfect time to try and take his son back, when there were plenty of gods in attendance who agreed that the father had rights over the child. Especially a demigod child.

"He will never go back to you," Cypress called, and the Fire God stopped. His shoulders tensed, but he didn't turn around. Cypress said, "Despite everything you've done to him, he's the most caring person I know. I thank the fates every day that I've had a chance to be in his life."

Still, Cindras didn't acknowledge what Cypress said.

Vine tendrils dripped from Cypress's skin, so he closed his eyes and focused on calming down. He couldn't attack Cindras, not if the Fire God hadn't attacked him first. He took a deep breath and said, "You're right that I don't deserve him, but you sure as hells don't either."

Cypress's green lightning dispersed, the vines whipping around his arms. He spun around and stalked away before the Fire God could answer.

Vaultus

Vaultus sat on his throne where he had adjourned with the Fire God. They'd left the two celestials to argue about the impending conflict, not wanting to be caught in a game of wits between the two.

"Thankfully, neither of those two helped make me," Vaultus said, rubbing his brow.

He'd sent Savos away as well, though his god-touched friend had protested. He didn't agree with the king being alone with the temperamental Fire God, but he'd gone to tell Hastia of their visitors.

Cindras eyed him, silent as a grave. Neither Falkar nor Torstan had shaped the Fire God either, Vaultus knew, but Cindras had worked with Falkar before. He was curious to see what the Fire God could tell him about the winged celestial. Though he looked in the prime of youth, Falkar was older than Vaultus and Cindras.

Vaultus cleared his throat, unsure what to say. He was excellent at starting conversations, but talking to the Fire God was like engaging with a volcano.

"Is it true?" Cindras rumbled, arms crossed.

"You'll have to be more specific," Vaultus said, sighing.

"You're weakening."

"Oh, that," Vaultus laughed, then coughed into his hand. Falkar knew about Vaultus's celestial-given power and was familiar with the ailment that troubled him. That had troubled him for thousands of years. Perhaps he'd told the Fire God. He said, "I am still the king."

"That's not what I asked." For being a force of heat and flame, the Fire God was cold down to his core. He would attempt to take Vaultus's throne if he thought he could.

"I don't think I heard a question," Vaultus said, frowning.

218

His black hair drooped around his face, and he knew he didn't look as magnificent as he once had. Even since the summit, he'd felt his body aching from having to contain the remaining celestial strength. He needed to give it to Bell soon.

"How are we supposed to function if you're gone?" Cindras asked. "The in-fighting will be catastrophic. The rumblings of rebellion have already begun, not to mention the fact that he escaped the Locker."

Vaultus was a bit surprised. He and Cindras had never seen eye to eye, even when they were first created. It was as though the celestials made them to be at odds forever. The Fire God seemed to despise everything and everyone, doing his duty as the chief Elemental god but taking no joy in it. He was quiet and taciturn, never giving his opinions on policy, never adding to the conversation at summits. They'd existed together longer than the other gods, and yet had never had more than a few private conversations.

And there was the messy business with his children.

"I've made arrangements for if I become incapacitated," he said, staring at Cindras.

The Fire God snorted. "If you think the old gods will follow that boy —"

"I will not speak of Cypress with you," Vaultus warned. "I know your feelings about him, and your good sense is clouded by resentment."

The Fire God fumed. Vaultus could feel the heat coming off him and waited for a blast of controlled rage. He could fight Cindras even though he was weakened, but he would rather not waste energy on something so asinine.

"You would dare bring up my son, when yours is the one who kidnapped him."

"Kidnapped is an interesting word, Fire God," Vaultus growled. "When for all accounts and purposes, Oken went willingly."

"So says the Forest God."

"So says your son," Vaultus spat back. "I'm uninterested in arguing about this. If your son wanted to stay with you, he would have. I know how many of the old gods feel about this matter, particularly since Oken is only a demigod, but I won't stand for it any longer."

He paused, collecting himself. Savos and Hastia would be furious if he exerted himself too much.

"If you have nothing constructive to say, you can go back and reattach your collar to Falkar's leash."

Vaultus waved a dismissive hand at the Fire God and stood. He had no time for this. It was foolish of the celestials to think they could work together. Maybe it was time to bring the younger gods into the deliberations. Though reckless and sometimes insensible, they would have new ideas and wouldn't challenge Vaultus about such trivial matters.

"You think I don't know that my son despises me?" Cindras said, not backing down. "Everything I've done was to make him stronger. He can hate me all he wants. I don't care. So long as he's prepared for whatever will seek to destroy him."

"I'm glad to hear that your child's feelings mean so little to you," Vaultus said and walked away. "I suppose the same goes for his poor mother? Where is the woman? Did you make her wait outside for you?"

He had probably gone too far. It wasn't his job or place to comment on the personal lives of other gods. The Fire God brought out his ugly side.

Cindras didn't say a word. His shoulders heaved with anger, but he made no move to confront the king. Vaultus shook his head in disgust and left the throne room, leaving the Fire God to find the exit.

Cypress

"You know what I advised," came an angry voice from Vaultus's chambers.

Cypress needed to speak with his stepfather to try and get answers Torstan wouldn't supply. He'd been thinking about it since that morning when he'd failed in their sparring. What good was training if he didn't know what he was preparing for?

"And it doesn't make a difference now, does it?" That was Vaultus. So, the first voice was Savos. Cypress had never heard the god-touched man's voice above a whisper, but it was how he'd imagined it, calculating and icy.

"If only you'd chosen Desh. He could have handled the power and wouldn't have been distracted by a pretty face."

Savos's disapproval hit Cypress hard, but why was he talking about the God of Peace? Had Desh been an original candidate for the celestials' gifts? Not likely, since he wasn't an old god. He was probably Savos's choice for the power now. Cypress thought of Desh: tall, steadfast, optimistic, everyone's ideal god. He was a little older than Cypress and very strong.

"I have chosen Bell, and that's the end of the matter," Vaultus said, voice harsh. Vaultus never spoke like that to him.

Cypress cleared his throat after knocking on the sitting room door. Both voices quieted, and he entered, eyes down.

"Vaultus? I needed to ask you something," he said, taking in the room.

Vaultus sat in his favorite armchair near the large picture window, the garden resplendent outside. He was encased in light, skin glowing like when Cypress first met him, but his eyes were blank and tired.

221

Savos stood nearby, arms crossed, back to the king. He glared openly at the Forest God, lips a thin line. Cypress thought he resembled a large bird of prey assessing its next meal.

"I'll leave you two alone," Savos said, voice dripping with disappointment. He shifted away, Vaultus reaching for him as though he wanted to say one more thing.

Vaultus settled back in his chair. "How much of that did you hear?"

Cypress winced and went to sit beside him in his mother's chair, which faced the king. He wrung his hands and said, "Just the bit about Desh."

Vaultus nodded. "Desh is a fine god and Savos has a soft spot for him, but he's not the one I chose. Try not to dwell on it."

Vaultus sounded spent, as though he'd run ten marathons. It was like at the summit when he was forced to spend three days at his best, trying to hide his infirmities.

"All right," Cypress said, but he frowned. "Vaultus, do I really deserve this?"

"Hmm?" the king asked, eyes closed and head leaned against the chair's back. "Deserve?"

"Wouldn't Desh be a better choice? He's one of the most powerful younger gods."

"By that measure, I should have given this gift to Bashima," Vaultus scoffed. "I chose you because you have a gentleness the others lack. You care about the world and don't get caught up in petty squabbles."

"Neither does Desh," Cypress muttered.

"He is an exemplary god," Vaultus said, smiling. "But so are you. You'll be fine." He paused and took in Cypress's downtrodden appearance. "Something else troubles you."

"What Torstan said about Oken."

"I thought that might be it," Vaultus said. "Torstan is a celestial. They have little use for emotions, though they attempt to understand them. Don't listen to his opinions on love. Hells, don't listen to mine either."

Cypress coughed, thinking of his mother. She loved Vaultus, had been married a long time, but they were more like friends than lovers. Cypress wasn't sure if the king had ever been in love. Vaultus loved his mother, but it wasn't the same as Cypress's feelings for Oken. There weren't many people Cypress could talk to about his relationship. His friends were disasters, and Bashima laughed at him and made jokes for the most part. It felt awkward to speak about it to his mother or stepfather.

Vaultus tapped Cypress's knee and said, "What's the point of defending the world if you have to do it alone?"

Cypress nodded and asked, "Why won't you tell me everything? The celestial who escaped from the Locker. That's what this is about, right? Why I have to take all the power at once?"

Vaultus gazed out the window. He seemed to be having an internal argument. Torstan must really have the reins.

"It's okay if you can't tell me," Cypress said, "But if I knew —"

"The celestial who escaped from the Locker is the one who injured me," Vaultus said.

"I thought that was the Sun God, Malrias," Cypress said. "During your fight with him."

Cypress tried never to think about those days so long ago, when the gods fought some of their own as well as displaced demigods, trying to wrest the sun's power from Malrias. Cypress heard the screams, smelled burning grass, saw Bashima pulling on his arm, eyes wild and flaming crimson, Cabari's yellow lightning arcing across a battlefield.

"That certainly didn't help," Vaultus said, laughing. Golden blood fell from the corner of his mouth, and he wiped it away quickly, trying to hide it from Cypress. "Trapping him took almost everything I had, but it was because of the celestial that I was already weakened. That celestial never agreed with his brethren, ceding power to the gods and ascending. It wasn't his plan for the world they'd created."

"And Torstan knows about this?"

"Of course," Vaultus said. "The celestials were a tight-knit group until most of them wanted to ascend and leave the world to the gods and humans. They'd completed their eons-long project and were ready to retire, I suppose. A few of them disagreed with that, and one of them was the most dangerous being in existence. Once he realized the others planned to leave, he decided that he could take complete control and rule over the world. Everyone, everything, would be his."

"Hells..." Cypress said and trailed off. This was the celestial who had been in the Locker for so long.

"And now he's out," Vaultus said. "He's not as powerful as he once was," he added, seeing Cypress's troubled expression. "I did plenty of damage to him in our initial battle after the celestials gave me their power. He was furious, of course. How could the supreme celestial be defeated by a mere god? Something his kind had created? The fact that he didn't know his brethren betrayed him was my only advantage, which is now gone."

"He almost destroyed you...and you gave me this power," Cypress said, perplexed. Too many questions he'd had for centuries were unfolding, and he found himself ill-prepared. He wet his lips and said, "Knowing that he might come for me someday? Why would you do that to me?"

He stood and stalked away, but Vaultus retained some of his vitality and sped in front of Cypress, wrapping him in a hug. Cypress struggled against the king, his stepfather, not wanting to hear any more. It would be more lies.

"Does my mother know?" Cypress asked when he finally managed to break away.

Vaultus looked ashamed, his face pale. "She doesn't know about Ouranios, no. That's his name, the celestial. Hastia knew I was severely injured, but she also thinks it was from Malrias."

"But Savos knows," Cypress said, frustrated.

"I'm sorry that I've saddled you with this burden," Vaultus said, his large body hunched. "But we needed someone worthy. A god who wouldn't flinch from responsibility."

"But you didn't give me a choice," Cypress said. "I didn't think I was worthy to succeed you, but I went along with it. I couldn't bear to see someone else ruin what you've built. But this is different. He's in hiding? Building his alliances back up?"

Vaultus put a large hand on Cypress's shoulder, and it trembled.

Cypress leaned his head against his mentor. "What if I can't beat him?"

This time, he let Vaultus embrace him. It was going to take a while to process the information. How was he supposed to tell Oken? He couldn't tie Oken to him if he had to fight an all-powerful celestial, even if Vaultus said he wasn't as strong anymore. How would Vaultus know? The celestial might have been rebuilding his power while in confinement.

"No need to worry," Vaultus said, patting his head, careful to avoid the horns. "Because I will be here."

But Cypress wondered for how much longer.

Interlude

Jace

For their fifth date, the Lightning God wanted to show him something, and no, not something weird or gross. Or so he promised. Jace wasn't too sure.

After his argument with Shako, Jace took a step back from Cabari, telling him he was busy or that his father was on high alert whenever Cabari asked to see him. His resolve crumbled with each letter the god sent him, notes talking about his day and how cute he thought Jace was. He meant to throw them on the fire when he finished reading, but Jace was unable to toss them into the flames.

He'd curl his fingers around the soft paper, drinking in Cabari's words. Then he hid them under his mattress. Why did he blush with excitement every time another secret message arrived?

Jace wasn't sure how Garyn was doing it, but Veles had yet to mention anything about the influx of mail, so Garyn must have some covert delivery channels. Jace appreciated it, though he had a feeling the

Messenger of the Gods read every damn word before sending the messages on.

One day, when his father was greeting a large incoming group of shades and Niall was away, Jace wrote to Cabari. He almost threw it away. Was he supposed to play harder to get? Had he ruined his chance by not replying right away to Cabari's last letter? Should he agree to meet at some mysterious location?

Just be cool, he told himself. Don't write a damn novel.

So, Jace wrote: "Sounds good. When?"

Right after he sent it, doing some minor coercion on the shade in charge of outgoing mail, his sister appeared. She shifted in front of him as he left the shade's office, a bright smile plastered on her face.

"Whatcha mailing?" she asked. Nim was about one hundred and seventy years old, still a kid. She looked around eleven human years old, her long pink hair tied up in a ponytail with a red bow, green eyes wide and inquisitive. The grin plastered on her face was wide and mischievous, and Jace wondered if she knew exactly what he'd been doing.

"None of your business, Squirt," he said. He strode past her, messing up her hair.

"You're sending love letters, aren't you," she said, falling into step beside him. Jace tried to keep his face blank, but he could feel the flush stretching across his cheeks.

"No." He didn't have an excuse ready, so he kept walking, hoping she'd get bored.

"Yes, you are," she said in a sing-song voice. "That's so romantic!"

"Do I seem like the romantic type?" Jace said, groaning. If Nim thought she was annoying him, she'd follow him all the way back to his room and might push her way inside to continue tormenting him.

"Not really, but you never know!"

Real nice, he thought.

"I was sending a letter to Oken," he said. A reasonable excuse. "He's a demigod, like us."

"I know who Oken is," Nim said and rolled her eyes. "That's so boring. I was hoping you were having a torrid affair with the god Papa keeps yelling at you about."

"Where the hells did you hear about 'torrid affairs'?" Jace asked, shocked and a bit flustered. And when had she overheard Veles chastising him about Cabari? Was he blushing even more?

"In a book," she said. She patted him on the back and went on her way. "Bye!"

Jace had barely made it back to his room when a scroll appeared on his bed. Damn, that was quick. He sat on his bed, legs crossed, and opened the seal, unfurling the scroll.

"Today?" was all it said in Cabari's flowing script.

So, Jace found himself topside, waiting for the Lightning God. He was in an open field near the Temple of the Sun, somewhere he'd been before and could shift to easily. Now that he'd defied his father again, Jace felt nervous.

The first four dates were straightforward: meals together in small villages where they wouldn't be recognized, although the tavern owners and patrons gave them wide berths. Cabari couldn't help but stand out, so even if people didn't know he was a god, they sure as hells knew he wasn't one of them. But this felt different, stepping across a boundary his father most definitely would not approve of. What were a few meals with someone? They could be friends. But this?

A slight wind announced Cabari's arrival as he shifted in, and Jace felt static electricity nip at him. Not enough to make his hair stand up, but the Lightning God liked to make his presence known. What a show-off.

"Hey Jace," Cabari said, bright and cheerful. Always so damned cheerful. Cabari wasn't dressed in his usual tight leather trousers and fitted tunic. He wore loose black pants and a slouchy shirt with a wide neck that showed off his collarbone. Jace felt an intense urge to touch that collarbone.

Nothing had happened since Cabari kissed him at Bashima's and Shina's wedding. Cabari hadn't even tried to hold his hand, hadn't brought up the kiss.

Two kisses, Jace reminded himself.

I'm not good enough for you...

Jace shook his head. He needed to think clearly. Curse the Lightning God's effortless ability to make Jace insane.

"Hey," Jace said, hands in his pockets.

"Chatty as usual," Cabari said, laughing. He strutted up to Jace. "You look great,"

Jace raised an eyebrow. What should he say? He couldn't tell the Lightning God how much his casual look was driving him crazy.

"I feel a little over-dressed," Jace said. He'd worn his usual dinner date outfit: simple black trousers and a long-sleeved black tunic.

Cabari laughed and looked him over, eyes gleaming. "Not in the least!"

Those were the looks that betrayed the Lightning God, the ones full of barely-contained hunger. He might have thought that Jace didn't pick up on it, but Jace was watchful. Especially when it came to Cabari's eyes.

Cabari touched Jace's elbow and said, "I told you I wanted to show you something. It's the best kept secret in the world."

"Should I be scared?" Jace asked, smirking.

"Maybe," Cabari said, waggling his eyebrows. "Just kidding. It's gonna be great. Mind if I shift us there?"

Jace eyed Cabari. This was the moment. He should say no and go back to the Underworld. He felt a pull toward Cabari that he didn't like but couldn't resist. All the more reason to leave. Cabari would be disappointed maybe, but he would get over it. He had plenty of people in the world to pine after him, who would love to hop into bed with him. Jace didn't want to be one of those poor fools.

Instead of leaving, he shrugged and said, "Sure."

Hand outstretched, Cabari smiled that damned dazzling grin, and Jace reached out and took the god's hand. Cabari looked away for a moment before they shifted, the sun hitting his profile, and Jace's breath caught in his chest.

Cabari landed them in a forest, sounds soft and inviting, running water nearby. They were surrounded by lush trees; the ground covered in cushy moss and short grass. Not at all what Jace had predicted.

"Where are we?" he asked, gazing around. The shadows were deep but somehow comforting, and sunlight peeked through the treetops, illuminating a narrow path.

"My favorite place in the world," Cabari said. He tugged on Jace's hand then dropped it, moving up the path. "Come on."

Jace missed the god's hand clasped around his and flexed his fingers. He wasn't used to touching people. He hugged Nim all the time; she wouldn't settle for less than his complete attention. No one else ever made contact with him. His father was caring but not big on outward displays of affection. Niall never acknowledged Jace's existence if he could help it.

Following Cabari along the path, Jace noticed that they were getting closer to the running water he'd heard when they appeared in the forest. The sound became a roar, echoing deep through the trees. What the hells was Cabari playing at?

They emerged into a large clearing, a waterfall clamoring over a high cliff, emptying into a pool of dark blue shimmering water. There was no way the pool was natural; sparkling like the night sky strewn with starlight. Some magic lived here, ancient and unknowable. The water threw mist into the air, obscuring the shore but for a flat area close to where they stood.

Now that they were out of the trees, it sounded almost musical, the way the water cascaded downward, and Jace longed to turn the effect into music. It would suit his violin, the way the sounds flowed so seamlessly. Or maybe his flute would be better. He could write an entire symphony about this place.

"Do you like it?" Cabari asked. Somehow, the waterfall didn't dull their voices. Jace had almost forgotten the Lightning God was there. He must have seen the complete awe on Jace's face.

"It's beautiful," he said, voice almost a whisper.

"No one knows about this place but me," Cabari said. He walked toward the pool, so Jace followed.

"This is…unexpected," Jace said when they reached the pool's edge. Up close, it was even more stunning. The water glistened with bits of light; tiny diamonds embedded in dark blue.

"Where did you think I was taking you?" Cabari asked, laughing.

"Your bedroom," Jace deadpanned, hands on his hips. He wasn't quite sure what Cabari expected of him. What was the purpose of showing Jace a place so dear to him?

"Jace," Cabari said, "If you try hard enough, anywhere can be a bedroom."

He started to take off his shirt and Jace backed away. What the hells? The presumptuous asshole.

"What are you doing?" Jace asked, an edge in his voice.

Cabari threw his shirt to the side, and Jace tried not to look at his chiseled body. He was rapidly losing that battle.

Cabari said, "Swimming, obviously." He slid his trousers down and thankfully wasn't naked underneath, though part of Jace hoped he might be. The skin-tight black shorts didn't leave much to the imagination, however.

With a sly wink, Cabari dove into the water.

"Are you trying to seduce me or something?" Jace asked when Cabari reappeared, water glistening off his hair. Cabari snickered, treading water, and gave Jace a reproachful look.

"Why? Is it working?" He dipped under the water again and darted off.

Jace snorted. It most certainly was, but Jace didn't have to jump in right away. He walked around the pool, taking in the clearing. The plants around the pool were greener than anything Jace had ever seen, including the masterful arrangements Cypress created for the Temple of the Sun. He might not have seen much of the world, but this place made him think he didn't have to see much else.

Birds sang in the trees, adding their voices to the waterfall's bass timbre, and the smell of muggy humidity filled his nose.

Cabari let him wander. Jace heard splashing from the pool, but the god didn't say anything. From the corner of his eye, Jace watched Cabari do a languid backstroke. He seemed content with swimming alone, being in his favorite place.

And he'd brought Jace here.

He's probably brought a lot of people here, Jace scolded himself.

Jace swallowed, the two parts of himself grappling with each other. Rationally, he had to believe that the Lightning God unveiled this place to anyone who didn't break easily, people who weren't taken in by his charms. The other part of his mind reminded him that Cabari probably didn't make this much effort, if he even needed to make an effort. Humans would fall all over themselves to be with a god, no majestic waterfall needed.

Fuck it.

Jace went back to the pool's edge and stripped off his tunic, tossing it near Cabari's. Taking a deep breath, he shucked his trousers too, grateful that he'd worn nicer underwear. He marched to the edge and glared down at Cabari, whose mouth hung open, unashamed as he ogled the demigod.

"Turn around," Jace said, self-conscious.

"Is all of your hair that color?" Cabari asked, giggling. Seeing Jace's narrowed eyes, he spun around in the water, muttering, "I've already seen almost everything, jeez."

"Water and lightning don't exactly mix," Jace said, shaking his head.

"Electric eels do just fine," Cabari said. "Just call me the God of the Eels!"

Jace laughed out loud, making Cabari spin back.

"Did you just laugh?" he asked, delighted.

"Absolutely not," Jace said, hiding his smile. "If you electrocute me, I swear."

"I promise not to electrocute you," Cabari said, holding up one hand.

Jace slipped into the pool, the water cool but not uncomfortable, and found that it had no bottom, at least not one his feet could reach. He was held up, not sinking, as though the water was supporting his weight. It felt like swimming through dense air. Cabari wasted no time, sending a splashing wave over Jace's head.

Sputtering, water dripping from his hair, Jace swam after the god, swearing obscenities he hoped Nim would never hear. Cabari cackled and swam away, but he let Jace catch him and dunk him under. When he came up for air, Cabari's eyes were shining gold with glee.

"Wasn't sure you knew how to swim," he said.

"The Underworld has rivers, you know. The human world too," Jace said and rolled his eyes. He was suddenly aware of how close they were, skin almost touching, and he swam backward.

"I'm glad," Cabari said. "Otherwise, this would have been a terrible date."

"What is this place?" Jace asked, ignoring the date comment.

"Oh, you know," Cabari said. "A meteorite landed here a really long time ago. Made the lake up there." He nodded up toward the waterfall. "Not sure exactly what happened, but the water took on properties of the meteorite. That's why we're so floaty."

"Did you see it happen?" Jace asked, surprised.

"I'm not that old!" Cabari splashed him again. "I found it when I ran away from home. My parents are a real drag."

Jace nodded. He knew a thing or two about that. Cabari seemed to know that he'd hit a rough spot, so he splashed Jace again and dove under the water before Jace could grab him.

They swam for a while, climbing out and diving back in, chasing each other around. Cabari chattered about how he found the clearing, the first time he dared swim in the strange water, how it made him giddy when he drank it.

"Don't try it, unless you want a two-day high," Cabari said, laughing when Jace's eyes widened and he covered his mouth. "Don't worry, you have to drink a lot."

After an hour or so, Jace said he needed a break and pulled himself out, tousling his wet hair. It fluffed around his head, wild no matter how wet it got. Shit. They didn't have towels.

Cabari hopped out too and snapped his fingers, two towels appearing in his hand. Jace gave him an incredulous look as he took one, and Cabari shrugged. He said, "What? I was prepared for almost anything."

Cabari dried his hair a bit then spread his towel on the ground, toppling over onto it. "Swimming always makes me tired," he said, laying on his back and covering his eyes with an arm.

Jace looked down at him, the god's skin gleaming from the water, the small sparkles standing out against creamy white.

"You just gonna stare all day?"

Jace startled. He set his towel out beside Cabari and sat, watching the waterfall. Cabari didn't say anything, his breath going in and out, a steady rhythm. Jace felt the pull again, that tension in the air between them.

"Why did you bring me here?" He asked after a few minutes.

Cabari didn't answer right away. It reminded Jace of the night of the wedding, him not responding to a tough question. The god's lips on his, searching, needy. Cabari was sober now. There was a tautness to him, like a violin string ready for a bow strike.

Eventually, Cabari said, eyes still closed, "I wanted to show you, I guess."

Jace lay down on his towel and stared up at the sky. Clouds passed by, unaware how nervous Jace was, indifferent to his internal struggle. Cabari made things feel easy, his nature carefree and friendly. It didn't seem like he was struggling at all, besides that latent tension. Cabari wasn't arguing with himself about being here with Jace, or at least Jace couldn't detect it.

"How does this work?" Jace asked.

Cabari turned his head, looking at Jace beside him. "How does what work?"

"Me. You," Jace said, eyes on the clouds.

Was he really doing this? What exactly was he asking? He didn't want to push, didn't want to appear too invested. His heart pounded, and he was sure Cabari could hear it. Cabari lying beside him made Jace think about hands and lips and teeth and longing.

Cabari propped himself up on an elbow. He gazed down at Jace, his hair a dancing corona around his head. His eyes shined bright yellow, and Jace knew that the god desired him, but that wasn't the problem. What did Jace want? What did he need? Cabari wasn't the monogamous type, even if he liked someone. Even if he thought he didn't deserve someone.

He was bound to move on to the next person, the next conquest. Eventually. Yet Jace still wanted him, wanted to tie him down as long as he could.

"I don't need you to be my boyfriend or anything," Jace said, averting his eyes, cheeks flushed.

He was aware of his bare chest, of Cabari directly above him. His long legs spread out on the towel, hair very much mint green everywhere. So much skin, open to the air. He felt so naked.

Cabari leaned down and caught Jace's lips with his own, one hand reaching behind Jace's head and lifting it to a better angle. Jace let him.

If he thought Cabari knew what he was doing after the wedding at the Temple of the Sun, it was nothing next to the way he kissed now. Cabari kissed like a gymnast, as though every movement of lips and tongue mattered, and Jace was drawn in, moving forward into the kiss, parting his lips and accepting everything Cabari was waiting to give. He closed his eyes and fell forward, though his mind told him to hold something back. He couldn't.

Jace reached for the god's waist and pulled Cabari down so he was on top of him, his legs parting, feeling damp skin touch his own, his arms clinging around Cabari's shoulders. Cabari's hips teased at him, dipping forward then away, until Jace wrapped his legs around Cabari and drew him in. Cabari's hands were in his hair, scratching along his scalp, and Jace moaned into the god's mouth. Tiny sparks flowed along Cabari's body and through his fingers into Jace's hair. He had never felt anything so intoxicating. It terrified him.

Cabari pulled away, looking down at Jace. His pupils were blown across his eyes, and yellow lightning shimmered across his skin. Was it real? Or was it an effect the god used on all his conquests?

"You're a really good kisser," Cabari said, a lilt of surprise in his voice.

He doesn't remember, Jace thought. We've already kissed and he was too drunk to remember.

"Yeah," Jace said. "I've heard that before."

A flash went across Cabari's eyes, as if he were jealous of some imaginary person who had kissed Jace before him. Like he thought Jace was unclaimed territory and was pissed to find out otherwise. Jace felt an electric hum encase them, and his arm and leg hair stood on end. There was a hint of savagery in the Lightning God's eyes, something Jace had glimpsed in his father and Niall once or twice. The unrelenting power of the gods, so used to getting what they wanted and damn the consequences if they didn't.

"It's that jerk Shako, isn't it?" Cabari said, and Jace was taken aback by the venom in the god's voice. It was possessive and grating, and Jace felt his dick stir. Cabari felt it too, and his power raced over his body in yellow-gold bursts. The air smelled like ozone and sharp lemons, and Jace took a deep breath, savoring Cabari's scent.

Jace glared up at the god, daring him to make the next move, his hands still thick in black hair cascading with lightning bolts.

Make me believe that you want me, he willed toward Cabari, his fingers moving down and scraping hard across the god's back.

That was all the invitation Cabari needed. He moved faster than Jace thought possible, the latent power coursing through his limbs, glowing yellow. Cabari grabbed Jace's arms and braced them against the ground, breath coming fast and uneven, his eyes explosive. Jace had never seen a god show their true form, not even his father, and it was breathtaking.

Cabari's face became a beacon of light, his eyes fully golden, the delicate slashes of his cheekbones becoming sharp, terrible and beautiful. He let go of one of Jace's arms and traced a line down Jace's side from chest to hip, and Jace's body obeyed, tilting up. The hardness between them was enough to make Jace come immediately, but he bit his tongue. He needed to wait. It would be so embarrassing if he came too fast.

Cabari's visage became a blur for a moment, his face darting to Jace's neck to sniff and then moving away, the highlights in his hair slicing the late afternoon light, and Jace didn't know what might happen. Would the Lightning God take him without preamble? Without asking?

Breathing slowly yet heavily, body tensed, Jace reached up with one hand and touched Cabari's cheek, rubbing his thumb across the charged skin. The blazing light left Cabari's eyes, replaced by uncertainty, something rarely seen in a god's face. He'd lost control a bit, showing his true face, which must have been troubling for a god like him.

Cabari's thumb hooked around Jace's underwear, but he looked down, eyes fully yellow. He said, "Are you sure?"

Jace grabbed Cabari's face and drew him back into another kiss, and the god's hand moved deftly, pulling Jace's underwear down in one stroke. He broke their kiss and fell back, slipping the underwear off as if it had never existed in the first place. Cabari's fingers tingled across Jace's feet and calves, ignoring his already hard cock. He inched upward, eyes ablaze, taking in every inch of Jace. He lay back, his leg muscles tense, and Cabari kissed along Jace's legs, from his calves to his knees to his thighs, savoring the delicate skin, sucking on his inner thigh.

Jace nearly lost it, scrabbling for the towel, his fingers like claws. He'd never felt something so intense, something so out of his control.

Cabari's mouth left his thigh, and Jace let out a huge breath. The god surged forward and kissed him again, drawing one of Jace's legs out and away, his hand teasing at Jace's dick, stroking, prodding, sliding with the pre-cum and rubbing it over his fingers, driving Jace crazy. Jace reached and grabbed the god's hips, tugging at his shorts, needing to see Cabari completely. His ass felt incredible, muscular and supple. Cabari let Jace tear away his shorts, his demigod strength asserting itself, and the god grinned, feral and craving. If Jace had any doubts that Cabari wanted him, that look struck them all away.

"Have you ever touched yourself," Cabari asked, mouth dipping to Jace's ear. His voice was like honey, low and sure. Jace nodded, though he was a sexual novice compared to the Lightning God. Cabari interlaced his fingers with Jace's, saying, "Show me."

Jace brought the god's hand down, grazing his harder-than-fuck cock, sending shockwaves through his body, but he knew that wasn't what Cabari meant. He went lower, tracing the skin between his hardened length and his ass. He hadn't experimented much with himself besides awkwardly jerking off in his room, but Jace went for it like he knew what he was doing. It didn't matter. Once he was close, Cabari took over.

He placed Jace's hand on the towel, saying, "That's mine."

He lunged forward and shoved his tongue down Jace's throat, sliding one finger inside. Jace jolted up, but Cabari held him down, kissing him until Jace melted, the tension in his muscles easing.

Cabari took his time, stretching Jace, sliding a second finger inside him then a third, all while kissing him as though his life depended on it, lips soft and tongue hard.

Jace grasped the towel with one hand and dug his fingers into Cabari's hip with the other, waiting for what he knew was coming. It hurt a bit, but the ache was dull and innocuous next to Cabari's lips and surprisingly gentle hands.

Cabari's lips left Jace's and trailed down his neck, sucking as he went, moaning onto Jace's skin, muttering, "So fucking tight. You're so hot, gods, I can't stand it."

His roving fingers hit something inside Jace, and his hips bucked, wanting the god's touch to never leave him. Cabari smiled, sharp canines gleaming, and Jace heard the waterfall's cascading call, begging for a composition, needing Jace to write its story in music.

Jace reached between them and stroked his aching dick, needing release, but Cabari pushed his hand away, grinning. "If I can't make you come by myself then what's the fucking point?"

"Then do it!" Jace yelled, indigo light blazing in his eyes.

Cabari's pupils blew again, and Jace felt electricity flowing through him, hitting every vital part of his body. Not enough to cause damage, but it was like Cabari was a part of him, directing his pleasure. Cabari pulled his fingers out and guided himself inside Jace with a deft thrust. Jace's hips rose to meet him, and he lunged forward and bit Cabari on the shoulder, his legs wrapping tighter around the god's back, and Cabari raised Jace's hips so he could go deeper.

"Fuck. Me. Gods," Cabari said as he moved his hips, grinding as far into Jace as he could. Jace held on, trying to keep a grip on his sanity. Fuck it felt too good. He couldn't get used to this.

Don't get used to this.

Unsatisfied with his position, Cabari pulled out, dislodged Jace's hands, and flipped Jace over, angling his hips up. Jace groaned as Cabari got to his knees and gripped him, stroking his side.

He said, "You are seriously something else," before sliding himself back inside.

Jace braced himself and pushed back. It felt amazing, even if it was slightly painful, like a mix of everything Jace expected. Cabari was firm but not rough, rubbing his back, whispering encouragement, telling him how amazing he was.

But still, Jace didn't come. A part of him hungered to take the Lightning God for himself, and he held onto that feeling, no matter how Cabari rubbed against his deepest self, he would be the one to decide how things ended. His toes curled as the Lightning God slammed into him again and again, and he waited. Soon, they were on their sides, Cabari still inside him, panting. He hadn't come either, also holding onto his pleasure.

"Is your prostate made of stone or something?" Cabari asked, impressed. He drew his hand down the small of Jace's back and kissed his shoulder blade. "You're fucking fantastic," Cabari said and nuzzled Jace's ear.

As Cabari relaxed for a moment, Jace saw his opening. He shoved himself forward and flipped Cabari over, straddling the surprised god, pinning Cabari's hands as he had done to Jace.

"My turn," Jace said, smirking. Cabari's smile blazed across his face, and he leaned back into the towel.

"Gonna wreck me, Jace?" Cabari asked, a dare evident in his tone. He pulled his hands free easily and dug his fingers into Jace's thighs. "You're welcome to try."

"Are you sure that was your first time?" Cabari asked, dazed.

After a few hours of grappling together, each fighting for the upper hand, god and demigod lay next to each other, spent and sore, chests heaving. Cabari suggested the pool, and they slid into the dark blue water. The Lightning God's skin glowed from within, and Jace couldn't help but stare. Cabari was the most magnificent being, perfection in one body.

Cabari caught him looking and swam closer, wrapping his legs around Jace like an octopus, shoving his face close until their noses were almost touching. He smiled, licked his top lip, and leaned in, kissing Jace as they floated in the water, both still naked. Jace's cock became lively again, and Cabari broke away.

"We can't stay here forever, Jace," he said, though his tone suggested that's exactly what he'd like. "Can you scrub my back?" Cabari snapped his fingers and soap appeared in his hand. He really was ready for everything.

Jace swam behind him, taking the soap. He lathered his hands and massaged Cabari's back and shoulders, trying not to lose himself in the soft skin dotted with light freckles. He moved closer and hugged the Lightning God to his chest, and Cabari giggled but allowed Jace to hold him.

After a moment, Cabari swam away, a roguish glint in his eye. "Your father hates me. You know that, right?"

Jace blinked, treading water. He said, "So?"

"So, you asked how this works," Cabari said, splashing him. "Between you and me."

Jace stayed silent. This was it. The Lightning God was already tired of him. It wasn't worth the effort or the risk, pissing off the God of the Dead, just for a piece of ass.

Jace swam away and pulled himself out of the pool, Cabari yelling at him. "Hey! Don't get all quiet on me now!"

Cabari leaped out of the water and landed in a crouch next to Jace. He looked like a lynx, water glimmering on his pale skin. He stood up and ambled next to Jace, tapping him on the chin.

"Where do you think you're going?"

"Back home," Jace said. He pushed past Cabari and grabbed his clothes from the ground, not bothering to towel off first. He pulled on his trousers and tunic but felt eyes on him. "What?" he asked, not looking at the god. Where the fuck was his underwear?

"Do you not want to see me again?" Cabari asked, scoffing like that was impossible.

Jace frowned, his clothes clinging to his body, hair a disheveled mess. He didn't move or answer.

"I'll take that as a yes," Cabari said. He paced in a line, naked, thinking. Jace watched him, wanting to swoop in and toss the god over his shoulder, take him into the forest and have his way again. Although Cabari could definitely fight him off.

"I guess our only course of action is to keep it secret," Cabari said. He stooped and picked up his clothes, sliding the loose trousers and shirt back in place, making Jace let out a shallow whine. He covered his mouth, hoping Cabari hadn't heard.

Cabari smiled at him and said, "You can always come over to my place, but if you're more comfortable in the Underworld, we're going to need to make some…arrangements."

He sidled over to Jace, confidence oozing from every pore, and put his hands in Jace's shirt. He dragged Jace into a kiss, jamming his tongue into Jace's mouth. Jace pushed back with his own tongue, not willing to admit defeat.

"You're way too damn hot," Cabari said when they broke away from each other. His eyes flickered with deadly electricity, yellow lightning arcing over his body. "How am I supposed to deal with that?"

Chapter Fourteen

Jace

Bashima had only gotten quieter and angrier since Jace had been at the Temple. He snapped at Oken for asking simple questions during lunch and dinner, though Oken ignored him and made conversation with Jace instead. He was like a bomb with a lit fuse, except they had no idea how long the fuse was.

It started the day Bashima collapsed in the throne room. They'd been having lunch, Bashima staring moodily out the skylight, watching the noon sun shine down on them. Oken was talking about the book he was reading, mentioning that Jace might like it. Bashima peered at them occasionally but didn't join them in chatting. Jace thought Bashima was somewhat grateful to have company, but he was approachable as a porcupine.

One moment, Oken was commenting on the rice Shefu made for them, the next, Bashima was on the floor, his food scattered. The Sun God was on his hands and knees, eyes unfocused and dark red. His body quaked with small spasms, and the candles flickered around the throne room.

"Bashima!" Oken yelled and ran toward the god, but Jace grabbed him.

"You don't know what's happening," Jace warned. Oken shrugged him off and went to Bashima's side, not touching him, but hovering nearby.

"Al—Al—Alaric—" Bashima muttered, his skin igniting with yellows, oranges, and reds. His palms lit up, and Jace winced. The Sun God could decimate both him and Oken, and he might not realize it until it was too late.

"He's talking about Alaric," Oken said, backing away toward Jace. "What do we do?"

"I don't think we can do anything," Jace said. He looked around the throne room. No shades to be seen. They'd left him and Oken alone with Bashima.

"We can't leave him like this," Oken said, as the Sun God's body became encased in light. "He could destroy the temple!"

"And us with it!" Jace yelled. "We need to get Kuroi before he explodes!"

Before Jace could drag Oken away, the light flickered out, leaving Jace with large black spots traveling across his eyes. He blinked and rubbed them, saying, "Fucking hells, what was that?"

Bashima sat on the floor, chest heaving, staring at his shaking hands. The light faded from his skin, and his eyes gradually returned to normal.

"Bashima?" Oken asked, moving forward. The Sun God's head swiveled toward them, and he looked like a wounded animal, one who didn't recognize that two demigods weren't threats. He growled at them, showing his teeth, and Oken stopped, saying, "It's Oken. I live here."

Which must have been the right thing to say, because Bashima quieted, narrowed his eyes, and waved a dismissive hand at them. "Don't fucking remind me."

He wouldn't tell them what had gone wrong, just that he was tired and that they should leave him the fuck alone. A strange sound came from him, high and sensitive. Kuroi appeared in the throne room soon after, kneeling next to the keening Sun God, and he shooed them away. Jace was glad to get away from the volatile god, but Oken looked worried.

A week later, they were in the dining room, repeating the usual routine. Bashima was surly, and his mood was even affecting Tika, who glared at the far wall, not paying attention to the Sun God or the two demigods who were apparently ruining her day.

Jace felt bad for the shades; Kuroi had them on full-time Sun God watch, making sure he wasn't wandering off during the day and bothering the shades as they worked. Keeping an eye out for more outbursts. Even Emilia was ill-tempered, the Sun God's moodiness having lost its appeal. She stood against the wall behind Oken, frowning. If Emilia was in a bad mood, they were all lost.

Kuroi shifted into the dining room, face harried, and he bent and whispered something to Bashima, who rolled his eyes hard and said, "Tell him to fuck off."

"I tried that already, Master Bashima," Kuroi said. "Not in those exact words."

Cabari burst through the dining room door, yellow lightning coming off him and arcing across the ceiling.

"Kuroi! That was really rude! I'm just here to —" The Lightning God paused, taking in the scene.

Oken had continued eating as though nothing was amiss. Bashima rested his chin in his hand, bored, and Kuroi looked like he might explode. Jace felt the blood drain from his face.

"Jace?" Cabari said, and a static charge went through the room, making all their hair sway with energy. Oken's hair was affected more than Jace's or the Sun God's, and he touched it, fascinated.

"Knock that the fuck off," Bashima said, and Cabari calmed himself. After a few moments of silence, Bashima said, "Well? What do you want?"

Cabari

Jace was in the Temple of the Sun. Having dinner with Bashima. And Oken was there. What was he supposed to be doing? He'd completely forgotten.

"Huh?" Cabari asked, eyes locked on Jace, who wouldn't look at him.

"We're trying to have dinner," Bashima snapped and threw a grape at Cabari, which bounced off his chest and rolled under the table.

"Hello, Cabari," Oken said, waving. He went back to his dinner without a second glance.

"Oh, uh," Cabari mumbled. Jace's shoulders were tense, his lips pursed in a thin line. Cabari said, "Right, Cypress sent me to check on Oken." He produced a small scroll from his jacket.

Oken stared at him, eyes alert, interest in his meal gone. "You've seen Bell?"

"Not as such," Cabari said, rubbing the back of his neck. "He's at the king's temple. Told me not to go there but that he needed to get this to you." He held out the scroll, but Oken made no move to leave the table and take it. "Okay." Cabari laid the scroll next to Oken and turned to Bashima. "He had one for you too."

The second scroll was larger, and Cabari had a vague idea what Cypress had written. The Forest God had been cagey in his note, but he hinted at a big problem brewing, something Vaultus wasn't ready to discuss with the younger gods. Cabari hated being out of the loop. If the problem worried the king, then every god deserved to know what was going on.

Unlike Oken, Bashima stood and marched over to Cabari, snatching the scroll from him. He opened it, read a few lines then rolled it closed in a snap, his eyes darting around the room. Kuroi stepped forward and Bashima handed him the letter. The god-touched man shifted away, taking the important news with him. Cabari cursed under his breath. So close.

"Tengu's errand boy now?" Bashima sneered, and Cabari laughed.

"Hardly. Cypress never asks for anything. He wanted me to see how you were doing too. With Alaric being gone. Where is he by the way?" The empty chair at the table made it seem like Alaric's ghost lurked in the room.

Bashima's eyes flared with color, and Cabari took a step back. "Fine, don't tell me," he said. Cabari glanced at Jace, who stared down at his plate. Oken was watching now, maybe sensing the strain between them.

"Jace," Cabari started. The demigod's eyes shot up at him, shining indigo. The usual bags under his eyes had diminished a bit, but he was the same Jace: handsome, angular face; greenish hair a whirlwind; closed-off expression. Cabari said, "Can we talk?"

"You're talking now," Jace answered, his hands turning to fists on the table. Oken and Bashima were silent, and Cabari wished that Oken would make an awkward comment or that the Sun God would blast him in the face. Anything to get him out of the room. But he also wanted to talk to Jace. He hadn't seen him in so long.

"I…I just…" Cabari stuttered, trying to find the right words. "I hate feeling this way."

Jace said, "I'm not responsible for your feelings."

Cabari's cheeks blazed. Jace throwing his own advice back at him stung. Why did he have to be so quick? So smart? So Jace?

"I wanted to see you, but I didn't think —"

"Stop," Jace said and stood. His chair nearly fell over. "Just stop. I don't want to see you."

Cabari moved closer to the table, but Bashima raised an eyebrow at him. Was he doing the wrong thing? Should he have left and said nothing to Jace? But he wanted to. He needed to hear the demigod's voice, even if he was pissed off.

"I know you're pissed," Cabari said, hands up. "I said some things."

"You can do and say whatever you want," Jace said.

"I'm trying to say that I miss you, all right?" Cabari said.

Bashima put his face in his hands and shook his head. Why the hells was he shaking his head? Wasn't it right to tell the truth? What made Bashima the relationship expert? Shit. He'd just thought about relationships and Jace at the same time.

A shadow passed over Jace's face, pain and regret and anger. He collected himself and said, "I thought I could handle it, that I'd be okay with it, but I'm not." His voice was low and layered with sadness, and Cabari wanted to grab him and shift them away from this audience, but that wasn't what Jace wanted. Jace said, "I wanted you, so I told myself I'd get over it."

Cabari wasn't used to feeling guilty for doing what felt natural to him. Sex was the thing he was best at, besides storms, and he wouldn't be content with one person. It wasn't an option. Ugly emotions clawed at him, tearing into his heart, making it difficult to breathe.

"I'm not sorry for who I am," he said.

Jace shook his head, as though amazed by how stupid the Lightning God was.

"I don't want you to be sorry for who you are. You should do what makes you happy. I can't be a part of it. Stop trying to make that happen."

Jace had at least been thinking about him. Not all was lost. Cabari could salvage this situation. He wasn't sure how, but there had to be something.

"What if we —"

"No," Jace said and held up a hand, signaling Cabari to stop. "If I let you talk to me, you could talk me into anything."

Jace walked toward the dining room door, hands in his pockets. He paused as he passed the Lightning God, and Cabari's body screamed at him to reach out, to touch Jace. His arm, his shoulder, his face. Anything.

Jace sighed and said, "When I hear your voice, I can't forget you. It's too hard." Jace's shoulders slumped, something Cabari had always noticed, but Jace had stopped doing it around him. Now he was back to the self-conscious posture.

"If I could erase your face from my memory, I would. It would save me from this."

Cabari's vision bled with yellow flares.

Erase the Lightning God?

He lashed out and gripped Jace's bicep, squeezing hard, fingernails digging into Jace's bare skin. Jace stared at his hand, his face like a bruise.

"You're hurting me," he said and tried to wrench away.

Cabari's grip increased. Why wouldn't Jace listen to him? Why was he making this so hard? He felt like his insides were on fire, like he couldn't focus on anything but the pain he was experiencing. Why did he feel this way? Why wasn't Jace trying to make it better between them? He was trying, dammit!

What was he doing? Cabari thought he heard a tea kettle screech and lost his focus.

Bashima snarled and Cabari felt the air grow chilly. His mind cleared, and he looked at Jace's disappointed face and dropped the demigod's arm as though it burned him. Bruises were already forming.

"I'm..."

Jace grunted in disgust, back straightening, and said, "You were right, I am too good for you." He stalked to the door.

"Wait!" Cabari yelled. "When did I say that?"

What the hells was Jace talking about? The Lightning God would never say anything like that.

Not even turning, Jace said, "The first time we kissed, you asshole."

Jace slammed the door, leaving the enticing woodsy scent Cabari had always liked. Images flashed through his mind: falling off the stage at the wedding, Jace holding him up as they walked down a hallway, hesitant lips on his, waking up next to Jace in the morning.

"Fuck," he said.

Bashima snorted and threw himself back in his chair. "You ever put hands on someone in my house again, I'll skewer you on your own temple."

Cabari stared at Bashima. He would deserve it. Why had he done that to Jace? It was like he'd been possessed.

"You know the way out," Bashima growled.

Before Cabari could move, Oken was beside him. He patted Cabari's arm and said, "He really did like you. I think he still does, otherwise he wouldn't be so mad."

Cabari blinked at Oken, who hadn't really spoken to him before. Oken gave him a small smile, his eyes full of pity.

"He said you made him laugh and didn't make him feel bad about himself. That's why he liked you. I don't know if that helps or not. But I agree with Bashima. If you touch my friend again, I'll set you on fire."

Bashima

The Lightning God left, thank the fucking heavens. Bashima sat back down, uninterested in finishing his dinner but not wanting to go to his chambers. Seeing Cabari grab Jace brought back unpleasant memories, and he'd rather avoid his bedroom at the moment. Thinking of his husband made his heart lurch. He needed a distraction.

"Zebra Head," he said.

Oken had also resumed his seat after pushing Jace's empty chair into the table. Tika and Emilia had barely moved during Cabari's ridiculous outburst, but Bashima could tell they were nervous. Anytime a god lost control, even for a second, was terrifying for shades.

"Yes, Bashima?" Oken ate a plateful of fruit skewers, sliding each piece off the stick then using his knife and fork to eat it. He was so weird.

"What did Tengu write to you?"

"What did he write to you?"

Unnerved by Oken's lack of outward emotion and quick rebuttal, Bashima didn't know how to answer. Tengu couldn't keep his damn mouth shut, so Oken probably knew everything the Forest God had written to Bashima, except for the bit about the insane celestial that might try to blast them all out of existence.

That was information Bashima hoped Tengu had gotten wrong.

He said, "Nothing good. We're going to be gearing up for something big soon."

"Indeed," Oken said. He put down his utensils and unrolled the small scroll.

His eyes moved fast over Tengu's crooked script and read, "'Oken, whatever you do, stay at the Temple of the Sun. Bashima will keep you safe. Your father's here at the king's temple in secret meetings they won't let me in on. He asked about you, but he shouldn't bother you so long as you're at the Temple of the Sun. Please, stay there.'"

It seemed like Oken would speak more, but his lips clamped shut, jaw tight. He tucked the scroll in his pocket.

When the shades had cleared the table, Jace reappeared, his eyes bloodshot, reminding Bashima of the God of the Dead. It was uncanny. All the demigod needed to be his father's duplicate was to deliver a stern lecture.

"I'm sorry I caused a scene," Jace said. "Now that Cabari knows I'm here, I'm going to leave."

"Ugh," Bashima said, arms crossed. "If I'd known it was that easy to get rid of you, I would've called that moron the first damn day."

"Bashima," Oken said. "That was mean."

"Don't make me kick your ass out too," he growled.

"You've never once kicked me out," Oken reminded him.

Bashima's skin glowed in annoyance. He had to admit that it wasn't too bad having the demigods around, even if they brought heaps of trouble with them.

"There's a first time for everything," he snapped and shoved out of his chair, storming toward the door. Before he walked through, he heard Oken ask Jace where he would go.

"I might go see my sister and Shako," Jace said. "At the Temple of Time."

Chapter Fifteen

Falkar

Falkar drummed his fingers on the table, chin in his hand. If he had to hear the Fire God whine about how pointless their mission was one more time, he might snap. He hadn't been able to find out much at the king's temple, no information he didn't already have. His feathers were unable to break through the defensive alchemy spells that surrounded Vaultus's private chambers and the throne room, and Cindras told him nothing about his private meeting with the king.

Torstan was unusually cagey too, talking in circles about the Forest God. Cypress. Falkar hadn't seen much of him since that first day, dropping leaves in his wake after trying to tell the celestial off. Orn saw Cypress more often as he ran around the temple perimeter with that odd god-touched of his, or doing exercises, but Cypress disappeared whenever the Augury got too close. Very wise. Unfortunately.

"Why did you bother coming if you're going to bitch about everything?" Falkar asked, one wing pointing at the Fire God.

Cindras's sneer would have flattened lesser beings, but Falkar was immune to his tantrums.

"I'm pointing out valid concerns," the Fire God said, flames igniting over his face and head. "What is our plan? We've only succeeded in agreeing there's a problem."

"You're not wrong," Falkar said, thinking.

Neither Vaultus nor Torstan had explained Cypress's role in the upcoming inevitable conflict with Ouranios, though Falkar suspected the Forest God already contained some of the gifted celestial abilities. If that was the case, then they were all fucked.

As far as Falkar knew, no one could handle that amount of power except Vaultus. The king had been made to withstand almost anything, but Ouranios snapped Vaultus like a twig before the king gained a hard-won victory. What chance did the Forest God have?

Cindras huffed. The Fire God had no love for Cypress, that much was plain. Every time his name came up, erratic flames shot from Cindras's body.

Falkar said, "What do you make of the Forest God's involvement? There are no other gods his age around here."

Snorting, Cindras said, "His mother lives here."

As though that solved everything and wrapped it up in a nice bow. The Fire God was smarter than this, but he let his emotions cloud his judgment.

"I doubt that's the only reason for his presence," Falkar said.

"So long as he's here and my son is elsewhere, I could not care less about the Forest God."

Not this again too.

Cindras never shut up about his kid, the amazing Oken, the perfect demigod. Yawn. They didn't have time to worry about wayward family members. Not when one of Falkar's relatives could wreak havoc at any moment.

"You need to get your shit together," Falkar said, voice a drawl. "Or it won't matter where your kid is. If Ouranios is at full power, he'll be able to destroy any temple anywhere. So, shut the fuck up about your kid and tell me what you really think."

Cindras looked murderous, but Falkar made a twirling gesture with his finger: I don't have all day.

"I think Vaultus means for the boy to take over for him," the Fire God said, lips a slash on his face. "Which is a foolish mistake. None of the older gods will follow him. He's weak. And young."

Falkar nodded. Cindras was perceptive, even if he didn't understand the exact scope of the situation. The Fire God didn't know about the gifted celestial powers, and Falkar hoped he never would.

"I agree," Falkar said, stroking his chin. "I have no idea how powerful he is or his disposition. Though he stood up to you." He smirked at the Fire God, whose face remained like stone. Falkar went on, "Vaultus must have his reasons. We need to find out what those are."

Cindras stood from the table and said, "I need to attend to something first. I'll return in a few days."

"Where the hells do you think you're going?" Falkar asked. "This is the most important place in the world right now."

"I don't ask you about your business, celestial," Cindras said. He stomped away and Falkar didn't bother to call him back. The Fire God would do what he wanted, whether Falkar tried to stop him or not. He'd be back. The thrill of battle strategy was too tempting.

"Not that you haven't wondered," Falkar muttered.

Where had Orn gotten off to?

Cypress

Cypress did a back-flip off the garden wall, landing cleanly. Taking a deep breath, he let it out before moving on to his next set of exercises. He was supposed to be practicing with the vines, but Torstan told him to avoid using them while Falkar and the Fire God were at the temple. Cypress thought that was dumb. Who knew when they would leave? Was he supposed to stop training entirely? Wasn't it of the utmost importance that he continue? He wished the celestial would make up his damn mind.

Wiping sweat off his brow, Cypress settled into a crouch and pushed off from the ground with explosive force. He leaped atop his mother's tall hedges and raced across them, trying not to disturb the branches. He could cheat and ask the hedge to hold him up, but he was supposed to be working on his reflexes. He dodged around on the hedges until he went all the way around the garden five times, dashing here and there, fast, but not like Torstan. He flipped off the hedge when he completed the last circuit, fingertips digging into the soil when he landed. He could feel the grass talking to him, tone excitable and proud of him. At least someone was paying attention.

"Bell!" Vaultus strode toward him, his movements exuberant. He was back to his usual buoyant self, at least for now. "Do you have a moment?"

Cypress nodded, still not content with how Vaultus had treated him. They hadn't had another chance to speak alone, not with Falkar snooping around, his student hiding away in the shadows at every turn.

Cypress was sick of Orn's face popping up while he trained. He was sure the young Augury was nice enough, but Cypress had to restart his sets after running away from him.

"I need to apologize to you," Vaultus said, sitting on a stone bench. He beckoned Cypress over. "I've given you very little time to come to terms with everything, and it's not fair."

"I get it," Cypress said, eyes down. He understood why Vaultus held things back from him, but he didn't accept it. He should have had a choice.

"I know you understand, but I did to you what the celestials did to me, pushing responsibility on you without asking, and I have no idea how to make it up to you." Vaultus smiled at his stepson, resting a hand on his shoulder.

"You can't," Cypress said. He shrugged off the king's hand. "I know you feel bad, but that doesn't change anything."

"I wish I had been more honest with you," Vaultus admitted. "I'll give you the choice on whether you'd like to accept the last of the power."

Cypress stared at him. Was that even an option?

"Don't you have to give them to me?"

Vaultus shrugged his massive shoulders. "That was the idea. If I keep them, we run the risk of my body giving out, then the additional strength will be out of reach for you. I have to give it freely. You can't take it forcibly."

"So, then it's not really a choice," Cypress said, voice rising. "You know I can't let that happen."

"I could help you fight if I kept them," Vaultus said, eyes far away, perhaps recalling a glorious battle.

"You can barely make it through one day without Mom or Savos," Cypress said. "You'd last about five seconds in an actual battle."

"Give me some credit, young man," Vaultus said, appalled. "I'd at least take some enemies down before I expired."

Cypress looked away. He knew Vaultus couldn't actually die, but what awaited him was almost worse than death. Torstan had at least explained that. Once Vaultus's power failed him, he would fall into a dreamless sleep and never awaken. Like what happened to Chronas. Was that the future that awaited him as well? He shuddered and rubbed his arms, tracing the scar on his right arm.

"The Fire God has gone," Vaultus said. "He is expected to return, but Falkar doesn't know where he's gone."

Cypress bit his lip. He hoped Cabari delivered the messages to Oken and Bashima. Would the Fire God risk attacking Bashima at his home again?

"But Falkar is still here?" Cypress asked.

"Mmm, a most annoying development. He moves too fast, knows too much. Or at least discerns too much. He's a damn menace."

Cypress laughed. Falkar looked like a young man who would rather be home napping than the shrewd tactician he was. Cypress often caught Falkar observing him, so he stayed far away. Cypress ate his meals in his room or his mother's, away from prying questions. Luckily, Falkar hadn't asked for him. Vaultus would've needed a pretty good excuse for his absence besides the fact that he didn't like talking to people he didn't know well.

"I think you should give me the power," Cypress said, and Vaultus's head jerked up. "We don't know if Falkar will leave. At least the Fire God is gone."

"When?" Vaultus asked.

"Might as well do it now," Cypress said, sighing. That way he'd have the rest of the day plus the night to process the added strength. He'd hopefully be able to hide the fatigue the next day. "Same as the last time?"

"Yes," Vaultus said. He drew a short dagger and slid it across his palm. As golden blood seeped from the wound, he whispered an incantation that Cypress recognized from the first time Vaultus had given him the power. The blood gleamed, shimmering in the morning light.

"This is the last time?" Cypress asked, and Vaultus smiled, but it barely reached his eyes.

"The last time," Vaultus agreed.

Cypress nodded. This was it. There was no going back after this. He would become the target of the celestial known as Ouranios. He doubted he had a chance to defeat something so powerful, but Vaultus had put his faith in Cypress. He would try his best not to let the king down.

The blood didn't taste like anything, it scratched Cypress's throat as he swallowed it, gagging slightly. Drinking blood wasn't a pleasant experience, and knowing what this meant made it harder to keep down.

Vaultus clapped Cypress on the back, and they sat together in the sun, neither speaking.

Neither of them noticed a dark figure in the shadow of the garden wall, its eyes blazing, ready to tell Falkar everything he'd seen and heard.

Interlude

Oken

Oken ran through the halls of the Temple of the Sun as though a terror chased him, his feet slamming into the black stone, arms pumping. Bashima had warned him about shifting into the throne room while he was working, so Oken respected that wish.

But he needed to see Bashima.

He and Bell had been in his room chatting about what they would do over the weekend, when the Forest God's body became rigid. He stared off into space, and Oken shook his shoulder, asking what was wrong. Their usual connection wasn't working, so he couldn't feel what Bell was experiencing.

After a few minutes, Bell's eyes lost the dazed quality. He said, "My temple" then shifted away without further explanation. Oken wasn't sure what Bell meant, but he'd received a wave of nausea when Bell came out of the trance before he disappeared. He fought back a gag and massaged his throat.

It was almost sunset. Hopefully, Bashima would listen to him.

He made it to the throne room and burst through the doors. Bashima sat on his throne, still in deep meditation. For some reason, he'd worn his formal uniform that day, and the golden chest piece nearly blinded Oken when the final beam of sunlight hit it.

"Bashima!"

The Sun God stirred, his eyes fluttering open. As he focused on Oken, the demigod could feel the heat coming off him.

"What the fuck, Zebra Head?" Bashima said, rubbing his eyes.

"Bell left! Something's wrong!"

Bashima snorted and said, "Not my problem if he finally got bored with your weird ass."

"He went into a strange trance," Oken said, rushing up to the throne and getting in Bashima's face. Bashima shrank back, not used to anyone invading his space. Oken knew he sounded hysterical, but he had to do something. "Then he mentioned his temple and shifted away. He looked terrible. And I felt like I might throw up."

"Calm the fuck down," Bashima growled. "If he said something about his temple, that's probably where he is."

"We need to go right now," Oken said. He made to grab the Sun God's arm, but Bashima drew back, hissing.

"You want me to leave the temple?" He sounded afraid, and Oken didn't have time to coax the god to leave. He knew it would be difficult, what with Bashima's tendency to hunker down in his den and never peek outside, but Bell needed them.

Before Oken could argue, he felt like a spear pierced his chest, driving the air from it. He coughed and collapsed on the floor. Bashima knelt beside him in an instant, eyes wide.

"What the fuck? What are you doing?"

"Bell…needs me," Oken said. His hand shot out and clamped onto Bashima's arm, and he shifted them away.

They landed in a heap in the forest that surrounded Bashima's mountain, wheezing.

"Why the fuck did you do that?" Bashima shouted, trembling as he leaped away from Oken. "If I hadn't redirected us here, you could have killed yourself! You can't shift all the way to Tengu's fucking temple!"

"I'm sorry," Oken said, lying flat on his back. "But we need to go. The trees, they were screaming."

Bashima glared down at Oken, muttering under his breath.

"If Tengu isn't fucking dead, I'm going to kill both of you," Bashima said and shifted them to the next spot. It didn't take them long, and Bashima shifted them near the temple entrance instead of the forest. An intense wave of heat hit them, enough for even Bashima to recoil. Walls of flame burned around the temple, the trees like twisted, scorched claws jutting from the earth. The wood shrieked and exploded as the fire became too much, the inner moisture boiled away.

"HOLY FUCKING HELLS!" Bashima yelled. He shoved Oken toward the temple and shouted, "Tengu!"

His voice cut through Oken, but he was more focused on Bell. He reached out, searching for any feeling from the Forest God, and felt a flicker nearby. Oken pushed past Bashima and unleashed his ice, covering a massive area with one wave of his hand. The fire went out, the ground and trees covered in a thick, icy layer. Surprised, the Sun God flew back, his palms glowing.

"Warn me before you do that!"

Oken ignored him and stepped away from the temple, furious, his right side emitting freezing air. He stalked around the main entrance, shooting ice at any flames he saw, smothering them. He couldn't save the trees, but he needed to find Bell. Bashima followed after him, searching, calling Bell's name.

"Find him," Oken said when Bashima caught up. "I need to stop the fire."

Bashima nodded, an impressed expression on his face.

Oken circled the entire temple, stamping out flames with ice. He hated fire, even though it was a part of him. How could this destruction do any good? What was the purpose? He was thankful the blaze hadn't touched the temple and hoped the shades inside were okay. His heart broke for Bell, who'd grown the trees that surrounded his temple from seeds, tended them as saplings. He'd often watched Bell speak to the oaks, maples, ashes, and evergreens like old friends, his smile contagious.

"Oken!" Bashima rarely called him by his actual name. Oken shifted back to the temple entrance, searching for Bashima.

"Get your ass over here!"

Bashima found Bell, almost in the burning forest. It looked like Bell had tried to crawl away from the flames, most of his clothing burned away, his skin covered in ash, his hair singed. A nasty red burn covered Bell's right arm, jagged and angry. Oken could hardly bear to look at the injury. He touched his face, where he wore his own scar.

Bashima held Bell in his lap, his eyes wild, colors flying across his skin too quickly for Oken to catch all of them. He looked feral.

"Did you put the fire out?" Bashima asked, voice deadly. He looked at Oken as though he blamed him for the disaster and clutched Bell close.

"It's out," Oken said. "The temple wasn't damaged from what I could tell. The shades should be all right."

"Good," Bashima growled, still eyeing Oken. "We need to get him back to my temple. My healer is better than his."

Bashima stood, hoisting Bell in his arms. The Forest God keened, and Oken shook, picking up on Bell's fractured mind. Bell couldn't focus on anything, his eyes roving around the clearing. His instinct cried out to his trees.

Oken made to take Bell from Bashima, but the Sun God snarled at him and said, "You've done enough."

Oken stepped back, but frowned, expression determined.

"I'm not tired, if that's what you think," Oken said. "I can carry him."

Bashima blinked, seemingly not understanding Oken. He shook his head, cursing. "Just grab onto my arm, you dumb shit."

Chapter Sixteen

Cabari

The Temple of Lightning pierced the sky, a gleaming citadel of white stone. Most of it was a facade; Cabari and his shades lived in the bottom half, while his throne room was at the apex, but there was nothing in between. The temple had been constructed so the Lightning God could conduct his work at the summit and not injure anyone, for the shades could be hurt by his electrical storms. The height wasn't an issue, because Cabari could shift to the top when he was home, though he didn't rely on a locus of power like some other gods. He didn't consider the temple his home so much as the place he stopped by on occasion.

Jace had never been there.

Why was that?

The demigod never asked, but Cabari hadn't suggested it since their first time at the waterfall. It would have been a much better idea than sneaking into the Underworld or clandestine meetings in secluded outdoor hideaways. Though Jace seemed to enjoy whenever they spent time out in nature, calling them their "camping trips."

Stop thinking about him, Cabari told himself, smacking his face. He hates you. I know, I thought that would be impossible. Everyone loves me!

His mind laughed at him.

Everyone except Veles.

What parent actually liked the person fucking their kid? Not that he'd be screwing around with Jace anytime soon. Maybe never. Never. That didn't sound right. Maybe he should send Pressa a message…but that wasn't what he wanted. Maybe go cruising around a new village, find a likely new paramour…that didn't sound fun either.

What was wrong with him? Was he broken? Did the demigod break him?

Thinking about Jace's long stork legs wrapped around him, his stupid lips making their way down his chest, fingernails digging into his back did the trick, making him semi-hard in an instant.

Gods dammit. What the hells was he going to do?

Cabari grabbed his head with both hands, trying not to tear out his hair, holding in a scream. He'd scare the shit out of his shades if he lost it. Watching them scurry around in terror wasn't as amusing as it sounded.

As he dragged his feet up the ivory steps to the main entrance, Cabari put his head back, taking in his temple. Maybe he could renovate it or something. That would be a nice distraction.

Before he reached the top step, his lead shade staggered from the entrance, babbling to himself. He stood in front of Cabari and waved his arms.

"You don't want to go in there, Master Cabari," Isaac said, looking back over his shoulder.

"Can't you see I'm tired. I was only gone a day. What's the worst you all could have done?"

Insulted, Isaac said, "By all means, I wish you the best of luck in your current circumstance."

Cabari didn't like the sound of that. Isaac was rarely sarcastic.

"You." The voice made Cabari's blood stop flowing. Shit.

The God of the Dead emerged from the main entrance, hair whirling around his head like dark clouds, eyes red and piercing.

"Veles," Cabari said, casual, unconcerned. Or so he hoped.

"Where is my son?" Veles nearly ran into Cabari, a tower of rage.

"Back off," Cabari loosed lightning across his skin, which Veles shut down with a flick of his wrist. Shit. Fucking damned alchemy.

"If you try that again, I'll rip your arms off and shove them up your ass," Veles threatened, his hands curled into claws. "If you don't produce my son in one second —"

Cabari didn't step back. Veles could threaten him all he wanted. He hadn't violated any godly rules. Fucking his son wasn't a crime.

He said, "Lost something, have you? He's not here. This is the last place he'd go." Cabari crossed his arms, knowing that Veles wouldn't believe him. What was he, some villain holding an enchanted prince in his tower?

"If he wanted you to know where he went, he would have told you." Knowing how to get under the other god's skin, Cabari sneered and said, "What the hells did you do to make him leave anyway?"

"That's none of your concern."

"Shouldn't it be yours?"

Veles had a lot of nerve accusing Cabari of taking his son, especially when his husband was a damned prick who couldn't keep his bullshit opinions to himself.

"Excuse me?" Veles's voice lowered. Cabari was risking extreme bodily harm, but he'd had a long day.

"You're kidding me, right? That letter?"

Veles paled and he lifted his chin in the same imperious manner Jace sometimes did. He said, "You read it?" There was curiosity hidden beneath his contempt. Not that Cabari would oblige him of the letter's contents, even though it would hurt the other god.

"Oh yeah, it was a fucking page turner. Your husband is so kind and understanding."

"How dare you —"

"I'm gonna stop you right there," Cabari said and stepped up to the God of the Dead. "I might not be a paragon of virtue, but I'm not the one who's been tormenting Jace since he was born."

Veles's eyes blazed with hatred. Being called out for being a shitty parent sucked, but he needed to hear it. It wasn't entirely Cabari's fault that Jace ran away, and he wouldn't take all the blame.

"Jace deserves more than being 'put up with.'"

"I love my son," Veles said coldly. "You know nothing about my family."

"That's great and all, but then why don't you know where he is?"

Veles seethed, but his hair settled back around his shoulders, and his eyes lost the red sheen.

Cabari shouldered past the other god and marched into his temple, Isaac regarding him with an impressed expression.

Before he shut the door, Cabari said, "He was at the Temple of the Sun, but I doubt he's still there. Maybe you'll get lucky and he'll forgive you for whatever you did. Or didn't do."

He left Veles outside and leaned back against the closed door, heart beat skyrocketing. Isaac stood at his side and said, "I didn't think you had it in you."

Jace

"Nim's doing great," Shako said. "Her training is going well, but she tires out pretty easily. She's napping right now."

Shako led Jace down one of the white marble hallways of the Temple of Time, and Jace shivered. The temple was freezing, and he wondered how Shako handled it. He imagined Nim wrapped up in a thick cape with furry boots on her feet.

Once they reached the throne room, Shako asked, "You're not just here to see Nim, so what's up?" His tone held an edge, and Jace knew he had every right to be suspicious. Jace hadn't visited him or written since their disagreement about Cabari.

"I…" Jace wasn't sure what to say. He didn't want to admit that his friend had been right about the Lightning God, and he also didn't want to talk about Niall's letter. He looked around the throne room instead of continuing with his answer.

So, this was the place where Shina turned into a dragon the first time. The room had been cleaned up, the white marble veined with light blue pristine. But there was a sensation that bothered Jace. It happened whenever he came to the Temple of Time, but it was stronger in the throne room.

"It's colder in here," Jace said, and Shako nodded.

"Yeah, there's not much I can do about that, besides light a bunch of fires. The shades are too afraid to come in here. Hells, they're afraid of being in the temple at all. I think Nim's the only reason they stay."

Veles recruited new shades for the temple to assist Nim and Shako, a group of fifty or so. Jace had never seen them. They'd been chosen for

271

their age and experience, their hardiness. If Jace felt off in the temple, they must be experiencing even more off-putting sensations.

"How are you doing?" Jace asked, hoping to steer the conversation away from himself.

Shako sighed and put his hands on his hips. "Could be better. I have to be around Chronas all the time, and he creeps me out."

In order for his ability to work to its utmost potential, Shako had to physically touch the person to use their power. They kept Chronas's eternally slumbering body near the Locker. Shako had to go to the Locker at least once a day to rejuvenate his power by touching Chronas.

"Do they think you'll be able to leave soon?"

Shako laughed. "The gods do anything quickly? Why would they help me if they don't have to? It's easier to have me do it for them."

Jace looked away, but Shako shoved him with a shoulder. "Don't you ever get frustrated?"

"All the damn time," Jace said.

"I mean with the gods."

They were heading into a dangerous conversation, one of Shako's greatest hits. Even speaking about it was taboo, but Jace's friend didn't care.

"I know how you feel."

"Whatever," Shako said, knowing Jace wouldn't engage with him. He walked toward Chronas's throne. Behind it was the entrance to the Locker. Shako had already done his duty for the day, so Jace didn't know what he was doing. Maybe he knew Jace wouldn't follow him in.

"Your father was here," Shako said, turning his head as he walked. Jace ran to catch up with him and spun Shako around.

"When?"

Shako shook him off, frowning. "Not that long ago. He's worried about you. I couldn't even tell him where you were."

"I was at the Temple of the Sun," Jace admitted. His father came after him. And he was worried. Was it time to let Veles know he was okay?

"Oops," Shako said. "I suggested Cabari's place."

"You what?" Jace gripped Shako's tunic and pulled him in. "Why the fuck would you do that?"

"Lay off." Shako shoved him hard this time, making Jace stumble back. He'd forgotten how strong Shako could get when he was mad.

"Sorry," Jace muttered. "Did he go there?"

"How the hells should I know? He was pretty pissed though. He thought you'd broken up with him."

Jace clenched his jaw, teeth clicking together. Of course. It was about this again. Shako wasn't going to drop it. He wanted to antagonize Jace into reacting. Well, he wouldn't do it. He'd had enough of mouthy jerks to last five lifetimes.

"I'm gonna go wait for Nim to wake up," he said.

"Come on," Shako said, throwing up his hands and dropping them to his sides. "I'm sorry, okay?"

"No, you're not. You want me to tell you that you were right. Does that make you feel better?"

Shako gazed at him and bit his bottom lip. His cheeks flushed, blue eyes guilty.

"It's not like I wanted him to hurt you," Shako said. "But gods are all the same. You think they asked me if I wanted this job? Sure, your dad's nice enough, but he dragged me here to rescue that red-haired guy, and I barely got a thank you before they said I live here now."

Jace hung his head. He knew how Shako felt. His father asked him to help interrogate the shades and god-touched from the Temple of Time, and he'd been happy to do it. At first. After the first few dead-eyed shades, he'd become uneasy, but he wasn't comfortable asking his father if he could quit.

"Doesn't it piss you off that we're not allowed to use our power unless it's convenient for them?"

"I don't like using my power at all," Jace said, and Shako snorted.

"Our abilities aren't flashy, but they're sure fucking useful to the gods," Shako spit out. "And now they've got your sister roped into this thing. Aren't you furious? She's not even two hundred."

"It pisses me off, but what can I do? What could we do about it? They'd crush us like bugs if we said anything."

"All I'm saying is this job is draining," Shako said, touching Jace's shoulder. "And it's not right to make Nim do it. Not right to ask her to do it."

"Do what?" asked a sleepy voice behind them. "Hi, Jace."

Nim stood behind them, rubbing her eyes. She wore a long-sleeved dress with wool leggings, her hair up in the usual ponytail. She must have put it in while drowsy, because it was crooked.

"Hey, Squirt, come over here," Jace said. Nim obeyed and clomped over, eyes lidded.

"What are you doing here?" She asked as Jace fixed her hair.

"Came to see you," he answered, securing her hair with the red ribbon. "All set. Have you been behaving? Has Shako been nice?"

Nim giggled at Shako's outraged face. "He's been okay. I'm glad to see you. It's really boring here most of the time."

"Where are your tutors? Isn't there supposed to be at least one god here?" Jace asked, looking at Shako, who shrugged.

"They have a day off once a week," Nim explained. "And then I get to rest. But I heard a weird noise outside my window, so I came to find Shako."

Shako stood beside Jace and said, "It's probably something hitting the cliff again." He turned to Jace. "Lots of debris comes in from the sea. It rams against the cliff and makes rocks fall. Sounds freaky when it happens in the middle of the night."

"Want to show me your room?" Jace asked. Nim wasn't a fan of letting Jace into her room in the Underworld, but she seemed younger here, like she'd regressed a hundred years or so and still wanted to follow Jace around.

"I guess," she said, eyes narrowing. "Promise you won't snoop?"

"Ha! Yes, I promise." He crossed a finger over his heart and smiled.

A loud crash came from the hallway, followed by a scream, and they jumped.

"Hells, what've the shades gotten into now?" Shako walked toward the door, but a shade appeared in front of him and pushed him back.

"Master Shako! You must run!" Her eyes were filled with terror.

"Calm down," Shako said, grabbing her shoulders.

"Mistress Nim!" The shade yelled when she saw the girl. She raced over. "Please! Get her away from here! We can't shift outside for some reason. There are people in the temple."

Jace could barely understand the shade through her panic. Her eyes darted around the throne room as though looking for places to hide.

Shako asked, "Have you lost your mind? Jace, can you try shifting outside?"

Jace held Nim's hand, and she looked up at him with confused eyes. He attempted to shift and nothing happened.

"Shit," Shako said. "Has to be some sort of alchemy. I can't shift either." He turned to the shade. "Did you see anyone?"

"No, sir," the shade said, voice quivering. "I can't find anyone else. No one's in the kitchens or the other rooms. All the shades are gone." She wailed and covered her eyes. "This place is cursed!"

Glancing around the room, Jace wondered where they could go. Where was the safest place in the temple?

"Shako, open the Locker. We can hide in there until whoever it is goes away."

"What if that's why they're here?"

They looked at each other. They had no idea what threat they faced. Jace grasped Nim's hand. "Jace, can you let go?"

Jace startled and relaxed his grip. He said, "Sorry, Nim, but please stay by me. We're leaving. Somehow."

Shako nodded. "You two need to go. They might be after Nim. It could be anything."

"What about you?" Jace asked, dread flooding his senses.

"I need to keep the Locker closed." Shako's voice was grim but determined.

"Just leave it," Jace said. "We all need to get out of here."

"Go get help. I can barricade myself in the Locker. If something breaks through, I'll shift out and find you. I promise."

Another crash sounded outside the door. This time, a loud thud came, and the door shuddered. Something was ramming the door.

"You can still shift inside!" Shako yelled over the din. "Nim, take Jace to your room. Now!"

"Wait!"

Nim listened and they appeared in her bedroom.

"Shit!" Jace said, dropping his sister's hand. "Why did you do that?"

"We need to get away, Jace," she whispered. "The temple's telling me something's wrong. There's a fire..."

"Where?" Jace asked, shaking Nim by the shoulders.

"I don't know," she cried. "It feels hot. I can't understand the temple all the time yet."

The female shade appeared next to them, sobbing.

"He made me leave," she said, weeping freely. "Please go. I'll do my best to hold them off."

The bedroom door burst open, and a woman came through, small and lithe as a cat. Eyes calculating, the woman reached for a long whip-like cord at her hip, and a grin split her face.

"More demis?" she asked, unfurling the cord. "Come with me, girl."

They'd come for Nim. Jace knew how to fight, but he couldn't do it without endangering his sister. He had only one choice.

"Who are you?" he asked, activating his ability.

"Great question," the woman said, then she froze, a victim of Jace's ability.

Jace's voice resonated around the room, "Get into that wardrobe and don't come out."

The shade gaped at him. Nim clung to his hand, staring at the strange woman who Jace had mentally incapacitated. The woman marched over to the large wardrobe, opened the door, and stepped inside. She closed the door with a soft click.

"That won't last forever," he said. "Let's go back and get Shako."

"You can't," sobbed the shade. "That horrible man set the throne room on fire."

Shako

What a fucking day, Shako thought.

He rubbed his arm where the asshole had burned away his tunic sleeve and some of his skin. Half of the shirt was gone, singed away by dark purple flames, and he was fairly certain he wouldn't be using his injured arm for a while. He flexed the hand and pain shot through his body, doubling him over.

"Fuck!"

This was what he got for listening to gods.

The door to the Locker wouldn't last long against the massive guy who'd crashed through the throne room's solid doors; covered in heavily veined muscles, the guy looked like his skin had been flayed from his body, leaving the muscle behind. But he wasn't as much of a problem as the fire prick. Shako might be able to use the fire ability, but it wouldn't do him much good. The Locker was a hell of a prison, and there was no back door out.

Chronas's slumbering body lay on the floor, having been knocked off the table where they'd put him after Shina defeated him. The former Time God's face was expressionless, his unfeeling eyes closed. Shako touched Chronas's foot, taking in more of his power. He had to keep the Locker closed as long as possible.

The temple was probably trying to help with the intruders, but it didn't answer to Shako. It barely liked Nim. The loyalty of buildings was fleeting.

Shako looked behind him at the rows upon rows of condemned beings. Mostly shades who'd done severe evil in life and death, they slept in their little cages, eyes forever open and seeing. There were a few demigods too, those who'd broken gods' rules. Shako suspected there were even some gods inside, though he hadn't been able to find them in his wanderings.

Before he could think of a defense, the door broke open, half of it falling to the floor with a deafening clang. Shako got to his feet, holding his injured arm. Whoever they'd come for in the Locker, it had to be someone bad.

Shako thought of Jace and Nim, trying to escape the temple. He needed to buy them time as well, give them a chance. If the prisoner was released, they could hurt Nim and his friend.

Always just a friend, he thought and giggled. Fuck that green-haired moron anyway.

"What are you laughing at?" asked the muscular man, who grabbed the other door and tore it from the wall, throwing it back into the throne room.

"Your ugly ass, obviously," Shako said, grinning. "Get the fuck out of my temple."

A harsh chuckle erupted behind the muscular one, and Shako cringed. His arm ached and shrieked at him. His mind told him to run, but Jace needed to get away.

Stay away from here, you idiot, Shako thought, get your sister out of here.

Jace had a nasty habit of not listening to good advice.

"Get the fuck out of the way," the dark voice ordered, and the muscular man backed away, glaring.

The fire user appeared in the doorway, his skin a mess of scrawled tattoos. Alchemy marks? If they were alchemy spell marks, they were done in a child's scrawl. Even his face was marked with purple, swirling tattoos. Some even whirled over his eyelids, lighting up his pupils. Messy black hair flew around his head, much like Jace's. He smelled like charred meat.

The man surveyed the room, ignoring Shako for a few moments. Once he'd taken in everything, the man turned his cold eyes on Shako. "Aren't you a demigod?"

Shako blinked. Not exactly what he'd expected.

"What of it?"

It was taking all his strength to ignore the pain in his arm and keep the invisible walls up around the prisoners, but the invaders didn't know that.

"So, what are you doing here, doing a god's bidding?" scoffed the fire user. He approached Shako. Good, Shako might be able to touch him and gain his full power.

"Seemed like a good idea at the time," Shako sneered, lowering his shoulders.

"You've got balls, at least," the man said, cracking his jaw. "Not exactly what I'm here for, but you want a way out from under your overlords?"

"Huh?" This day was getting weirder by the moment.

"The gods can go fuck themselves, but I've got a soft spot for people like me."

The man scratched his face and skin flakes fell like snow. Did part of his tattoo disappear? The purple ink danced across his skin, replacing the lost lines. Shako tried his best to hide his disgust.

"I'll give you one chance to let go of the Locker walls and come with us. You'll be able to do what you want, whenever you want. No more shackles on your power."

He only had one shot. Shako nodded and looked around as though he were pondering the offer. Chronas's body mocked him from the floor, his face forever set in sleep. When Shako turned back to the fire user he said, "Sure, sounds great."

The man motioned him forward and Shako went. He controlled his breathing as well as he could, considering the adrenaline racing through his body.

When he was close, Shako lunged, grabbing the man's forearm. "Gotcha."

The man was fast. He grabbed Shako and threw them both from the Locker before Shako ignited purple flames across his body. Muscular guy yelled a curse as they launched past him.

"Brann! What the hells are you doing?"

The fire user — Brann — grinned at Shako, his teeth white against his tattooed skin. Inked flames sang across his skin, playing on his jawline. But these makeshift tattoos were like sketches. Shako might have a chance. The room burned around them in every shade of purple imaginable. The heat oppressed Shako, and he tried to focus on maintaining his hold on the Locker.

"I love a recruit with some fire," Brann said and threw Shako off him, sending him flying across the throne room. Shako landed hard on his back, knocking the wind out of him. The purple fire died on his skin as he fought for breath, though it still raged around the room. How long would it take to burn itself out if the asshole didn't stop it?

Brann walked toward him like he was on his way to the kitchen for a snack, like he had all the time in the world. The flames parted for him. "Where's the girl?" he asked when he was closer, looming over Shako.

"She's long gone," Shako wheezed. He ignited the purple flames along his arm and aimed them at Brann, who sidestepped the fire with ease. He jammed his foot on Shako's injured arm and pressed down hard, making Shako scream.

"Interesting ability you've got," Brann said, cocking his head. "That'll be a nice addition to our little collection."

"I'll never join you," Shako said, laughing.

"Who said I was offering? That option's off the table." He leaned down. "But first, release your hold on the Locker."

Shako gritted his teeth and tried to shove Brann's foot off his arm. Brann swooped down and grabbed Shako by the tunic, hoisting him in the air with ease. Shako's feet dangled, trying to find purchase.

"Fuck you."

"You're really not my type," Brann said, lip curling. "Just let go. It's not that hard. Is this really something you want to die for?"

"Shako!"

Fuck.

Both Shako's and Brann's heads turned toward the busted throne room doors. Through the flames, Jace's hair swirled, his eyes wide and scared. Nim wasn't with him. Hopefully she was with the shade, far from the temple. Of course, Jace hadn't been able to leave.

"And who's this?" Brann asked, licking his lips.

"He's nobody," Shako said. He closed his eyes, concentrated on honing the fire ability, and sent out a massive burst of purple flames, engulfing himself and Brann. The asshole cackled as they burned.

The last thing Shako heard was Jace screaming his name.

Veles

Veles scowled. Bashima had been ruder than ever, which was saying something. The young gods had attitude problems, so why was Veles cursed with interacting with more than one of them in less than twenty-four hours?

Cabari. The Lightning God.

His body shook with rage just thinking about him. Veles knew his son wasn't telling the entire truth about what happened between them, and he'd wanted to torture the little shit within an inch of permanent unconsciousness. But Cabari voiced some uncomfortable truths he'd had no right to speak out loud. Who was the Lightning God to tell Veles about his son, about his family? Some cheap, impulsive godling with no tact and a reputation in the toilet. Veles knew Cabari hurt his son in some way, had dangled affection then pulled it out of reach, probably whispering promises and oaths the entire time.

No. He couldn't think about that or he might go back to the Lightning God's temple and rip it down stone by stone. He needed to find Jace and tell him to come back home. Veles wanted to give his son some space, but he'd been gone too long, and with no word to let his father know he was okay.

And the Sun God. Why Vaultus gave such an important role to a younger god made zero sense to Veles. Surely, there was an older god, more responsible, less volatile, that would have been a better guardian to the sun. Veles had to admit that Bashima had done a decent job through the centuries, despite his isolation after the death of his human companion.

It seemed finding a new partner did little for his prickly personality. He hadn't even let Veles into his temple when he'd gone looking for Jace.

"What the fuck, is this a damn hotel?" Bashima had yelled at Veles from his main doors. "Your kid took off about a day ago. Good fucking riddance."

"Where did he go?" Veles had asked through clenched teeth, his fists shaking at his sides. The blatant disrespect.

Something had flashed through the Sun God's eyes before he answered, "The Temple of Time." Then he slammed the door in Veles's face.

Of course. He'd chased his son all over the place and now Jace was back where Veles started. He shifted toward the Temple of Time, furious with his son for taking him on this circuitous route. Why couldn't he have said where he was going? Why were children so difficult?

The roaring sea hit Veles's ears like a thunderclap when he landed, the black waves crashing into the cliffside where Chronas's temple — no, Nim's temple now — had been built. The white marble glistened against the black cliff, and violet flames licked across it, encasing the entire structure. Like night itself was consuming it.

Veles choked on his next breath and almost fell to his knees.

Gods, no.

His children.

Interlude

Veles

Veles was terrified. How was he going to tell his husband what he'd done? It was a vague memory distorted by an alcoholic haze. He'd been able to ignore the nagging feeling in his mind for months, unsure what exactly happened. One moment, he'd been in a human tavern, drowning himself in liquor. The next, he'd woken up outside the Temple of the Dead in the Underworld, his clothes and hair a mess. He recalled the bartender, a woman with an annoying laugh and mint-green hair, asking him to marry her. He'd told her he was already married, but that made her laugh harder.

She'd shaken her head at him and asked, "That Then why are you here?"

Had he really said it? Yes, he thought he had: "My husband…doesn't want children."

The bartender nodded, her eyes filled with understanding, but that was her job. Chat with patrons, hear their woes, pour the drinks. It hadn't stopped there, apparently.

Ten months later, she'd lit a beacon and said a prayer to the God of the Dead. Veles would normally avoid such summons. They usually didn't work, but it made the humans feel better to chant to a higher being every now and then.

The bartender at least knew what she was doing: She burned a yew tree branch, a black swan feather, an owl's skull, and chrysanthemums. Realizing what village the incantation originated from, Veles decided to see what she wanted. Because it had to be her. With mischief in her eyes and a ready smile.

When he appeared, she didn't jump like most humans would. She grinned at him, holding a bundle in her arms.

Veles sighed. If this was a prank, he was going to curse the woman into oblivion. "You summoned me?"

"Well," she said, a bit of doubt on her face now that he'd spoken, his voice heavy with power. "I wasn't sure if he was yours at first. Didn't want to bother you, ya know, if it wasn't you."

Veles tensed. What? The bundle in her arms stirred, the blanket rustling.

Oh shit. Oh gods. No.

She stepped toward him and motioned for him to take what she held. A soft cooing came from its depths, and Veles stopped breathing. What had he done? He was such a fool. Niall would never forgive him.

"He doesn't bite," she said, amused, thrusting the baby into his rigid arms. Flustered, Veles yelped and clung to the bundle, bringing it in close to his chest. He'd never held a child before, except a full-god child, and they were sturdy. There was hardly any way to hurt a godly baby. This one had human fragility. How should he hold it? What if he crushed it?

She noticed his panic and touched his arm. "It's okay. Just relax. If you wake him up, he'll scream his head off, so let's try not to do that."

Veles looked at the human, her eyes kind. He asked, "How do you know…"

"He smashed a table with one swing a few weeks after he was born. That might have been the first clue," she said, sarcastic. "At least he got my hair." She pulled the blanket back from the baby's head a bit, and wild mint-green hair fell out, curling around his face. His eyelashes were thick and a purple so dark they might have been black. He was so small.

"He's really mine?"

"I wouldn't have called you otherwise," she said. "If he'd been a human baby, I would've raised him on my own. But there's no way I can deal with a demigod by myself."

Veles nodded. Demigods had enhanced strength and sometimes developed powerful abilities. It was almost impossible to know what powers a demigod would manifest, if any, and a human woman would have no chance teaching the baby how to handle it.

"I'll take care of him," she said. "Don't worry. You don't have to be involved if you don't want that. But I could use help when he, you know, starts acting weird."

"It's not weird," Veles said, voice low. She dared call his son weird. He pulled the baby away, but she clicked her tongue at him.

"Don't get all high and mighty with me," she said and crossed her arms. "It might be normal for gods, but the humans in the village won't know how to handle it. Once he can control whatever abilities he has, it will be easier. They'll accept him if I tell them to. I own the damn tavern and know everyone's secrets."

"I can take him with me," Veles said, gazing down at the sleeping baby. His mouth was set in a small scowl, his little eyebrows scrunched up on his brow. Such a serious little thing.

Her eyes widened, and she made a move toward Veles, who backed away. Her humor vanished in an instant, replaced by fright.

"Please don't take him," she pleaded, reaching out her hands. "He'll need his mother."

A million thoughts cascaded through Veles's mind. He had an idea of how Niall would react to the news, and it wasn't good. A baby didn't belong in the Underworld. Maybe when he was older.

She was mortal, after all, and wouldn't live longer than a hundred years. He would have eternity with his son. Why steal him away now when his husband might retaliate in some way? Veles didn't think Niall would hurt a child…on purpose. What if he lost control and accidentally damaged the baby? There were plenty of human-world fears to deal with as well, but the woman seemed smart and capable. She would do everything in her power to make sure the child grew up well.

"If I allow this," Veles said, "I will be able to see him whenever I wish."

"Of course," she answered. "He needs his father too. I didn't plan on keeping him from you."

"And when the time comes…he'll come live with me."

She frowned. "I thought your husband didn't want children."

Veles looked away from her and touched a gentle finger against the baby's cheek. He stirred but didn't wake, sighing and settling against Veles's chest.

"That doesn't matter," he whispered.

"I know you gods aren't big on names, but I'm calling him Jace. It means 'compassionate.'"

"That's beautiful," Veles said and felt tears forming.

"I assume he'll take your name of course," she said. "But for now, he'll have mine. Fitzgerald. My name is Nessa Hirikomi Fitzgerald. It's quite a mouthful, so call me Ness."

Veles snorted. He'd never been on a first name basis with a human. It was odd, but he could humor her. Someday. "Whatever you say."

But now, he had returned to the Underworld, and he had no idea what to tell his husband. He could feel his son's weight in his arms, so slight and frail, skin like paper.

The thought of losing him trumped every fear he'd ever experienced. If Veles could die, he would gladly do it for that tiny form wrapped in a blanket. Niall would have to accept what had happened, because Veles wouldn't give up his son.

He found Niall in their bedroom, packing for a work trip. He'd be gone for weeks, trying to settle a dispute between some southern gods. Bustling around the room, his husband was content, preparing for a normal part of his job, having no idea Veles had upended their lives.

"Niall," Veles said. He closed the bedroom door quietly. No need for the shades and god-touched to hear the imminent verbal explosions.

"You're back," his husband said, beaming. "I wasn't sure if you'd be here in time for dinner, so I asked the kitchen shades to save you something. I guess we can eat before I leave." He came over, gave Veles a quick kiss then went back to packing. "How was it? Just a random summoning? I have no idea why you humor those humans so often."

"Niall." His tone made Niall pause, hands midway into his bag. Niall turned around, a frown forming.

"Did something happen? Are you okay?"

"I'm fine," Veles said, rubbing the back of his neck. This was harder than he thought. "I need to tell you something."

"You're scaring me."

Veles moved to the bed and sat, Niall standing by his bag. He let the silence form between them like an ocean, distant shorelines caught between a widening gulf. This changed everything. Nothing between them would be the same. It had been a massive mistake, but all Veles could see was his son's wispy green hair, tiny fingers wrapping around one of his.

Sighing, Veles said, "Remember that fight we had a while back?"

"Define 'a while back.'" Niall's tone was acidic, his eyes narrowed in suspicion.

"Almost a year," Veles said, wincing.

"The fight where you called me an unreasonable ass and stormed out of the Underworld like a child? The one where you wound up drunk on the front stoop the next morning?"

"That's the one."

"What did you do?"

Niall's accusing voice was like broken glass in Veles's heart. They'd been together forever, almost since their creation. They argued like any married couple, but they always found a way to make up and come back together, stronger. He doubted that would happen this time.

"I made a mistake," Veles said and reached for his husband's hand. Niall pulled away.

"Did you cheat on me?"

The hurt. The pain. Worst of all, the disbelief. Niall never thought Veles would be unfaithful. It wasn't a possibility. They were married. They were two halves of one person.

"I don't remember," Veles said, desperate. "But...yes."

Niall nodded, muttering to himself.

"I'm sorry," Veles said.

"Oh, I can tell," his husband snapped, glaring at him. "You wouldn't be the first god to disrespect their partner like this, and you won't be the last. What happened?"

"I got drunk."

"Fucking hells, Veles. That excuse?"

"It's what happened," Veles said, letting annoyance creep into his voice. He stood up and went to his husband, who walked away, fuming.

"Since you can't handle your alcohol, I believe you. Who was he? Some random human? Is that who summoned you? Needed another round?"

Veles couldn't meet his eyes. "It wasn't a man."

Niall was shocked, his mouth hanging open. "You fucked a woman?"

"Is it that hard to believe?" Veles was rapidly losing control of the conversation. Soon, the yelling would start. Perhaps the throwing of furniture.

"Considering you never have, I'd say I'm a little surprised, yes." Niall put his hands on his hips. "Wait. She summoned you now? After how long?"

Veles's face fell. Niall arrived at the inevitable conclusion before Veles could confess.

"Oh, my gods." Niall's blond hair flew around his head, his rage growing. "What have you done?"

"I'm so sorry," Veles said, rushing to his husband and grabbing his arms. Which was a mistake. Niall lost it. He shoved his husband away with such force that Veles hit the far bedroom wall and slid to the floor.

"Not only did you cheat on me," Niall said, advancing on Veles, his eyes blown full black, "it was with some human female whore. And you got her pregnant with her demigod spawn." His hands had become claws, his teeth like daggers. "I'm going to kill her," Niall seethed, his voice a menacing growl. Vele's husband was gone. "And then I'm going to kill that thing you made."

Veles launched himself at the creature that used to be his husband. It shrieked at him, clawing his clothes, biting toward his face. He'd never used alchemy on his husband, but Niall was out of control. All Veles could think about was his son, keeping him safe. Niall was in a rage, and there might be no stopping him if he got away from Veles's grasp.

Veles's eyes burned red, staring into his husband's blackhole eyes. "Stop," he said, using his power. His power was almost infinite, could stop any god in their tracks. He'd learned at a young age that alchemy was his only weapon against those more powerful than him, and so he became alchemy's master. It was like being in the calm center of a storm. Niall's hair fell, and his eyes faded back to normal, gazing at Veles like he didn't know him.

"I will not permit you to harm my son."

Niall didn't try to pry Veles's hands off him. He watched his husband, red rising in his cheeks, shoulders quivering. He pursed his lips and said, "Is that so?"

"If you try," Veles said, "I will leave you."

"Fine," Niall said. He shrugged out of his husband's grip, grabbed the bag from the bed, and walked toward the door. "Don't bother leaving. I'll go."

"Niall —"

"Don't worry," he said, scornful. "I won't hurt the brat."

"I changed my mind," Niall said, turning around. They stood in a forest, in an opening in the trees. Ness's house was nearby, smoke coming from the chimney. She'd moved further from town to accommodate their son's growing strength. And his mysterious ability to get people to do what he wanted. Veles had a notion what it could be, and the boy had luckily not used it on his mother yet. Or so she thought.

Veles sighed. It had taken twenty years, but he'd finally convinced his husband to meet his son. He ran a hand through his hair, which had become shot with more gray over the two decades of constant fighting and cold silences. He said, "You've come here, why not stay? For me?"

"Don't pull that." Niall glared at him. "I should never have agreed to come. He's your son, not mine."

"I know that —"

"Daddy!" A joyous shout from across the open backyard. Jace looked like a ten-year-old child, though it had been two decades since his birth. Gods and demigods aged differently than humans, so there was no telling how his growth would proceed. He could physically age another ten years overnight. His green hair had grown longer and swirled around his head in a riotous cloud, much like Veles's had when he was younger.

Veles tensed and looked at his husband, whose face had gone rigid and cold, his hands fisted at his sides. He watched the child race up to them, whose eyes were wide with excitement.

Veles knelt down and let Jace run into his arms, the boy throwing his arms around his father's neck. "Daddy, you're late," he said in a child's giggle.

"I'm sorry," Veles said, hugging Jace tightly. "I'll try to be on time next time. You're getting big."

"Yup," Jace said, letting go. His eyes were a deep indigo and very bright. He knew no hardship, just loved running around outside and playing with the neighboring kids. Under his mother's supervision of course.

"Have you been listening to your mother like I told you?"

Jace avoided his eyes and said, "A bit. Sometimes she scolds me."

Veles laughed and ruffled his hair. "That's because she's the mom and you're the kid. I hope you're not getting into any trouble."

"No," Jace laughed again and shoved Veles's face away as he tried to kiss his cheek. "I haven't gotten into trouble in forever! Gross, Dad!"

Niall stood behind them, and Veles felt his eyes boring into them. Now that Jace was in his arms, bringing his husband seemed like a terrible idea.

"Who's that, Daddy?" Jace's face remained lit from within, his smile infectious, as he regarded Niall. Veles took a deep breath and stood up.

"Jace, you remember when I told you about my husband?"

"Yes," Jace said, suddenly shy and hiding behind Veles. "Hi." His voice was light and sweet and so innocent. He gave Niall a little wave.

Niall was stunned, not speaking. It was odd for him not to have words. He could talk to anyone, spin a tale, end an argument with a jest, effortlessly effervescent. Now, he couldn't string together a few words.

He looked from Veles to Jace, the boy's hand clamped firmly on his father's arm. Veles could tell that his husband was fighting a breakdown in front of his son, trying so hard not to make a scene.

"I can't do this," Niall whispered and shifted away.

"I don't want to be tied to you forever," she scoffed, tossing her green hair. "I only joked about marrying you, for godsake."

"That was a real crowd-pleaser," Veles said, rolling his eyes. "Are you sure? You could be with Jace."

"Don't tempt me with that bullshit," Ness said, flicking a towel at him. "I love Jace, but I'd be miserable in the Underworld as a god-touched. You know that. I'll become a shade like I'm supposed to. You better get me a good job or I'll haunt you."

Veles laughed, rubbing his eyes. "What are you going to tell him?"

"He already knows how I feel, Veles." Ness walked around the bar and shoved his shoulder. She'd never been afraid of him, despite the fact that he could blink her out of existence in a moment. She said, "Jace will be fine without me. And he can come see me if he wants. It'll be good for him to live with you, see that side of his heritage."

"I'm not so sure about that," Veles said, shrugging.

"Niall?"

"Who else?"

She messed up his hair and walked back to wipe down the bar, getting ready for the day. "So long as you promise to keep our son safe, I'm not worried about your husband. Jace's a tough kid. He can take care of himself."

"Speaking of that, has he made any friends?"

Ness gave a small shake of her head. "He spends a lot of time with that Shako kid. You know, the other demigod who lives a few villages down the river? The mouthy one?"

Veles winced. Ugh, yes. The son of the God of Memory who conveniently forgot he had a son the instant he learned of the boy's existence. As far as Veles knew, Shako was relatively harmless and had an interesting ability. He could imitate other gods' powers for a short time, though that limit might increase as he aged. Veles vowed to keep an eye on Shako, especially if he was going to spend time with his son.

"I'm not going to live forever," Ness said and threw her towel at him. "Maybe Jace should come visit you for a weekend, get used to the business of the Underworld."

His son was inconsolable, which wasn't surprising. Ness died peacefully, much older than anyone had expected her to live, in her bed, one last joke upon her lips as she passed. Jace wanted to stay in his house, the only home he really knew, but Veles wouldn't allow it. He was only eighty years old, much too young to stay on his own, and his power was growing along with his height.

Jace could now look his father in the eyes and had developed a stern personality to match, claiming that his mother had been the loud, social one. He walked around the temple, slouched shoulders, hands in his pockets, mumbling non-answers to anyone who spoke to him.

Veles's god-touched tried to make conversation, but his son remained sullen and unknowable. Where was the bubbly boy Veles knew?

The only thing that cheered Jace up was visiting Shako, the other demigod, who'd grown into a nuisance. Shako hated the necessary restrictions on his powers, had flaunted the rules numerous times, relying on Veles to get him out of trouble. And he was always smiling. Even when he was angry, the boy plastered a grin on his face and got on with it. A stark contrast to Jace, who couldn't seem to muster an expression past semi-apathetic.

Since he'd moved into the Underworld, dark circles formed under Jace's eyes, but he claimed he was sleeping fine. He didn't want to see his mother's shade either, perhaps angry at her mortality.

Veles didn't know what else he could do. He talked to his son whenever he could, asked him how his day was going, did martial arts with him, listened to him play the flute, made him do his lessons and practice his ability. Which turned out to be a sort of mental power: mind-reading and astounding coercion.

His progress with it was extraordinary, exhibiting excellent control. Veles had to help with Jace's training, because he was the only one the ability didn't work on. Veles expected that it wouldn't work on gods. For now. With the speed Jace was mastering the skill, it wouldn't be long before Vaultus would want to see him and make Jace show his power. Then Jace would go on the list of known demigods.

One day, after they'd completed a session and the shades had gone, Veles felt Jace trying out his ability on him, like invisible fingers tickling his mind. He'd lashed out with his own power, knocking Jace on his backside.

Standing over his son, livid, Veles said, "Never. Do that. Again."

Jace glowered at him, bottom lip stuck out. "You didn't have to push me," he muttered.

Veles knelt beside him, grabbing his arm. "Yes, I did. You need to understand. Demigods who use their abilities against gods get a one-way ticket to the Locker. Being my son might get you leeway. Once. But don't count on it. Vaultus may be the king, but the other old gods weigh in on his decisions, and he has to appease them."

Jace's expression didn't change, defiance spreading in his eyes.

"Do you understand me?" His grip tightened on his son's arm. Veles needed to get this lesson across, more than anything. Jace's ability was more dangerous than any physical power. Gods would fear him if they knew he could take over their minds.

Jace wrenched his arm from Veles's grasp and shifted away. Veles rolled his eyes. He was really sorry that he'd taught Jace how to shift.

Nim never stopped crying.

Veles lay in bed, staring at the ceiling, Niall snoring beside him. He took a series of deep breaths, waiting for Nim to quiet, though it might take hours. It never bothered Niall, who said it was necessary to let babies cry through the night and not coddle them.

Veles couldn't believe the baby was in their temple, one room over. She'd been with them for a few months, her mother having passed away soon after the birth from the strain. Niall couldn't bear to leave her with the woman's family, though he hadn't planned on being in the girl's life at first.

Their argument about Niall's retaliation had been brief, probably not what Niall expected. But what could Veles say? He'd cheated on Niall first, and while he was hurt that his husband chose revenge instead of communication, he couldn't bring himself to rage at him. Niall smacked his husband's chest again and again, begging Veles to get angry, asking for him to scream and threaten. When Veles didn't, Niall had gone away for months, leaving Veles alone with the sullen Jace. Who still wanted to go by the name Fitzgerald, rejecting his godly name.

Veles rubbed his eyes, wishing he could be a better husband and father. It was so much harder than he'd expected. Niall had told him for thousands of years that children were difficult, that he was happy just to have his husband. That they didn't need children. Sometimes, Veles wished he'd listened to Niall. Then, he felt terrible and tried to hug his recalcitrant son, who bore the hugs with long, drawn-out sighs.

Nim cried. She was a sweet baby, very beautiful, with pink hair and large green eyes. During the day, she toddled around her playroom, cooing and giggling at the god-touched in charge of watching her, and she adored Niall. He was a bit perplexed by the affection but smothered her in kisses and gifts. So many toys. More toys than one room could hold.

Veles looked over at Niall snoring beside him.

The wailing stopped. Veles's attention snapped to the door. Nim never quit. Not until early in the morning. It was like she knew when they were putting her to bed for the night and raged against the injustice of her crib.

Trying not to disturb Niall, Veles slipped out of their bed and tiptoed to the door between their room and Nim's. Niall didn't move an eyelash as Veles slid through the door and closed it gently.

A single candle burned in Nim's room. Standing beside her crib was Jace, holding her in a blanket against his chest, her tiny hand holding onto his shirt collar. He spoke to her in a low voice, but Veles didn't catch what he said.

Jace eventually noticed Veles at the door and clutched Nim tighter. "I can't let her cry," he said.

Veles smiled and walked toward them. He pulled the blanket away from Nim's face. She slept soundly against Jace.

"She's so little," Jace said, rocking her.

"You were that small once."

Snorting, Jace went to sit in the cushy chair in the corner, maneuvering around Nim's mounds of toys. Veles felt a pang in his chest; Jace never had this much extravagance in his youth. His son didn't mention it, probably didn't even notice, but Veles wished he'd showered Jace in this much love.

"You can give her to me and go back to bed if you want," he said.

Jace shook his head, gazing down at Nim. "That's okay." He curled his legs up under him and leaned back against the chair, his tired eyes shining deep indigo.

"I love you," Veles said.

Jace looked up at him sharply. He allowed Veles a rare smile. "I know, Dad."

Chapter Seventeen

Alaric

Alaric wanted to do anything but train. He'd rather be back in town shopping with Loralei. It would be less tortuous than training with Daruk and the silver dragon. So, he thought he'd try out what they bought in town.

Loralei had taken him to the village of Kamaishi, which was much bigger than Togarashi and had more shops and artisans. It was lively and bustling and filled with people and new smells and sounds. Alaric found himself distracted by everything: the stall selling meat pies, a band playing in the town square, kids running around and playing games, a shop that only sold glass figurines, one that had odd animals on display that people could buy as pets. Loralei let him look and smell and even bought him a meat pie when he gave her the "huge-eye puppy begging," as she called it.

"We're not here to eat everything in sight," she scolded fondly. "We're here to get you something to help with the rut so you don't try to hump Daruk's leg again."

"It was only the one time," Alaric mumbled, blushing scarlet.

They'd been wrestling, Daruk teaching Alaric some new fighting moves with his scales activated, when he'd lost control for a moment.

"Once was quite enough for my mate." Loralei laughed and patted his arm. "And I don't mind doing your laundry, but there's been a lot of mysterious red fluids on the sheets."

Alaric gulped. He had been having sleep-humping incidents. He'd offered to help with laundry, knowing what it was, but Loralei told him to stop being a big baby. It wasn't the first time she'd had to deal with dragon cum.

"I figured we'd need to come here eventually," she said as they walked through town. "And I need to do a little food shopping. We're almost out of salt and flour."

"Does Daruk ever come here with you?"

"Not often. No one's around from when he was young. It makes him a little sad. He's not like me, wasn't born almost immortal. He misses his normal life sometimes."

"I get how he feels," Alaric said, hanging his head. Not that he'd give up his life with Bashima, but he wondered how it would feel once his family and old friends were gone.

"At least he has another dragon-touched to bother him now," Loralei said and smiled.

"Yeah. Even if he thinks I'm a moron."

Loralei burst into raucous laughter and pulled him into a shop with shaded windows and no sign. It was the oddest place Alaric had ever been. It was fairly dark and smelled nice, like spices and trees found deep within a forest. But it was covered in mysterious, odd items.

"Is that...a penis?" Alaric asked, shocked, seeing a group of sculptures on a shelf.

Loralei snorted when she looked where he pointed. "Relax. It's not a real one. It's a sex toy."

"What is it made of?" Alaric was mystified. There were such things you could buy? In a store?

"Probably wood and leather," Loralei said, pondering. "The base is made from wood, and the craftsman covers it in soft leather. Maybe not as great as the real thing, but people have needs."

Loralei shoved him with her shoulder, shaking her head at his naivete, and went to the counter to find the shopkeeper. Alaric's eyes widened as he wandered around the store. There were a variety of elaborate costumes along with the sex toys, including one that looked like a unicorn and another one that suspiciously reminded him of Bashima.

"Role-play," came a quiet voice behind him, and Alaric jumped. He spun around, and a small woman stood before him, short enough to only reach mid-torso. "Hm, I guessed you were a big one."

"Beg your pardon?" Alaric backed away. She was an unusual woman, covered in a blue robe and hood so only her face showed. It was impossible to tell her age, but her large blue eyes belied wisdom Alaric might never achieve. They were rimmed with heavy, dark blue kohl, and Alaric thought of his early days at the Temple of the Sun.

"The costumes," she said, motioning to a rack of clothing. "Were you interested in something along these lines?"

"Gods, no! I'm sorry, not that someone wouldn't be interested in them. Just not me. At least, not right now. Loralei!"

He couldn't tell the woman that his husband had outfits that were far superior, then he imagined Bashima in his formal armor and started drooling, a bulge forming in his trousers. The woman stared appreciatively at his crotch, and he covered himself with a hat from the nearby rack.

"I don't think that will hold it, but you can always try," she said, winking.

"Hello Mrs. Hudson." Loralei approached them, grinning at Alaric's discomfort. "What's with the hat?"

The woman smiled. "Back so soon?"

"I'm not shopping for myself today. My friend is in need of the specialty item that your husband makes." She looked Alaric up and down then looked back at the penis-model sex toys. "He's probably smaller than my partner. Maybe a medium?"

"Hey!" Alaric said, embarrassment growing. He moved from one foot to the other, wanting to flee. But Loralei would make him come back. Loralei raised an eyebrow at him, and he sighed, saying, "That's fair."

"Come in the back room, young man," Mrs. Hudson said. "Let's get you measured."

Measured? Loralei hadn't mentioned anything about getting measured. He followed the woman but pleaded non-verbally with Loralei, eyes wide. She grinned and waved at him. So unhelpful.

"I'm here to help you," Mrs. Hudson said as she led him behind a curtain to a back room whose walls were covered with dark blue velvet fabric. It smelled like lavender, very soothing. She went on, "If you're in the same condition as that demigod and her mate, you're the ones we opened this shop for."

She brought Alaric to a small table and bade him sit.

"My husband is a highly-skilled textile alchemist," she explained. "He makes everything in this shop and doesn't ask questions. Excepting the necessary ones, of course. Otherwise, how is he to please his customers?"

"Umm." Alaric wasn't sure how to answer. This was so strange, though he felt oddly comforted.

"I am also an alchemist," she said and gestured around the room. "My specialties are herbal remedies and potions. Are you feeling more relaxed now?"

"A little," Alaric admitted.

"It will be fine, young man. Sexuality is very natural, yet many people find it difficult to discuss."

She brought out an item from under the table to show him. It was a box with a sturdy frame and built-in handles and a soft, cushioned center with one hole. Oh, dear gods. He was supposed to fuck that? He imagined his husband cackling at the thing and nearly collapsed into giggles.

"You can laugh all you want," she said. "Sex is inherently funny. If more people realized that, the less seriously they'd take themselves. The more fun they'd have with their partner. And more pleasure."

"This is the craziest thing I've ever seen," Alaric said, poking the device.

"I doubt that," she said. "We make a variety of sizes. Normal humans can use them of course, but Loralei and her partner are our chief clients. These are made to last, imbued with spells that keep them clean and let you do what needs to be done. They do wear out eventually, but it should keep for at least three seasons."

Seasons? Did she know about ruts? Did she know what Daruk was? She seemed to at least know that Loralei was a demigod. How could they trust a random shopkeeper with their secret?

"We get plenty of other animal hybrids as well," she said, raising an eyebrow. "Don't think you're the only one we've seen. They also benefit from our knowledge."

"Okay," he whispered. If she could help him, it could solve a lot of his rut issues with Bashima. His dragon brain was unimpressed, grunting in the back of his mind that he didn't need the stupid contraption. His mate was perfect and wonderful and could handle anything. He told his dragon self to shut the hells up.

So, they'd found him a rut aid in his size — maybe not as big as Daruk but still commendable, definitely bigger than a medium, Alaric thought — and went back to the cottage. Daruk had gone to the nearby lake to fish and would be back to train before dinner. He left a note for Alaric to be ready to attempt his own dragon trance.

Anxiety ate at Alaric. Try his own trance? Was that possible? Could Daruk and Kamaishi teach it to him? He'd done well on the silver dragon's other tasks, but this one worried him. What if he couldn't do it?

A low whine formed in his chest and he wished Bashima was there. He thought about the costumes displayed in the alchemist's shop and imagined his husband welcoming him home, hips draped in the black and gold kilt he'd worn when they first met. Which switched on his damn dragon brain. Saliva pooled in his mouth and he snarled. He shouldn't think about Bashima when the god wasn't around; it made him hard and pissed off, and jerking off didn't satisfy the dragon inside.

His eyes found the bag from the shop, and he regarded it, his dick almost hard. He had time before Daruk got back. Maybe he should try it. The dragon brain roared at him to put his dick in the damned thing, since it was already there, and Alaric tore into the packaging, sniffing the toy. It didn't smell like Bashima, and he cringed, hissing and accidentally scenting the room. It smelled of moss and a forest after a storm. Daruk would yell at him for that later, but it was too late now.

Might as well at least give it one go. He took off his trousers and sat on the bed, his dick interested in the toy, fully hard and throbbing. He'd need to get Bashima's scent on it, then it might be easier to accept. As he eased himself inside the soft part, bracing the toy with his hands, his normal mind turned off and the dragon took over. He growled and thrust it onto himself. It almost felt real. At least it was soft and a little warm, nothing like his husband, but it would do the job. He bit his lip and lay on his back on the bed so he could thrust up into the toy. It felt good…really good. If he closed his eyes and pictured his husband, he almost felt normal.

It is normal, the woman's voice echoed through his head. How you deal with sex is unique to you, but everyone has similar experiences. Sex is normal. You are just fine the way you are.

He whimpered as he slammed into the toy again and again, hoping to satisfy his urge. As he kept going, Alaric's claws and jagged teeth came out, his dragon-touched scales emerging. Probably not the best idea for the toy, but he didn't try to stop.

"Alaric! I've been yelling up the stairs for ten minutes!" Daruk's voice in the hallway. Shit.

Daruk burst through the door and locked eyes with Alaric, his mouth hanging open like he was going to yell again. Alaric snapped at him, tasting the metallic tang of Daruk's scent on his tongue. He growled, warning Daruk to get out of his territory. As he registered what Alaric was doing — mid thrust into the toy — Daruk's eyes bulged and he roared, slamming the door.

"It's my house!" He yelled, stomping down the stairs.

Alaric couldn't stop until he came or he'd be irritable, so he kept at it, making his scales recede. He didn't want to break the toy and he shouldn't get used to having sex in his hardened form. Bashima wouldn't go for that. When he finally felt the heat pool in his belly and his body stiffened as he came, Alaric saw the ruby-colored cum burst from the toy. As he removed his spent dick, the fluid disappeared, taken care of by the cleaning charm the woman had touted. He turned the toy over in his hands, but the cum was gone.

At least he'd taken care of that issue, but now Daruk was going to torture him for sure.

"No, no, no, that's not it at all."

Alaric fell over in the stone circle, spreading his arms and legs out like a starfish. He let out a breath, and smoke escaped his nose.

"Don't blow smoke at me, hatchling." Kamaishi loomed over him, casting his shadow upon the circle. Daruk looked on, checking out his nails instead of coming to Alaric's aid.

"I didn't mean to," Alaric grumbled.

"You need to be able to enter the dragon trance on your own," the dragon said, waving a single claw in Alaric's face. "You won't be with Daruk all the time. Do you understand the importance of this?"

"Obviously," Alaric said. "But I'll be calling Togarashi, right? You really want me to do that?"

"Harrumph, he may be a poor excuse for a teacher, but he is your dragon." Kamaishi settled his bulk on the grass and lowered his head to the ground so it was level with the two dragon-touched. "He won't think it's odd that you haven't contacted him since your turning. He attends to his own pleasures, but he will come if you call."

"And he'll come if I call him in Daruk's trance?" Alaric was skeptical. Shouldn't he need to be in his own mental space to summon his dragon?

"If he could hear your poor excuse for a call, he would."

Alaric sat up and glared at Daruk, who hadn't spoken in an hour. The jerk had groomed himself, checking each of his scales for tarnishing, preening. He was obviously cranky about the incident with the sex toy.

Daruk noticed him staring and said, "What?"

"You could be a little more helpful."

"How? It's your task."

Alaric stuck his tongue out. He crossed his legs and closed his eyes. He could do this. Control his scent, concentrate so Togarashi would feel his mental voice reaching out, focus everything on picturing what the ruby dragon looked like.

"Wrong again."

"Ugh!"

Alaric opened his eyes and stood, pacing around the circle. He and Daruk no longer needed to hold hands within the trance. That impressed Kamaishi at first, but since Alaric caught onto things quickly, he'd expected the redhead to succeed at a breakneck pace. Alaric could hardly keep up with the lessons. He'd been able to control his scenting, which the dragon made him do in his sleep as well. Daruk had been stationed in his room for a week and would smack him in the face with an evergreen branch if he scented in his sleep. Kamaishi said it would be more difficult to do while rutting, but it would help with his urges if he could learn to regulate his scent.

"Don't you wish to spare your god a little pain?" Alaric had pouted at the dragon's teasing words while Daruk laughed.

"His god is such a weakling! Can't even handle one rut. What's he going to do for your next one? Send you on another vacation?"

The teasing continued until Alaric threatened to tell Loralei.

Kamaishi rumbled with glee at that. "Even I fear Loralei," he said. "She is more frightening than many dragons I know."

After a week of smelling like a pine tree, face covered in sticky sap, Alaric made it through a night without scenting. To get back at Daruk, he'd scented all over the ground floor, rolled around in his chair, and hid his favorite boots. Daruk chased him around the yard while Loralei sunned herself near the chicken coop. When Daruk saw her, he said she needed to cover up, even though she wore a thick cloth bandeau around her chest. It didn't matter that Alaric wasn't interested, he was still in a rut and might not be able to control himself. Loralei then chased Daruk around the yard while Alaric lay on the ground laughing.

She'd yelled at her mate, brandishing her fists. Not stopping her pursuit, she'd said, "Don't let him make fun of you, Alaric! His cum is silver when he ruts and it tastes like shit!"

"Why would you tell him that?" Daruk had wailed at her, mortified.

Alaric tried to think about Togarashi again, bring himself back into focus, but he was too agitated by Kamaishi's casual admonitions and Daruk's jibes.

"Why is this so hard?" He asked Daruk. "I should be able to get it."

Daruk shrugged, smiling. "I can't cloud-dance. Maybe this is something you're going to have trouble with."

He was just happy that Alaric found something he couldn't do after three attempts.

"Great. The one way to communicate with my dragon and I can't do it."

Kamaishi snorted, his scaled eyelids clicking as they closed and opened, and said, "You will be able to do this at some point. All dragon-touched could do it. Not all dragon-touched could cloud-dance, which I've explained to Daruk numerous times."

Daruk rolled his eyes. "Having two of you to gang up on me is great, have I mentioned that? Three, if you count Loralei."

Before Alaric could spit snark back at him, Kamaishi's head perked up, his eyes alert and shiny. His eyes and ears darted erratically, his tongue sliding in and out like a serpent's.

"Is everything okay?" Alaric asked.

"No," Daruk said and stood up. "Something's coming."

"Go now," Kamaishi said. "Return when you can. I don't like this smell."

They emerged from the trance, sitting in the stone circle. Daruk leapt to his feet, surveying the yard and clearing, but there was nothing to see. It was the same as when they'd entered the trance: warm breeze blowing through the trees, birds calling to each other, smoke coming from the cottage chimney as Loralei made dinner. Two dragonflies buzzed around their heads, wings moving too fast for Alaric to see. He didn't smell anything different about the clearing, but he wasn't as good at detecting scents as Daruk.

"I don't like this," Daruk said. "Kamaishi isn't usually wrong."

Alaric looked around. "Everything seems all right."

"Let's go check on Loralei and make sure."

They started toward the cottage when everything went quiet. The birds stopped chirping. The dragonflies disappeared. Even the chickens weren't squawking. Alaric couldn't hear any insects buzzing.

"Yeah, that's not normal," Alaric said, taking a defensive stance. His scales began to emerge as he reached out with his senses, feeling the area around them.

"Another one? How splendid." The voice sent a million daggers into Alaric's spine and he yelped. Daruk grunted beside him, silver scales crashing through his skin, claws out. Alaric's knees hit the grass and he grabbed his head, trying to dislodge the chilling voice.

"What do you want?" Daruk growled, moving in front of the prone Alaric. How was Daruk still functioning? Alaric could barely move besides keeping his ears covered.

"I came seeking the famous last of the dragon-touched, but it appears I've gotten two-for-one."

Sweating, Alaric managed to look up.

Standing near the cottage was a man in a long dark cloak buttoned up to his throat. A grin stretched across his face, but where his eyes should have been, there was smooth skin, gouged where his eyes used to be. He had no ears that Alaric could see, and his hands were covered with blackened skin. When he looked at the man, all Alaric could feel was fear and pain. There was also the sense that this body wasn't the man's true form, like a shimmering mirage over a monster's maw.

He wanted to run but couldn't. He couldn't do anything. He was helpless. Like a rabbit caught in a snake's spell.

This was no human man.

"Daruk," Alaric managed, trying to stand. His scales had receded.

"Shut up and stay down. It's a celestial. I can feel his power resonating off mine."

Alaric shuddered. A celestial? The things Cypress told him about? The beings older than gods? What was one doing here? And he was looking for Daruk, a dragon-touched.

"If you leave now, I'll forget about the intrusion," Daruk said. Alaric thought his boldness was faked, but Daruk wasn't putting out much of a scent. A true dragon-touched. Alaric must smell awful; he was so frightened.

"Can't we have a civilized conversation?" the celestial asked, spreading his arms in a welcoming gesture. His voice was cutting as a blade. "We are basically brothers. Of a sort." His smile widened, showing enormous teeth. Alaric thought the man might devour them both before they had a chance to run.

"There'll be no talking between us, celestial," Daruk growled. "None of you showed interest in helping me in the past, so I'm not obligated to you."

"That's a pity," the celestial said, shrugging. "I was going to ask you nicely to come with me, but I'm not opposed to violence."

Loralei came out the door with a broom and yelled, "What the hells is taking you two so long? Get in here." She halted when she saw the celestial facing off against Daruk, and he tilted his head far to the side.

"A demigod as well? My spies are so inadequate these days."

Daruk roared and charged at the celestial who jumped away, laughing. Now that he was preoccupied with Daruk, Alaric felt the mental hold break. Maybe that was what Daruk meant by his resonating power. How had Daruk fought against such an onslaught?

Alaric stood and transformed, hardening his entire body. Loralei shouted something at him, throwing down the broom. She raced over to him, not taking her eyes off Daruk and the celestial circling each other.

Daruk snarled with each lunge, but the celestial was fast, dodging every move with ease. It seemed like he was playing with Daruk. And he was enjoying it.

"What is that thing?" Loralei yelled when she reached Alaric's side. "Daruk said it was a celestial! What should we do?"

"A celestial here? Impossible." Loralei licked her lips, and Alaric could tell that she was trying to think of what to do. She couldn't get in the middle of the brawl or risk getting torn apart.

"He's not a god," Alaric said, voice shaking. His scales were trying to retreat again, and it took a massive effort to keep them in place. They were his only protection, and he needed to shield Loralei.

"I've never seen anything move like that," Loralei said.

The celestial caught Daruk as he lunged again, grabbing him by the throat. Daruk writhed in his grip, eyes shining silver.

"I grow tired of this." He tossed Daruk aside like he weighed nothing and advanced toward Alaric and Loralei. "Maybe you'll be easier to persuade if I take them."

"Alaric!" Daruk yelled from the ground, struggling to get back on his feet. "Take Loralei and go! Run!"

"Alaric, is it?" the celestial asked, as though he'd gotten a juicier piece of meat. "The new Sun God's plaything?" He laughed, dark and high-pitched, and Alaric groaned. "The Sun God tamed a dragon? He'll be much easier to deal with now that I've got you."

"No!" Daruk screamed and ran at the celestial. He had no choice but to turn and meet the dragon-touched head-on, fingers on one hand transforming into jagged black chains. Alaric was reminded of Cypress's vines as the chains twisted around Daruk, binding his arms and clinging to his neck. The celestial squeezed and Daruk shrieked, trying to claw and bite the bindings.

"That won't do you much good," tsked the celestial. "Aren't you dragon-touched supposed to be strong?"

The brand on Alaric's back glowed like a star, blazing through the afternoon sun, and it caught the celestial's attention. His smile faltered for a moment, then it returned.

"Ah. That's interesting."

"Go!" Daruk pleaded.

Alaric thought of Bashima. What would Bashima do if Alaric was captured again? He'd burn down the world looking for Alaric, tear down every mountain, drain every ocean. He'd lose himself completely if Alaric didn't return.

"I'm sorry," he whispered. Alaric grabbed Loralei around the waist, braced himself against the ground, then vaulted into the air. Loralei pounded on his hardened arms, crying, yelling at him to go back. She struggled against him, her strength draining his resolve, but they couldn't save Daruk. Whatever that thing was, there was no beating it.

The celestial's laughter followed them into the sky, and he yelled, "Brillant!" But he didn't follow. Alaric was thankful for that. Maybe celestials couldn't fly. Or Daruk was giving him more of a problem than anticipated.

"Alaric Shina! Get your ass back down there now!" Loralei sobbed, her blows ceasing. "We can't leave him. We can't."

Tears ran down her face, landing on Alaric's scales. He released the scales back to his tanned skin.

"He told us to go," Alaric said, voice trembling. "I'm sorry I couldn't do anything. I'm useless."

She didn't answer, sagging in his arms as he flew. Alaric hoped that Bashima was still blocking him. He hadn't felt fear reverberating through their connection, so maybe the Sun God had listened when Alaric said to close himself off completely.

Bashima

"What the fuck is my life? Seriously, Kuroi. What. Is. Fucking. Happening?"

Bashima stormed out of the throne room, the sun setting, his work completed for the day. Kuroi followed, arms behind his back. Through their connection, Bashima could feel Kuroi's irritation. Not with Bashima, at least not yet. Everyone was on edge. They all wanted Alaric to return so things could get back to normal.

He stalked down the hall to the main doors, throwing up a hand signal so they would open. The doors didn't want to listen and stayed shut.

"Fuck! Just open up! It's fine!"

Kuroi tutted beside him. "I told you it wasn't working."

"I'm here now, so open the fucking doors!" He cursed at the temple. He felt the walls humming around him, uncooperative. After a few moments, they accepted the Sun God's order and slowly opened, but only enough to let one person in or out at a time.

"For fuck's sake."

Bashima squeezed through the narrow opening, coming face to face with the Fire God. Cindras stood on the landing, arms crossed, a haughty look slashed across his face.

"First Veles, now you," Bashima growled. "You need to start paying me to babysit your damn kids."

The Fire God didn't try to hide his vexation. Flames burst around his head and massive shoulders as he glared down at Bashima.

"Well?" Bashima asked. "My temple's not a huge fan of yours, so say what you're gonna say and get the hells out of my sight. Oken's not coming out, and you're not coming in."

"May I see my son?" A tremulous voice came from behind the Fire God.

A woman with delicate features and blueish hair emerged from behind the Fire God. Cindras could hardly look at her, as though her very presence pained him, this tiny slip of a woman. Oken's mother.

Bashima's mouth hung open, and Kuroi cleared his throat beside him. Bashima hadn't noticed the god-touched man leave the temple and jumped.

"Master Bashima," Kuroi said. "Might we let the lady in?"

Cindras turned his back on them and looked out over the valley, not intending to enter. Bashima nodded and let the woman pass through the door. The temple sighed as she entered, and she smiled. Bashima followed her inside, dubious of the Fire God's true intentions.

"He's probably at the dinner table," Bashima grumbled, not sure how to address her.

"He always was a punctual boy," she said. "My name is Marlana in case you were wondering."

The air around her carried a coldness, though her serene face was warm and heartbreaking. Bashima wanted to comfort her, tell her that everything would be okay. He saw a lot of her in Oken, her paleness, the quiet that surrounded her. It was unnerving, just like the demigod.

She was one of the rare god-touched who exhibited an incredible power, unaided by a talent with alchemy, which was probably why

Oken was so gifted. With his father the most powerful fire-type god and his mother like this…there was no telling how strong Oken could become.

Bashima led her through the temple. He asked if she'd prefer shifting, but she shook her head, taking in the temple.

"You have a beautiful home," she said, touching a wall as they passed. The ceiling above sparkled with constellations.

"Uh, thank you," Bashima grunted, uncomfortable. No wonder Cindras was so anxious with her near him. She was ethereal and bewildering. And so sad. It came off her in waves.

When they entered the dining room, Oken was seated, waiting patiently for Bashima. The Sun God could tell that Oken missed the green-haired one, though it had only been a day. They'd kept each other entertained, hardly bothering Bashima at all. Oken had gone to his room and hadn't come out after Jace left.

"Oken." The word escaped Marlana's lips like a prayer, and the demigod looked up, shocked.

"Mother?" He stayed seated, timid. "Are you really here?"

Bashima snorted. "I sure hope she is, or I've been talking to a mirage." If he could even call it talking. She was about as chatty as Oken.

Oken stood and strode over, clasping her hands. He was much taller than Marlana but seemed like a child next to her, his face open and innocent. Bashima took a step back. He and his mother had almost no relationship, and when they did meet it was to spit and snarl at each other. He didn't comprehend the tenderness in Marlana's eyes or the hope on Oken's face.

"Do you have time to talk?" she asked, eyes glistening. "We haven't seen each other in a while."

"Not since the summit," Oken said, which made Marlana wince.

"Your father…"

"It's okay, Mom. I'm okay." Oken glanced at Bashima, who had discomfort radiating off his skin. "We can go to my room, Bashima. I can get something to eat later."

"I'll have Shefu save you something," Bashima mumbled, which made Marlana smile again.

"Thank you for taking care of my son."

"Sure." Bashima waved them away and went to sit at his place at the table. They were gone in an instant, and Bashima felt the room's emptiness like a weight pressing on his chest. The vacant chair at the other end of the table mocked him.

Oken

"This is quite lovely," Marlana said of Oken's room. She walked over to his bed and touched the duvet, running her fingers across the fabric. She sat down on the bed and took the stuffed cat from its place on the bedside table. "You kept this?"

"You made him," Oken said, watching her from across the room. She nodded and put the cat back, surveying the rest of the room. Her eyes landed on Kuroi's painting, and she sighed.

"It's kind of the Sun God to let you stay here, but why aren't you with the other one? With green hair. The Forest God."

"Bell is away," Oken said, hands at his side. "He told me to stay here." After Oken betrayed him and ran away to the Temple of the Sun, but he didn't want to admit that to his mother.

Marlana nodded. "Cindras was at the king's temple. I didn't see him, but Cindras mentioned that he was there. Are things well between you two?"

Did she know something was wrong? Why would she ask that?

"We're fine."

Marlana nodded but didn't pry further. "Are you enjoying your time here? The Sun God is…unique."

"He is very strange, but it's fun to tease him." Oken smirked. "He gets very annoyed with me on occasion, but he's never kicked me out."

"What fine qualities in a host," Marlana joked, surprising Oken. He'd never heard her use humor. "He and the Forest God are friends?"

"I wouldn't go that far."

Oken thought about Bell and Bashima and how they interacted. Bashima treated everyone similarly, with exasperation and hostility. But Bell often bore the brunt of his bad tempers.

"They grew up together, and Bell never gives up on him."

"That's nice," his mother said. She seemed wistful, as though part of her wasn't in the room. Maybe the other half of her was with his father.

Oken wondered why his mother stayed with his father, had chosen to become a god-touched instead of finding some peace as a shade.

She spoke again, "The Forest God may have need of you soon, Oken. There are things happening at the king's temple. The god-touched there are distracted and frightened. And I met Resk, the young man staying with you at the Temple of the Forest."

"You did?" Oken was taken aback. Bell had taken Resk to the king's temple? It wasn't like they were bound together by the god-touched ritual like his mother and father.

"Peculiar boy," she said. "He asked about you as well and said that Bell was doing well after the 'incident.'"

Oken flushed and pursed his lips. Marlana tilted her head, inquiring.

"Are you sure you don't want to talk about it?"

Oken slumped onto the bed next to his mother and sighed. "We had a fight. Before I came here."

Marlana took his hand in hers. "That's a natural thing for couples to do."

"We never fought before," he said, pouting. "I didn't like it. But I was so angry."

"That's normal too," she said, giving a gentle laugh. "I'm angry with your father quite often."

Oken took his hand back and said, "Why don't you hate him?"

If the question shocked her, Marlana gave no indication. She smiled her forlorn smile and gazed at Kuroi's painting.

"I never expected much from my life. I was a princess but far down the line of succession, so all I had to look forward to was a life of boredom and service to my family. I could dance, sing, paint, sew, flirt in the courtly manner. The ideal noble lady. Catching a husband would have been easy for me, but that wasn't what I really wanted."

Oken imagined his mother, young and lovely, pining for adventure from her castle home. Feeling like she was trapped. She'd traded one prison for another.

"Don't look so sorry for me," she said and touched his cheek. "Your father isn't an easy person, but in the beginning, he doted on me, brought me gifts, anything I desired. And he was so happy when each of you children were born."

"But it didn't last long," Oken said. His fingers curled into fists, nails digging into his flesh.

"The only way your father knows how to show love is to make sure you'll survive."

"That's…that's bullshit, Mom."

He didn't often curse, but he was thankful he'd learned so many colorful phrases from Bashima. His mother was delusional, trying to make her life seem less awful than it was, to make her relationship with his father not a nightmare.

"I want —"

"I can't listen to you talk about him," Oken said and stood. "He treats you like a servant. Dahlia is the only one who can stand to be around him. Have you even heard from Asher or Iris? In centuries?"

Marlana hung her head and sighed. "My greatest failure was letting him hurt my children. I know I'm a terrible excuse for a mother. I wasn't strong enough for you."

"And you loved him, so you let him do it."

She didn't speak.

"Is he here?" Oken asked.

"He won't bother you," Marlana said, standing and smoothing her dress. "He promised to stay outside and wait until I came out." She went to the door, ready to go. "It's not that I don't hate the things he's done. But he gave me you, so I can't hate him completely."

"I'm sorry too, Mom. That I can't get you out of there."

She was stuck, forever tied to the Fire God. She would have to endure until she decided she'd had enough.

"You should try to make up with your Forest God," she said. "He's very fond of you."

She didn't bother going through the door, simply shifted away, leaving Oken confused.

When had his mother met Bell?

Chapter Eighteen

Jace

Jace shifted inside the Temple of Time's main entrance, and when he landed, he stumbled and fell onto the hard marble. He stared at the cold floor and screamed, closing his eyes against the thick smoke that billowed around him. Fire chased through the temple's halls, nearly at his heels. He could feel it approaching the entrance. What kind of flames were these? They weren't burning out at all, growing, though there was no fuel. That man, the tall slim one. Jace hadn't gotten a clear look in the throne room, but he recalled black hair and strange skin. And the laugh. Jace would never forget the madness in that laugh.

Shako's final blast sent Jace flying away from the throne room doors, and he'd shifted in mid-air, not sure if he'd land in a safe place. Luckily, the fire only singed him, but he could smell burning hair and was having trouble breathing.

Coughing, he slammed through the main entrance doors, which were luckily not barred, hoping that the female shade had gotten Nim back to the Underworld.

Nim hadn't been impressed with that idea, but he told her that he needed to get Shako and couldn't do it if he was worried about her too.

Please Nim, he thought. Please be home safe.

Despite the heat from the temple, a cold blast of sea air hit Jace when he went outside, the salt and briny smell making him sneeze. He thanked the gods again that the main entrance hadn't been closed off. He had no idea why they couldn't shift out of the temple, but he hoped he'd be able to once he got outside. Since Nim and the shade were nowhere in sight, he figured it was possible.

As he surveyed the nearby cliffs, searching for a good place to shift, a massive burst of heat hit him from behind, and Jace flew across the entrance's stone platform, skidding close to the edge.

The God of Time had made sure it was almost impossible to gain entrance to his temple, which left only a small space for visitors to land. Jace braced himself before his legs went over the edge and breathed out hard. The violet flames licked out, engulfing the temple like they meant to consume it whole. The fire didn't move past the white marble, but Jace felt like it was leering at him, hungry. He staggered to his feet, body shaking.

Shako…

There was nothing he could do for his friend, except hope that he'd survived somehow. He'd find a way to get back in after he found help. He wouldn't leave Shako to the mercy of those people.

"Jace!"

Jace spun around and saw a shape running across the cliffs in the distance, hair flying behind him. Then the shape disappeared, and his heart paused. Was that?

His father appeared beside him, wrapped his arms around Jace, and shifted them off the ledge. They landed on the nearby cliff and collapsed to the ground, the wind biting at their skin.

Veles took Jace's face in his hands and yelled, "What were you thinking? Leaving and not telling me where you'd gone?"

His eyes were bloodshot and wild, fear overwhelming in their depths.

"We have to go back for Shako!" Jace said, dissolving into tears. He crumbled into his father, hugging him fiercely, sobbing. Veles's thick beard scratched against his cheek.

"I'm so sorry, Dad. I'm sorry! Did Nim make it back to the Underworld?"

"She's not inside the temple?" Veles asked, the panic leaving his voice for a moment. "Thank the heavens."

"I sent her out with a shade," Jace said, clinging to his father's tunic. "Before the fire got so bad."

Veles put a hand in his son's hair and tried to sooth him. "It'll be okay. You'll be okay."

"Shako's still in there," Jace said, pushing away from Veles. "I left him."

The flames encased the temple, bright, hateful purple against the black cliff. How were they going to get inside? Jace scrambled against his father, trying to stand, but Veles held him fast.

"Let me go!"

"You can't go in there," his father said. "Not until we can put the fire out."

"Please! I can't leave him! Dad, let me go!"

"We need to get away from here," Veles said.

"I can't! What if he makes it out and no one's here to help him? He was doing what you gods wanted him to do!" Jace cursed and struggled to no avail. "We can't abandon him. If you take me away, I'll just come back."

Veles held him for a few minutes until he stopped straining against the embrace, and Jace wept in his arms, whispering, "Please don't make me go."

Soft footsteps approached them, someone small running, and Jace and Veles looked up to find Nim barreling toward them at full speed. She was alone, her hair billowing behind her, having come loose from her bow. She looked fierce and unafraid, and Jace had no idea how she was so strong when they'd almost been kidnapped and only just escaped the blazing temple.

She launched herself at them, knocking them over, and yelled, "Don't you ever do that again! Don't you ever!"

When she hit them, the tears started, and her words were lost in muffled cries. Veles took an unsteady arm away from Jace and pulled Nim in. She burrowed closer, trying to get in the middle. She didn't look hurt, just a few bruises from shifting and bumping into things. Veles sat them up as Nim sobbed.

"Tell me what happened," Veles said, his eyes on Jace over Nim's shivering head.

"I don't know," Jace admitted. "Someone attacked the temple, and they knew exactly what they were doing. We couldn't shift outside, only around inside the temple."

Veles tensed. "Do you know what they wanted?"

"One of them tried to take Nim," Jace said, nodding at his sister. "I'd never seen her before, but she knew we were demigods. Why would they want Nim?"

Nim shuddered between them and continued crying.

"And Shako?"

Jace's breath hitched in his chest. He didn't want the last thing he remembered about his friend to be the terrified look in his eyes.

"He stole the purple fire," Jace said. "It had to be the guy I saw in the throne room...I think they were trying to get in the Locker." He paused and glared at Veles. "They were left alone. Shako and Nim with a bunch of shades. Where was the god who was supposed to watch over them?"

Veles looked away from his son, shame in his eyes. He didn't answer.

"Because Shako's a demigod and doesn't matter, you all forgot about him, right? You're too busy to help him keep the Locker closed, leaving him alone to deal with it, having to touch Chronas's body every day."

Jace ripped himself from his father's grasp and stood, facing the still-burning temple.

"Don't!" Veles said, pulling himself and Nim from the ground. "It's too late."

"You don't know that," Jace said.

"The entire temple is burning. Don't scare your sister."

Jace turned around, and Nim gazed up at him, begging him not to go.

"Nim, where did the shade go that I sent with you?" he asked.

Nim grimaced and bit her lip. "I told her to go to the Underworld and get Papa."

Jace stiffened. The last person he wanted to see was his stepfather. Those judging eyes, the indifferent words. He'd hug Nim and cry over her and make everything about him. Then he'd whisk them away back to the Underworld, Shako an unfortunate casualty.

"I'm not leaving," Jace warned his father. He put power behind his voice, the spidery, coercive tendrils that could work their way into anyone's mind. Even a god's. Jace didn't care that it was forbidden or that his father could easily strike back. Veles's expression was grim, but he nodded.

"You don't have to do that, son," Veles said. "I won't make you leave."

It didn't take long for Niall to find them. Jace sat near the cliff's precipice, watching the flames cascade around the temple, keeping out anyone who might stage a rescue. The man who caused the fire couldn't still be inside. He must have gotten what he came for. How powerful was he to keep this fire going?

Veles stood back with Nim, speaking softly to her.

"You have to save Shako, okay?" she said. "He's Jace's best friend, and he was always really nice to me. I don't want him to be dead."

For some reason, Jace thought of Cabari and wished the god was with him. He used to curl up against Jace like a cat, purring, even when they hadn't had sex. Sometimes they'd lay on Jace's bed, Cabari's warmth spreading into Jace's entire body. Now he wished for Cabari's arms around him, telling him everything would be all right. Not that the Lightning God would do anything like that. He didn't like Shako, who was only a demigod. One more mortal being gone from the world. What was that to a god?

There was a whooshing sound, and Jace hoped for a second that it would be Cabari. Why did he keep torturing himself like this?

"Nim!" Niall yelled, appearing nearby, his long hair tied back. He ran to his daughter and scooped her up into a hug. Nim put her arms around Niall's neck and patted his back, trying to calm him down.

"I'm okay, Papa," she said. "Jace saved me. He used his special power on this woman who wanted to take me away."

Veles's head jerked in Jace's direction, his eyes wide. Jace knew what that look meant: you used your powers without permission. But what was he supposed to do when he was in danger? Let himself and

Nim be taken? Wait for a big, strong god to show up and protect them? Because that hadn't worked so well for Shako.

"My gods, the temple." Niall's voice held frightened awe. "What kind of fire can do this?"

"The really hot kind?" Jace suggested. He stayed sitting on the cold ground and pulled up the harsh grass, twisting it in his fingers.

"Jace…" Niall rarely said his name, but Jace ignored him. He didn't need a lecture right now or a self-righteous comment about staying out of trouble and not using his ability. "I'm sorry."

"Don't worry about it," Jace said without thinking. His automatic response to most everything. Don't worry, you didn't hurt me, I'm tough and can handle it.

The last time he'd spoken to Niall, Jace had said the truth: that he hated him. At least that was how Jace felt in the moment. He didn't want to hate his stepfather, not when Veles loved him so much. It wasn't fair to set them at odds.

"I'm sorry." Niall sat beside him on the cliff's edge and touched his shoulder. Jace moved away, a reflex, not used to the contact. Niall flinched and didn't try to touch him again. "The shade who came to me in the Underworld, she said that you did everything you could to save them."

"Nim's my sister," Jace said, putting his chin on his arms, which laid across his knees. "And I couldn't let the shade be destroyed for us. She deserved a chance too."

Niall threw his arms around Jace, who shrank back, alarmed. Tears ran down his stepfather's face, gratitude written there. Unsure how to act, Jace let Niall embrace him, his body rigid. He glanced at Veles, afraid. Why was Niall acting like this?

His father looked shocked and stood still, as though he was looking at a dream he'd always wished for. Nim clomped over and hugged

Niall, pressing her cheek into his back. Eventually, Veles made his way over and sat next to Jace, draping his arm across his son's shoulder. His body shook, but he held back the tears. Niall was weeping enough for all of them.

Cabari

Hours had passed by the time Cabari heard about the disaster at the Temple of Time. The rumor filtered to him through Alora, who shifted directly to his temple to ask what the hells was going on and if he knew anything.

"What do I care about the Temple of Time?" Cabari had asked. He'd been through the emotional wringer in the last few days and wasn't interested in the white marble monstrosity. He lounged on the couch in his sitting room, head on a pillow, feet up on the table. Alora had shoved his feet off the table and plopped next to him.

"You didn't hear?" Alora asked. "It's been on fire for hours. And the really weird thing, it was purple fire. Have you ever heard of that? They finally found Cindras to put it out."

Cabari sat up. "Is Nim okay? Jace's sister was living there, right?"

"I don't know if she's okay," Alora said. "No one knows anything. Garyn hasn't been answering me since he told me the fire was still going. Bashima and Cypress never bothered to answer me either. And none of the old gods will tell me shit."

"I've got to go."

"Wait! Think about it. What can you do to help? Your power isn't made for something like this. You'll be in the way. And we aren't supposed to know about it."

"Sorry, but I can't just sit here and do nothing."

"You think I don't want to see if they need help? I'm not going to get Garyn in trouble. They'll know he told me about it."

"I'm not asking you to go," Cabari said. "But something weird is going on. It can't all be a coincidence. All those messages Garyn was seeing between the older gods. Cypress hiding away at Vaultus's temple, not wanting Oken with him...we need to find out what's going on."

Alora stood and nodded. "I'm going to head over to Garyn's. He'll be pissed but he'll get over it."

So, the Lightning God found himself back on the freezing cliffs that surrounded the Temple of Time, bereft of almost all life besides hardy, tough grasses. The wind blasted around him, whipping his hair around his head. Alora had been wrong that the fire was still going, but the formerly pristine white temple was covered in ash; Cabari could barely make it out against the dark cliff side. He shaded his eyes from the gusts and looked around.

And saw Jace. That mint-green hair was unmistakable. His heart plummeted to his feet. Jace stood on a nearby cliff with three others; they looked like Veles, Niall, and maybe Nim. Cabari had never met Jace's sister, but her pink hair blew with the wind, and she had her arm around Jace's waist, her head against his arm. They all stared at the temple as though it might do something. Cabari thought it might fall into the sea at this point, if it had been ablaze for hours. He took a step forward.

"Lightning God." A gruff voice behind him.

Cabari spun around, yellow energy coursing through his body and over his skin. The Fire God and a man with large silver wings. Cindras watched him coldly, scowling, but the winged man regarded him with open fascination.

"Cindras," Cabari said, testing what the other god would do. "I suppose you know what's going on?"

"So curious," said the winged man, a gleam in his eyes. "What brings you all the way out here?"

There was no accusation in the man's question, but he made Cabari nervous. Something about him felt wrong.

"Heard there was an emergency. I thought I might be able to help."

"Hmm you 'helped' here the last time, didn't you?" the winged man asked.

The Fire God glared at him with so much contempt that Cabari thought he might be set ablaze.

"I was here, yeah." He needed to be careful. The older god and his strange companion were suspicious of him, and he hadn't even done anything wrong!

"You were about to interrupt Veles and his family," the Fire God said.

Cabari bit the inside of his cheek, but gave Cindras a challenging look. What did he care if Cabari wanted to go and see if they were all right? If Jace was okay?

"And?"

"Leave them be," Cindras growled and turned away. "You'll do them no kindness. They're waiting to see if the other demigod's body turns up. They don't need you butting in."

"The other demigod?"

Shit. Shako. He was at the Temple of Time too. Keeping the Locker shut.

"You've got to be shitting me. The Locker."

The winged man smiled at him, feathers flying from his wings and heading toward the temple. "What about it?"

"Was it destroyed by the fire?"

"Who said there was a fire?" Winged man was sharp. Too quick.

"Is that a secret?" Cabari countered, crossing his arms.

"Not anymore, apparently." The winged man's tone was light and conversational. Cabari imagined that he could talk a person into anything, could coerce the deepest secrets from someone's mind without even trying.

"I know some shades escaped before…when Chronas got taken out. And I'm guessing some other nasty shit too."

"Perceptive," the winged man said, and Cindras snorted.

"Come on, Falkar. We need to go through the temple again, now that it's cooled down."

Falkar. Who the fuck was Falkar? The winged man tipped an imaginary hat to Cabari and followed the Fire God.

"Wait!" Cabari ran up to Cindras, who glowered down at him like he was an insignificant insect. "What fire-type god uses purple fire?"

Falkar's face betrayed nothing. That cool, collected smirk remained on his face.

Cindras ignored Cabari and kept walking.

"You didn't answer me," Cabari said.

"None of them," The Fire God said and stomped away, but Falkar contemplated Cabari for a moment longer.

"You shouldn't make him mad, you know." The man's wings fluttered in the wind, a few more feathers dashing across the cliffs.

"I don't really care."

"The Lightning God, huh?"

Cabari didn't like the way Falkar was giving him the once over. It wasn't because he thought the Lightning God was attractive. Cabari was used to those admiring looks. He tore his eyes away from Falkar and gazed at Jace and his family. If only he could tell Jace that he was sorry.

"Cindras is a jerk, but he's right. Don't bother them now. That demigod who was keeping the Locker closed, Shako? He's probably dead. The kid with the green hair seems pretty broken up about it."

Falkar's grin was gone, and he cocked his head at Cabari. "Why are you so interested?"

Jace beside him, the waterfall crashing nearby, his hesitance, the feel of his hand on Cabari's cheek. Their fingers intertwined as they let their bodies dry off in the pool's dark, mysterious water.

Why did you bring me here?

"Like I said, I just thought I could help." Cabari needed to focus, not get lost in memories that would never be again.

Falkar blinked at him, disbelieving.

"Sometimes the best thing we can do to help is to not do anything." He took off and flew after the Fire God, leaving Cabari to ponder his wisdom.

Chapter Nineteen

Bashima

Bashima paced around the throne room, waiting for Tengu's reply. No one seemed to know what the hells was going on. The Temple of Time had been decimated by a mysterious fire, but whoever knew about it was keeping their normally gossipy mouths shut.

Alora contacted him again from Garyn's temple, worried about Cabari for some reason, mentioning that Garyn was trying to figure out as much as he could without reading too many messages. Which made no sense. The moron usually had no problem sifting through everyone's mail. What had his ass in a bind about this?

So, the Sun God wrote a quick note to Tengu at Vaultus's temple, hoping he'd answer. If there had been another deliberate attack on the Temple of Time, that could only mean that the escaped celestial was on the move.

But what did they want? And was it the same celestial Tengu was worried about?

Veles hadn't told Bashima much after the incident with Chronas; only to watch out for anything strange, if it seemed like they were being watched. Bashima had been afraid that Veles thought his husband would be a target, but nothing was amiss for them besides Alaric's damn rut.

Bashima was tempted to let down his soul connection block, just a little. Needing to feel what his husband was going through was a test of patience for Bashima, one he hoped never to experience again. But Alaric was busy, trying to learn how to be a dragon-touched. He needed to let Alaric be until there was concrete news.

Bashima paced faster, cursing Tengu as he walked in circles.

Tika watched him from beside the throne, sympathetic. The sun would be down soon, and then he could berate Tengu with messages until he answered. She would personally deliver them if needed, though it would pain her to be so far away from the Temple of the Sun. Bashima told her not to be ridiculous, that he'd never ask her to do that. She'd been so patient with him these last weeks, no doubt sick of his ever-changing moods. The day when Alaric's soul blasted him had been difficult, trying to keep himself under control and not reach back out to his husband made him grasp at endurance he didn't know he had.

"I can't do that to him, Tika," he'd said, grasping his head. "It was like being torn apart. I have no idea what he was doing, letting his guard down like that."

"You said it didn't feel like he was in danger," Tika said.

"That's the only reason I didn't go find him."

"He'll be okay, Master Bashima. And when he's finished, he'll come right home."

"I wish I knew how long it would be."

And now he wished he had gone and found his husband.

These rumors and rumblings of an escaped celestial, Tengu going through more training with Vaultus and that old bastard Torstan, and the latest crap about the Temple of Time…too many things were happening at once. Hells, even the Fire God was acting weird. What was his deal with bringing Oken's mother to the temple and not insisting on seeing Oken himself?

And fucking Zebra Head locked himself in his damn room again. Hadn't even bothered to come to dinner after his mother left or lunch the next day. Or another dinner! Was he even eating? Why was Bashima worried if the demigod was eating? Bashima was such a mess without Alaric.

A humming rang through the throne room, stopping Bashima in his tracks, then a clanging went off in his head; the main doors were opening.

NOW WHAT? Who could it possibly be now?

Also…why had the doors opened without his or Kuroi's permission? Damn temple. Always thinking it was being clever.

Kuroi appeared from behind the throne, nodded at Tika, and sighed. "The doors are opening. I'll see what's the matter and come right back. Don't concern yourself, Master Bashima."

Visitors. Parties. Demigods, old gods, new gods. Would his temple be a damn way station forever?

Bashima looked up through the skylight, watching the red leach from the sky as light pinks and purples took over. He closed his eyes and took a deep breath, letting the sun go. His favorite time of day. There was always peace in a sunset.

A tremor went through the temple, and Bashima staggered. Tika let out a soft cry but held onto the throne so she didn't fall. Her eyes met Bashima's, wide and afraid, knowing he hadn't caused the quake.

Kuroi shifted back to the room, clutching two forms: an unconscious auburn-haired woman and Alaric, whose eyes were bloodshot with fatigue.

No. He should have felt his husband come back, even while blocking him. How had his body and mind not known Alaric was so close? And yet, there was no mistaking the fiery red hair, the scar over his eye, that spicy aroma laced with autumn apples.

"Khresh," Alaric whimpered, reaching for him, then he collapsed, falling from Kuroi's grip.

"Master Shina!" Kuroi, panicked, looking from Alaric to the woman in his arms, her face smudged with dirt and tear tracks.

Bashima released his soul block and felt endless exhaustion roll over him, and he fell to his knees by the throne. Alaric wasn't giving him coherent thoughts or emotions, just draining weariness. Bashima threw the block back up before he could faint and crawled to his husband. He dragged Alaric's head into his lap and touched his forehead, his face, his hair, still not believing it was him.

"Who is she?" Bashima croaked out, arms shaking.

"I have no idea," Kuroi said, staring down at the woman. "Shina…he flew at me through the doors and told me to take her, but he couldn't say anything else. It seems like he's been flying for hours."

"That can't be the other dragon-touched," Bashima said. "Alaric said he was male." He brushed his husband's hair back and kissed his forehead. "What happened to you out there, Red?"

Alaric

Alaric woke up in his bed and wondered if it had all been a dream. But for his aching body, he might have believed it.

He'd flown them to the Temple of the Sun without stopping, barely able to stay in the air near the end, but he had to get home, had to get back to Bashima.

He feared for himself and Loralei the entire time, paranoid that the celestial was behind them, that he'd been able to fly after all. Alaric felt phantom fingers on his legs, his shoulders, his neck and fought the screams of terror that wanted to escape. The panic nearly made him fall twice, and Loralei's fearful warnings reverberated through his head.

"We need to rest, Alaric. You can't go on like this."

"I can't stop," he'd said. "We need to tell my husband what happened as soon as possible. I don't know any temples that are closer."

He regretted having to leave his scarf at the cottage. The map might have been able to direct him to a nearby god's temple. The only ones he knew were his home and Cypress's Temple of the Forest, which was farther than the Temple of the Sun.

So, he'd pressed onward for two days, straining from carrying Loralei, thirsty and panting. They were safe in the air, or so he hoped. Nothing came after them or attacked them. They flew over rivers and villages and rolling hills, not speaking much. Loralei slept fitfully the first night and tried to stay awake the second, talking to him, encouraging him since he wouldn't land. Alaric knew she was uncomfortable and sore, but she didn't complain. She wept often, trying to keep quiet and still, not bringing up that they'd left Daruk to be captured. Or killed.

He wanted me, Alaric thought as he pressed himself into the familiar mattress. When my brand lit up, he felt it somehow...

Alaric took a deep breath, inhaling his husband's sage and citrus candles, relishing in the familiarity. Cautiously, he searched for his wards and realized they were down. When did that happen? He'd tried so hard to keep them up, which lessened his reflexes, but he hadn't wanted Bashima to leave the temple and try to find him.

The celestial talking about the Sun God replayed in Alaric's mind over and over. How Bashima would be easier to control if the celestial had Alaric.

Shuddering, Alaric sat up, the duvet falling from his bare chest, the golden chain and piercings hanging like weights. A shadow fell over the bed and a low growl went through the room as something hurtled at Alaric. Something with blond hair and penetrating eyes.

"Khresh —" Alaric's voice was shoved from his chest by the sheer force of Bashima's embrace. His muscular arms wrapped around Alaric's shoulders, face buried into his neck, and Alaric felt hot tears on his skin.

"You are never leaving me again," the Sun God rasped, clinging tighter.

Alaric sighed and nestled into his husband, who moved so he was sitting in Alaric's lap, not letting go. He petted Bashima's hair, running his fingers through it. Gods, he'd miss touching him. He purred deep in his chest and released all the positive energy he could muster, enveloping them in his love. Bashima pressed back with his own emotions, allowing them to join together in a mosaic of pure feeling. The brand glowed on Alaric's back, and Bashima ran his fingers across it, making Alaric rub the claiming mark on his husband's shoulder.

"Better not do that," Bashima said, shuddering, his voice quiet. "You're still weak, and I haven't slept."

Alaric took a deep breath and put up some of his wards, easing Bashima from him, both essence and body. He took in all of his husband: tired orange eyes, pouting mouth, gracefully curving neck that he wanted to nuzzle, his soft black tunic and trousers. Alaric had even missed Bashima's feet, his toenails painted black.

"Zebra Head did that," Bashima grumbled when Alaric touched his toes.

Alaric laughed and said, "It's not like you've never painted them before."

"Yeah, well, no one else ever did it…except you."

Bashima traced Alaric's scar across his forehead then pulled his husband's head down so he could kiss it. Closing his eyes, Alaric breathed in his husband's scent, sweet and rich and smokey. So different from Daruk's. His eyes flew open.

"Is Loralei all right?" he asked, grabbing Bashima's shoulders to make him focus.

Bashima frowned, disappointed to already lose his husband's full attention. "Is that the woman you brought with you?"

Alaric dislodged Bashima and stood from the bed, tossing back the duvet, thankfully wearing trousers. He brushed a hand through his hair and said, "Yeah, is she okay? How long have I been asleep?" Alaric bustled around their bedroom, searching for a tunic.

"Just through the night. She hasn't come out of her room yet," Bashima muttered, still sitting on the bed. Alaric felt the pang through their connection and whirled around, needing to comfort his mate. He sat back down and hugged Bashima, rubbing his back. Damn, that bond worked a little too well sometimes.

"Babe, I'm sorry," he said. "I wish we had time for a proper welcome home. But something happened to the other dragon-touched. I don't even know if he's dead or just captured."

"What?" Bashima sprang from the bed, skin blazing with sun colors. "You were in danger?"

"Why else do you think I flew all the way here?"

"But I couldn't feel you," Bashima said, panicking, "I shut you out and didn't even know!"

"I told you to do that, it's okay," Alaric put up his hands in a peaceful gesture. "I'm glad you couldn't, because it was awful."

Bashima looked away. He was going to hold onto his guilt for a while. "So, who's the woman?"

"Daruk — the other dragon-touched — she's his mate. Loralei. I had to take her with me, otherwise who knows what the celestial would have done."

Bashima's emotions hit Alaric hard: utmost dread and something else he tried to hide...concern for Cypress? Alaric put his wards up, needing to re-focus, and his husband winced from losing the connection.

"A celestial attacked you?" Bashima asked, flexing his hands. His palms glowed.

"That's what Daruk said it was." Alaric shuddered. "It was like a demon out of some story. Looked kind of human but it definitely wasn't. And he came for Daruk, was looking for a dragon-touched."

"Did he see you?" Bashima's hands reached for Alaric's face, his eyes desperate.

Alaric nodded. "He knows who I am, saw me transform and fly off with Loralei." He paused, Bashima's hands shaking on his skin. "He knew my name. When Daruk told me to run, he screamed at me to take Loralei, and he said my name. And the celestial knew I was your husband."

Bashima's head fell, and he let Alaric go, cursing under his breath.

"Do you know who he is? What it is?" Alaric asked, not sure that he wanted to hear the answer.

"There have been a lot of weird things happening since you've been gone," Bashima growled. "It's all starting to make sense, but I'm missing pieces of the whole." He glanced at Alaric and sighed, saying, "The Temple of Time was nearly destroyed, burned from the inside out. I don't know much. No one is saying shit about it besides rumors and guesswork."

Hearing of the Temple of Time was enough to make Alaric blanch. Was Chronas really gone? Could gods be destroyed by fire? He swallowed hard.

"I should go see Loralei. If she's awake, she'll have no idea where she is or what's going on."

"I'll come with you."

"No!" Alaric put a hand up, making Bashima's eyes go wide. Alaric grimaced and said, "I don't want to overwhelm her, and she's not the biggest fan of gods."

Bashima crossed his arms and scowled. "Does she know you're married to one?"

"Don't be like that, of course she knows I'm married to you. I told her and Daruk all about you."

And defended you more than once, but I'm not getting into that any time soon.

"She's a demigod?"

"Yes," Alaric paused and pursed his lips. "She had a shit life, mostly because her goddess mother abandoned her. I know you don't mean her any harm, but she'll be scared. I'll introduce you to her when I've had a chance to warm her to the idea."

"You're more concerned about her than me." His husband's bottom lip stuck out, skin crackling with energy. Was he jealous?

"My first priority is always you," Alaric said. "No matter what. You think it'll do you any good if she freaks out the first time you meet her? If she doesn't trust me because of it?"

Bashima grunted and stalked out to the sitting room. Alaric took a deep breath and remembered that his husband had been without him for weeks, not knowing what he was doing, and that he'd hit Bashima with a massive soul bond strike right before telling him to cut off their connection completely. The Sun God hadn't burst from the temple and come after him. He'd trusted Alaric enough to let him continue learning.

"Hey," he said, following Bashima. "I missed you."

"Oh, you missed me?" Bashima asked, standing by the window, the sun rising behind him. He looked painfully beautiful, even though he was cross with Alaric. Nothing could make him ugly in Alaric's eyes.

"I never want to be away from you again."

Alaric traversed the room and swept his husband into a kiss, which Bashima didn't want to return at first. He tried to push Alaric away, but Alaric could hold his own. He growled into the Sun God's mouth, parting his lips with his tongue, eyes on Bashima's. The Sun God snarled in reply but grabbed his husband's back and pulled him in, locking their hips.

"What did you miss most about me?" Bashima whispered as they pulled apart.

"Every part," Alaric said, kissing his husband's neck. "Your eyes, your lips, your nose." He inhaled deeply, smelling Bashima's arousal. "The way your hair smells."

"That it?" Bashima dragged Alaric's lips to his and opened his mouth but bit Alaric's top lip hard enough to draw blood.

Alaric's dragon brain wanted to take over, his rut instinct still strong, but Alaric had learned how to control part of his urge. Instead of biting back like he wanted, Alaric licked the blood from his lip and grinned at Bashima. If he wanted to be an asshole, Alaric could be one too.

Claws emerged from Alaric's hands and he shredded Bashima's trousers off, grabbed his husband's ass, and hoisted him up onto the windowsill. Surprised, Bashima held onto Alaric's shoulders, fingers digging in. Alaric kissed him again, rough, and ran his hand up

Bashima's shirt, pinching his nipple. Bashima rolled his body forward at Alaric's touch, trying to wrap his legs around Alaric, but he pulled away and knelt, spreading Bashima's legs.

The Sun God was almost fully hard, so Alaric licked along his inner thigh, eyes up, watching his husband's reaction. Bashima glared down at him, pupils blown across his eyes. Alaric adored that Bashima could look so pissed and so in love at the same time. He dragged his claws lightly down Bashima's legs, and his husband hit him with an explosive emotional charge strong enough to break through his defenses. Alaric felt all the yearning, anxiety, and rage that Bashima had held onto for weeks, nearly knocking him off his feet. Bashima's fear that Alaric wouldn't come back was overwhelming. As was his gratitude that Alaric had come back.

Alaric stood and leaned into his husband, whispering in the shell of his ear. "I won't ever leave you again."

And he would try his hardest to keep his word, though someday they might have to part again. Bashima rested his chin on his husband's shoulder, and Alaric reached for his hardened length, stroking him, retracting his claws. Gods, he'd missed touching Bashima. The Sun God jutted his hips forward and murmured but Alaric soothed him, "It's okay, we'll be okay."

Bashima groaned as Alaric's touches increased in speed, fingers tightening, caressing his husband until he was fully hard.

"Keep going," Bashima moaned, and Alaric wanted to do anything for his husband in that moment.

The dragon quieted inside his mind and body, and he hugged Bashima to him as he worked his erection, massaging through the pent-up worry and anger until he felt Bashima tense up. Bashima pumped his hips forward in rhythm with Alaric's touches until he was ready, then he whispered, "I'm coming."

Alaric held onto him until he came. Bashima was crying; Alaric felt hot tears on his neck.

He let go of his husband and knelt once more, licking him clean, purring, sending out his calmest thoughts. When he was finished, Alaric wrapped Bashima's legs around his waist and carried him to their bedroom, the god still crying softly. He set Bashima down on the bed then stripped off his shredded and soiled clothes and climbed into the bed, hugging his husband into his chest so Bashima could rest his head on Alaric's chest.

They lay together for some time before Bashima said, "I'm so sorry, Red."

"It's okay, babe. I wouldn't have married you if I couldn't handle your moody ass."

Bashima shook in Alaric's arms and said, "No, I'm sorry. For all the things I did when you were still human."

Alaric tensed, uncertain where Bashima was going with this. He rubbed Bashima's back and wove their legs together.

"Babe…"

"Jace was here," Bashima interrupted. "He ran away from home or some stupid shit. Came to find Oken. Cabari showed up, didn't know Jace was here, and things got…intense."

Alaric kept silent. He was curious what Jace had been doing there but would ask about that later. Had he and the Lightning God broken up? Alaric needed to focus on his own problems. It was Bashima who needed his attention now. His husband was trying to tell him something important, was building up to it.

"They argued. Cabari grabbed Jace's arm, hurt him…" Bashima's body felt so tense, like he hadn't relaxed in years. He melted into Alaric, his voice full of barely-contained emotion. "I did that to you. I hurt you. I could have killed you." Shuddering sobs wracked Bashima's body, quaking their bed. "Why didn't you leave? It makes no sense. Why did you forgive me?"

Alaric's mind flashed with the memories from that day: Bashima's feral rage, his words like knives, his rough hands on Alaric's body. The pulsing temper-quakes that had shaken the entire temple. Fading sunlight in the stable, the Sun God leaving his sanctuary, trying anything to convince Alaric to stay with him. Alaric remembered the smell of his sweat in the stable, the way Bashima's eyes pleaded, how unsure he was of his decision, the ache to run away and never look back.

Alaric sighed. "I forgave you, because if I hadn't, I definitely would have left." He hugged Bashima, trying to calm his shaking body. "I don't know exactly why I stayed, but I knew it would kill me if I left."

"It would have killed me too," Bashima said. He pulled away from his husband, face covered in tears, his eyes puffy from weeping. "Jace said that he was too good for Cabari. You're way too good for me, but I promise I will love you for all of my life."

Alaric let his wards down and encased Bashima in everything he was feeling, and the Sun God answered, his skin shining with color. Alaric's brand ignited on his back as he leaned in and kissed Bashima, threading his fingers in blond hair.

After staying in bed for longer than they should have, Bashima went to the throne room to refocus his power and start his workday. They'd cleaned each other up, using the urn full of warm water and soft towels from their washing table, memorizing each other's bodies like they'd done so many times before. Bashima didn't mention the new bruises that covered Alaric from his dragon training, but he eyed them with concern. Alaric would tell him everything later. For now, Bashima needed to direct the sun, and Alaric had to talk with Loralei.

Matthias met him near the guest wing, frown lines etched on his face. The shade gave Alaric a quick hug and asked if he was all right.

"Kuroi said you flew too long," Matthias said, chastising Alaric.

"I did." Alaric flexed his arms over his head, stretching the muscles. "But I didn't have a choice. I would have taken more rest, but it wasn't possible."

"Mm," Matthias muttered. "I had someone check on the young woman earlier this morning, but she was still asleep."

Alaric nodded and clasped Matthias's arm. "She's not that young, my friend. You should come in with me. At least she'll have another friendly face. She…doesn't like gods."

"And you brought her here?" Matthias drew back, alarmed. "You do know that your husband is a god? Does she have abilities we need to worry about?"

"Just a little extra strength."

Alaric smacked Matthias on the back and knocked on Loralei's door. It only took her a moment to throw the door open, green eyes shining, fists up. Alaric didn't budge. He smiled at her, seeing that she'd at least used the wash table to clean the dust and dirt from her face. He hated thinking that she was alone and dirty and tired.

"Alaric," she said and dragged him into the room. She tried to close the door, but Matthias followed, squeezing through the gap. Loralei raised a fist at him, but Alaric gripped her hand.

"He's just a shade! It's okay! Ugh. Not 'just a shade.' Sorry Matthias."

"I'd rather she knew I'm not a threat than be offended by something that minor," Matthias said, smirking.

"Did we make it? To your home?" Loralei asked, agitated. Alaric looked around the room. She hadn't touched much, but she'd put on a clean tunic and leggings. Her gingery hair was loose around her shoulders.

"We got here yesterday, around sunset."

"Where is…" She retreated from Alaric and went toward the center of the room, defensive posture in place. She moved like a boxer, much more refined than Alaric's or Daruk's fighting stances.

"Khresh has to work," Alaric said, raising his hands in supplication. "I told him that you needed time to adjust."

"And he'll listen?" scoffed Loralei. "I need to get out of here. I have to get home and find out what happened to Daruk." Anger flared in her eyes, and she scowled at Alaric. "I should never have let you take me away from him."

"I couldn't fight a celestial, and neither could you," Alaric pointed out, and Loralei raised her chin.

"You don't know that."

"Maybe not, but what do you think that thing would have done to you, especially once he found out you're Daruk's mate?" Alaric paused, letting his point sink in. "Daruk told me to run, so I did. If he didn't stand a chance against the celestial, there's no way I would have. He would have swatted me like a fly."

"A celestial?" Matthias asked, alarmed.

"That's what Daruk thought it was. He's the dragon-touched I went to find. Loralei is his mate." Matthias's eyes darted to the claiming bite scar on Loralei's shoulder near her neck, and she glared back at him.

"Did you tell Master Bashima?" Matthias asked.

Loralei snorted. "He makes you call him 'Master?'"

Matthias's lips closed into a thin line, and he said, "Master Bashima doesn't make me do anything. I choose to live here and serve him." He glanced at Alaric. "Shina can attest to that. I should go speak with Kuroi, make sure he doesn't need something." Matthias shifted away.

"It was just a question," Loralei said.

"You didn't have to ask it like that." Alaric rubbed the back of his neck and groaned. His entire body ached, and he had to make Loralei understand that they couldn't go back to her cottage.

"I'm grateful that you saved me," Loralei said, crossing her arms, "but I need to know what happened to Daruk. If anyone should understand that, it's you."

"We need time to recover," Alaric pointed out. "What if that celestial left sentries to watch for us? We can't waltz into a trap."

"Fine," she said. "You can go. I'd rather not look at you right now."

Alaric sighed but left her alone. He would find Matthias and apologize for Loralei's harshness.

Bashima

Their peace didn't last long. At sunset, Bashima stormed from the throne room.

Everything was happening too fast. He'd only just gotten Alaric to himself, and now they were being summoned to a secret meeting at the king's temple. The message was written by Vaultus's god-touched Savos, the creepy asshole, and instructed both Bashima and Alaric to report to the king in two days. He'd added that if Oken was still at the Temple of the Sun that the demigod should accompany them. Nothing else. Just the order to appear.

Tengu never answered him, and Bashima wondered if he was under strict orders not to send messages. It was amazing that he'd smuggled the two scrolls through Cabari, if that was the case.

"It's happening again," Tengu's message had warned. "I have a bad feeling that there will be war before the year is out."

Bashima recalled a blazing sky, bodies everywhere, the former Sun God's merciless laughter…

Bashima stalked down the temple halls to his chambers, wanting to clear his head of as many negative thoughts as he could before he saw Alaric. His husband hadn't bothered him all day; probably spending his time with the demigod woman.

Don't be a jealous prick, he told himself. Alaric isn't even mildly interested in that woman. Keep it together.

The temple buzzed around him, as though anticipating something. Perhaps it knew that Bashima would have to leave soon. Because there wasn't another option. He had to bring Alaric and Oken to the king's temple, which meant his three god-touched would have to go as well. Shit. Kuroi was going to be pissy about it. He'd gotten used to being in the temple, in his own domain. How would he fare when he wasn't the god-touched in charge? Bashima guessed, poorly. Shefu and Draiden wouldn't like it either, but Bashima had no choice. The royal temple was too far away to stretch their bond.

He had to break the news to his husband and Oken. Dammit. The demigod still hadn't stirred from his room, probably didn't know Alaric was back. Blowing a thick blast of air out his nose, Bashima stopped in front of Oken's door. Might as well bring him along. He knocked loudly.

"Zebra Head! Time to stop moping! Alaric's home!"

"Go away."

Had the demigod just told the Sun God to "go away?" In his own temple? In the room he let the demigod sleep in?

"Don't make me come in there and drag your ass out."

"You won't."

Calm. Calm. Calm. He was calm. He didn't want to blast down the door and beat the shit out of the demigod.

"Vaultus has summoned us to his temple," he growled, knocking again. "We have to go in two days."

"No, I don't."

That monotone voice had always irked Bashima, so lacking in feeling, an air of superiority about it.

"You're named in the message, so you're going! End of discussion!"

Bashima smacked his palm on the door once more then stalked to his chambers, muttering.

"Gods dammit, what the fuck am I supposed to do if he won't come out? Fuck. Fuck. Fuck."

"What's with the shouting?" His husband stuck his head out their door, curious. He'd spiked up his hair and braided it, which he hadn't done in a long time, giving him a fiercer countenance.

"Zebra Head won't come out," Bashima said, pushing past Alaric. He went to the sitting room and slumped on the couch. He held out the unfurled scroll to his husband, who'd followed him inside. Alaric's eyes widened as he read then he turned the scroll over. "That's it? No reason?"

"Nothing." Bashima crossed his arms and huffed. "Haven't gotten a summons like that in thousands of years. Not since…"

"You okay, babe?" Alaric sat down beside him, hand resting on Bashima's knee.

"The last time the gods were called and it wasn't for a summit, a lot of people got hurt, some died."

"A battle?"

"You could call it that. It wasn't just one battle. Started small, people disappearing, picking us off one by one, shit like that. The old Sun God, Malrias, he formed an army of shades and demigods, promised them freedom or whatever. As if he'd really free them. Fucking idiots."

Bashima put his head back, resting it on the back of the couch. "Gods can't die. I've told you that so many times. But you know there are worse things than dying." He trailed off, not wanting to make his husband think of the Time God. "Vaultus had to promote a lot of new gods after that. It's how I got my job. Most of the younger gods took over from older ones who…"

"Couldn't do the work anymore?" Alaric asked as he pulled Bashima's hand onto his knee and threaded their fingers together. "You don't have to talk about it if you don't want to."

Bashima looked away. His husband was too perfect, so understanding and accommodating. If it were him, he'd be demanding an explanation. Or at least vow to destroy whatever was making his husband upset.

"Why won't Oken come out of his room?"

"Hells if I know," Bashima said. "After Jace left, he got quiet. Then his mom showed up."

"What?" Alaric exclaimed.

"I know, weird. After she left — fucking Fire God was here too, but he didn't try to get in — Oken locked himself in."

"Is that why you were yelling at his door?" Alaric held out the scroll and Bashima nodded. "If he doesn't want to go…"

"He doesn't have a choice," Bashima grunted. "We don't either. Besides, if something's coming, I want to know exactly what to expect."

"Want me to talk to him?"

"It should be me, since he's in my temple. But if you want to come along it couldn't hurt."

Alaric grinned and kissed Bashima's nose.

"Anything to help."

"I'd prefer not to, thank you."

Bashima fumed at the closed door, losing his temper. Alaric took his hand and rubbed the knuckles, sending him shining encouragement.

"Zebra — Oken," Bashima said, after his husband gave him a look. "Can you please let us in so we can talk to you. Alaric is here."

"Welcome home," Oken said, but the door didn't budge.

"He's standing right there," Bashima said through clenched teeth, and his husband snorted. "It's not funny. Eventually I'll have to go in there and get him out."

"Let me try." Alaric said. "Oken? Is something wrong? Khresh said Jace was here…and your mom? Do you want to talk about it?"

Silence.

"He's being stubborn," Bashima grumbled, but the door opened slightly, a turquoise eye gazing out at them. Bashima crossed his arms and looked away, huffing, but Alaric grinned his sharp-toothed smile and rubbed the back of his hair.

"Are you okay?" Alaric asked.

"Not really."

"Can we come in?"

Oken took a moment to think, probably going to close the door in their faces. Bashima recalled Tengu stuck to the ceiling in his temple and thought maybe they should leave the demigod alone. Then, the eye disappeared and they heard Oken retreating into his room, but the door remained ajar.

"Finally," Bashima said, throwing up his hands.

"Don't be mean," Alaric said. "In fact, maybe don't talk."

Bashima pushed his bottom lip out, eye twitching. Alaric leaned in and kissed his nose then went into Oken's room. Following him in, the Sun God muttered under his breath.

What the hells did Alaric mean, don't talk?

Oken sat in a chair in his sitting room, staring out the window into the twilit sky. Maybe Alaric was right. He shouldn't try to make someone feel better; it wasn't in his skill set. The demigod was unreadable as always, but locking himself in his room was a new phenomenon. Oken enjoyed spending time with people, torturing them with his presence, so why was he secluding himself?

Alaric sat next to Oken on the couch and leaned forward on his knees. So open, so willing to let people talk to him. Bashima felt like his husband could get anyone to speak with him.

"You did your hair," Oken said.

"Oh, yeah." Alaric touched the red braids. "Hadn't done it in a while."

"Looks nice. I like all the braids."

"Oken," Alaric said. "What's going on?"

The demigod looked from Alaric to Bashima, eyes fathomless. Bashima let his gaze dart around the room so he didn't have to look at those eyes.

"I don't understand people," Oken said. "You all do strange things, say things to each other that hurt. Or you avoid talking about important things."

Alaric gazed at Bashima, biting his lip. How was he supposed to explain why anyone did anything? There was no rhyme or reason most of the time. People, whether gods or otherwise, did things that defied logic. Bashima still didn't know why his husband was with him, after everything he'd done to push the redhead away, and now Bashima was a clingy mess. Hardly the most appealing person in the world.

"Is this about your mom?" Alaric asked. "Bashima said she was here."

"She loves my father," Oken said, with disbelief in his eyes. "How can she love him when he did awful things to me? To my brother and sisters?"

Alaric opened his mouth but no words came out. Bashima was stunned by Oken's candid questions. The demigod didn't bother waiting for them to answer an impossible query.

"Cabari hurt Jace. After Jace said something he knew would hurt Cabari."

Oken's hands shook as he looked at them, and a tear ran down his cheek. Bashima could barely stand to look at him, the scar standing out against his pale skin.

"I don't know why people hurt other people," Alaric said. "Especially people they love. I try not to do it, ya know?" He patted Oken's knee, but the demigod pulled away.

"Bell doesn't want to marry me," he said, holding Alaric's gaze. "He won't tell me why. It has to be me, right? He's a wonderful person, so maybe he sees something in me that's not right."

"Ugh." Bashima couldn't stand hearing Tengu complimented that much. "Tengu isn't that great."

Alaric glared at him. "I thought I told you not to talk."

"It's the truth. Zebra Head is way easier to get along with than fucking Tengu." Bashima crossed his arms, rolling his eyes. "It's stupid to think he did something wrong when Tengu's just a fucking coward."

Oken's eyes blazed at the Sun God. "Bell is not a coward."

"Oh yeah? Then why won't he talk to you instead of blowing you off, hoping you'll forget or get over it or whatever?"

Alaric shook his head a fraction of an inch. If Oken got mad, so what? Maybe he needed a kick in the ass.

"Why do you even want to marry him when he's such a dickless chicken?"

Oken moved with incredible speed, getting in Bashima's face, ice running up his arm.

"Take that back!"

Alaric growled, and Bashima saw his clawed hands grab Oken's shoulders and rip him backwards.

Shit! The damn mating thing!

"Alaric! Stop!"

His husband hadn't completely transformed, but his eyes glimmered crimson and the brand glowed on his back like a signal fire. He breathed hard, glaring down at Oken, who he'd thrown on the couch. Oken stared back, ice covering the couch where he'd landed, his scowl a jagged gash.

"Both of you need to calm the fuck down," Bashima said, groaning. His husband's head spun toward him, and Alaric was at his side in an instant, sniffing at him.

"Are you okay?" Alaric asked, voice a whine.

"I'm fine! Gods, why are you smelling me?"

Oken snorted from the couch, and Alaric blushed, realizing how he'd behaved.

"Sorry, Oken," he said. "I guess I need a few more rounds of training."

Oken shook his head and sighed. He said, "You two make it look so easy. Like your love can't be contained. And you fit together like two pieces of a very confusing puzzle. Jace said something to me, that Bell and I were a perfect couple. But what if that was all on the surface? What if it's not strong all the way through?"

"Fuck," Bashima said "Is that what you're worried about? I've known that moron for a really long time, and he's never given as much a shit about anyone besides you." Bashima wanted to tell Oken about his soul bond with Tengu, but that wasn't his job. "He wouldn't be with you if he didn't want to be. He's not that nice."

Oken's eyes were wide in surprise. He looked so young, and Bashima cursed Tengu for bringing the demigod to his temple. Caring about people was too hard.

"And your dad's an asshole," Bashima said, unable to stop talking. "And you can't control how your mom feels. It's stupid, but at least you don't have to live with them anymore. Ha! You're stuck with Tengu."

"At the moment, I'm stuck with you," Oken said. "I still don't understand."

"Neither do we," Alaric said, cutting off Bashima from giving more advice or opinions. "People aren't easy to figure out. It's tough most days to understand why they act a certain way then completely change the next day."

He sat next to Oken and jumped a little at the cold. Oken apologized as he got rid of the ice, and Alaric continued, "Bashima and I aren't perfect. You and Cypress aren't perfect. There's no such thing as a perfect couple. You've gotta figure out how to be together, if it makes sense to stay together."

Oken nodded. Bashima could tell that he was trying his best to listen, but words only did so much. Especially when the words weren't coming from the person he actually wanted to talk to.

"The summons, to the king's temple," Bashima said. "It sucks, but we need to go. Tengu will be there and you can talk to him. Or not. It's up to you. But you have to go."

"I know," Oken whispered. "I'm afraid of what they'll ask me to do."

"What? Why?" Alaric asked, alarmed. He looked at Bashima, who shrugged. He had no idea what the demigod was talking about.

Oken took a small scroll from his pocket. "Bell told me to stay at the Temple of the Sun, if at all possible. He's worried that the king will ask me to do something dangerous."

"That's what the rest of the message said?" Bashima growled.

"And some other private things." Was Oken blushing? "He said that I should be careful what I agree to do, even for the king."

Chapter Twenty

Cypress

Cypress glanced at Vaultus, trying to gauge how weary the king was. Since he'd transferred the last of the celestial strength, the king was able to keep up his ruse for only a few hours. There would be no more battles for Vaultus, and he knew it. Cypress caught the king staring at him during meals, his eyes glimmering with sadness, and he hoped his stepfather didn't regret giving away his power. Cypress didn't feel different. It had taken a long time for the first celestial-given power to awaken in him. Perhaps it wouldn't even get a chance to emerge this time.

They waited for the first arrivals, those who'd been summoned to the war council. Not that the younger gods knew why they were meeting. Savos sent out the messages with little detail, and Cypress knew Bashima would be fuming.

He hadn't been able to send more notes since his last two, which he'd sent to Cabari to keep Torstan off his scent. The celestial knew to watch for anything going to the Temple of the Sun, and he would have

356

instructed the shades to destroy any messages addressed to the Sun God. The shade in charge of the post had given Cypress an odd look, but the Lightning God wasn't on the "do not send" list, so he ignored Torstan's mail embargo. Except now the Forest God wasn't allowed to send anything.

He asked if Bashima could come a day earlier than the other gods, and Torstan had rolled his eyes but allowed it. The Sun God couldn't stop their deliberations, couldn't stop the other gods from answering the summons, even if he wanted to.

Cypress had no doubt that Bashima would be against open war with the celestial. He was an excellent fighter, but the last conflict with the former Sun God cost their world too much, and Bashima had his own temple to protect, his own people to worry about. Cypress would have to make him understand that this fight was to protect everyone. He hoped that Shina might be able to push that point home. Though he was new to the world of the gods, Shina had an innate sense of duty; he would talk Bashima into at least hearing the king out.

Savos pushed through the throne room doors, indubitable frown in place, his eyes glowing, and he led the Sun God and his husband inside.

Bashima was dressed for travel, his cloak drawn around his throat, heavy boots for the marshy land that surrounded Vaultus's temple, and a hood covering his blond hair. The hood fell back as he entered, Shina at his side, red hair set in commanding spikes and intricate braids. He smiled whereas Bashima scowled, crimson eyes watchful and curious. He wasn't as bundled up as Bashima, arms bare, but his dragon blood kept him warm no matter the climate. Cypress hadn't seen Shina since he'd gone on his dragon-touched search mission, and he was a little surprised to see him back already. But he appeared more confident as he stood tall with the Sun God. They would all need to talk in private later.

Torstan cleared his throat beside Vaultus, who sat in his throne. Hastia was seated next to him, as always, and she smiled at Bashima and Shina. At least the first arrivals were people she knew and loved. This council would be stressful enough for her.

"Bashima, my boy!" Vaultus said and stood, arms outstretched. The Sun God couldn't contain a small smile for the king, and he approached the throne, his husband steadfast beside him.

"You two are such a striking pair," Vaultus added, "It seems married life agrees with our Sun God."

Bashima rolled his eyes as he stood before Vaultus and accepted a hug. Shina grinned as Vaultus pulled him into an embrace as well, his body creaking from the king's strength. As they moved back, Shina glanced at Cypress then motioned behind him, inclining his head.

Oken stood in the throne room doorway. His feet moving of their own accord, Cypress raced past everyone and up to Oken, throwing his arms around the demigod's neck. Why did he come? Cypress warned him to stay at the Temple of the Sun.

He heard Torstan snort and say, "So, that's an Oken."

Oken's body stiffened, and he grasped the Forest God's arms, shifting them away.

And into Cypress's bedroom. Cypress didn't bother with a hello. He pulled Oken's lips to his and kissed him like they'd been apart for centuries, hard enough to bruise. Oken kissed him back, hands searching Cypress's back, fingers scraping against his heavy tunic. It felt like they were frozen in time together for a moment, just them with no worries from the outside world. Oken didn't let Cypress kiss him for long. He pushed the Forest God away, his face a mystery, his soul blocked off, even when Cypress sent an inquisitive tendril of his own soul outward.

"I'm still mad at you," Oken said. He shoved off his trousers and kicked them away, ripping his tunic off as well. Cypress sputtered where he stood. What was he supposed to say? Should he also get naked? Oken said, "Well? Take your clothes off."

"Oken..."

The demigod marched over to him and pulled his tunic off, glaring at the offending trousers, which Cypress quickly pushed down and kicked off. Oken was dead serious about whatever he planned to do, which excited Cypress to no end. He'd started getting hard the second he'd seen Oken, so he was well on his way to being ready.

Oken got in his space, towering over the Forest God, his eyes blazing. He said, "Lay down on the floor."

"Okay..."

"No talking. I'm going to ride you until I come."

Cypress's bottom lip quivered. This wasn't how he'd pictured their reunion, but it was better than being stuck to the ceiling with ice. He tried not to think about that. He might say something stupid, and he really wanted to have sex. They would be talking about it after. Maybe.

He lay down on the soft rug near his bed — why couldn't they use the damn bed? Not that he would question Oken — and Oken descended on him, kneeling over Cypress's legs, stroking his cock, getting it how he wanted it. When Cypress tried to reach for the demigod's thigh, Oken smacked his hand away. No touching either apparently. Cypress fisted his hands at his sides and gulped.

"Don't worry," Oken said, "I'm prepared already."

Before Cypress could protest, Oken closed his eyes as he sheathed himself, and Cypress's fingernails dug into the carpet. Oken's warm walls slid and constricted around his length as the demigod slid himself up and down, breathing heavily, eyes still closed. Cypress wanted Oken to look at him, give him any indication that he was doing this because he wanted him, not just to get off.

It felt so good to be this close to Oken again, but he seemed far away. Cypress resisted reaching out again.

He doesn't want to hear you talk, so he definitely doesn't need your touch. This is all your fault...

Oken started rubbing himself, groaning at the sensation as he touched himself and rode Cypress, faster and faster. Neither of them had had sex in weeks, so it probably wouldn't take Oken long to finish.

Tears formed in Cypress's eyes, but he pulled them back and closed his eyes. He couldn't look at Oken like this. His back and ass dug into the rug, and he wanted to escape the discomfort, escape the pain in his heart. Oken was doing this because of Cypress, because he couldn't be honest. Cypress still didn't know what he wanted, but it definitely wasn't this disconnected mess. He'd give anything to go back to the night where Oken asked him why they weren't married. He'd make sure Oken knew how much he was loved.

"Bell," Oken said, whispering. "We're floating."

Cypress's eyes shot open, and Oken was gazing to the side, thighs gripped tight against the Forest God's body. Opening his fists, Cypress reached out, but the soft carpet wasn't there. Nothing was there. Fuck! What was happening? They weren't that far off the floor, but there was air between them and the rug, and Oken's feet couldn't reach the floor.

Oken cocked his head to the side and said, "This is new."

"Shit," Bell muttered. "Must be from the celestials."

He wasn't sure how to get down without jarring his dick in the process. If they fell to the floor, it wouldn't hurt too much, perhaps. Cypress wasn't willing to bet on Oken's reflexes, and he might shoot them into the floor instead of landing gently.

Oken stayed silent while Cypress tried to figure it out. Oken had been with Cypress when the vines first manifested, when Cypress nearly went through a ceiling by jumping. Oken had been there for everything. Cypress had the power for three thousand years, but the strength didn't come until he met Oken. Something in Cypress's mind awakened then, a primal urge to protect. Maybe that's why the powers had slept: they weren't needed until Cypress had something he wanted to fight for.

And now Oken was slipping away from him.

Cypress locked his eye's on Oken's, pleading for him to say something. He sent out another bit of his soul, hoping to coax Oken out. Not that he would know what Cypress was trying to do, because he hadn't shared that with the demigod either. He was so stupid.

Help me.

Oken sighed and said, "It's okay, Bell. Just let go."

The Forest God let the tears fall, and Oken looked away. Concentrating on not falling, Cypress lowered them to the rug, breathing fast, sweat beading on his forehead. Oken's feet touched, and he grabbed Cypress's hips, leveling them out, helping Cypress to the floor. When they were down, he pulled himself away and staggered to the bed.

"I can remember almost every time you've touched me," Oken said, avoiding the Forest God on the floor. "And I used to count your freckles, but there are so many, I could never get them all. So, I decided that I'd try and kiss them. I thought it would take a thousand years. I'm still not done finding them."

Cypress covered his eyes with a hand, weeping. This felt so final, like Oken was letting him go. No emotions came from Oken; Cypress couldn't feel a thing. If it was over, he had to let Oken leave. There would be no begging, no pleading. He couldn't do that to Oken. It wouldn't be fair.

"I can survive without you," Oken said, conviction in his words. "But I don't want to."

Cypress shot to his feet and grabbed Oken, his instincts overwhelming his good sense. Oken could blast him away, ice or fire, and he would deserve it. Cypress would take the burns if that's what was meant to happen, but Oken didn't shove him away. The air didn't turn icy with his discontent. He took Cypress's face in his hands, wiped away the tears, and dipped forward to kiss him, hands in messy green hair. Leaves went everywhere. He broke away and turned around, facing the bed and put Cypress's hands around his waist, drawing them lower.

Green light flew across Cypress's body, and he couldn't contain it. He bent Oken over the bed, caressing and kissing down his spine, spreading the demigod's legs further. Oken cried out in pleasure, and Cypress clenched his teeth. Go slow, don't hurt him.

I don't think you can hurt me, Bell...

He leaned into each thrust, going slowly, taking his time. Oken braced himself and moved his hips in time with Cypress, taking everything, sighing with relief, as though he'd missed the closeness too. Cypress knew he'd hit the right rhythm when Oken shuddered beneath him and tensed, so he didn't stop. Oken had been close before, so it was easy bringing him to climax. His fists bunched in the duvet as he came, and he said Cypress's name. When he did, Cypress felt the heat growing inside release, and he thrust inside Oken once more, clinging to the demigod's back.

Spent and feeling boneless, they collapsed onto the floor in a heap. Cypress smoothed Oken's hair away from his forehead, showing the dark red scar and gleaming turquoise eyes. Oken gazed up at him, still closed off. Cypress had no idea what he was feeling.

"This doesn't change anything," Oken said. "I don't want to be without you, but I can't be with you right now either."

"Then why did you say that?"

Oken could survive without the Forest God, but he didn't want to. That's what he'd said, right? Didn't that mean that Oken wanted them to stay together?

"We both needed this," Oken said and moved away. He went and grabbed a towel from the washing table in the corner and wiped himself down. "I meant what I said. I've meant everything I've said. I just want you to be honest with me."

Cypress opened and closed his mouth. Before he could confess everything, let the truth fall from his lips like rain, an image flashed through his mind: Oken rampaging through a battlefield, face calm, his ice and fire decimating people left and right, not caring if they were ally or enemy. That was what was coming, what Vaultus probably expected. Unleashing Oken would be perilous, but it might help achieve victory. It's what Oken's father would want, what he'd worked for: his glorious creation devastating the world. No matter what, Oken would survive, and he'd try to protect Cypress while he was surviving.

It would destroy him.

Cypress swallowed and said, "Vaultus wants me to lead everyone once he's gone. And he thinks it will be soon. Something bad is coming, and I'm not ready. None of us are ready."

"Even if we're not together, I won't let anything happen to you."

Oken's utter conviction scared the Forest God more than anything. What if Cypress fell against the celestial? What if eternal sleep was all his future held? He couldn't tie Oken to him. He couldn't tell him about their soul bond. He couldn't marry him. Oken would remain at his side forever, even if the Forest God was no longer really there. He'd become a living ghost.

"I want you to go away," Cypress said, and Oken's eyes widened. Not what he'd been expecting. "Run away from this and don't look back."

Oken stalked toward Cypress and slapped him across the cheek. Shocked, Cypress touched his face, the swelling already starting. Oken collected his clothes and shifted out of the room, hopefully to the baths where he could get dressed away from prying eyes. Cypress closed his eyes and wished he'd never agreed to accept Vaultus's offered gifts.

Jace stared around the throne room, holding his breath. The king's temple was full of light and opulence, much different from the Underworld or the Temple of the Sun. Veles and Bashima preferred simplicity, whereas Vaultus couldn't get enough statues and greenery inside his halls. The throne room was no different: dozens of intricate, realistic statues made of bronze, gold, and stone; flowers erupting from ceramic vases, no doubt furnished by his wife; ornate incense diffusers that filled the room with a pleasant, masculine scent.

A massive conference table sat in the middle of the room, two large chairs at the head for Vaultus and his wife. The table held enough space for forty gods, but Jace wasn't certain how many were invited. He wasn't sure why he'd been summoned, but Veles guessed it had to do with the attack on the Temple of Time, something Jace wasn't ready to discuss.

They didn't find much inside the Temple of Time once Cindras subdued the flames. It was a burnt husk; everything not made of marble reduced to dust and cinders. Jace secretly hoped the woman he'd coerced had gotten out. He was against killing someone, even if she had been trying to kidnap Nim.

The entire Locker was destroyed, and they didn't know if the intruders managed to escape with prisoners, or if that was their mission. The Locker was a massive empty space, all the transparent cells gone, no bodies. Cindras said the fire was hot enough to reduce a demigod body to ashes, but that a god's body would be left intact. So, Chronas's body had been taken, and any gods that had been kept there.

There was no sign of Shako, no remains. Not that his whereabouts were a priority.

The Fire God told Jace of Shako's fate as he stood on the desolate cliff with his family, Cindras gruff but not without sympathy. He at least pretended that it was a loss, and said that Shako was brave to stand his ground against such a strong foe.

It meant nothing.

If only the god who was supposed to be watching over the temple had been there. They couldn't find her anywhere, Rozlyn, one of the Earth Elementals. Her distraught husband didn't know what happened. She was due to return home after her week of watching the two demigods and hadn't sent word that she was leaving the temple.

Nim, unfortunately, wasn't much help. The gods never told her anything, only greeting her when they arrived and left. Rozlyn hadn't bothered to say good-bye, but Nim said she was nice, so Veles expected that she'd been compromised somehow. Another missing person.

One of Vaultus's god-touched led Veles and Niall to the table, and Veles nodded at Jace to follow. They sat close to the table's head, putting Jace between them. Niall had been strangely protective over Jace since the fire and had argued with Veles that Jace shouldn't have to accept the summons. He was just a child. Jace wanted to agree with him, but he also wanted to help.

His father and stepfather were anxious, wondering what Vaultus was up to. They shared conspiratorial glances whenever Jace pried too far, and they changed the subject. So, they at least knew something was up. There hadn't been a summons like this in ages. They could barely contain their anxiety.

He'd overheard them talking the night before they left, getting everything in order for the trip. Luckily, the king's temple wasn't too far from the Underworld, so Veles's god-touched could stay and do their work, but there were still issues. Vaultus requested that Nim come as well, but that he understood if they weren't comfortable with it.

"Absolutely not," Niall had said, throwing an extra tunic into his bag. "It's bad enough that Jace has to go. Get eaten alive by the rest of the old gods. What is Vaultus thinking?"

"That this is an emergency and he needs every piece of information he can get," Veles said, grim.

"I don't give a shit if the damn sky is falling. Asking children to do this is ridiculous."

"Jace isn't a child anymore," Veles said, trying to keep his voice low. "He's expected to follow the rules, just like us. It's nice to see you like this, though, in his corner."

"He's still a sullen little shit," Niall said, snorting. "But I suppose he's our sullen little shit."

Now, he was seated between them, Veles's sunken eyes surveying the gods around the table, Niall chatting animatedly with Mo, the God of Food and Wine, beside him.

Almost every seat was filled, and Jace recognized most of them from the summit: the Gods of Peace and War, Desh and Raphe, partners in everything; Rizu, the Water Goddess, with her was Insjo, the Goddess of Lakes, with long green hair and large eyes that rarely blinked; Vesper, the Air Goddess, who waved at Jace, smiling; Alora and Garyn, who acknowledged him though seemed surprised he was there.

Bashima and Shina entered last with Oken, and Jace almost stood up. Vaultus even called Oken! At least there was another demigod with him, probably here because of Cypress. Where was the Forest God, anyway? Waiting to come in with the king and queen?

Oken ignored his seat and went to Jace. The Sun God nodded at Jace, and Shina gave him a massive smile. His hair was spiked up and impressively braided, making him a threatening presence. At least Shina was back; no need to worry about him being far away on whatever mysterious errand he'd been undertaking.

"Jace, I'm glad you're all right," Oken said, coming up behind him. Jace stood and moved away from the table, his father's eyes not leaving him.

"Do you know why we've been called here?" Jace whispered. "When did you get here?"

"Just yesterday. Bashima wanted to get here a day early so he could talk to Bell. Not that they've let him. Something bad happened, or is going to happen. Bell didn't...tell me either."

Oken averted his eyes and looked at the conference table, perhaps searching for his partner.

"Great, so we're in the dark." Jace pushed his lips into a thin line and said, "Is everything okay with Cypress? And you?"

"Bell told me to leave," Oken said, hardly loud enough for Jace to hear. "He thinks it's dangerous for me to be here. But I'm not going anywhere. I want to know what's going on."

Jace nodded then heard his father clear his throat. Veles beckoned him back to the table, and Jace noticed that some of the other gods were watching him and Oken. Demigods at godly events were too unusual not to observe.

Alora whispered something to Garyn, who nodded. Their eyes kept darting to the throne room doors, and there was an empty chair beside Alora.

"We better sit down," Jace said. "Stick with Bashima, okay? I have a really bad feeling about this."

"I certainly wasn't going to sit with my father."

Oken took his seat next to Shina, who patted his arm, encouraging. Bashima's eyes wandered around the table, his familiar scowl set in place. He looked like he might spring up onto the table at the slightest provocation. They were seated across the table from Jace and his father and stepfather, so at least Jace had some friendly faces to look at. This meeting was sure to devolve into gods arguing and hurling insults at each other. He was glad of his place between Veles and Niall.

Vaultus entered the throne room at last, and everyone stood, Veles pulling Jace up by the sleeve. He was more nervous than Jace had ever seen him, jaw clenched, and he held onto Jace's sleeve for a while before letting go.

Queen Hastia wasn't with Vaultus, which sent muttering up and down the table. At his side instead were the Fire God, Cypress, and two figures Jace didn't recognize. One was an elderly man with bright eyes and long hair tied in a ponytail, the other a handsome man with large silver wings and hair that shimmered like rose gold. Neither of them sat at the table. They situated themselves off to the side and looked over the table, perhaps checking that everyone had obeyed the summons.

Cindras terrified Jace, with his massive shoulders and icy glares. He stood at the chair to Vaultus's right, and Cypress, who looked like he might throw up, stood to the left. He wasn't with Vaultus at the head; Queen Hastia's chair remained empty. The king glanced at the queen's place, blinked, and finally sat. There was a weight about him, his shoulders slightly sagging, his hair not as shiny, eyes dimmed. It was like he'd aged a thousand years.

What the hells was going on?

Before everyone sat, the throne room doors burst open. Heads turned to watch the Lightning God enter, wearing a determined smirk, yellow energy crackling over his body.

"Sorry I'm late," he said, sauntering to his place beside Alora. Jace couldn't breathe. He'd hoped Cabari wouldn't be at the meeting, and he could tell that his father was less than pleased to see the Lightning God. Veles's hands became fists at his sides, and Jace felt Niall take in a quick breath and poke his husband behind Jace's back, warning him.

When he was in his place, Cabari finally noticed Jace, and a flush formed on his cheeks. Static electricity coursed over the table, and some of the gods squawked in irritation. The Lightning God yanked his hands away from the table, and Alora tried not to laugh, shaking where she stood. She leaned over and whispered something to Cabari, who flushed. Garyn glanced at Jace then quickly away.

Let them laugh at me, Jace thought. It's only one meeting. I can do this.

"I'm going to murder him," Veles whispered under his breath.

"Dad, it's fine," Jace said, leaning close to him so no one could hear.

But it most certainly wasn't fine.

Seeing the Lightning God was the last thing Jace needed. Cabari was going to hear his story, if that's why Vaultus had summoned him, hear about Shako, and Jace couldn't bear to see the Lightning God's smug face. At least he didn't look happy to see Jace either, flustered and rearranging his jacket.

"Now that we're all here," Vaultus said, a reprimand in his tone, "we can begin."

He motioned for them to sit.

"My associate Torstan will lead this meeting, as he is much more knowledgeable on certain topics we need to discuss. Cindras is my second and also speaks with my voice. Within reason."

The Fire God crossed his arms and glared at everyone, gaze avoiding his son. Cypress pursed his lips, and he stared down at the table. He looked exhausted and worried, his green hair wilder than usual, brown leaves drifting to the floor behind him.

The elderly man who'd come in with the king stepped to the table but didn't sit, leaving the winged man to observe in the background.

"As Vaultus said, I am Torstan," he said, his voice gritty but pleasant. "I'm a celestial. In case anyone here doesn't know what that means, I'm very old."

A few laughs around the table, the older gods nodding. Jace looked at Bashima, whose entire attention was on Torstan, and he looked livid. Jace knew what celestials were, but he'd never seen one. He hadn't thought they'd look like an old man. He expected celestials to be either too beautiful or too terrible to look upon.

"You've been summoned here because one of my brothers is once again at large."

The older gods shook their heads, and the younger ones looked confused. Bashima and Shina didn't seem surprised by the news, but the other young gods stared at Torstan like he'd gone mad.

"We've been in contact with the old gods," Torstan continued. "Because they were around during the first incident with this celestial. They know what's at stake."

"And why are you only telling us now?" asked Vesper. She was a younger god, very new to her position as the head Air Elemental. "I assume you've known for a while, since this event is so organized. You all know what's going on?"

She turned to Rizu, who hung her head. The Water Goddess was as old as Vaultus and Cindras. Jace thought she was shivering.

"We're telling you now because it's time," Torstan said. "Though things could have moved faster if the celestials had known of our brother's escape immediately."

More murmurs. Veles shifted in his seat.

Escape?

"This celestial, calling himself Ouranios, has been in the Locker for eons," Torstan explained. "The king put him there himself, and many of you fought beside Vaultus during that long battle. We always expected that one day he would find a way to escape, and due to an unfortunate incident with the former God of Time," he looked pointedly in Bashima's and Shina's direction, making the redhead bite his lip. "He is now out of our reach."

Jace was impressed that Bashima kept his composure at such an open insult.

"Is he forming an army, like he did last time?" That was Mo, seated beside Niall, whose face had gone white.

This was out of Jace's realm of understanding. A celestial who Vaultus fought and captured had gotten out when Shina transformed into a dragon for the first time…did everyone here know that? No, Cypress said it had to be a secret. They all thought Shina was a god-touched who'd gone berserk, an unfortunate accident. Even his father thought Shina was god-touched.

Had his father known what escaped the Locker? Jace glanced at Veles, who shook his head slightly. Don't draw attention to us yet.

"We can only assume that he will try," Torstan said. "This time we know what he's capable of, and he should be weakened by his time in the Locker." The celestial looked down the table at Veles and said, "God of the Dead. Your son was present at the Temple of Time. Can he explain what happened there recently?"

Every god turned their gaze on Jace, and he stiffened from the attention. It didn't matter that this was the scenario he'd expected; he felt like a zoo exhibit, and the gods' eyes felt like needles on his skin. The only one not looking at him was Cabari, who fiddled with his jacket.

No one was going to help Jace. His father couldn't, not when Jace had been asked a direct question. Jace was very aware that he and Oken were the only ones in the room who could die.

Niall touched his arm and said, "Do you need a moment?"

Jace shook his head and took a deep breath.

"I was at the Temple of Time visiting my sister, Nim. She's being trained to become the next Goddess of Time. My friend —" He paused, stumbling over Shako's name. He needed to speak for his friend, or no one would. They needed to understand what he went through.

"Shako was stationed there as well, to keep the Locker closed. They were alone. Two demigods in that temple, with only a bunch of shades to help them." He clenched his fists under the table and willed himself to go on, though a few of the gods muttered. "And the intruders knew exactly where and when to attack."

"How do you know that?"

A haughty voice near the end of the table. Skaadar, the God of Destruction. He had blue-black hair done up in a top knot and contemptuous yellow eyes, the pupils slit like a cat, and wore thick black gloves made from leather. He leaned back in his chair and tapped his gloved fingers on the table, seemingly unconcerned with the meeting going on around him. The gods next to him fidgeted, perhaps anxious to be away from his dangerous hands.

"How else would you explain a precise attack, when the god assigned to protect them was gone?" Niall asked, voice rising. "My daughter was there." He practically hissed. "Let my stepson speak. Isn't that the reason you called him to this war council?"

Niall turned his attention to Vaultus, who nodded.

Torstan said, "Until he's through speaking, keep your thoughts to yourself. There will be plenty of time to discuss matters once we've gone through the evidence."

Skaadar said no more but crossed his arms and shrugged.

"Um," Jace started again, his composure flagging. "We couldn't shift outside. Shako and I tried, but we could get around fine inside. All the shades were gone too, that's what the female shade who escaped with us said, so the warning came too late. Shako told me and Nim to go. We shifted to her room, getting away from the throne room, from the Locker, but one of the intruders came right to Nim's room. They knew what they were looking for," he said, glaring at the God of Destruction, who wasn't moved by Jace's frustration.

"I…I used my ability on her, after she said she would take Nim."

The gods tensed.

A demigod using his power without permission?

Veles must not have a short enough leash on him.

Surely it was fine that he used it just this once.

If they let one demigod get away with it, where would it end?

"If I hadn't used my power, we wouldn't have gotten away," Jace said, voice clear.

Cabari finally looked up at him, but Jace couldn't read his expression. His usual lively energy had faded.

"We can talk about that later as well," Torstan said. "Escaping capture was your first priority, especially if they wanted your sister."

Jace nodded and said, "I told Nim and the shade to leave, that I was going back for Shako. He stayed in the throne room to keep the Locker closed. He was trying to keep everyone safe from whoever — whatever

— you locked inside. The last time I saw him, he was holding off the man who set the fire. He was tall and thin, and something was wrong with his skin. It looked badly burned. Before I could help Shako, he stole the man's ability and blasted the entire throne room. I had to shift away."

He swallowed, remembering the man's laughter, Shako's eyes filled with fear and purpose.

"I got outside, and the fire tore through the rest of the temple. That's when my father found me."

Veles wrapped an arm around Jace's shoulder and whispered to him, "You don't have to say anything else." He turned to the assembled gods and said, "Cindras arrived later, maybe two hours, and he was able to staunch the fire."

"We found no one alive in the temple," the Fire God rumbled next to Vaultus. "The Locker's contents were either destroyed or taken by whoever invaded the temple. Without knowing the number of attackers or what abilities they might have, it's impossible to know if they took anything from the Locker. Excepting the two gods: Malrias and Chronas's body. We found no trace of them."

Small conversations erupted over the table. Jace chanced a look at Shina, whose posture had been alert since Torstan brought up the Temple of Time. His cheek twitched as he listened to the gods speak, their voices getting louder as each one attempted to be heard.

"Are you saying that the former Sun God is out too?"

"What good would it do for them to take Chronas's body?"

"Is anyone searching for these attackers? Is there any way to find out who they were?"

"Cindras, which one of your fire gods lost their damn mind and joined the enemy?"

The handsome man with the silver wings crashed onto the middle of the table, startling several gods. Veles put an arm across Jace's chest, pressing him back into his chair. Shina hissed and stood, trying to block Bashima, who swore and told him to sit back down.

"We all need to calm down," the man said, curling his wings back onto his body. "It won't do any good to fight amongst ourselves. That's what Ouranios wants."

"Who the fuck are you?" Bashima growled, finally getting Shina to sit.

"Me? Oh, I'm just a bystander who's here to help."

"Bystander my ass," the Sun God said. "We get it, this shit is bad. What the fuck do you expect us to do? Thank our lucky stars that you finally decided to tell us what's going on?"

"You have a lot of nerve, Bashima," sneered Skaadar. "Wasn't it your…husband…who caused this problem in the first place?"

Bashima snarled and stood, this time Shina trying to calm him. Shina pulled on his husband's arm, whispering to him. A dim light came from beneath Shina's tunic, drawing the winged man's attention. Jace almost didn't catch it, but he'd been watching the silver wings, fascinated. The winged man definitely moved a fraction of an inch toward Shina. When Bashima finally sat, the glow faded. It didn't seem like anyone else noticed it.

"Falkar, get off the table," Torstan said, exasperated. The winged man shrugged, bowed, and flew away to his place off to the side. Torstan continued, "Falkar is a celestial, like myself. And he's right. I wish there'd been more time to tell you what's been happening these past few weeks, but keeping information contained was essential. The enemy could be anywhere, and they could have spies amongst us. Some of you knew for months that something was amiss, and yet you didn't see fit to tell the remaining celestials."

Vaultus sat up straight in his chair, but he seemed uncomfortable. A few of the older gods averted their eyes.

"We have no idea what's to come," Torstan said. "We only know that Ouranios isn't going to disappear from the world. He doesn't want to ascend. He wants to rule. You younger gods may remember the conflict with Malrias. Ouranios is worse. There is no way to quantify how bad this situation is. We're counting on all of you to do your part."

Vaultus finally spoke up, "We will be communicating with gods from other parts of our world, telling them to stand fast. We won't pull them from their temples if we don't have to."

Torstan nodded. "It would only complicate matters to have outside gods here. Instead, we need to reach out to every god in the vicinity, see if they've seen or heard anything. Gather intelligence."

"Shouldn't we be making our own army?" Mo asked, and Raphe, the God of War, shook his head.

"We should only have soldiers who want to fight," Raphe said, voice quiet.

Jace strained to hear him.

Desh, the God of Peace, nodded and spoke up, "Raphe is right. When we fought Malrias, he had countless shades in his ranks. We could try the same thing, but it might prove ineffective. He gave his soldiers incentives that we can't, even if he was lying to them. If we fielded soldiers who didn't want to fight, the enemy would roll right over them."

Mo agreed but countered, "But he also had a large cadre of demigods following him. They don't need much of an incentive to fight full gods. Shouldn't we try to recruit them instead? There have to be at least a hundred or so out there, ones who don't live in the temples. They'd be a great resource."

Jace sat lower in his chair and looked at Oken, who hadn't said anything yet. He met Jace's gaze and held up his hand.

Don't say anything.

Vaultus sighed and said, "I hoped to save this issue for later, but since it's been brought to the group's attention, I propose that we send an envoy to the demigods. Recruitment would be the priority, but I would settle for neutrality."

"Neutrality?" scoffed Skaadar. "What good would that do?"

"I would of course prefer if they fought with us," Vaultus said. "But if we can keep them from joining Ouranios, I would accept that." The king regarded Jace and rubbed his chin. "I haven't had the chance to speak with their parents, but I had young Jace and Oken, the Fire God's son, in mind for this mission."

"What?" Veles shot to his feet. "That's out of the question. My son and Oken are too young —"

"You'd send two untested demigods?" Rizu asked. "Shouldn't we vote on a more suitable option?"

"If we send a god," said Cindras, his voice cutting through the others, "the demigods won't listen." Flames danced across his head and shoulders, and he glared at Veles. "It's not up to us if they want to accept the mission, it's up to them."

"How can you say that?" Veles asked, shocked. "What if they're attacked, out there searching for demigods who don't want to be found?"

"My son can handle himself," Cindras rumbled.

"You don't have to do this," Veles said to Jace, grasping his shoulder.

"It's a waste of time, unless they agree to join us," Skaadar drawled, and Jace wanted to punch him. The gods were discussing him and Oken like they weren't in the room, as though they hadn't been invited to join the same table. Even his father was trying to speak for him. The mission would be dangerous, but if Jace was with Oken, he thought they'd be fairly safe. Unless they couldn't use their powers.

"I'll go."

Everyone quieted and stared at Oken. Across the table, Bashima fumed silently, and Shina looked horrified. Jace was grateful that he couldn't see Cypress's face, but green light flickered around the room for a moment before dissipating.

"Oken," Shina said. "You don't have to."

"If Jace goes, I'll go. He's better at talking to people, and I can protect him." Oken's countenance was set, and Jace gave him a nod.

Better at talking to people? They were both terrible at that! What had he just agreed to?

Veles crashed into his chair and gripped Jace's leg, silently pleading with him to decline the mission.

"I want to help," Jace said, and his father's fingers tightened before they let go.

"You're the telepath, right?" Skaadar again, his yellow eyes cold. He looked up the table at Vaultus and said, "Why waste that ability? If the demigods refuse to fight, he should brainwash them into coming back with him. Easy enough. If he can do it."

Jace's mind fractured. Use his power on other demigods? Was that why Vaultus wanted him to search for them? Was this a big trick? How could they ask that of him? Right, like they'd ask. It wouldn't be a request. It would be an order.

Niall and Veles were speechless, mouths open in horror.

Cabari barked laughter, the first sound he'd made since sitting at the table. Jace's eyes widened and he scowled at the Lightning God. What the fuck was he laughing at? He had no right to have an opinion on anything to do with Jace.

"How would you like it if someone did that to you, Skaadar?" Cabari asked, acid in his tone.

"He's just a demigod," Skaadar said, flipping his hand, dismissing Cabari. "Not likely it would work on us. Besides, we're going to need all the fighters we can get, and I'd personally prefer that a bunch of demigods stood in front of us than sit back and watch us get our asses kicked."

"This is the exact reason why the demigods wouldn't want to fight," Cabari said. "Gods using them when it's convenient, letting them rot when it's not."

Jace watched the conversation bounce between the Lightning God and Skaadar. What the hells was Cabari going on about? Did he actually believe what he was saying?

"Why else do they exist?" Skaadar asked, smiling.

"Not for you to play with, asshole," Cabari sneered. "As if you could even keep your dick up long enough."

The smile dissolved from Skaadar's face, and he pulled at a glove.

"That's enough," Cindras said. "Skaadar isn't wrong. We need able fighters, and some of the demigods may prove useful." He looked at Vaultus, who wouldn't meet his eyes. "We knew it might come to this. The danger is too great to let them sit this fight out."

Silence dropped over the group.

Jace couldn't believe it. Were they really going to make him do it? He could agree then...not go through with it. There had to be a way to convince the demigods to join them without using his ability.

Even his father and Niall had no words. Veles fumed beside Jace, fury darkening his features. Shina looked ready to mutiny, and Bashima's brow furrowed, but they had to protect their secret. If the gods knew about Shina's enhanced power, they would make a plan for him as well. Jace didn't blame them for not speaking up and making themselves targets.

"No one else going to say anything?" Cabari asked. When he received no response, he said, "If you ask him to do this, I'm done."

Alora tugged on Cabari's sleeve, but he pulled it out of her hand.

What was he thinking? If Cabari left, he'd be in violation of the king's order. They'd eventually go after him, subdue him if they could. A rogue god was about as useful as a demigod who flouted the rules. Jace wished that Cabari would look at him. He needed to know if Cabari was serious, if he meant what he said. If Jace could get him to look over.

The room was still. Yellow lightning played over Cabari's body and he stood and stormed from the throne room.

Jace wanted to leap from the table and follow him, but his father grabbed his arm.

"Let him cool off," Skaadar said, chuckling. "He's not going anywhere."

Jace watched the throne room doors ease shut.

He didn't notice Falkar's wings dart through.

Chapter Twenty-One

Cabari

Cabari's thoughts and doubts spun in his head in a whirl, and he jumped from one worry to another. He couldn't believe what he'd done. Had he really walked out of the king's meeting?

Niall was right, it wasn't a meeting, it was a damn war council, and he should be a part of it, but what he'd heard made his stomach churn. Who the fuck was Skaadar to dictate how the king should run things? Why hadn't Vaultus spoken up, when it was obviously wrong to make Jace use his ability on other demigods?

He paused in his furious retreat. Shit. Would he have felt that way if he didn't know Jace? If the demigod had been sitting across the table, a stranger, would Cabari have taken the same stance?

He liked to think so, but that wasn't realistic. When had he ever cared what demigods did or said? He didn't care what anyone did, so long as they didn't try to tell him what to do. He'd never bothered to hang out with demigods besides Jace and Oken. But Oken was attached to Cypress, so that was the only reason Cabari interacted with him. And when had he bothered to notice that the gods dumped their half-human kids? Jace and Oken were anomalies, living with their parents.

That's what happened to Shako, right? Ignored and abandoned by his godly parent. Hadn't Jace mentioned something like that once?

They'd actually wanted to have a discussion about Jace using his damn ability when he and his sister, a child, were in danger. Why was that an issue? Any god would use their skills against an enemy. Why be so up in arms about a demigod doing it, if it was in self-defense?

"Ugh!"

All this was making his brain hurt. He hadn't expected to see Jace in the throne room. It never crossed his mind. Then there he was, sitting between Veles and Niall, looking miserable but so handsome…and stupid Alora teasing Cabari about the accidental static charge.

"At least you don't like him," she'd muttered at him, giggling.

He couldn't muster the wherewithal to tell her to shut up. He did like Jace. Way too much. It was distracting and annoying and he couldn't get within two feet of him, not with Veles circling him like a guard dog.

Hearing what Jace went through in the temple, how hurt he was that the gods not only failed his friend but also his sister, tore at Cabari. Jace sounded in pain, truly understanding how little the gods cared about demigods. Cabari could have volunteered to help protect Shako and Nim when they'd been secluded at the Temple of Time, but it wasn't something he considered. Why would he? He was a selfish asshole.

He needed to go back in that throne room and make sure the gods didn't make Jace promise to do something he'd never forgive himself for. Cabari turned on his heel, intending to march back into the meeting, and ran right into Falkar. The celestial stayed put as Cabari bounced off him.

"Fucking hells!"

"Already regretting what you said, Lightning God?" Falkar's voice was a casual drawl, as though he found Cabari interesting but not enough to make much effort. Yet he stood in the way, barring the hall back to the throne room.

"Not in the least," Cabari snarled. He didn't have time to chat with the celestial. That's why the winged prick had seemed so strange when they first met: Falkar didn't give off the same energy as a god. He was ancient and perilous, someone to be avoided at all costs.

"Then why go back? You said your piece, now stick to it."

"The fuck do you care? I didn't hear you agreeing with me."

Falkar gave him a small smile. "What good would that do? The king won't listen to me. Torstan has his ear. Besides, I doubt that kid would use his ability on a fellow demigod. It's not in his nature."

"You don't know a thing about it," Cabari said and made to shove past him, but Falkar stuck out his arm and stopped him again.

"Sure, I do. It's my gift to understand people." That cocky grin again. His wings fluttered and a few feathers dislodged and flew away of their own accord.

"What would a celestial care about a demigod? Or a god, for that matter?" Cabari asked.

"Plenty." The grin disappeared, and Falkar' eyes gleamed. "I have a proposition for you."

"Not interested."

"Hear me out. Torstan didn't mention it, because he's not supposed to, but my job is intelligence gathering. I'm in charge of finding out what Ouranios is up to."

"Good for you. Can you get out of my way?"

"I don't think so," Falkar said, pondering. "Let's take a walk." His arm snapped out, and he grabbed Cabari's bicep, shifting them away.

"What the fuck?" Cabari yelled as they landed outside among the topiaries. He ripped his arm from Falkar' grip.

"Sorry about that, but lots of prying eyes and ears in there."

Another figure emerged from the shadow of a nearby hedge, the strangest person Cabari had ever seen: he had a bird's head covered in feathers and a sharp beak; observant eyes, searching the area; draped head to toe in a black cloak.

"We're alone," he said, and Cabari could have sworn the bird-guy's voice echoed.

"Excellent! Lightning God, this is my student, Orn. Don't let his visage frighten you. He's actually quite charming."

"I'll leave you to your business, but be aware, the darkness awaits." Orn swooped away back into the shadows.

"Pleasant guy," Cabari said, sarcastic.

"He really is, once you get to know him," Falkar said, beaming. "Us birds have to stick together, you know." He winked and shook his wings.

Cabari scowled at him and crossed his arms. "Why won't you leave me alone?"

"I think you show promise, Lighting God."

"You can call me Cabari. If you're so interested, you must have at least bothered to find out my name."

"Name?" Falkar laughed. "I do enjoy how you gods took to the mortal notion of naming each other. Where did yours come from?"

Cabari flushed, the red creeping down his neck. It was none of his damn business.

"What do you want?"

"Right to the point. I like that in a god." Falkar beckoned him toward the hedge, further shielding them from sight. "You're the exact person I need to assist me in infiltrating Ouranios's inner circle."

Cabari laughed. What in the hells was he saying?

"You're laughing, but it's true," Falkar said, smirking. "You're not close with your parents, you have few close friends, no spouse — or partner if that's the word you prefer — no children. You could disappear off the face of the world and hardly anyone would notice. Or care."

"Since you've put it so nicely," Cabari said. He shook his head in disgust and tried to move away. Falkar grabbed him again, fingers like talons.

"Did you mean what you said in there? Or are you just in love with Veles's son?"

"What?" Cabari hissed, pulling his arm free. Panic filled his body, but he froze. He should try and get away, but something held him there.

"I'm not the one who set off a static charge in a room full of gods who would kill to know my business. Or weaknesses."

"It was an accident," Cabari grumbled.

"Sure." Falkar paused, perhaps rethinking something. "You showed up at the Temple of Time, by yourself. Fairly interesting on its own; I'd especially like to know how you found out about the fire, but you gods are well-known for your gossip chains."

"So, what if I was there? That's not a crime."

"Oh, it's not just that you were there," Falkar said. "When you noticed Veles and his family, you did this peculiar thing: you paused. You see, most busybody gods would've wasted no time in bothering Veles. What would they care that he was there with his family, one of whom they would know was living in the temple and probably witnessed what happened?"

"One pause and you base my whole character off that?"

This celestial was an idiot.

Falkar said, "Hardly. That pause only meant that you're capable of decency. To tell you the truth, I was more impressed with your questions. And you weren't afraid of Cindras, which is quite a feat."

"Cindras is a dick and a bully, but you don't mind hanging out with him."

"The Fire God has his purposes."

"Like agreeing with Skaadar? You're talking decency, where the hells was decency at that meeting?"

"Ah, so you did mean what you said," Falkar said, triumphant. "Although it could be about the demigod boy."

"He does have a name, asshole."

Falkar waved his hand, as though Jace's name was a minor detail he needn't bother with.

"Your inability to understand your own feelings isn't my problem. It doesn't matter at this point; you stood up for a demigod. That's an anomaly I'm intrigued by. Self-sacrifice isn't usually in a god's vocabulary. Are you willing to keep going?"

"And help you infiltrate a celestial's stronghold? You're out of your damn mind."

"Whether you like it or not," Falkar said, poking Cabari in the chest, "Jace — yeah, I know his name — is going to be sent on that mission. He could refuse, but I think you know he's not going to back down. He wants to help bring down Ouranios. Do you?"

"Obviously, otherwise why the hells would I show up here? I knew some bad shit was going down." He brushed Falkar's finger away. "I fought against Malrias. I'm no coward."

"I didn't think you were. You just need to get your priorities straight. It won't matter if Jace finds the demigods and convinces them to fight if we don't know what we're fighting. He can die, or did you forget that?"

Cabari paused with his rebuke. Falkar was trying to manipulate him, play on his fears. Of course, he knew that Jace could die. He just didn't like to think about it.

"You could do more than wait until they tell you to join a battlefield. You could be useful."

Cabari sighed. He could try and stop Jace from leaving. Hells, Cypress was probably livid with Oken, especially if he warned him beforehand to stay out of this mess. But Jace would hate Cabari for intervening. Enough of his life was controlled.

"What are you planning to do? I'm not following you with some half-assed plan."

Falkar smiled. "I would never approach Ouranios directly. Although I wasn't involved in his last failed bid for power, he wouldn't appreciate another celestial making contact. So, I'm going to find out where he's keeping Malrias and finagle my way in."

"You think that's why they attacked the Temple of Time," Cabari said. "To break out the last Sun God."

"Among other things." Falkar seemed pleased with his deduction. He said, "Malrias's demigod followers were in the Locker too. I'm sure they'll enjoy freedom. They were after Niall's daughter as well. For what purpose..." He shrugged.

Cabari shuddered.

It had taken everything they'd had to take down the old Sun God. Malrias had demigods chomping at the bit to join him, so full of promises. Which was probably what Vaultus was afraid of. Maybe the younger demigods would flock to Malrias's side. Ouranios would hardly have to lift a finger to get the forces he needed to fight if the demigods believed Malrias was the better option.

Cabari remembered being chosen by Vaultus to be the new Lightning God, soon after the final battle with Malrias. Cabari had blood all over his face and hands, from people he'd either killed or wounded. After his predecessor fell in battle, Vaultus needed a new Master of Storms. She was forever sleeping, as close to death as a god could get. Such a waste.

"And what am I supposed to do?" he asked Falkar.

"You'd come with me, as a peace offering."

"You're insane," Cabari said, mouth hanging open. "As a captive or like I'm joining them?"

"How does the word 'traitor' sound to you?" Falkar lifted an eyebrow, his smile gone. Now that he'd snagged a co-conspirator, he was serious.

"Like shit, but it's better than being a captive."

"You'll need mobility in the group, wherever we end up. Can't do that locked in a cage. I don't know what they'd expect from you, or if they'll even accept you, but they'll want to recruit gods. They might be desperate enough."

"Great, you're risking my life on a hope that they'll think it's totally normal that I would defect to their side."

"Come up with a good enough reason, and they might believe you." Falkar patted his shoulder. "Just don't spout any of your pro-demigod sentiments. There's no way in the seven hells they'd believe a god cared about demigods. Say you got bored or something."

"You celestials made the gods, right? Little late to complain about us."

"We didn't think you'd all turn into selfish assholes," Falkar said. "If you think you're up for this, go back to your temple and get what you need for a short journey. Go to a place no one knows about and wait for two days. I'll give you one of my feathers so I can find you."

"I know a spot." Cabari took the proffered silver feather, which was heavier than he'd imagined. It glittered at his touch, sending sparkling light around the garden. He stuck it in his jacket pocket.

"Don't tell anyone where you're going or what you're doing. Secrecy is of the utmost importance. The only ones who'll know you're not actually a traitor will be me and Orn."

"You want everyone to think I defected…because of Jace."

"I doubt they'll think that's why you left," Falkar said, tilting his head. "Why would they think you love anything other than yourself?"

"Fuck you."

"Hit a nerve? If it makes you feel better, the kid feels something for you. Whether it's hatred or something else is too hard to tell. Intense emotions are harder to read, but it was written all over his face when he saw you." Falkar flapped his wings, preparing to take off. He said, "I'm leaving now too. Torstan can't know what I'm up to, in case he's interrogated at some point. Don't speak to anyone, just go. I mean it. Don't try to see the demigod kid. Everyone has to believe you've flipped sides, even him. I'll be in contact soon."

Falkar soared up into the sky, and Cabari watched until his silhouette faded. He knew exactly where he could go. But first, he needed to head to his temple and grab some things. Isaac was used to him being gone for extended periods of time, so he wouldn't think it odd if Cabari stopped by then left immediately.

The water was as he remembered, not that it ever changed. The dark blue color speckled with crystalline spots was as constant as the sunrise. The clearing was quiet and dim, early evening settling over the forest, and Cabari dropped his small pack near the spot he and Jace always lay after swimming. He could almost imagine soft indentations in the grass from their towels.

Stop. It won't help.

But Cabari found it was impossible to come to the waterfall and not think of Jace. The demigod didn't let on, but it became one of his favorite places too, and Cabari was proud that he'd given Jace some happiness. Anything to break through that sharp exterior.

Once, not long after their first time together, Cabari brought Jace back to the waterfall and its magical pool, hoping to entice him into more entanglements. Jace pushed Cabari into the water fully-clothed when he'd tried to kiss him, which should have pissed Cabari off. Instead, he couldn't stop laughing. He'd nearly choked on water as he cackled, enthralled with Jace's audacity. No one ever tried to stop the Lightning God from kissing them. Jace was going to be a challenge every single time.

He leapt from the pool and shook himself like a dog, spraying Jace, who yelled adorable obscenities at him.

"That's what you get for ruining my clothes!"

"They're not ruined," Jace said, rolling his eyes and shoving damp hair from his face.

"Nope, ruined, better take them off." As Cabari stripped off his tunic and trousers, Jace shoved him in again. This time, Cabari was ready and grabbed Jace's hand, landing them both in the floaty blue water.

"Ha! Better take yours off too, I guess."

Jace splashed him, trying to hide a smile, his hair nearly covering his eyes.

"You're such a dick," he said, chuckling.

"Who pushed who in first?" Cabari asked, faking indignance.

Jace rolled his eyes again and climbed out, shucking his clothes. Then he dove back in, his body curving gracefully. He was more naturally athletic than Cabari and moved easily through the water, like he was born to it. Cabari was a strong swimmer, but he had water god lineage to draw on. Jace made every movement seem effortless, especially if he didn't think anyone was paying attention. If he noticed Cabari watching him, his posture and body attitude changed back to sullen indifference.

"Why do you do that?" Cabari asked, doing a smooth breaststroke up to the demigod.

"Do what?"

"Whenever someone's watching you, you get all tense and..." Cabari made a disinterested face, trying to imitate the demigod's usual expression.

Jace snorted. "That's not what I look like."

"Oh, it is."

Jace stared at him a moment, his eyebrows bunched together, then got out of the pool. He spread out a towel they'd brought and collapsed onto it.

Retreat-and-avoid was Jace's chief defense against tough questions. Or questions he didn't like. Cabari didn't think he was prying. He'd already seen the demigod's entire body and fucked him into near catatonia. What other secrets could he have?

Cabari got out of the pool and toweled off his hair, putting the towel down beside Jace's. Once he'd lay down, he stared into the sky, fiddling with his fingers. He hated long silences. Jace seemed to thrive on them.

"You're a really good swimmer," he blurted.

Hells, why did I say that? Just sit still for once.

"Thanks?" Jace said, sighing. "My mom taught me. She was the best swimmer in our village."

"My mom's a water-type goddess and she couldn't be bothered to teach me," Cabari said. "Just chucked me into the ocean and hoped for the best."

"What?" Jace sat up, staring down at him. "I know you can't drown, but seriously! You could have been hurt."

Cabari shrugged. "I told you my parents suck. My dad's an air-type, so I don't sink fast. Not that it impressed them. The only thing they were proud of was when I showed capability with weather manipulation, combination of water and air powers."

"That's cool," Jace said. Cabari could tell he was still floored by the being-thrown-into-a-large-body-of-water-as-a-child situation, but at least he was talking. He lay back again and asked, "Two abilities. Like Oken?"

"Ha! No. It's common enough in gods to have a combination of their parents' powers. It's unheard of in demigods. There's no one like Oken. Not that I've ever heard of."

"That must be lonely."

Cabari furrowed his brow. He'd never thought about it that way. "He seems like a pretty together guy."

Jace scoffed but didn't offer a comment.

Was Oken not a together guy? He was so mellow, it was hard to say. Cypress was the jittery, nervous one.

"It must have been boring at the Temple of Fire," Cabari said. "For him to pick up and leave with Cypress."

"I guess boring is one way to put it."

Cabari didn't want to guess what that meant.

"Is it boring in the Underworld?"

They hadn't settled on an iron-clad way for the Lightning God to visit Jace in the Underworld, so he was curious.

"Very."

"Glad I could rescue you," Cabari said, grinning.

Jace didn't answer, and Cabari couldn't think of another thing to say. His flirting didn't work on Jace, at least not his usual style. Jace more often than not laughed at his attempts. It was both confusing and frustrating. And also very enticing.

Cabari reached out and ran a hand down Jace's side, still damp from the pool, and Jace didn't move, didn't flinch away. Progress! Dammit, but it should have gotten some reaction. Jace's eyes were closed, his breath even. So, Cabari threw caution to the wind and searched further, fingertips tracing the band of Jace's shorts, flitting under to touch the soft skin beneath.

"Want me to throw you in the pool again?" Jace asked, voice unreadable.

"Dare you to try."

Instead of tossing the god into the water, Jace reached for Cabari's hand and guided it down beneath his shorts, and Cabari ran his fingers through the soft green hair as he went. Jace's body arched slightly at the touch, not giving too much yet.

Jace knew exactly what he wanted, which turned Cabari on more than anything. Jace liked to be in control, craved it, wanted to direct the Lightning God how to pleasure him, and Cabari was more than happy to go along. For the most part. None of his other lovers were so sure of themselves in that way.

So, not to be completely told what to do, Cabari enjoyed teasing Jace, pulling away a bit when the demigod wanted him to move forward, tickling him, running his fingernails down his cock instead of stroking it, which made Jace growl low in his chest. It was such a sexy sound, that wanting-but-not-getting frustration. Seeing Jace impatient was intoxicating.

When Cabari finally circled his fingers around Jace's halfway-to-hard length, the demigod shuddered and let go, letting the Lightning God take over. He massaged and stroked in a languid motion, in no hurry, savoring the sounds coming from Jace, his breath finally quickening.

Jace reached into the nearby bag and dragged out a phial of oil, deft fingers un-stoppering it. He upended the small glass container, and oil dropped into his palm. It smelled like Jace, woodsy and peppery, and yellow light played over Cabari's skin. Jace ignored the light burst and slid his hand back down his shorts, adding his hand to Cabari's for a moment, sliding the oil onto himself and Cabari's fingers. Then Jace lifted his hips and went straight for his ass, which was unacceptable.

Cabari released Jace's hard cock and flipped onto him with godly speed, pinning the demigod's hands beside his head. "Didn't I tell you that's mine?"

Jace smirked up at him. "Who's to say I haven't been experimenting on my own?"

Cabari gasped in feigned surprise. "You misbehaved? Naughty."

Jace shrugged as best he could with the Lightning God holding him down. He said, "What are you gonna do about it?"

"Go so slow you'll be begging to come."

Cabari bent forward, feeling Jace's hardness between them, making Jace moan as he pressed down harder with his pelvis. He rubbed his nose against Jace's, savoring the confused arousal in the demigod's eyes, then kissed the corners of his mouth, the swooping bow of his lips, the full bottom lip. Jace tried to connect their lips, but Cabari was too quick, dipping lower, trailing fluttering kisses down Jace's neck and collarbone. He released the demigod's hands, which found Cabari's hair and brushed through it, scraping his scalp.

For how tough Jace was on the outside, he had a gentle touch, his fingers long and agile. He was letting Cabari take the lead for now, but the Lightning God was ready; Jace could turn the tables on him fast. Taking one nipple in his mouth and the other in his hand, Cabari drew some new noises from Jace, a low whine that started in the back of his throat, and he arched up, grabbing Cabari's hands.

"It's not nice to grab," Cabari scolded him. "Maybe I should have tied you down?"

"Too bad you didn't think that far ahead," Jace whispered, voice low, not releasing him.

"Bad Jace!" Cabari pulled free and spun around, using his knees and legs to pin Jace's shoulders and arms. "Now I'm gonna take longer."

Cabari loved how tall Jace was, because he could stretch his full body on top of him.

"Fuck, I forgot how strong you are," Jace muttered, trying to move Cabari's legs.

"Powerful thighs," Cabari said, giggling. He ran his hands down Jace's sides, traced his abs and his delicious vee-shaped muscles that led downward. He slid Jace's shorts off. Cabari's pupils blew at the sight, but he needed to keep it together. He'd promised exquisite torture, and that's what he would deliver. He touched every inch of skin, caressing Jace's inner thighs, which tensed at the sensations, and Jace moaned again, sending trills of excitement through the Lightning God.

"Please, touch me," Jace groaned.

"Begging already? Thought you'd have more stamina than that," Cabari teased, laying down on Jace and lavishing him with slow, exaggerated licks.

"Fuck, what are you doing to me?"

"It's your own fault, such a rule-breaker," Cabari said.

He made the mistake of easing up the pressure on his legs, and Jace's arms were free in an instant. He tore the Lightning God's shorts off with a grunt and grabbed his hips, pulling him backwards. Okay, it wasn't a mistake, because Jace's tongue jammed into him, sending Cabari into a pleasure spiral. Just as nimble with his tongue as he was with his hands, the demigod was merciless, holding his hips in a death grip. Cabari's dick hardened in an instant.

Cabari regained his sanity long enough to lean forward and engulf Jace's waiting cock with his lips, sucking and drooling everywhere. So much for making him wait. Jace's body tightened as the Lightning God bobbed up and down on his length, skimming it with his teeth, and he released Cabari's hips and fell back, swearing. As he was inhaling that beautiful dick, Cabari slid his oiled fingers inside Jace, getting a roar of surprise.

"You-better-fuck-me-or-I'm-going-too-arghhhhh!" Jace's cry as Cabari hit his prostate made a group of birds soar from the nearby trees, cawing their displeasure.

"You want it?" Cabari asked, coming off Jace's cock.

"Yes! For godsake!"

"I won't make you say please…this time," Cabari laughed. He turned back around, spread Jace's legs, and rammed into him. Jace's long legs wrapped around Cabari's hips as he thrust forward, and he sat up, gripped the back of the Lightning God's neck, and pulled him into a fierce kiss.

Fucking hells, Jace kissed like a demon was after him.

Jace lay back, pulling Cabari with him as he shoved himself inside Jace again and again, keeping their lips locked. Jace's breathing was heavy now, hot against Cabari's cheek, and he sent his hands searching down the Lightning God's back, scratching him raw.

Jace didn't warn Cabari when he came, splattering them both with cum, and he fell back, nipping the god's bottom lip. Cabari held up his thighs and kept going, saying, "Gods. So tight. Gonna. Come. Inside. You."

Jace nodded, dazed from his climax. Seeing Jace's fucked-out eyes sent Cabari over the edge, and yellow electricity flowed through his body and over his skin. He contained his power so he didn't hurt Jace, but as he came, Jace's hair stood on end with the static charge.

He lay still, chest heaving, on top of Jace, who raised an unsteady hand and tapped his shoulder, appreciatively, before the hand fell back to the ground. They lay like that for a while, regaining their breath.

"It's borderline criminal that Veles hides you in the Underworld," Cabari said. He eased himself out and laid his chin on Jace's chest. His fingers played with Jace's hair, twisting it lightly.

Jace snorted, eyes closed. "He doesn't 'hide' me."

"Then why haven't you been anywhere?"

Jace tensed again.

Shit. He'd said the wrong thing. What could he say to change the subject?

"I've been here," Jace said. Cabari barely heard him. Cabari snuck up further and pushed soft green hair off Jace's forehead, sneaking one kiss right in the center.

Indigo eyes stared up at him, surprised. Jace asked, "What was that for?"

"Can't I just kiss you? Jeez." Cabari rolled his eyes.

"Not without an ulterior motive," Jace said and laughed. Before Cabari could serve him a rebuke, Jace leaned up and caught his lips again, closing those cursed indigo eyes.

Ulterior motive? What the hells? Well, it was kind of fair. For some reason, Cabari didn't want Jace to think of him that way. What could he do that wasn't about sex?

"Wanna see me make a storm?"

After washing up in the pool and dressing, Cabari stood in the center of the clearing, Jace off to the side, eyebrow raised.

"Isn't it dangerous for me to stand here?" Jace deadpanned, as though Cabari would forget the most important part of weather manipulation: don't put anyone in danger from your electricity.

"Normally, yes, but I'm part air god, remember. It's not as easy for me as my dad or Vesper…just watch, okay?"

Jace smiled and crossed his arms, hair a messy cloud around his head.

Holding out his arms at his sides, Cabari took a deep, calming breath, and rose from the ground. Jace's eyes bulged, his mouth falling open.

He better be careful or I'll put my dick in there, ha!

"Um, you're flying?"

"Air manipulation," Cabari said, grinning. "But basically, yeah. I have to go a ways up, so my lightning doesn't direct toward the ground instead of the sky."

He shot into the air, Jace yelling below him.

Cabari loved this part of his job. He wasn't technically supposed to make it storm in that region that day, but whatever. He never deviated from his plan, what was one time? As he rose higher, Cabari expanded his lightning over his body, letting it fly off his fingers as he directed the bolts into the clouds. Yellow energy flew from one cloud to another, igniting along the way, making a glowing cage in the sky. Drawing on his water god abilities, Cabari pulled the moisture in the air into the clouds, fattening them. As the lightning worked its way through the clouds, the air became dense with energy and water vapor. The first thunderclap roiled through the sky, and Cabari smiled. His job was done.

He descended, and Jace ran up to him, shaking. "What the fuck? You can't just fly away and send lightning everywhere!"

Thunder cracked and lightning slashed the sky.

"I didn't do that," Cabari said, laughing, as rain crashed down into the clearing, soaking them. Jace gaped at him, arms raised, droplets pelting him, water dripping off his clothes and hair. It ran down his face, blurring his handsome features. But Cabari could see a huge grin.

Jace spun in a slow circle, eyes closed, face up to the sky, letting the rain hit him. He brought his hands to his face and rubbed his eyes and cheeks, as though he wanted to absorb the falling water into himself. Cabari's heart lurched and he grasped his chest. What the hells was that?

Jace turned his head, met Cabari's eyes, and laughed. A genuine cry of joy.

The Lightning God opened his eyes to his uncertain present, the sound of rainfall fading from his ears. Had Jace really smiled at him like that? It felt like a dream, a faraway mirage. There was no way they'd gone from that sparkling memory to their current fractured state.

Cabari took out Falkar's feather and twirled it in his fingers. He had no idea what was waiting for him, but if plunging off a cliff into the villains' den would help save Jace — help save everyone — he had to do it.

And if he ever wanted to see those damned indigo eyes again, he'd better learn to play a villain.

Chapter Twenty-Two

Cypress

As the other gods left the throne room, Cypress tried to make pleading eye contact with Oken, but the demigod wasn't swayed. Oken stood with Bashima and Shina, arms crossed, surveying the room, avoiding both Cypress and the Fire God. He'd spoken briefly with Jace, probably making a plan to meet for their mission.

At least Veles and Niall looked as frustrated as Cypress. Cindras was fine letting his son go off and find the hidden demigods, some of whom might be as powerful as Oken. He hadn't batted an eye. Maybe because he knew what Vaultus had planned to propose. The king hadn't bothered filling the Forest God in on his plan.

After Oken and Jace agreed to go, Cypress lost track of the meeting. He heard raised voices, fists pounding the table, but remembered nothing. Vaultus could tell him everything later. Cypress had no intention of listening to them once they'd condemned Oken to a suicide mission.

Cypress had heard stories about demigod communities, most of which broke up after members couldn't get along. There had been a large group in the south, maybe a few thousand years ago, who had demolished each other over some ridiculous argument, the entire settlement gone in an instant. Nearby gods said they could see the blast for miles…

"Cypress," came Torstan's gruff voice.

"What?" Cypress refocused, pulling his eyes from Oken. Torstan glared at him, expression wry.

"Were you listening to any of that meeting?"

"I heard enough," Cypress said. "When were you and Vaultus going to tell me?"

Torstan ignored the question and said, "We need to go over some things with the Sun God. Tell him to wait. I'm sure he's in a hurry to get his husband out of this hornet's nest, but he needs to clear up a few things."

Cypress gulped. What did that mean?

He walked over to Bashima and Shina, and Oken backed away, piercing Cypress's heart. Oken didn't want to be around him, that much was plain.

"What do you want, Tengu?" Bashima growled. Shina gave his shoulder a shove, and Bashima sighed. "What was the point of us coming a day early when you wouldn't even talk to us?"

Cypress grimaced, "Torstan and Vaultus wouldn't let me. They're —"

"Wouldn't let you? You could've found a way. You should have warned us that Vaultus wanted to recruit Zebra Head to that stupid mission."

"It's not stupid," Oken said. He didn't move closer to them, but he was paying attention.

"Uh, I didn't know about that," Cypress admitted. Bashima shook his head, not believing. Cypress stuttered for a moment and said, "Torstan asked if you would stay, Bashi."

Bashima's eyes narrowed into dangerous slits.

"Why?" Bashima glanced at his husband, light flickering on his skin.

"Further debrief I think," Cypress said, gulping. "Just us. Everyone else is leaving. Going on to their assigned tasks. So…you don't have to worry."

Bashima didn't say anything. Maybe this time he actually was worried.

Oken didn't leave with the others. As the Fire God passed him, flames raging across his body, Oken nodded. Cindras didn't stop, but his hand moved, as though he wanted to reach out to his son. He stopped himself and kept going. Cypress had tensed, ready to jump in front of Oken if he needed to, but the Fire God made no other moves.

So different from Jace, who'd been led out of the throne room by his father and stepfather, Veles and Niall forming a protective cocoon around him.

As the throne room doors closed, Savos appeared and cast a locking charm, keeping everyone out. It would stop Falkar's intrusive feathers too, though Cypress hadn't seen the other celestial since he jumped on the table.

Savos hastened to Vaultus's side, bending to whisper a question.

"I'll be fine. I can rest in a moment," the king said and waved Savos away, and the god-touched man obeyed, nodding at Torstan before disappearing again. He'd spared no glances for anyone else.

"Oken, son of Cindras?" Torstan beckoned the demigod to the head of the table where Vaultus sat. Bashima inhaled sharply, but Shina put a warning hand on his arm. Cypress eyed the king.

Vaultus raised his great head and sighed. He said, "I thank you for accepting the mission to recruit the demigods. It will take uncommon courage and tenacity."

"I'm up for it, your majesty," Oken said and bowed his head.

"None of that, now," Vaultus said, chuckling. "You've stayed in my temple more than once. Just call me Vaultus."

Oken nodded, but Cypress doubted he'd ever feel comfortable calling the king by name.

Vaultus went on, "Do you and young Jace have a plan? There's not much information we can give you, besides the few towns where we know gods have…"

"Left their half-human children?" Oken offered.

Vaultus coughed into his hand and nodded. "Torstan has the list for you. You may take it and proceed. The doors will open for you."

The celestial pulled a scroll from his long sleeve and handed it to Oken. He said, "Send word to the king's temple if you require assistance. We might not be able to send much help, but someone would come. I will, if need be."

"Thank you, sir," Oken said. "If we need help, I doubt there will be time to send a letter."

"Hm, you're probably right," Torstan said, chuckling. "Either way, let us know."

"So long as we can use our abilities, we won't need any help," Oken said and bowed again. He walked toward the throne room doors, ignoring Cypress's gaze.

Shina said, "You're not going to see him for a long time."

"I know…" Cypress said.

"Go talk to him. Now." Shina growled the last word, making Cypress jump.

"He doesn't want to talk to me," Cypress said.

"Such a fucking moron," Bashima muttered. "If Alaric did that, I'd kick his ass."

"Such a romantic." Shina drew his husband close to him, and the Sun God snorted.

"Fine. I'll be right back." Cypress said and trotted after Oken, who paused when he heard the Forest God approaching.

"You told me to go," Oken said before Cypress could speak, pulling him up short. "So, I'm going."

"I didn't mean like this," Cypress said, shuffling his feet. "I don't want you to get hurt."

Oken glared at him. "There's no way I won't get hurt with everything that's happening. What did you expect me to do, hide in your temple until the fighting ended?"

Well, it wasn't exactly what Cypress intended, but that sounded like a great idea at the moment.

"You've never seen another demigod besides Jace and your siblings. How are you supposed to do this?"

Oken sighed. "I knew you wouldn't believe in me."

"That's not it at all!" Cypress waved his arms wildly in front of him. "It's not that I don't think you can do it. I just…"

"I have to do my duty," Oken said. "Just like you." His eyes softened. "I know you can't tell me everything, but these powers Vaultus gave you, they're to fight the celestial, right?"

Cypress nodded and tucked his chin to his chest. Oken always knew, always picked up on why the Forest God was feeling happy or sad, or in this case terrified.

"I won't be here to protect you," Oken said. "So, try to be careful."

He turned away, but Cypress grabbed his hand. "If there's a demigod more powerful than you, promise me that you'll run."

"You know I can't promise that."

Oken didn't pull his hand free, and Cypress let down his walls a bit more, wanting to tell him. The soul bond would make Oken stay, if he explained it, what it meant. But maybe it was safer for Oken to be away from him, even if he was heading into danger. At least he'd be off Ouranios's radar. The closer Oken was to the Forest God, the closer he was to the celestial's wrath.

Cypress's soul retreated, drawing back into himself.

Oken blinked in surprise and stepped back, dropping Cypress's hand. He reached forward and clasped Cypress in a hug.

Tears rolling down his cheeks, Cypress whispered, "I love you."

Oken's grip increased for a moment, and Cypress wasn't sure if he'd answer.

After a moment that felt like an eternity, Oken finally said, "I love you too."

He dragged himself away and shoved through the doors before Cypress could say more. The doors slammed closed with Savos's spell, and Cypress held in a sob.

Torstan

Just what he needed, Torstan thought, two soul bonds. He rubbed a hand over his face, watching the Fire God's son flee the throne room, wrenching himself from Cypress's arms.

Why the gods and mortals insisted on these messy romantic entanglements was beyond the celestial's comprehension. When making both gods and mortals, the celestials hadn't thought much about emotions. They'd given both the ability to feel, to love, to hate, but they hadn't expected either race to take it this far.

Soul bonds. Hells. That was a side effect the celestials hadn't thought of. And now there were two. It hadn't happened in generations, yet here were two gods who'd chosen mortal mates. At least the Forest

God's bond wasn't as solid. Oken didn't seem aware of it. The Sun God and his husband were like twin stars, blazing with passion. And it was dangerous. Too dangerous to keep them together on a battlefield. Neither would be able to function if the other was present, too concerned for their partner's welfare. No matter what, a soul bond meant disaster. If Ouranios found out, he could exploit the connection, possibly enough to tip the scales in his favor.

Sending Oken away was the right choice. At least Cypress would be able to recenter himself.

He shook his head. No use thinking of that now. He'd have to find a way to separate Bashima from his husband.

The Sun God and god-touched human hunched together, conspiratorially, murmuring. Vaultus watched Cypress by the doors, not paying attention to the more troubling matter in front of them.

"Sun God," Torstan said, earning a scathing look from Bashima. "You may approach the king."

Bashima and Shina stepped forward together. The redhead seemed nervous. The Sun God's posture demanded respect, and Torstan knew he usually got it. Bashima was also a hothead who couldn't control his temper. Or so Torstan once thought. This Bashima was more contained, possibly the effects of his soul-bonded mate's nature spreading to him. Alaric Shina was a mystery, some village boy who'd caught the Sun God's eye...and toppled the God of Time. Something was definitely off.

Torstan needed to figure out what.

Alaric

The celestial zipped in front of him and Bashima, almost too fast for Alaric to see. For an old man, he sure could move. Alaric put an arm in front of his husband, who grunted in surprise. Bashima hadn't noticed Torstan zoom in.

"I don't believe we asked your husband to stay, Sun God. Wasn't it enough that we allowed a god-touched into the meeting?" The celestial's dour expression didn't change. He'd looked the same through the war council meeting, never smiling.

Alaric winced. Bashima wouldn't be happy with that. He said, "It's okay, I can go back to our room."

"No, you won't," Bashima snarled. "He stays with me."

"Torstan, it's fine," Vaultus said, exhaustion heavy in his voice. Alaric whimpered. The king seemed so weak.

"What we have to say is for you only," Torstan said to Bashima, not acknowledging Alaric nor what Vaultus said.

"You'll have to send me a letter," Bashima said. "Let's go, Alaric."

Before Bashima could move an inch, the celestial flew at him, with much greater speed than before. Alaric's reaction was pure instinct. He roared and grabbed the celestial's fist, stopping him mid-punch, stalking away from his husband, taking the threat with him. Growling, his scales tore through his tunic, exposing his upper body. He'd worn a pair of leggings from Kamaishi, so they stretched over his growing legs.

"Stop!"

Bashima's voice sounded far away. All Alaric could feel was the celestial's energy resonating off his own, much like the one who'd attacked Daruk. It buzzed in his brain, sending tiny shocks through his nerves, pounding at his heart: Threat. Threat. Threat.

The brand on his back went off like a beacon, sending dazzling gold light across the room. The celestial covered his eyes, but he was grinning like a madman, dangling from Alaric's grip. As though it didn't cost him much effort, the old man twisted out of Alaric's claws and landed nimbly on his feet.

Bashima tackled Alaric from behind, wrapping his legs around his waist.

"Alaric! It's okay. He's not going to hurt me, you idiot!"

Bashima pounded a fist on Alaric's hardened hair, and Alaric snapped at him. Alaric had to keep the celestial away from his mate at all costs. Bashima didn't understand. Alaric whipped around, trying to dislodge his husband.

"Shina!"

Cypress came out of nowhere, his vines curling around his arms. He scooped the celestial out of the way, which seemed to annoy Torstan, then stood in front of Alaric again, floating off the ground. "Shina! It's Cypress! We're not going to hurt Bashi! You know that!"

Alaric bellowed at the Forest God, saliva flying from his sharpened teeth, sending him backward from the force, but Cypress stopped himself, wrapping the vines around Alaric and Bashima.

"I don't want to hurt you!"

"Stay out of the way, Tengu!" Bashima yelled, cursing. "That's just gonna piss him off!"

A sudden calm descended on Alaric, and he stopped mid-leap. He'd intended to attack the Forest God, that much he could recall, but the rest was a serene vision in his mind, and he could hear far-off music, like a harp playing. He smelled citrus and sage, burnt sugar and smoke.

He collapsed, Bashima on top of him, and his scales receded slowly. Bashima panted and ran his hand down the brand, sending out soothing energy, telling Alaric it was okay. The glow dimmed. Cypress's vines released, and Bashima eased off Alaric's back, pulling him into a sitting position and dragging his head to his chest. The Sun God scowled, eyes darting in three directions, daring them to approach his husband.

"What in the seven hells just happened?" Vaultus yelled, standing by his throne. It happened so quickly, and the king hadn't moved far, He had retreated to his place of power.

Alaric closed his eyes and sighed. He leaned into Bashima. He'd lost control again. Daruk would be so disappointed in him.

"That," came the old celestial's voice, "is no god-touched. That's a gods-damned dragon."

"A dragon?" Vaultus's voice was fearful but skeptical. "There haven't been any dragons for…"

"Fifty thousand years," Cypress muttered. "He's not technically a dragon."

"Don't you start with your muttering," Torstan said. "It's obvious that you knew. This is even worse than them having a soul bond."

Bashima snarled like a wounded animal and shot to his feet, leaving Alaric cowering on the floor. His palms ignited with bright light.

The celestial knew. Somehow, he knew. Had Cypress told him? No, that didn't seem possible. Cypress hadn't told the king or the celestial that Alaric was a dragon-touched, so he certainly wouldn't bring up the soul bond.

"Enough of the theatrics," Torstan grumbled. "We're not going to hurt you or your husband. Not that I couldn't."

"Fuck you," Bashima said, his voice coarse.

Alaric hadn't heard Bashima this distressed in a while. He shut down his wards, so their bond could flow freely. If they had to escape, they needed to know what the other was feeling. Bashima wanted to run, but he was afraid of the celestial, and he felt betrayed by Cypress.

"He didn't tell anyone, Khresh," Alaric murmured from the floor. Bashima didn't move, his defensive stance prepared to decimate anyone who dared approach them.

"I wouldn't do that!" Cypress said, hands in the air. Green energy cascaded over his skin, and his wide eyes pleaded with Bashima to believe him. "I couldn't do that to you."

"You." Torstan marched over to the Forest God and smacked him on the back of the head. "You're going to get the same lecture as them. Not that it makes much difference. Your bond partner is gone, thank the gods."

Cypress stuttered incomprehensible syllables at the celestial, his eyes turning bright, shining green. Torstan smacked him again. "You think I didn't notice? I have eyes. Though you're in nowhere near as much trouble as these two."

He shook his head.

"What are you talking about?" Vaultus sagged down into his throne. "Dragons? Soul bonds? Those aren't real."

Torstan harrumphed. "Like hells they're not. We're just lucky that they don't occur very often."

Alaric reeled where he sat. This was bad. Cypress said that no one could know he was dragon-touched, Togarashi had warned the same. And their soul bond, what they'd tried so hard to hide…

"How did you know?" Alaric asked.

Everyone looked at him. Cypress and Bashima were frightened, their faces pale, although the Sun God was ready to rip out throats. Vaultus's mouth hung open, disbelieving. Torstan eyed Alaric like he might attack at any moment.

"The scales were a dead give-away," the celestial said.

"Not that."

Alaric's eyes gleamed, and every part of him screamed to kill Torstan. His brand glowed, light low, and Bashima hummed in his chest, trying to sooth his husband.

"That," said Torstan, "is harder to detect. Unfortunately for you, celestials can pick up on it if they're close enough and paying attention."

"Pick up on what?" Vaultus's voice was high and confused. Alaric felt bad for him, but this was serious. He and Bashima might have to flee and bar themselves in the Temple of the Sun. Or they might have to leave. He didn't want to think about that option.

"Vaultus, soul bonds are very rare, an unfortunate side effect of bestowing emotions on our creations," Torstan said and paused before addressing Alaric again. "When you use your bond, I can sense it. Your brand makes it even easier to see."

He marched over to them, and Bashima hissed, but Torstan waved a hand at him.

"I assume you've been claimed as well, otherwise the bond wouldn't be this strong. Shit. Dragon mates and soul-bonded."

He rubbed his eyes, and Bashima flushed, moving his shoulder back. Torstan laughed softly. He said, "Won't do any good to hide it from me. If he's a dragon, and you're this attached, he's claimed you. There will be no way to separate you two."

This time, Alaric growled a warning. Separate them?

"Don't make me use the sensory bomb again," Torstan warned. "It can pack quite a wallop if I want it to."

"Did he do something to you?" Bashima asked Alaric, alarmed. He put his hands on Alaric's face and turned it to the side, searching for marks. Alaric held onto his mate's hands and smiled.

"In a manner of speaking," Torstan said. Cypress had edged closer, listening. "I overwhelmed him with sensory memories. He would have sensed things that calm him, smells, sounds. I didn't hit you with too much force. No need to knock you unconscious, but don't do something that will force my hand."

Bashima helped Alaric to his feet, light flying across his skin.

"If you tell anyone about this —"

"Hells, boy, do you think I've lost my mind? The fewer people who know the better. Does anyone not in this room know about your soul bond?"

Alaric shook his head. Cypress looked like he might be sick. He must have been thinking of Oken.

"That's good. At least you had the sense not to shout about it." Torstan put his chin in his hand, thinking. "And that you're a dragon?"

"Dragon-touched," Cypress said, earning a glare from the celestial. "If you're going to talk about him, at least be accurate."

"A few people know about that," Alaric said, hanging his head. "But they won't say anything."

"Hells, if they were in the war council, they had the chance to do it and didn't," Vaultus said. He sounded exhausted and furious that they'd hidden something this important from him. "Had you planned on telling us? Do you have abilities that would make you an asset?"

Bashima snorted and said, derision in his voice, "So you could use him like you're using the demigods? No thanks. Alaric isn't a weapon you can order around, and I'm no demigod that you can scare into submission."

"We certainly won't try to make Shina do anything," Torstan said.

"Now that you know I'm a dragon," Alaric said, standing tall. "But if I was some lowly god-touched, you would have tried."

Torstan met his gaze cooly. He said, "Having a soul-bonded pair on a battlefield is reckless. You won't behave rationally, knowing your partner might be in danger."

"We're in danger all the time," Bashima rasped. "You think we don't know that being what we are could be taken advantage of?"

Cypress stepped forward, his green eyes full of purpose. He said, "Knowing about the soul bonds doesn't change anything."

He looked from Torstan to the king, neither of whom wanted to meet his eyes. Something was going on there too. Alaric and Bashima weren't the only ones keeping secrets.

The Forest God cleared his throat and said, "The situation is bigger than that. Bashima and Shina wouldn't put our mission in jeopardy, and Shina's power is still an asset."

"Like hells," Bashima said. "You're playing dedicated soldier now, but I won't let you use my husband."

"Khresh," Alaric said, putting a hand on Bashima's shoulder. He sent out a tendril of his soul, conciliatory. Bashima huffed but didn't say more. Alaric continued, "Since you know about me, I should tell you. I was training recently, with another dragon-touched."

Torstan's eyes lit up. "There's another?"

"We were attacked," Alaric said, and Cypress inhaled sharply. "By a celestial. One that felt a million times worse than you." Alaric nodded at Torstan, whose face fell. "He didn't have eyes — it looked like they'd been ripped out or something — and he'd come for Daruk, the other dragon-touched. Daruk told me to run, so…so I did."

"You saw him," Torstan said, shocked. "You saw Ouranios."

"I don't know who he was."

"No eyes." The king put his face in his hands. "It had to be him. He was out in the open, brazenly recruiting."

"And now he has a dragon." Torstan walked away from them, muttering under his breath.

"Daruk won't follow him!" Alaric said, whipping his head to look at the king. "He tried to fight. He tried everything he could!"

"There are ways for him to make this Daruk fight for him," Torstan said.

"I escaped with Loralei, Daruk's mate," Alaric said, pleading. "So at least Ouranios can't use her against him."

"That's one good thing about this situation," Torstan said. "He'll want the dragon to follow him freely, if he wants the full power potential, but he won't shy away from torture or coercion."

"He won't be able to make Daruk do anything," Alaric said, full of conviction.

There was no way Daruk would agree to anything that monster said. Ouranios could keep him locked up forever, and Daruk wouldn't budge.

"We can only hope," Torstan said. "As for you, Forest God. Get that power under control. Things are going to escalate. He's shown his face, and Shina escaped him. He'll need to make a move."

He walked toward the throne room doors, leaving them. "Good work with the vines."

The door closed after him, Savos's charm still in place.

"Cypress," Alaric started, but he wasn't sure what else he could say. The Forest God gazed at him, dazed. The determination that was on his face a moment ago melted when the celestial left the room.

"Bell, you're bonded with Oken?" Vaultus sat on his throne, worry radiating off him. "I'm so sorry that I volunteered him for that mission."

"Like Torstan said," Cypress mumbled, voice devoid of inflection. "It's better that he isn't here."

The Forest God fled the throne room, shoulders slumped. Alaric wished there was something he could do for his friend, but they each had a burden to carry. Speaking of.

"What did Torstan mean about Cypress getting his abilities under control?"

Bashima wouldn't look at Alaric. He moved from foot to foot, biting the inside of his cheek.

The king said, "Seeing that Bashima has kept his word, has kept my secret, means that we put our trust in the right god."

Vaultus stood and stepped down from his throne. He approached Alaric and Bashima, his gait slow. "Bashima can tell you everything. Don't be angry with him that he hasn't explained. I made him swear not to speak of it. If the other gods got wind of what's happening to me, even now, there would be mass panic."

Alaric wasn't cross with Bashima, but he was sick of the gods hoarding their secrets, thinking it was for the greater good. It was to protect themselves, and he wished they'd admit it. If Vaultus was weakened to the point where he couldn't lead, Alaric hoped there was a plan in place besides the Fire God being his second in command.

Vaultus gripped Bashima's shoulder and said, "Please keep an eye on Bell. You're being assigned with him, and Shina of course. With Oken gone, he'll need you." He patted Bashima on the back. "You may go."

What the king hadn't said was that he doubted he'd be around to watch Cypress, but Alaric didn't think he needed to say that to Bashima.

His husband's face was blank as they left the throne room, but his soul put out an avalanche of apprehension and uncertainty. Alaric clasped his hand and hummed, hoping he'd be able to help keep Cypress safe, whatever he was up against. Bashima's grip was like a vice, and he shuddered, bottom lip quivering.

Chapter Twenty-Three

Jace

Jace tried to think of when he'd been more uncomfortable or felt more awkward but was struggling to find a moment as ghastly as being in the Temple of Fire. Oken hadn't been in his first home in over a thousand years, yet he didn't hesitate before climbing the stairs and walking right in. Jace winced and shook his head. His friend didn't give two shits about protocol or lingering resentment. He needed to go to the temple, so he did. Jace didn't think it could be called bravery, per se, but Oken's fortitude impressed him. Maybe they had a real chance on this mission.

Cabari had told Jace that he'd never been anywhere, but he could now mark Cindras's temple off his list, and he planned never to return. The halls were dark, even though they were lit with massive torches, and every hall and room felt warm, dry, and intimidating. The shades bustled about their business, and the god-touched also marched the halls, seemingly proud of their jobs. At least the Fire God didn't mistreat his staff, or at least not from what Jace could see.

"They all look…"

"Content?" Oken offered.

Jace shrugged and stood to the side as another god-touched passed. He eyed the two demigods but did nothing to impede them.

"Yeah. It's weird, right?"

Oken continued down the hall, remembering exactly where he needed to go. He said, "Not really. My father was never abusive to them. He's a fair employer. They're devoted to him. His god-touched have been with him forever. Except my mother. She's the newest."

Jace wiped sweat from his forehead. He wondered where the Fire God was. If his god-touched were in the temple, he couldn't be too far away. He also thought about Marlana. Was Oken's mother nearby too?

Leading him down the halls, Oken took sudden turns and walked briskly, not paying attention to if Jace followed, so he stayed on his friend's heels.

Oken had been quiet since they'd left the Underworld, only answering questions, never offering conversation. Oken overhearing Jace's last conversation with his father might be on the "most embarrassing moments of his life" list as well.

They'd been in Jace's room, packing for the journey, and Oken sat on the bed, watching Jace search his room for things he thought might be useful. He was very excited about using his collapsible bucket, though Oken gave him a blank look when he demonstrated what it did. Jace labored over his flute and violin, but he knew they should only bring essentials. He sat in the chair in his music area and ran the bow over the violin's strings.

"My father thought music was a waste of time," Oken said. "Is it enjoyable to play an instrument?"

Jace set the bow down on the music stand and sighed. He stood and placed the violin on its stand. He said, "It usually is."

Oken nodded, not prying further.

Veles chose that moment to knock and come into the room. His eyes were bloodshot from lack of sleep, and he slouched over to Jace, ignoring Oken. His father wasn't angry with Oken, but Veles felt like Oken encouraged Jace to join the mission.

"Almost ready," Jace said, shuffling his feet.

His father's sour mood was also worsened because Niall was gone. He left the Underworld early that morning, his chief task to travel to the southern gods and apprise them of the situation. He'd agreed to Vaultus's request, though he voiced his displeasure and at a very high volume. Niall told Jace to stay out of trouble and to run at the first sign of danger. Then he'd hugged him. The hugging was still strange.

Nim hid in her room. She hadn't said much to Jace since finding out that he was leaving, just pouted at meals and wouldn't talk to him.

"If I could make you stay, I would," Veles said, pulling a thick coiled whip from behind his back. He handed it to Jace. "You're going to need this. Your practice one is worn out, and it's about time you graduated to the real thing."

"Dad, no this is yours." Jace tried to pass it back, but his father crossed his arms, his eyes shining red.

Veles said, "You'll need it more than me. I can request another."

Jace brought the whip to his chest and looked at the floor. His father was terrible at letting go, so the gesture was unexpected, but Jace appreciated it.

"That's an odd gift," Oken said, head tilted. He sat cross-legged on the bed, eyes inquisitive. "I wouldn't know. I don't get many gifts."

"It's not only a gift," Veles said, grumbling. "It's a weapon, for defense as well as offense. Jace doesn't have a showy ability like you, so he needed to work twice as hard."

"Dad!" Jace was mortified.

"You're right," Oken said, "I should feel lucky that I don't need a weapon." He looked at his hands, studying their curves. "I am the weapon."

Veles shifted uncomfortably and grunted under his breath. He said, "You're not a weapon, Oken. If your father said that to you, forget it. It's your power, and if it can help keep my son safe, I'm glad you have it."

Oken gave them a small smile. "Bell used to say that to me, that it's my power, and I can use it to protect people."

Veles cleared his throat and refocused on his son. "Leaving all this here?" He gestured at the music stand and instruments. A piece of sheet music caught his eye, and he picked it up.

Shit. Jace thought he'd gotten rid of that.

His father said, "What's this? Something new?"

"It's nothing," Jace said, grabbing it back.

Sensing his son's mood, Veles took a slight step back. He probably would have let it go, if this weren't Jace's last day in the temple.

"Would you play it for me?"

Horrified, Jace balled up the pages and threw them in the trash bin by the music stand.

"No!" Seeing his father's shocked expression, Jace said, "It's...it was for someone else. And it's not finished."

Veles's confusion drained, replaced by quiet fury. His lips pressed together. Jace brushed past him and went to the bed. He shoved the whip into the pack and slung it on his back.

"We need to go," Jace whispered.

Oken glanced between the father and son, appreciating that something had just happened between them that he didn't grasp. He got off the bed and walked out into the hall.

"You know he hasn't been seen for over a week?" his father asked, voice sharp and hard as a blade.

"You keep reminding me," Jace muttered.

He didn't want the last thing they said to each other to be an argument, but he didn't know what else to say. He knew why his father kept bringing it up: the Lightning God was shirking his duties, most dishonorable.

His father walked over and grasped his shoulders, making Jace look him in the eye. He said, "You know I want you to be happy. But my only concern right now is your safety."

"You don't have to worry about that, Dad."

Veles drew him into a hug, and Jace reluctantly put his arms around his father.

"I'll always worry about you."

Nim ran into Jace's room, sobbing, and tackled him with a hug, finally able to say farewell. Like she'd been waiting outside the door for an opening.

And now, they sought Oken's sister, Dahlia, hoping she might have a lead on other demigods.

Jace wasn't crazy about trying to find the demigods on Vaultus's list, but at least they were known quantities. Oken had a different idea, so Jace would let him pursue the option. At least with Dahlia they might have an in.

"Dahlia's room was about as far away from mine as you could get," Oken said, finally starting a conversation. "Iris's and Asher's were near hers."

Jace shivered. "Your father really kept you away from them?"

"I was too young to remember much about my brother and other sister," Oken admitted as they turned another corner. "Asher left when I was really little. I couldn't even tell you what he looks like. I remember Iris had white hair and an angry face."

"And that's who you want to find?"

Jace didn't think Oken was prepared for what would happen if they did find his sister. He said that Iris hated the Fire God and probably wouldn't welcome Oken if they found her.

"She might not try to kill me," Oken said. "Which is more than we can hope for with other demigods."

Great. Their best hope for finding a demigod was Oken's estranged sister who might not try to kill him.

Oken stopped in front of a door that resembled the others they'd passed. He knocked loudly, and someone squealed inside and ran to the door. Dahlia, Oken's oldest sister, flung it open and grabbed Oken by the shirt, pulling him inside.

"Baby brother!" She embraced Oken with such force Jace thought his head might pop off his body.

She was much shorter than Oken, and he patted her on the head, smoothing her white hair. There were flecks of red in her hair, the only similarity she shared with her father. She had a heart-shaped face and large gray eyes, her smile effusive. Jace wasn't sure the Fire God was capable of smiling.

"Hello, Dahlia," Oken said. "You got my letter?"

"Yes! And I can't believe you're here! I haven't seen you in so long." Tears leaked from her eyes as she released Oken, and she rubbed them away. "You got even taller, how is that possible?"

Oken tilted his head. "I suppose it's genetic." She giggled and smacked Oken's arm. He said, "Why did you hit me?"

"I missed you so much," she said, laughing. "Always so literal. And you must be Jace? Veles's son?" Dahlia extended her hand and Jace shook it. She was so different from Oken and the Fire God, bubbly and friendly.

"Yeah, umm…"

"Just as chatty as Oken, huh?" She winked at him and grabbed his hand. "I'm glad he'll have company on this mission, or whatever it is. Dad hasn't said much, and Mom sits in her greenhouse all day."

"Are they here?" Oken asked, voice quiet.

Dahlia fidgeted with her hands. "Why don't you come sit down. I called for some tea." She led them to her sitting room, which was bright and cheery, covered with floral paintings. "They're not here, but they didn't go far. There's a fire-type god who lives nearby that Dad needed to meet with."

"Right now?"

"He wanted to give you some space, I guess," Dahlia said.

Tea was ready, and Jace was grateful for the hot drink and snacks she'd set out. One thing they needed from the Temple of Fire was more provisions. They'd gotten a few things from the Underworld, but Oken said they could resupply from his father's temple.

"That seems unlikely," Oken said and sipped his tea. He seemed far away again, not looking at either his sister or Jace.

"He seems different," Dahlia started, but Oken cut her off.

"He's the same. Don't look for something that isn't there."

She bit her lower lip and sighed. "I just wish we could be a family, you know?"

Oken took a deep breath and said, "You will always be my family, Dahlia. I love Mom, but she can't leave him. She won't leave him, and I don't understand why she defends him. Or why you're trying to."

Dahlia didn't answer. She gazed down at the small table that held the tea things. Jace fought the urge to run out of the room. They needed to get what they'd come for.

"Oken thought you might have an idea where your sister is."

Dahlia set her cup down and said, "I know where Iris is, yes. But I don't think you should go there."

"Why not?" Oken asked, curious.

"She lives in a demigod community and they're pretty anti-god." Dahlia's cheeks flushed, making her look like she knew a secret but couldn't share it.

A community? Jace wondered how many demigods lived with Oken's sister. Could they complete their mission by traveling to one place? No, it wouldn't be that easy. If they hated gods, there was little chance the demigods would agree to join the conflict against Ouranios.

"We have to try," Oken said. "The king is counting on us. And once they hear what we're up against, I think they'll agree to come with us."

Dahlia let out a soft laugh. "I doubt Iris will agree to do anything a god wants her to do, but I hope she does, for your sake. I don't care much either way, I just want you all to be safe."

"None of us will be safe if the celestial takes control of the world," Oken said, tone firm. "I don't know if Dad told you, but that's what we're up against. This isn't a petty squabble between gods."

"A celestial?" Dahlia's eyes widened. "Dad didn't mention that, but he's been so busy lately. I've hardly seen him."

"Can you please tell me where Iris is?" Oken took his sister's hand, his eyes blazing. He was ready to move on to the next step. Jace wished they could spend more time with Dahlia, for her sake and Oken's, but that wasn't an option. They shouldn't stay too long in one place.

"You'd go looking for her anyway," Dahlia said. "They're about two hundred miles south of here, living in an abandoned temple."

"Do you know how many are there?" Jace asked, but she shook her head.

"Iris doesn't say much in her letters, just that she's okay. Says that she's happy where she is. She's with a group of people she trusts. Asks about Mom, and you too, Oken."

"And what do you say?"

"The usual. Mom's the same, but she was so happy to see you. If you could write to her once in a while, I think she'd like that."

"I'll think about it," Oken said.

"I'm never sure what to tell her about you," Dahlia went on, rubbing another tear from her cheek. "Only that I know you're okay and staying with the Forest God."

Jace gazed at his friend, whose face had gone white.

"You can write to me too," she said. "Dad won't stop your letters. He might have before, but like I said, he's changed."

Oken stood up abruptly, and Dahlia jumped to her feet. "Are you okay?"

"We should go," Oken said. "I don't want to waste too much time."

Jace groaned. His friend was terrible at this stuff. Dahlia's face fell, her hands shaking. "It's not a waste of time if you want to talk with your sister. We can stay a bit."

Shaking his head, Oken said, "I would like to, but this mission is too important. I'm sorry, Dahlia."

"That's okay," she said, sniffing. "It was so nice to see you. I'll get a map for you, for where Iris is staying."

"I promise I'll come back," Oken said.

Dahlia looked back at her brother, smiling sadly. "I hope you do."

They shifted away from the Temple of Fire, Oken holding Jace's arm. It would take them at least twelve shifts to get close to the temple ruins that Dahlia showed them, and the trip would drain their energy. Jace suggested that they camp for the night in a place he knew, and Oken agreed, though he was adamant that they move with haste the next day.

They landed in the familiar clearing, water falling behind them, birds calling from the trees.

"Oh," said Oken, and there was actual feeling in his tone. "This place is beautiful."

"Yeah." Jace walked toward the pool and gazed down into the dark water. Light played off the surface as the sun set, throwing dots of color on Jace's skin. He hadn't been to their — no, stop — this place in a while, but its magic hadn't faded. Not even the Lightning God could ruin the waterfall nor the dark blue pool.

"How did you find it?" Oken stooped beside him. "I can't see my reflection."

Jace laughed. "It's sort of magical." He dropped his pack next to Oken's and sat down. Taking off his boots and socks, he dipped his feet in the cool water and sighed. "Don't drink it, okay?"

"Cabari brought you here, didn't he?"

Jace bit the inside of his cheek and sucked in a deep breath. "Yup. But it's the safest place I know. No one will find us here."

"I'm sorry I brought him up." Oken joined him, dangling his feet in too. "It's not as cold as I expected."

"It's nice, huh?"

"Very. Thank you for bringing me here. It's a special place." Oken pulled his feet out and watched the water drip off his toes. "You had sex here, didn't you?"

Jace snorted and turned bright red. He shoved Oken with his shoulder. "Add that to your list of things never to bring up, jerk."

Oken looked hurt, his mouth drooping.

"Sorry, you're not a jerk." Jace rubbed his eyes. "I'm the jerk. I brought you here, you were bound to have questions."

"Without Bell, it's hard for me to remember the things that aren't appropriate to talk about." Oken brought his feet up and rested his arms on his knees, putting his chin on top.

Jace threw a pebble into the water, and ripples roved out from the center, flowing across the pool.

"My first time was here."

"Wow," Oken said, awed. "Mine was in a normal bedroom."

Jace choked on a laugh and clapped Oken on the back. "Somehow, I doubt your first time was normal. I don't think anyone's first time is. I know it's not supposed to be a big deal or whatever, but it felt pretty big to me."

"Who said it wasn't a big deal?"

Jace shrugged. "No one, I guess. I always thought I shouldn't work myself up over it. It's just sex, right? People do it all the time."

"But you hadn't done it all the time."

Cabari sure had, Jace thought and grunted.

He needed to let the Lightning God go, but it was difficult when the pool called to him, making him remember every time they'd swum here.

"Sex is natural," Oken said. "That's what I believe. But it's also special, if you think it is. Don't feel bad about having sex with Cabari."

"I don't feel bad!" Jace stood up and stomped away from the pool. He needed to set up the tent. Oken followed him, concerned.

"Then why does it seem like you do?"

"Can you just…not right now?" Jace glared at the other demigod.

Once Oken had an idea in his head, it was tough to dislodge. He was inquisitive to the point of being intrusive, and while he didn't mean any harm, he didn't understand that some things needed to stay private.

"Doesn't talking about it help?"

Jace whipped around, the tent a mess at his feet. "Do you feel like talking about your parents?"

"Would you like to talk about them?"

Dammit, wrong tactic. Oken might drive him insane on this mission.

"No. Well, I don't know." Jace threw his hands in the air. "Most people don't like discussing this kind of stuff. It's depressing."

"Oh," Oken said. He knelt by the tent and extracted the poles and ropes. "I can help."

They built the tent in silence, Jace trying not to look at his friend. Oken didn't say anything else, and when they were finished with the tent, he walked away, gathering stones and twigs and branches.

"What are you doing?"

"I'm going to make a fire," Oken said, as though Jace had asked a dumb question. "I can make sure the smoke doesn't show. And then we don't have to eat cold food."

Jace nodded. For a fellow shut-in who hadn't seen much of the world, Oken knew a lot about roughing it. They sat near the fire when it was ready and ate in silence. Jace normally didn't mind being quiet. The Lightning God was the one who couldn't bear staying still for one second. But sitting with Oken made the silence stretch on forever.

"I don't feel bad about sleeping with Cabari," he ventured, and Oken looked up, surprised. "I feel stupid." He threw a few more sticks on the fire.

"Why?" Oken asked. "You liked him. He liked you."

"He liked getting laid."

"You think that's all he liked about you?"

Damn, Oken had to ask the worst questions. Why had Jace said anything? The silence wasn't as bad as having to talk about Cabari.

"I don't know what he liked about me. But I guess it wasn't enough."

"It was nice of him to stand up for you at the king's meeting," Oken said. "Why would he do that if he didn't like you?"

Jace didn't want to think about that either. If he did, he might rationalize forgiving the Lightning God for being such a jackass. But

Cabari hadn't needed to say anything during the meeting. He could have sat there like everyone else, not caring about what happened to two demigods.

"I don't think a god would speak up for a demigod, not unless they had a reason."

"What does it matter?" Jace asked. "If it hadn't been me, he wouldn't have said shit."

"Exactly." Oken said it like Jace had proven his point for him. "He said it for you."

Jace scoffed. "He should want to stand up for all of us."

"That's a lot to expect from a god. Isn't it good that he at least defended you?" Oken let that sink in, and Jace had to admit he was right. Oken said, "I wish Bell said something. Not that he could. He couldn't stand against his stepfather. At least he didn't know what they were going to ask us to do."

"He didn't?"

Jace remembered the flash of green light that went around the throne room when Torstan and Vaultus proposed the demigod recruitment assignment. Maybe Cypress hadn't known.

"He said he didn't, and he wasn't lying."

"That's something," Jace said, and he thought about how he and Oken had chosen to be with gods, when gods dating demigods was so uncommon.

Then there was Bashima, who married a human. It was unheard of with the older gods to mix with other types of people; they either married each other or stayed single and fucked whoever they wanted. Maybe the younger gods were different, or at least different enough.

"I doubt Cypress wanted you to go traipsing over the world with me, trying to find people who don't want anything to do with the gods."

"He didn't want me to, no. But I don't think Bell knows what he really wants. There's too much weight on his shoulders. I only added to it." Oken looked into the fire intently. "But I couldn't roll over and accept everything without question. Look what's happened to my mother."

Jace clicked his teeth together. He didn't know enough about Oken's mother to comment.

"Your dad seems okay though," Oken said.

Coughing, Jace said, "My dad? He's…fine. Not the best at letting me experience things."

"But you can do all kinds of things!" Oken stared at him. "You can fight with that whip, right? And play instruments. And you write music? I can't do any of that. My father thought it was a waste of time. I can fight, but that's about it."

"When you put it like that, you make me sound like an amazing person. I'm just me."

Oken was wrong. There was nothing extraordinary about Jace. He could read minds somewhat and coerce them, sure, but he wasn't a fantastic composer or that good a fighter. He was pretty average for a demigod.

"That music you wrote? That you didn't want to play? Did you write it for Cabari?"

"Why do you keep asking me stuff like that?" Jace shouted, stood up, and paced around the fire, muttering to himself. Oken kept crossing the line, making him revisit memories he wanted to let go.

Cabari was ticklish, and he would shriek with laughter and beg Jace to stop when he attacked his feet and the backs of his knees. He called Jace a monster with no feelings as he fell onto the ground in fits of giggles…

"Because it seems important," Oken said. "I don't think people should forget important things."

Jace stopped pacing. Oken didn't want to hurt Jace's feelings or stir up bad memories. He meant well. "It was just an idea," Jace mumbled, kicking a rock into the trees, hands in his pockets. "Didn't really finish it."

"What was it about?" Oken stared at Jace, rapt. He wasn't used to having a captivated audience.

"Uh, about the waterfall…and…"

"Oh." Oken's eyes got huge. "Imagine if your dad heard you play a song about you having sex for the first time."

"You had to say it." Jace paused, about to yell at Oken, but he stopped.

Jace would be mortified if his father knew what the piece was about, so embarrassed he might skip the afterlife and go right to permanent death. He tried to hold in a laugh, imagining his father's face if he found out. Absolute fury.

He crumpled to the ground and cackled, letting his voice carry into the trees. He rolled around, tears rolling down his cheeks from laughing. He hadn't laughed in so long.

"Are you all right?" Oken stood over him, alarmed. "You seem to be in hysterics."

Jace gulped air and shook his head. "I'll be fine." He stopped rolling, laying on his back, and gazed up at the stars. "Let's get some rest. We've got a long trip tomorrow."

They slept well into the morning, lulled to sleep by the waterfall. Oken was agitated, but Jace didn't mind. It was the first good sleep he'd gotten in a while. As his friend bustled around, taking down the tent and shoving it into his pack, Jace took one last walk around the clearing.

The water called to him, beckoning for a quick swim, but they didn't have time. He went toward the waterfall, letting the sound cascade through his mind, savoring it. He might never come back, and he wanted to imprint the sensations on his memory. Oken called him over eventually, and Jace sighed.

"So long, waterfall," he whispered.

As he was about to go back to Oken, Jace spotted something in the grass near the pool. He stooped and picked up a feather, dark gray and heavier than a normal bird's feather. It was bigger than any bird's Jace had seen too. He shrugged and put it in his jacket pocket.

As he walked back to their makeshift campsite, now cleaned up, the fire's ashes spread across the grass, a cold wind knocked Jace back, and he tripped, falling to the ground.

"Oken! What the hells?"

But Oken couldn't answer him. He writhed on the grass by their packs, back arched, pupils blown black, and his right arm was covered in ice crystals and flames sputtered on his left. Snowflakes flew upward from his right hand, which was an icy claw.

No, no, no, what was happening?

Jace leaped up, but what if Oken accidentally hit him with his ice or fire? Jace couldn't defend himself from that. What could he do?

Think! Do SOMETHING!

Collapsible bucket! Oken could put out a fire with his ice, but they'd needed something to collect fresh water. It wasn't looking so dumb now, bringing the bucket along.

Jace skirted around Oken, whose jaw was clenched, his entire body shaking, and grabbed his pack. Jace tore through it and grabbed the bucket, sprinting for the pool.

Please work, please work, please work.

He skidded to the pool, dropped the bucket into the dark blue water, which sang to him. He was doing the right thing. It was all he could think to try.

Tears leaked down Jace's face. He raced back to his friend and upended the bucket of magical water on him.

Chapter Twenty-Four

Alaric

"Keep your eyes closed!"

"They're closed, all right? Sheesh. Don't let me run into anything."

"Like I'd let that happen."

Bashima held Alaric by the arm, steering him through the temple, and he'd already almost let Alaric hit numerous objects. Bashima pulled his husband out of the way in time, but it was jarring to get pulled off his feet with his eyes closed.

"What about that antique vase you knocked over?"

"That was me, not you," Bashima said, and Alaric could tell that his husband rolled his eyes. Alaric grinned and shook his head.

Bashima never celebrated his own birthday, and he didn't see the point of them. The three god-touched had made sure he knew how important birthdays were to humans, that Alaric would definitely expect something. So, he was overcompensating, almost giddy with whatever surprises he had in store for Alaric.

They could use some fun. It had been a little over a week since the war council meeting, and everyone was tense. Kuroi had been storming around the temple, lecturing the shades on proper protocol in case he and the other god-touched had to go with Bashima on short notice. He quizzed them constantly, and most of the shades learned to avoid Kuroi, knowing his daily routine. Alaric found Emilia hiding in the library numerous times, and Matthias only spoke in grunts and one-word phrases.

So, Bashima told Alaric he had a plan for his birthday and not to worry. Alaric tried to tell him that a birthday party didn't matter, considering what was going on in their world, but Bashima was insistent.

"I'm not going to have your first birthday ruined because some asshole wants to take over the world."

"Babe, it's not my first birthday."

"It's your first one with me."

Now, Bashima tugged on his arm again, and Alaric followed, trying not to peek.

"Why didn't we shift wherever you're taking me," he asked, giggling.

"This is way more fun," Bashima said.

He must have the evilest grin on his face, Alaric thought. Such a jerk.

"It'll be less fun if I break something. Either my ankle or some sculpture worth more than my whole village."

Bashima stopped him and grabbed his shoulders, facing him in the proper direction. He stepped away from Alaric and the soft breeze meant he'd opened some doors.

"Okay," Bashima said, excited. He grasped Alaric's hands and led him forward. Bright light hit Alaric's face and he leaned forward, appreciating the warmth. Bashima's grip tightened.

"You can open your eyes now."

They were standing in the middle of the throne room, sunlight falling through the skylight. At first, Alaric was confused. Why would Bashima bring him to the throne room? Then he saw it.

"Holy. Shit."

"Yeah, I thought it was a little excessive, but the temple does what it wants," Bashima said, fake grumbling. He crossed his arms and leaned back, admiring the sight.

Next to Bashima's throne was an identical seat, a solid sheet of gold running up to the ceiling, the same size, same color, but where Bashima's throne sported a sunburst pattern, the second had a stylized dragon roaring across the back. The matching thrones gleamed in the sunlight.

"Subtle," Alaric said, smirking.

"If you like that, you'll love this."

Bashima spun him around. Over the throne room doors hung a massive lifelike painting of Bashima and Alaric from their wedding day, done like an official royal portrait. Their eyes shone with luminous red and orange paint.

"Good gods! We're enormous!" Alaric ran over to the painting, neck craning as he looked up. "Kuroi, I assume?"

Bashima sidled up to him and slung an arm across Alaric's shoulder. "You guessed right. He said that he, Shefu, and Draiden already gave you a birthday gift, but then he unveiled this monstrosity. I didn't have the heart to tell him you'd hate it."

"Hate it?" Alaric yelled. "It's glorious!"

"Hells, you have terrible taste," Bashima said, pinching the bridge of his nose. "Anyway, Draiden has something else for you too. Shefu wanted to make you dinner, but I wanted to do that. So, we compromised."

"And Shefu's making dinner?" Alaric held in a laugh.

Bashima had proudly brought him a cheese and bacon omelet for breakfast, and Alaric was surprised how delicious it was, but his husband excelled at most things, so he shouldn't have been shocked that Bashima could cook.

"Shefu's making dinner," Bashima grunted under his breath. "I have something for you too, but I'll give it to you later."

"Ooooo sexy," Alaric said and waggled his eyebrows.

"Not that, your pervert. Well, yes that, but I have something else too."

Alaric stuck out his bottom lip, eyes shining and wide. He said, "Fine, but you better pull out all the stops. I'm going to go sit on my throne."

He skipped across the room and launched himself onto the huge chair. It wasn't the most comfortable thing in the world, but Alaric doubted he'd use it much.

"Why would the temple make me a throne? I won't be in here while you're working."

Bashima ambled up to him and lounged in his own throne. "You'll have to join me during the tribute ceremonies." The grin that slashed his face was criminal.

Alaric laughed and waved his husband away, but Bashima's smile stayed in place.

"You're not serious."

"I'm dead serious." Bashima grabbed Alaric's hand and squeezed. "Now we can be bored off our asses together. There's supposed to be one coming up next month, but…"

"Maybe the torture can wait another year," Alaric said, hopeful. He had no desire to watch the tributes fawn over his husband. What would that do to his jealous dragon side?

"You're worried that you'll get jealous," Bashima teased. He kissed the back of Alaric's hand.

"Sometimes having this soul bond is really annoying," Alaric said and sent his husband an emotional rebuke, and Bashima laughed.

They had dinner outside, down in the valley, once the sun set. Kuroi made sure they were comfortable under the canopy he'd designed to go over the dinner table and draped with hundreds of floating, twinkling lights. Bashima enchanted his standing harp to play during dinner, and it strummed in the background as everyone arrived.

Since most of the gods were gearing up for whatever Ouranios had planned, the party was small. Alora and Garyn were on time for once, bringing more wine than they could possibly drink. They greeted one another, hugging, trying to be upbeat when the future loomed over their heads.

"Thanks for coming," Alaric said, flushing. "We're all so busy."

"I'd much rather be hanging out here than going to more meetings. Or being stuck working," Garyn said, sighing. "I wasn't sure if I could leave my temple, but Alora dragged me out. Thank the gods."

"And we've never been to an actual birthday party before!" Alora said. "Oh. Shina. Who is that?"

She grabbed him by the tunic and dragged him from under the canopy, watching two figures approach.

Cypress had shifted from Vaultus's temple, bringing Resk the god-touched in tow. The Forest God had asked Alaric if it was okay to bring Resk with him, since it was boring for him at the king's temple. The other god-touched thought he was strange and avoided him. Not wanting anyone to feel left out, Alaric said Resk could join them. He wanted Cypress to be less stressed. With Oken leaving, he seemed dejected and lost.

"Uh, Cypress?" Alaric said.

"No, dummy, who's that with him? He's so tall..." Alora was practically drooling.

Alaric gulped and said, "That's Resk. He's a god-touched from the Temple of Time. Cypress sort of adopted him."

He left out the part about how Resk had assisted in his kidnapping; that would bring down the mood, and he wanted the evening to go as Bashima planned.

Alora glanced at Alaric from the corner of her eye. She said, "Didn't think Cypress would replace Oken that quickly, but what do I know?" She muttered something about the Lightning God and morons.

"No!" Alaric pulled her back under the canopy. "It's not like that! Resk didn't have anywhere to go. The other God-touched that Chronas made...they died. Veles asked Cypress if Resk could stay with him until they could find a better place for him."

"Oh, I can find a better place for him," Alora said, licking her lips. Alaric gaped at her as Garyn walked over, possibly sensing something was afoot. Alora said, "We've been looking for a third —"

"We have?" Garyn asked, raising an eyebrow.

"I've been looking for a third," Alora corrected herself. "Garyn didn't realize he wanted the same thing until right this moment."

"I did?" The wings at Garyn's elbows fluttered, showing his agitation.

"Look at him!" She peeked at Cypress and Resk approaching and shoved Garyn's face in the same direction. "He's perfect!"

"Cypress? Are you insane? He'd drive you right up a wall."

"What is wrong with you men?" Alora blew a breath out her nose. "The handsome, tall one, moron."

"What's that on his face?" Garyn asked, though his tone was appreciative.

"Eye glasses," Alaric said. He put his hands on his hips. "They help him see better."

Cypress and Resk made it to the makeshift pavilion, the god-touched awed by the simple display. His mouth hung open as he took in the tiny lights. Alaric was so used to Kuroi's alchemy that the lights were beautiful but expected, and he remembered when he'd first come to the Temple of the Sun, knowing nothing about gods or alchemy or much of anything outside the human world. Resk had only known what the Time God allowed. The least Alaric could do was show him that not all gods were bad, that there were still things in the world to admire.

"Hey, Cypress," Alaric said. He felt Bashima's tension from the table, from which he hadn't budged. He almost stood up upon seeing Resk, but Alaric sent him a calming thought. It was okay. Resk wasn't hostile. He wasn't a threat.

Alora shoved Alaric and the Forest God aside, positioning herself in front of Resk. Cypress squawked in protest, but Alora shushed him. She said, "Who's your gorgeous friend, Cypress?"

"Resk, this is Alora, Goddess of the Moon," poor Cypress sputtered, having no idea what was happening right in front of him. "Alora, Resk is a god-touched who's staying at my temple."

"That's so interesting!" She grabbed Resk's hand and led him to the dinner table, where Bashima watched them through narrowed eyes. Alaric imagined steam coming from his husband's ears and giggled.

"What just happened?" Cypress asked, shocked.

"Watch a true master at work," Garyn said, patting the Forest God on the back. He followed Alora to the table and sat across from her, smirking.

"She thinks Resk is cute," Alaric explained, rubbing the back of his neck.

"Okay…" Cypress took his seat at the table and Alaric was the last.

As he sat facing Bashima, Alaric noticed that his husband was trying not to look at Cypress, instead focused on the canopy, or the table, or even at Alora, who leaned so close to Resk while she spoke that she might as well be in his lap.

Resk made awkward chopping gestures with his hands as he answered her, and she gave him tinkling laughs and moon eyes. Alaric thought she'd flirted with him a few times. The way she'd been with Alaric was nothing compared to the sparkling creature invading Resk's personal space.

When Alaric sat, shades appeared around them, setting down covered dishes that smelled amazing. Matthias shifted next to him and leaned down, whispering, "Loralei prefers to remain in her room." Alaric nodded. He'd hoped Loralei would join them for dinner. She hadn't come out of her room once, still hadn't met Bashima. Alaric was surprised how calm his husband was about it, but he had more pressing matters to worry about than one demigod woman staying in the temple.

"We should begin," Alaric said, smiling.

They were missing people — Oken, Cabari, and Jace should be sitting at the table with them — but Alaric felt blessed to have a small moment with his husband and friends. His next birthday might not even happen.

"So," Cypress said, not having taken any food yet, "has anyone heard from him?"

They all stopped. Alora sighed and sipped her wine, and Garyn pretended like he hadn't heard. Resk didn't know what they were talking about, so he kept putting food on his plate.

Bashima cleared his throat. "Had to bring it up, didn't you, Tengu?" He grabbed his glass and gulped down wine, shaking his head.

"It's okay," Alaric said. He was curious as well and hoped Alora and Garyn might know something. "I'm worried about him too."

"He probably fucked off like he said he would," Bashima said. "Didn't think he had the balls, but he was pretty pissed."

"He hasn't contacted us," Alora said. "But it's not the first time Cabari's gone off on his own."

"That was during peace time," Garyn said. "Not when there's probably going to be a war declared any day now."

"Have you gotten anything from Oken?" Alaric asked Cypress, who shook his head and reached for a dish of fruit.

"It's better if I don't know where he is," Cypress said, voice monotone. He attempted to brighten his countenance, as though remembering that he was at a party. "But I'm happy we could celebrate your birthday. Gods aren't very good at that sort of thing."

"I suppose if you never die, there isn't much point in birthdays," Resk mused, looking up at the canopy.

Garyn snorted into his drink, spilling wine on the table.

"You've definitely got a point," Garyn said.

"And he's smart too," Alora cooed, shifting her chair even closer to Resk's. She winked at Garyn across the table and his wings fluttered again as he wiped up the wine.

Dinner went well, with no incidents besides Alora almost crawling into Resk's lap and knocking over a glass of wine onto the cheese tray. Resk didn't seem to mind, but he blushed scarlet the closer she got, and all Garyn could do was laugh.

Alaric had been wrong about the wine. Though he couldn't get drunk, the others could, and soon they were laughing and yelling at each other, even Cypress. Bashima only had a few glasses, so he mainly rolled his eyes and made snarky comments, but he smiled and indulged Alora blowing kisses at him.

As they stood to return to the temple, Alora pretended to fall over so Resk would catch her.

"Thank you! Such a gentleman." She quirked a brow at Garyn, who shrugged, and Alaric braced himself for what was coming. "Would you care to join Garyn and me for a drink in the temple?"

"We've had many drinks!" Resk said with enthusiasm.

Alora pulled his head down to her mouth and whispered something Alaric was glad he couldn't hear. That was the best birthday present the Moon Goddess could give him. Resk nearly lost consciousness from what she'd said.

"Cypress? Mind if we borrow Resk?"

The Forest God, also tipsy, waved at her and said, "Resk can do what he likes, I'm not his master."

He hiccoughed and braced himself on a chair. Alaric went to stand next to the Forest God, and Cypress shifted his weight onto Alaric.

Cypress said, "Thanks, Shina. This was nice."

"Uh huh. Khresh? Want to shift us up to the temple?"

Bashima cursed under his breath. "Some people can't hold their alcohol."

"Bashi," Cypress said, as Bashima grabbed his arm and draped it over his shoulder, hefting the Forest God off Alaric. "You're like my brother, you know? I love you."

"Fucking hells," Bashima muttered, and Alaric shook with contained laughter. "Don't you say anything," Bashima said, pointing at Alaric.

"It's my birthday," Alaric teased.

"Not for much longer."

Alaric kissed Bashima's cheek and grasped his arm as the Sun God shifted them to the temple.

After dumping Cypress onto Oken's bed, Bashima tugged Alaric out of the room and down the hall.

"He'll be okay in Oken's bedroom?" Alaric asked. "It might be weird for him to wake up there."

"Better than hearing whatever the hells Alora is getting up to. Besides, it's basically his room too. And if he freaks out, I'd rather be close by."

"Babe, you do care."

"You better pipe down if you know what's good for you," Bashima said, smiling. "Or you won't get your present."

Alaric gasped in feigned horror. "You wouldn't!"

"You bet that sweet ass I would," Bashima growled, throwing open their chamber door. "Before you jump me, I put your present in the sitting room."

"I have some self-control," Alaric said, nose in the air. He marched past his smirking husband to the sitting room. On the table by the couch was a wrapped package, the same iridescent paper Kuroi had used for his scarf. Thinking of the scarf, left behind at Daruk's cottage, sent a pang through him and Bashima was at his side in a second.

"Are you okay?"

"Yeah," Alaric said, sniffing. "It's been a long day. Not that I didn't love everything."

"We can go to bed if you want," Bashima said, concern layered in his voice. He took Alaric's hand. "Tell me what you need."

Alaric wrapped his arms around Bashima and kissed him, pulling him into an embrace. It hadn't been that long ago that they'd danced here together, when they'd been broken, trying to mend. He knew Bashima would do anything for him, even throw him a party when he'd rather spend the day alone, just the two of them.

"Nope, I want to open my present."

He made a show of looking the package over, oohing and ahhing for Bashima, who looked very proud of himself but also very nervous. Bashima fidgeted on the couch and ran a hand through his blond hair. He said, "I'm not great at this stuff."

"I'll be the judge of that," Alaric said and slid his fingers through the crease in the wrapping paper. Inside was a large book, fairly thick, with a black canvas cover. Embossed on the front was a black stylized letter A. It looked like a journal or a sketchbook.

"It's beautiful!"

"You haven't even opened it yet."

"I don't need to open it to know that I already love it."

Alaric leaned over and kissed his husband's flushed cheek then opened the book in the center. And his breath caught in his chest.

"Draiden helped me," Bashima said, voice shaking. "With the binding. He's better at that kind of alchemy."

Alaric paged back to the front, wanting to drink in the images. The book was filled with Bashima's sketches and line drawings, some of the mountain and surrounding valley, a few of the temple. But most of the pictures were of Alaric.

Alaric was brought back to the first time he had gone into Bashima's chambers, uninvited, snooping. He'd seen a desk covered in unfinished sketches, all human figures, graceful and strong, caught in motion. They'd all been of him.

"Khresh…"

His own eyes stared out of the book, deep and lifelike and made by an artist who knew his subject well. "This is the best gift anyone has ever given me." He set the book down on the table and took Bashima's shaking hand. "I'm not lying. It's the most thoughtful thing you could have given me. Thank you."

Alaric leaned forward and touched his forehead to Bashima's, sending him every loving feeling he had inside himself. The Sun God's skin lit up, throwing color across the sitting room, and he sighed.

"I was worried you wouldn't like it."

"You? Worried?" Alaric laughed.

"Only sometimes," Bashima mumbled. "Happy birthday, Alaric."

"I'll never get tired of you saying my name," Alaric said, purring deep in his chest.

"Oh yeah?" That devilish grin formed on Bashima's lips. "Alaric."

Alaric grabbed his husband and pulled him into his lap, nibbling at his neck, making chirping sounds in his throat. He breathed in deeply, inhaling every smell that made him think of Bashima, his skin charged with the sun's light.

"You get more dragon-y every day. So, you ready for your other present?"

Alaric couldn't form words. He let the dragon take over, rumbling in his chest. Hands roaming over Bashima's back, Alaric finally felt like he could relax and let the day go.

He was twenty-one.

Bashima snapped his fingers and the room dimmed, filled with small candles that illuminated the room like fairies in flight. Citrus and sage filled Alaric's nose, and he pulled away from his husband.

"You know I'm going to expect this all the time now, right?"

Bashima took Alaric's face in his hands and kissed from his forehead to his nose, making his way to Alaric's waiting lips. Before linking them, he said, "Whatever you desire, my love."

Alaric's eyes flared with crimson light, and Bashima connected their lips, laying Alaric back on the couch.

Alaric woke the next morning in their bed, every part of his body sore but satisfied. He stretched his arms, sitting up slowly so as not to wake Bashima. His husband slept next to him, blond hair a mess, snoring lightly into his pillow, and Alaric watched the steady rise and fall of his breathing. He traced shapes on Bashima's naked back.

"Good morning," came a rumpled voice.

"It is indeed," Alaric said. He snuggled into Bashima, chest against the Sun God's back, and intertwined their legs. He kissed the space between his husband's shoulders and hummed, content.

"Surprised you let me top so many times last night," Bashima said, smug.

"Well, it was my birthday, and I deserved to be lazy," Alaric said.

He hadn't felt the dragon trying to wrest control from him last night, so maybe his rut was over. Although, they had gone for at least four hours...

Bashima snorted into his pillow and groaned. "Did you have a good birthday? Is that what you're supposed to ask?"

"Ha! Yes, I did. Mainly because of you." He nibbled Bashima's ear, hands drifting below the covers.

"Hey, your birthday's over, husband," Bashima said, snapping his hips back, making Alaric laugh.

Alaric rolled over, releasing his husband. "Watch where you're throwing that bony ass, I'm very delicate."

Snorting, Bashima rose from the bed, and stretched, showing off every inch of himself. "You love my ass." He peered behind him at Alaric's devoted staring and laughed. "We can stay in bed all day if you want. Once the moron squad leaves."

"You don't have to work?" Alaric asked, skeptical.

"Obviously, but I can concentrate enough from here, now that I'm not exhausted. One morning won't derail that asshole's trip across the sky."

Alaric blushed and hid under the blankets.

"Nope, no hiding. Time to kick them all out."

It took longer than expected to get everyone out. In fact, it was noon before they departed. They'd spent a few hours over breakfast, poor Cypress forced to watch Alora parade a very shell-shocked Resk around the conservatory. Garyn sat in his chair, eyes closed, small smile on his lips. He sipped orange juice and listened to Alora gush about the young god-touched.

"You should come home with me. Cypress, is that against the rules?"

"Huh?" The Forest God could barely form sentences, he was so hung over. Alaric figured he'd had at least three bottles of wine the night before.

"Why don't we try dating a little first, Alora," Garyn said, and Alora pouted for the rest of the meal.

Cypress perked up after a few hours of greasy food and water, but he trailed dried leaves wherever he went, making Bashima mutter under his breath about the mess. The Forest God waited for Alora and Garyn to say good-bye and shift away, and then his eyes cleared a bit. He sent Resk on an errand to the kitchens before turning his attention to Alaric and Bashima.

"Neither of you have heard from Cabari? Really?"

Surprised by his lucidity, Alaric said, "No, nothing. Is something wrong?"

"He's not at his ugly-ass temple?" Bashima asked. "Alora and Garyn probably know where he is and don't want to say anything."

Cypress shook his head. "No one has seen him. Not since he left the war council meeting, after the thing with Jace."

"That was some bullshit," Bashima snarled. "At least Jace is smart enough not to fall for the 'what a god says is law' nonsense. There's no way he'd use his ability if he didn't want to."

Cypress nodded. "Oken would tell him not to, I'm sure of it. But the fact that Cabari has been missing since then isn't good. Falkar disappeared too. He left his student behind at the king's temple. Orn, he's the Augury. He has no clue where his teacher went or why he left. Torstan isn't talking, but he was annoyed that Falkar left without telling him."

"Celestials do what they want to do," Bashima said, shrugging. "As for the Lightning Moron, I'm sure he'll show up once he's done sticking his dick somewhere."

"Wasn't it weird that he spoke against Vaultus's plan?" Alaric asked. Cypress and Bashima avoided his eyes. He looked between the two. "Come on. Can we not with the secrets? Bashima told me everything about your celestial power, Cypress. Not like there's anything else to hide."

"You told?" Cypress punched Bashima in the arm.

"What the hells? Vaultus said I could!"

Cypress huffed, crossing his arms. "Fine. It's only fair. I know everything about you two."

"It's just…Cabari is fun and all. Seems like an okay guy, but he didn't strike me as the type to stick his neck out for someone."

"Don't be fooled by his attitude," Bashima said. "He's a moron, but he's a loyal fucker. He helped rescue you from Chronas. Not that you needed much rescuing."

"Which is why Vaultus is worried," Cypress said. "Cabari wouldn't abandon us."

"Maybe they pushed him too far?" Alaric asked. "He said he'd be out if they tried to make Jace use his ability against people."

Neither Bashima nor Cypress spoke. The Forest God sighed and walked toward a large flowering fern. He touched the leaves, thinking. He said, "If you hear from him, please let me know."

Before Bashima or Alaric could answer, Cypress's body went rigid and green energy spiked over his body. His eyes gleamed with dark green light. The fern's leaves crumbled to ash in his hand.

"My temple."

Cypress fell to the ground with a scream, his eyes changing from green to bright white.

His body spasmed, the whip-like vines snaking from his arms, spinning around his body, lashing out. More vines than Alaric had seen him use before, like thick spider legs. They tore through the nearby foliage, shredding plants and flowers.

"Tengu!"

Bashima made to run to the downed Forest God, but Alaric's dragon instinct took over. He shoved his husband out of the way, somehow knowing Bashima shouldn't be the one to touch Cypress's writhing body. Scales flowing over his skin, Alaric leaped to the Forest God's side, the vines whipping harmlessly against his hardened skin. Smoke billowed from Alaric's nose as he grasped Cypress's shoulders, intending to hold him down.

His head whipped back when his clawed hands touched the Forest God's skin, green light coursing through him. A whine formed in his head, and Alaric realized it was himself, keening from the amount of energy Cypress had unleashed. Alaric roared, pushing back, his brand igniting from the effort. He could faintly hear Bashima screaming at him to let go, to get away.

Come on, Cypress, come on…

An image flashed through his mind: violet flames cascading through thick walls, timbers shrieking from the heat, incoherent screams, a sickening laugh shredding his thoughts.

Then everything was golden light, and Alaric knew no more.

Epilogue

Bashima

Bashima knelt and rested his head on the raised platform, holding in the scream he wanted to unleash. He clenched his fists and drove them into the stone, wanting to destroy it. He deserved better than this. They all deserved better.

His body shaking, the Sun God stood and looked down at the peaceful face, wishing they had more time. He adjusted the shroud, smoothing it over the broad chest.

Weren't gods supposed to be invincible? Never-fading? Hadn't that been the one thing promised to them by their creators? Yes, you carry immense responsibility, but you will remain young, strong, beautiful, able to reign supreme over other beings.

But what did that matter if they could end up like this?

"Bashi?"

That voice. Like a knife in his heart. Bashima took a deep breath and turned around.

Tengu.

He stood at the throne room doors, one arm in a sling from the seizure he'd withstood, face and arms littered with lacerations from the vines that almost tore him apart as they'd attempted to keep his body safe. What good was a defense that could hurt you? What good was the power of celestials if Tengu couldn't control it?

Bashima thought of Alaric resting in their guest room, unable to walk without assistance. It brought back unfortunate memories of his husband's recovery after the Time God almost killed him, and Bashima put up his wards — as Alaric called them — hoping to spare his husband from the despair that coiled in his heart.

Why did Alaric always have to rush into the fray? He'd pushed Bashima out of the way, making sure he was the one to wade through Tengu's vines, the things slicing at his hardened scales, not sharp enough to wound a dragon-touched.

But what happened when Alaric touched Tengu…Bashima had no idea. Alaric's brand went crazy, encasing his entire body with golden light, covering both him and the Forest God, forming the shape of a massive dragon, too bright for Bashima to look upon. He'd yelled at Alaric, cursing his stupidity, unable to get close enough to help.

The burning light left a scorch mark on the floor when it finally went out, leaving Alaric sprawled next to Tengu, who had stopped thrashing. Both of them lay still for almost ten minutes, eyes wide open but not seeing, before Alaric stirred, groaning.

He'd had his wards up, shielding Bashima from whatever he experienced, holding onto Tengu for dear life. Alaric didn't remember what happened from the point when his brand lit up to him waking up on the floor.

Now, Bashima scowled at the Forest God standing in the doorway, freckled face desperate, tears welling in his green eyes. He wanted to beat the shit out of Tengu, pound his stupid face until those tears went away, until he could forget what he'd promised Vaultus.

He's going to need you…

Fuck that. Bashima had his own damn problems, like his idiot husband who had more courage than sense. Ugh, but he couldn't ignore the king's final request, and stupid Tengu would do the same for him if their roles were reversed.

"Is Hastia okay?" Bashima growled.

"She's…out in the gardens with Savos. She doesn't want to talk to anyone or see anyone, but he won't leave her."

Tengu's voice was flimsy, as though he'd forgotten how to speak. Certain words eluded him.

"That bastard was here a while ago. Wouldn't let me in at first."

Tengu didn't answer right away. His eyes drifted to the platform where Vaultus lay. Whatever was left of Vaultus, King of the Gods. Bashima hoped the king was far away so he wouldn't see what happened to them without his guiding presence. Bashima wished him a pleasant rest, for Vaultus not to witness the world he'd helped make fall apart.

Savos had placed Vaultus's body reverently before his throne, dressed in his battle armor, arms crossed on his chest, as though he was sleeping. Eyes closed, he might have been. The king's face was drawn, his cheekbones sharp, the illusion of good health stripped away. His hair flowed around the platform past his shoulders. Bashima reached out to touch it but pulled his hand back.

It wasn't real. It couldn't be real. Not yet. It was too soon. He couldn't recall the last thing he'd said to the king, but he was sure it was in anger.

"Torstan wants to talk to you before…" Tengu said, trailing off to a whisper.

"Yeah, whatever." Bashima stalked across the room, his boots clicking on the tile. He never wanted to be in this room ever again.

"It's important."

Bashima stopped beside the Forest God, his hands shook, fingers like claws. Punching Tengu wouldn't make him feel better, wouldn't change anything. And the asshole was still weak from his episode. Tengu couldn't, wouldn't, fight back. He'd let Bashima pummel him into unconsciousness, maybe hoping he also wouldn't wake.

"Maybe if he'd done his damn job, this wouldn't have happened," Bashima said and waved a hand and walked away, leaving the Forest God alone with his stepfather's body.

The shades were terrified, fleeing from the Sun God's presence. Bashima was surprised there were any left, was shocked that the only casualties from the attack were the king and the celestial. Although he wasn't sure about the god-touched.

The temple was untouched for the most part, except for the gardens, where Vaultus and Hastia had been taking breakfast together. The grounds were virtually demolished from the fight: twisted branches, hedges full of holes, trees upended. The flowers had been trampled, petals like blood on the grass.

Torstan knew exactly what happened, but Bashima heard that the king ordered Savos to take the queen and escape, that Ouranios was only there for him. He wasn't interested in a goddess and one god-touched man. At least that was the gossip in the temple. Bashima had cornered a shade when no one would tell him what happened, and all she knew was that there had been an attack on the king and Savos saved the queen.

Bashima walked through the temple halls, and it was darker than usual, as though the building dimmed itself, recognizing its master was gone. The flowers and plants had wilted in their vases, and no one had removed them.

They'd put Torstan in the king's personal guest suite, but he was alone when Bashima entered. He expected the room to be crawling with medical shades, but it was empty. The air was cool, the open window letting in a soft breeze.

"Sun God," came a wheezing voice from the bed. "Wasn't sure if you'd come."

Bashima snorted and approached the bed, taking a seat on the chair next to it. He said, "Since you're the only one who knows anything, might as well visit before you get to die."

Torstan laughed, which made him cough, silvery blood trailing down his chin. "You speak so boldly for a young god. I can see why Vaultus liked you." He coughed again. "I've held on for as long as I can, but it's time for me to ascend. My brothers and sisters await me."

"What did you want to tell me?" Bashima glared at the celestial. Why didn't he save Vaultus? Why couldn't he? Too weak to stop Ouranios. Too old to be of any use.

As though knowing what Bashima was thinking, Torstan smiled. "This would have happened eventually, you know. Vaultus was prepared for it, as was Hastia."

"Being prepared doesn't mean they were ready," Bashima snarled.

Had the celestial said the same bullshit to Tengu? Was that why he was moping around like a lost ghost?

"No one is ever ready for death, Sun God. We crave more life, even as we yearn to move on."

"Thanks again for not giving us that option."

Torstan ignored him. "There are a few things I need to discuss with you before I ascend. But I'd like to explain what happened to Vaultus.

Cypress knows everything, but he'll need someone to share the burden with him. Vaultus wished for that person to be you."

"Didn't expect to get taken out this quick, did he?"

"We knew Ouranios would make his move, and so he did. It was well-coordinated. We think it happened the exact same time as the attack on the Temple of the Forest. We got off lightly."

"How the fuck you figure that?" Bashima asked. Wasn't it enough that their leader was gone? And now Torstan was choosing to die rather than stay and help them. And Tengu's temple...It couldn't get much worse.

"He didn't capture Cypress. Or your husband. And Oken is still out there, even though we haven't heard from them. If he'd been injured, Cypress would know through their bond. So long as the Forest God is functioning, we have a chance."

"Tengu's a damn mess," Bashima groaned. "It would be better if Oken was here."

"Easier for you, perhaps." Torstan sighed and closed his eyes. "Vaultus fought like a hero of old. I doubt Ouranios was expecting him to put up much resistance, because he came alone. At least, we saw no one else with him."

"Of course, the king fought," Bashima said, disgusted with the celestial. "What were you doing? Watching from the sidelines?"

"We fought together, as best we could. Vaultus hasn't moved like that in centuries. When he saw Ouranios nearly tear me in half, you should have seen him." The celestial's eyes shone with pride, but all Bashima could think was that it was a mistake and a waste. Torstan went on, "My brother is much like Cypress is now: so much power that he's taken over the centuries, stealing from his celestial family. With one crucial difference, Cypress took that power from Vaultus so he could do good in this world. And the power can't be forcibly taken from him."

"Why's that important?"

"A piece of Ouranios's power lies in Cypress now. He will defend that power for as long as he can, and Ouranios will try to capture him unharmed so he doesn't lose that power. Most likely, my brother believes that he'll be powerful enough to take that last piece of himself back. Without Vaultus to oppose him, to rally the gods, he might get that chance. Cypress is woefully unprepared."

Bashima couldn't believe what he was hearing. They'd cursed Cypress with this power, turned him into a vessel against his will, and now Torstan was bashing him.

"Tengu's going to end up on a slab next to Vaultus."

"That's what we're trying to avoid." Torstan hacked into his hand violently. He settled back into the bed and said, "Cindras is an able commander, and the gods will follow him, but he lacks Vaultus's charisma. He's going to need allies, particularly the younger gods."

"The Fire God's an asshole. None of the younger gods will listen to him."

"That's where you come in. You and the God of Peace. You're to be the commanders under Cindras."

Bashima couldn't contain bitter laughter. He said, "You've lost your mind. Desh makes sense. Put him and Raphe together and every single god will line up behind them. Why me?"

"The young gods respect you. And Cypress can't be in the forefront. You need to keep him with you and make sure he doesn't lose control."

"How the hells am I supposed to do that? He has massive celestial power plus his own."

Torstan's eyes leveled on Bashima's, and he noticed silver lines threading their way across the celestial's face like infected veins.

Torstan said, "You'll find a way. Your husband stopped Cypress's reaction, correct?"

"I won't make Alaric do anything like that again. He still can't walk on his own, and it's been three days."

Torstan shook his head. He said, "He shouldn't attempt it lightly, but he has the blood of dragons flowing within him, and there's much we don't know about his kind. Practically nothing. From what Cypress told me, in that state, your husband was probably the only one who could have helped him."

Bashima recalled how stupid Tengu couldn't stop muttering about purple fire when he came out of his stupor, and he'd made Bashima shift him to his temple, begging, not realizing that Alaric was knocked out next to him. Had helped him.

Bashima did the only thing he could: called for Kuroi to watch his husband while he ferried the stammering Forest God to his temple.

Torstan brought Bashima out of his revery, saying, "And now, for the difficult news."

"None of that was difficult news?" Bashima asked. He crossed his arms and looked away. This was all too much for him. Lead the younger gods? He wasn't made for that.

"Whatever happens, you must not allow Cypress and Cindras's son to fully claim their soul bond."

"Huh?" Not at all what he'd expected the old celestial to say.

"Oken doesn't know about it, and you should insist that Cypress keep it that way. They're already connected, no helping that now —"

Bashima interrupted, "You mean Oken could have felt that seizure?"

They needed to find him and Jace. They could be anywhere, not knowing what had happened or why. Jace wasn't a dragon-touched, so Oken could seriously injure him.

"Cypress would know if anything went seriously wrong. Tattoo that on your brain. Do not search for him and Jace. They have their own mission. It's not as crucial as yours, but you may have need of the demigods before long."

"They deserve to know why it happened if Oken felt it."

Bashima thought back to when Alaric's soul tidal wave hit him, how disorienting it was, and he'd known what was happening. Oken had no idea how tied to Tengu he was.

"Focus on your task, Sun God. Because I won't be here to do it for you. And you can't rely on Falkar. He's attending to his own affairs. Keep Cypress safe. Do not let him tell Oken about their soul bond."

"Wouldn't it be better if he knew?"

"Once Oken knows and accepts the bond, which he will, it can never be broken."

Bashima scoffed. "It's not like they'd regret it. Tengu would do anything for that Zebra Head bastard. I'm the same. I'm never leaving Alaric, and they'd have to kill him to make him leave me."

Torstan reached out, lightning quick, and grabbed Bashima's wrist. His grip was intense, and Bashima tried to pull away. The silvery lines on Torstan's skin flashed.

"If your husband dies, so will you."

Dark red light flew over Bashima's skin, his orange eyes shining. "You're lying."

"I wish I was," Torstan said. "If he chose to ascend at some point, you would live on, because you'd know it was coming. You'd have time, like Vaultus and Hastia, to prepare yourself. But if it was sudden, and the shock was too great, you would die."

"You've lost it, old man. Gods can't die. Even Vaultus isn't completely dead. He's stuck in that body."

Torstan smiled sadly. "It has happened before. One of the first gods we made fell in love with a human, and she accepted him, braver than any human who has been born since. What did she know of the power of the gods? What did she have to fear, partnered to a god? Courageous, shrewd, an able fighter. And fragile. When she perished in a battle, that's when we celestials knew we'd made a mistake giving you emotions, this insane ability to love."

"So what? We can love. What does that matter?"

"The ability to love also gives you the ability to grieve, which you know all too well."

Bashima growled and jumped to his feet. "I've heard enough. Just ascend or whatever. We'll take care of the world, just like we always do."

"Listen to me, Sun God. The soul bond between that god and that human woman, the first to ever exist, is why the land was broken, why the waters flow differently. His despair broke the world apart, his madness flooded the lands, and when he died, unthinkably, he killed every mortal creature we'd created with the force of his pain."

"You're making this shit up to scare me."

And it was working. All Bashima could think of was Alaric rushing headlong into danger, not thinking about what could happen to him, not caring, so long as he was helping someone. Bashima didn't care if he was the one who died, but if Alaric was taken from him…

Livid light flowed on his palms, and Bashima found it difficult to contain his rage.

"Even now, thinking of your husband dying, it's enough to make you forget yourself, to leave reason and logic far behind."

Bashima calmed himself and felt a pang of alarm from Alaric.

Shit, his wards had come down a bit. Bashima sent out a soothing thought, telling his husband everything was okay. The redhead sent him an uncertain, suspicious feeling, and Bashima chuckled. Alaric knew him better than that. Bashima needed to get to their room before Alaric's stupid dragon brain made him try to find his husband.

"As the Sun God, you hold incredible power, power that could disrupt this world if you let it go," Torstan said, his voice faltering. "Imagine what someone like Cypress could do if his bond partner died."

Bashima was silent.

"I'm not trying to break you and your husband apart," Torstan said, sighing. "It's too late for that. But it's not too late for Cypress."

"Why did you do this to us? Make us this way?" Bashima whispered.

"We wanted to give you things we didn't have, make you better than us," Torstan admitted. "We didn't realize how strong these…emotions…could be. It's why we made the older gods skeptical of mortals, told them not to mix together, that humans were inferior to the perfect gods."

"But then gods married each other," Bashima said. "You didn't get rid of the emotions. Couldn't the same thing have happened?"

Torstan said, "There has never been a soul bond between two gods, nor two humans. It takes an immortal and a mortal to make the bond form. But it doesn't always happen. Not many gods choose mortal partners. We celestials haven't had to worry for thousands of years. We hoped that it was an unfortunate fluke, a flaw in the design."

"And now there's two," Bashima said.

"Now there are two." Torstan coughed again, and the silvery lines darkened. "It is almost my time, so you must go. I wish to be alone for my ascension."

Bashima swallowed hard, trying to keep his emotions in check. He threw his wards back up.

"I didn't want to burden you with all of this, but there's no one else. Keep Cypress safe and warn your husband not to be so careless with his life."

Leaving the room, Bashima glimpsed a brilliant silver light and had to look away. The celestial would be gone, leaving no trace behind, unlike the king. As the light faded, Bashima wondered what it would feel like to know you were dying. And what might wait on the other side.

Bashima made his way back to the throne room. He needed to check on Tengu before collapsing into bed beside his husband. Dammit, he didn't want this, didn't want to worry if the Forest God was trying to slit his wrists in front of the king's forever-sleeping body. It wasn't his damn job.

Then why had he agreed? Both Vaultus and Torstan expected great things from him, but would he be able to deliver?

"I hate this place," Bashima muttered, pushing the doors open.

Tengu sat on the dais of Vaultus's throne, knees to his chest, face buried in his arms. He'd removed the sling, which sat next to him, useless. His green hair shone in the candlelight, and leaves fell softly beside him.

Walking toward him took everything Bashima had. His mind told him to run, to take Alaric home and never look back, but he couldn't do that to Vaultus. He owed the king so much. The least he could do was make sure fucking Tengu didn't implode.

He slumped down next to the Forest God, but he didn't move, face still in his arms.

"I'm sorry about your temple," Bashima mumbled.

When they'd arrived at the Temple of the Forest, Tengu had fallen to his knees and thrown up. What the flames failed to do a thousand years ago, they'd completed their work. The temple walls were charred, the wood pockmarked with smoking holes, and it had collapsed in on itself. The trees nearby were unharmed; like the fire knew what to destroy.

The ruins creaked and moaned, like a dying animal in its final throes. Tengu called to his shades for hours, walking around the ruin, trying not to step through the piles of ash, and Bashima didn't stop him. There was little hope that anyone escaped. It hadn't taken long for the fire to bring the temple down.

"Dasari," Tengu had pleaded, finally falling to the ground. He dug his fingers into the ashen ground, sifting through it, searching for who knew what. All Bashima could do was watch him weep. Bashima thought of his husband back at their temple, of his god-touched and the shades who served him so loyally. At least Resk hadn't been at the Temple of the Forest, he was safe. And Oken was gone too.

"Thank you," Tengu said, raising his head and bringing Bashima back to the present. Tears shined on his cheeks. Vaultus's throne loomed behind them. "Is Torstan gone?"

"Yeah. Blaze of glory and all that noble shit."

They sat in silence, Tengu for once not fidgeting. It was weird. Weirder than normal between them.

"There was nothing you could have done," Bashima said, twisting his fingers together. "If you'd been there, you would have gotten hurt. Or worse."

Tengu laughed, but there was no humor in it. "Things can always get worse, right?"

Bashima wasn't used to the Forest God acting so apathetic. He was a ball of nervous energy, curious about the world around him. It was like taking the celestial's powers drained him of everything that made him Bell Cypress.

"How's Alaric?" Tengu asked.

"He'll be fine. If he keeps being a heroic idiot, though, I may have to divorce him."

That made Tengu laugh in earnest, and he wiped the tears from his cheeks. "Like he would let you divorce him."

Bashima nodded, smiling. "He's stuck with me, and I'm stuck with him. We're lost causes."

"At least you're together," Tengu sighed. "Veles will be here soon. He hasn't heard from Jace, and he's worried, but there's not much we can do but wait for them to make contact."

"Oken's okay, right?"

"It's so weird when you call him 'Oken.' As far as I know, he's okay. I don't remember much, but I think I'd feel if he was really hurting. Cindras hasn't mentioned anything, but I doubt Oken would write to him."

Bashima took a deep breath and let it out through his nose. "What do we do now?"

The throne room doors slammed open, and the two gods were on their feet in a second, green and orange energy crackling on their skin.

"Calm down." A voice like razor blades down their backs.

Both Bashima and Tengu froze where they stood, unable to move. Bashima felt panic stream through him, and he fought to keep his wards up, but this guy made every cell in his body want to run and hide. If Alaric felt Bashima's fear, he'd do everything he could to make it to wherever Bashima was.

Wards. Up.

"Shit," Tengu said through clenched teeth.

A man strode into the room, tall and lean. His chin was like a spear point, his eyes shards of onyx. A ragged mask covered his face and black leather strips coiled around his muscular arms. He wore thick black trousers and tall boots, a blood-red cloak billowing behind him, and his dark hair fell into his eyes, unkempt and wild. He moved with a slight slouch to his back, as though he was prepared to strike against an attacker, his gait feline. His entire body was draped with bladed weapons, and a long, slim sword was slung across his back.

He stopped in front of the raised platform where Vaultus's body rested, his face unreadable.

"What do you want?" Tengu strained out, face flushed, teeth bared in a silent snarl.

The man didn't acknowledge them. He stared down at the king and the minutes ticked by. Bashima's body began to shake from staying in place, and he grunted. That got the man's attention, and he glared at them, releasing his hold on them with a languid blink of his eyes. This was a being who truly felt no fear. Bashima sagged over onto the Forest God, who grabbed him, holding him steady.

"Why are you here, Pyato?" Tengu demanded, his green hair whipping around his head.

"To see how much damage Torstan has done," the man said, his voice like gravel. "To see how badly he failed my creation."

"You told Vaultus you'd never come back here," Tengu spit out, the spirit flowing back into him. Bashima had no idea who the newcomer was, but he was dangerous, definitely another fucking celestial. Just what they needed, and this one seemed way less helpful than Torstan or Falkar. And Tengu was talking to him like he was the one in charge, as though the celestial couldn't take their heads off.

"So I did, Inheritor," he said, glowering at Tengu. "But the time has come."

Pyato spread his arms, indicating Vaultus's slumbering form. "This was just the beginning. And you're not ready for what's coming."

To be continued...

465

Acknowledgements

I started this series during Covid, a terrible time of isolation where the only connections I had were through Zoom calls. Since I had so much time on my hands, shouldn't I have been writing? Stalled on a different book project, I returned to my roots: fan fiction. What began as a simple dialogue exercise between characters grew into this sprawling monster of a book. I turned thousands of words into separate volumes and let my friends read the stories. Thank you to my friends across the United States for reading and encouraging me to keep going. Eva and Christine, who got me going. Stacie and Brenda, who fell in love with pure Alaric and cranky Bashima. Jess, who recently asked me where the heck was book two. Don't worry, Jess. It's here.

To my supportive family who told me to pursue my dream of getting my PhD. Don't worry, I'm also working on that project. To my PhD supervisors who understand that I have multiple teapots screaming at me to take them off the fire. To my fellow PhD candidates, thank you for your support when you're all as busy as I am.

To everyone at Between the Lines Publishing for your relentless patience and kind words of encouragement. This series wouldn't be possible without your belief in it.

Lastly, to my readers. Whether you were there in the beginning when this story was in its infancy or if you've recently joined me on this journey, thank you so much for your support, comments, and reviews. Every time I see your love for these characters, it drives me forward.

Colleen McMillan is a Minnesota native who currently lives in Cardiff, Wales. She also calls Paris her second home, but don't tell the Parisians. She was educated at the University of Wisconsin, River Falls and received her Master's Degree in Creative Writing at the University of Kent, Canterbury in England. She is currently studying Gothic Literature at Cardiff University.